M000267124

More Alternative Truths

Stories from the Resistance

Edited By

Phyllis Irene Radford

Rebecca McFarland Kyle

Lou J Berger

Bob Brown

Cover Design

C. Thom Coyle

B-Cubed Press
Benton City, WA

Copyright

Foreword © 2017 by David Gerrold

Orangemandias © 2017 by Adam-Troy Castro

The New Colossus public domain by Emma Lazarus

The Right Man for the Job © 2017 by K.G. Anderson

I Am Woman © 2017 by Jane Yolen

How Dangerous is Republican manic-depressive disease? Both bipolar phases are destructive, but the manic ones kill? © 2017 by David Brin PhD.

The Diplomatic Thing © 2017 by Esther Friesner

Doctor Republican's Monster © 2017 by Jim Wright

A Letter from The Federal Women's Prison © 2017 by Stephanie L. Weippert

One of the Lucky Ones © 2017 by Wondra Vanian

A Beautiful Industry © 2017 by Stuart Hardy

Queens Crossing © 2017 by Lou Antonelli

Small Courages © 2001 by Eric Witchey, First Published: "The Runner" in *America's Intercultural Magazine after 9/11*

The Nompers copyright © 2017 by Rebecca Mix

The Ten Commandments Renegotiated © 2017 by Jim Wright and Bobby Lee Featherston

Illegal Citizens © 2017 by Irene Radford

During the Lockdown, After the Lockdown © 2017 by Michael Haynes

A Sonnet on Truth © 2017 by Philip Brian Hall

Drafting the President © 2017 by Lou J Berger

The Politicians © 2017 by Mike Resnick

A Modest Proposal for the Perfection of Nature © 2005 by Vonda N. McIntyre, First Published in *Nature: Futures* 3 March 2005

Conspiracy of Silence © 2017 by Philip Brian Hall

HMO by Karin L. Frank © 2017 by Karin L. Frank

Being Donald Trump © 2017 by Bruno Lombardi

America Once Beautiful © 2017 by Brad Cozzens

America First © 2017 by Tais Teng
Trickster Times © 2017 by Jane Yolen
Final Delivery © 2017 by Kerri-Leigh Grady
No Tanks © 2017 by Jane Yolen
Remembering the Bowling Green Massacre © 2017 by Steve Weddle
Treasures © 2017 by Rebecca McFarland Kyle
Tweetstorm © 2017 by Manny Frishberg and Edd Vick
The Tinker's Damn © 2017 by Edward Ahern
Wishcraft.com © 2017 by Elizabeth Ann Scarborough
A Woman Walks Into a Bar © 2017 by Jill Zeller
America Year Zero © 2017 by Gwyndyn T. Alexander
Future Perfect © 2017 V.E. Mitchell
How to Recognize a Shapeshifting Lizardman (Or Woman) Who Has Been Appointed to a High-Ranking Government Cabinet Position © 2017 by Kurt Newton
I Didn't Say That © 2017 by Jane Yolen
Non-White in America © 2017 by Debora Godfrey
Desperate Resolve © 2017 by John A. Pitts
You Are Weighed in the Balance © 2017 by Rivka Jacobs
Priorities © 2017 by C.A. Chesse
The Healer © 2017 by Melinda LaFevers
Triple R Presents © 2017 by Colin Patrick Ennen
Donald Where's Your Taxes © 2017 by Susan Murrie Macdonald and Elizabeth Ann Scarborough
A Spider Queen in Every Home © 2017 by Mike Morgan

All rights reserved.
Copyright 2017 Robert L. Brown and B Cubed Press
Interior Design (E-Book) Vonda N. McIntyre
Interior Design (Print) Bob Brown
Cover Design C. Thom Coyle
ISBN: 978-0-9989634-3-3
Electronic ISBN 978-0-9989634-2-6
Frist Printing 2017
First Electronic Edition 2017

Editors' Note

American identity. An unofficial theme of this anthology. So many of the stories ask what America has become? What will it be? Will it devolve into a Russian style Oligarchy or will we rise to the challenge and use our hearts, our minds and our votes to return to a rational democracy, of, by, and for the people. No one knows for sure.

In 1883, Emma Lazarus gave one vision. A land free of pomposity. Where the tired, the poor, the tempest tossed could be free. A land at odds with the American reality around her. A reality where, less than 20 years after the defeat of the Confederate forces, the return of white nationalism loomed large, voting rights were stripped, a land where the Civil Rights Law of 1875 was ruled unconstitutional by a court determined to end the reconstruction era. This ruling denying the people rights that were not returned to the citizens of this country for nearly 90 years with the passage of the Civil right act of 1964.

Like 1883, we see challenges, dangerous and hateful challenges, to the civil rights gains of the last generation, a determination to put the boot back on the neck of millions of Americans. To restore an un-natural order.

This book is part of the resistance to the rolling back of progress of equality and civil rights in our era, as to our everlasting shame, was done in hers.

It is our privilege as the editors of this work, to honor Ms. Lazarus and the words that made her immortal.

The New Colossus,
by Emma Lazarus 1849-1887

Not like the brazen giant of Greek fame,
With conquering limbs astride from land to land;
Here at our sea-washed, sunset gates shall stand
A mighty woman with a torch, whose flame
Is the imprisoned lightning, and her name
MOTHER OF EXILES. From her beacon-hand
Glows world-wide welcome; her mild eyes command
The air-bridged harbor that twin cities frame.

"Keep, ancient lands, your storied pomp!" cries she
With silent lips. "Give me your tired, your poor,
Your huddled masses yearning to breathe free,
The wretched refuse of your teeming shore.
Send these, the homeless, tempest-tost to me,
I lift my lamp beside the golden door!"

Your appreciative and humbled editors, Bob Brown, Lou J Berger, Phyllis Irene Radford, and Rebecca McFarland Kyle
11/11/2017.

Table of Contents

ACKNOWLEDGMENTS

To the Readers.
Without them we are but words.

To the Writers
Without them, we are but ideas

To the Teachers.
Without them we are nothing

Foreword

David Gerrold

"What is truth?" asked Pilate—and then he washed his hands, as if by washing his hands, he could also wash away the troubling question.

It may be, however, that "What is truth?" is the ultimate existential question.

Philosophers, both classical and contemporary, as well as various self-appointed gurus of cultural ephemera, have pounced on the question from a variety of directions. Truth can be divine, it can be revealed, it can be discovered, it can be known—or truth is defined only by peer review, or it's a subjective perception, or maybe ultimate truth can't be known at all.

There. Does that clarify anything?

What it clarifies is that we don't know. What it demonstrates is that truth is like a handful of lime Jell-O. If you squeeze it too hard, it oozes out between your fingers—and whatever you thought you were holding onto is now just a sweet sticky mess that you are left licking off your fingers.

The question of truth is irrevocably linked to the harder question, "What is reality?"

That one's a little easier. There may or may not be an objective physical reality in the universe. Maybe. Some scientist-philosophers have suggested that the entire universe is a holographic projection and that we are all characters in a cosmic role-playing game. Others have asked why anything exists at all? Why not nothingness? To which others have answered, we don't exist—we are just possibilities being played out. And if I follow this train of thought any further, my brain starts to hurt.

Descartes—you may have heard of him—considered the question of consciousness at length, but all we know of his deep and deliberately methodical inquiry is the punch line. "I think, therefore I am." Or, in contemporary terms, "I think I think, therefore I think I am."

Some philosophers even believe that consciousness itself is an illusion produced by timebinding—by the accretion of memories and the need to protect those memories as a tool for survival. (It's useful to know that mates and bananas are good, hyenas and lions are bad. Those who didn't remember this didn't survive long enough to reproduce.)

Are you beginning to see how slippery this particular bar of soap is?

Don't worry about picking it up, the universe has already bent us over. Life itself is a practical joke. About the time you start to gain even the slightest smidge of what passes for wisdom, you're too old to do anything with it—and then you die.

Okay, let's assume there is a tangible reality, a physical basis for what we experience. It's out there. Whatever it is.

But at the same time, we are not designed to *experience* that physical universe.

Our hearing is limited to a range, at best, between 20 and 20,000 cycles, whatever the mechanisms in our ears can resolve. Most of us do not hear tones above or below that range.

Our sight is limited to a specific range of colors, what the rods and cones in our retinas can sense. We do not see infra-red or ultra-violet. We do not see the frequencies beyond those.

And there are so many different scents floating in the atmosphere that our noses are unable to detect that I can't even find an appropriate metaphor to suggest that range.

There are other things that occur in the physical universe that we are not designed to sense. We do not see the faint light of the Andromeda galaxy in the sky, even though it covers a greater arc than our own moon.

We don't see X-rays or radio waves, we don't hear the low grumbling of elephants. We don't feel radioactivity. We don't sense magnetism or electricity.

We don't see Kirlian auras. And who knows what else we don't sense because we still don't have the prosthetics—the technology—with which to detect it.

So, the world that any of us exist in is a subjective one, not just limited by our sensory equipment, but designed by their deficiencies.

And it gets even worse than that. We live in a reality that has been defined by our language as well.

We are creatures of language. We conceptualize everything, we codify it, and we use language to pigeonhole our experiences, adding relative judgments to everything we experience. We don't experience heat and cold as sensations, we experience things as too hot or too cold. We don't experience flavors as sensations, we experience them as too spicy or too sour or too sweet—or sometimes even, just right—and all those things are judgments that create a world-view, a mind-set, a set of biases and prejudices and beliefs. We train ourselves to live in a reality that we create ourselves. We're making it up as we go. And as soon as we make it up, we think that's what reality is.

At least, that's what some contemporaries think.

But even if we disregard that thesis, no matter what thesis about reality we choose to live in... ultimately, it all boils down to this: *everything is a conversation.*

We live within our perceptions of reality, and they become our conversation.

(Don't take my word for it, test it out yourself. Get back to me when you can.)

Still with me?

If everything is a conversation, then what is truth?

In some philosophies, truth is what we can all agree upon. And history tells us how that works out. There were times when a majority of people agreed that Jews were vermin, blacks were inferior, women were too emotional to be trusted with a vote, and LGBT+ people were perverts by choice and sinners in the eyes of God.

That particular philosophy, that truth is something that we can all agree on, is fundamentally flawed. It creates evil in the world. It allows us to justify behavior so vile that even a reality TV host would be embarrassed. (Well, some reality TV hosts.)

So, no—we can't go there.

If we're looking for truth, we have to limit ourselves to evidence-based conversations. And we have to be careful about our evidence. We have to focus on a reality that can be measured and tested and verified by independent experiments. That's as close as we're ever going to get to hard-cold reality and the conversation that expresses it.

Today, we live in a world of conflicting conversations, a world in which truth has become a relative commodity. People argue from philosophical illiteracy, "Well, that's your truth, it's not mine." And in politics we have heard people who use their position of credibility to argue, "We are entitled to alternative facts."

No, you are not entitled to "alternative facts."

No one is.

There are no such things as alternative facts—that's a polite way to say "lies." In fact, it's a lie about lying.

The impolite way to describe it is "bullshit."

Truth is not relative. Reality is not negotiable. And the world does not run by magical thinking.

Magical thinking is common to three-year-olds. "Step on a crack, break your mother's back." Until one day you realize that your mom is perfectly fine and you can step on all the cracks you want—that stepping on cracks is completely irrelevant to her health.

But there are people—so-called leaders—who believe that merely saying something into a microphone makes it real.

Bullshit.

Saying that "trickle down creates jobs" is a lie. It doesn't. We have twenty years of evidence that it's a self-serving lie, it loots the wealth of the middle class, and ultimately creates the kind of economic disparity that put the French aristocracy out of business.

Saying "if the president does it, it isn't illegal" is a lie. Congress appointed a special prosecutor to disprove that one.

And saying, "I'm the best," when the evidence demonstrates you're the worst—it's not just a lie, it's such a huge steaming pile of fetid bullshit that even a reality TV show host should hesitate before speaking that one aloud.

But reality TV isn't about telling the truth. It's about selling you a brand.

Television, as we know it today, isn't about entertaining you—it's about convincing you that you smell bad, that you aren't good enough, that you're broken and need fixing—and if you just buy this thing, this hyper-hyped, color-enhanced, sparkly distraction from reality, then you'll be all better, you'll be *there.*

Bullshit.

There is no *there*. There's only *here*. And what you do in the here and now is the only where and when that affects what's possible—and no TV commercial, no pitchman, no con man, no self-inflated, pompous, reality-TV bluffoon is ever going to sell you anything that will make a difference in *your* life. He's in business to make a difference in *his* life. He's in business to make a profit, nothing else. He's the one who gets the gold-plated toilet seat, not you. You're not his partner, you're his resource to be exploited.

He's a con man.

Understand this—a con man preys on your ignorance and your greed.

Anyone with a little larceny in their heart is fair game. An honest man will walk away, shaking his head in disgust, appalled that anyone could be so stupid as to fall for the lies, the bullshit.

But we live in an age of calculated desperation, because the con man and his enablers can't win when people are effective and succeeding, when people can see that their hard work will get them to their goals.

No, the con man and his enablers need people to be desperate—because when you're desperate, you do stupid things. When you're drowning, you grab for the first thing that looks like a life preserver, even if it's an anvil.

The con man knows how much you want a ticket to paradise. That's his wedge into your consciousness, that's where he turns the conversation to his advantage. That's when he promises you the golden ticket. It's a very special golden ticket. It's just for you. Nobody deserves it as much as you do. Because you're so special.

That's the conversation. And it works because you're desperate—because you allowed yourself to believe the decades of lies and bullshit that shout at you from billboards, that pour from the tabloids at the supermarket checkout stands, the lies and bullshit that spew from radio and television and pop-up ads on your laptop—all the lies and bullshit that masquerade as news and information. It works because your sense of what's true has been buried under humongous mountains of calculated bullshit.

And worst of all, it works because each and every one of us is hard-wired from birth with a specific kind of listening. "What's in it for *me*?"

If the promise is big enough, if the golden ticket glistens just right, if all of your questions and objections are dismantled and deconstructed before you can finish assembling them—they've got you.

Your common sense gets overwhelmed.

Whatever conversation you think you have about life—you don't. Not anymore. You have the sum total of all the free-floating conversations that have been poured into your head by the purveyors of bullshit, all the conversations that have settled into your consciousness unquestioned and unexamined. Those are the conversations of con men: "Those lazy immigrants are coming here to live off welfare and steal your job."

Bullshit.

That word, that beautiful vulgar word—it's your only defense against the conversations that other people use to control you. You're either living in your conversation—or theirs. And if their conversation is about greed, if it's about fear, if it's about hatred, if it's about wallowing in a negative view of the world—*it's bullshit.*

Today, at the time of this writing, we have a choice between evidence-based conversations and huge steaming piles of bullshit masquerading as conversation. Each and every one of us, we have a choice between a conversation that relies on research, facts, logic, and a smidge of compassion—or a conversation based on wishful thinking, fear, hatred, and polarization.

That's why this book exists.

Science fiction is a conversation of ideas. It's a conversation of possibilities. It's a conversation that says the way things are is not the way they have to be.

Science fiction is a metaphorical conversation about the world we live in—one that points to desirable futures and warns against painful ones. It's a breakwater against the inescapable sea of bullshit, all the crap that erodes the shores of rationality. It's a deliberately subversive way to expose the consequences of evidence-null dialogues, the fictions and false realities of con men.

Read this book as a whack upside the head with a clue-by-four. It's an alarm bell, but it's also a hopeful effort. Because its existence is a demonstration that we still have the right to consider alternatives—and warnings.

We still have a chance to choose. We still have a chance to do better.

We still have a chance to create a conversation of mutual respect, compassion, and partnership for a future that works for all of us, with no one and nothing left out.

At this point, I would normally say, "Read. Enjoy." But I think it's probably much more appropriate to say, "Read. Think. Think hard. *Then act.*"

Especially *Act.*

David Gerrold, Aug 29, 2017

Orangemandias

Adam-Troy Castro

I met a traveler from an antique land,
Who said—"Two vast and trunkless legs of stone
Stand in the desert. Near them, on the sand,
Half sunk a shattered visage lies, whose frown,
And wrinkled lip, and sneer of cold command. . .
Tell that its sculptor well those passions read
Which yet survive, stamped on these lifeless things,
The hand that mocked them, and the heart that fed;
And on the pedestal, these words appear:
'Look. I have a very good brain.
I know more about ISIS than the generals.
That was the biggest inauguration crowd in history.
Global warming is a Chinese hoax.
Anybody who says anything otherwise is spreading
fake news.
Stop investigating me! Investigate Hillary!
What I say goes, you losers!'
Nothing beside remains. Round the decay
Of that colossal wreck, boundless and bare
The lone and level sands stretch far away.

The Right Man for the Job

K.G. Anderson

The chief of staff for a U.S. senator paused in the kitchen doorway, a bottle of chilled Sauterne in each hand.

"I can't believe we've come to this."

His wife, a political advisor to the 2016 Clinton campaign, pulled trays of desserts out of the stainless steel refrigerator.

"You mean Trump?" she said.

"No!" With a jerk of his head, he indicated the formal dining room down the hall of their Silver Spring home. "I mean a séance. *Really*?"

His wife, her features drawn with stress and exhaustion, shrugged.

"Why the hell not?" she asked. "People keep saying 'If only Molly Ivins were here! If only Walter Cronkite could see this!' So I figured, why not? We'll call them back to help us!"

"But. . . a séance?" her husband said.

"You have a better idea?"

He shrugged. Together they entered the dimly lit dining room and joined the ten high-ranking Democrats seated around the damask-draped oval table. Conversation stopped when a late-middle aged woman in an evening gown, shawl, and black silk turban appeared in the opposite doorway. She took the chair at the head of the table and extended her be-ringed hands to the guests on either side of her.

"Turn off ze lights," she said. "And ve shall begin."

The host, seated at the foot of the table, leaned over and whispered to his wife.

"Nice touch, the Eastern European accent. I hope she's not a friend of Melania's."

"Shut up, dear," his wife hissed. She clasped his hand, somewhat more tightly than necessary, and the séance began.

~oOo~

The bright yellow river raft bumped the dock, and a sturdy woman clambered out. She wore jeans, a chambray shirt, and a down vest. Her reddish-blonde hair was tied back in a ponytail. She waved enthusiastically to the dapper, balding man sitting at a table on the front porch of the rustic lodge.

"Hiya, Adlai," she called as she strode up the lawn.

"Hello, Molly." He folded the copy of the *Washington Post* he'd been reading and rose to give her a peck on the cheek.

"You get the call from that séance?" She flopped down in a chair across from him and raised an eyebrow. She had a wide grin, sparkling blue eyes, and a Texas twang.

"Oh, yes. They must be getting desperate."

She nodded. "Apparently it's desperate times back there."

“Coffee?” he asked her. He looked back toward the open door into the lodge.

“I’d take a beer.”

Seconds later a tall waiter appeared with a pot of coffee for Adlai Stevenson II and a chilled brown bottle of Lone Star for his guest. “Good to see you again, Miss Ivins.”

She waved away an offered glass and took a long pull from the bottle. “Pretty soft here in the afterlife, isn’t it?”

“Delightful,” he said. “And so you know, I haven’t the slightest desire to go back and help what currently passes for the Democratic Party deal with this Trump idiot. As my father said when he served as vice president, ‘Your public servants serve you right.’”

Ivins grinned. Then she leaned forward, face serious. “Never met this Trump guy, didya?”

“Thank heavens, no. I left politics in 1965.”

“Trump isn’t really in politics,” Ivins wrinkled her nose. “He’s more of a celebrity. Had a TV show. It was all about him bullying people and then firing them.”

“Charming. I guess that’s what it takes to get elected these days.”

Ivins sipped her beer, squinting out at the river. It looked a lot like the Colorado but wasn’t, really. “I missed the boat on Trump, you know. Had him in my sights. It was the run-up to the 2000 election and I joked, in the *Texas Observer*, about him ‘being treated as though any reasonable citizen would consider voting for him.' Adlai, I *joked* about that. And look what happened. Boy, was I wrong about Trump."

"I'd say you were right about Trump, but unduly optimistic about the American voter."

"I don't know." She gave a deep sigh. "It is the stories we don't get, the ones we miss, pass over, fail to recognize, don't pick up on, that will send us to hell."

Stevenson gestured to their pleasant surroundings. "This is hardly hell. Unless you've been rafting on the River Styx."

"Point taken," Ivins said with a grin. "But apparently they've now got hell back where we came from."

"Wasn't it always hell," he said. "Somewhere?"

The phone in the lobby of the hotel rang and the tall waiter appeared in the doorway. "Mr. Stevenson, they're calling from that séance again. What should I tell them?"

"Oh, lord, don't tell them I'm here," Ivins said. "There's no way I'm going back. I wrote hundreds of columns, dozens of books, and obviously nobody listened. What about you, Adlai? You going back?"

Stevenson waved away the waiter. "Not me. Not again. I made three runs for president, you know. I'll always remember that poor woman who assured me that I 'had the vote of every thinking American.'"

Ivins hooted. "As the story goes, you told her it would take a lot more than that."

Stevenson peered into his empty coffee cup. “These days, it might take an act of God.”

“Speaking of which, you think we should get in touch with Walter?”

“Why not?” Stevenson brightened. “It would be good to see him again.” He went into the lodge and took a London Fog raincoat and a fedora from the coat tree. Ivins kicked some of the dirt off her hiking books and hid a smile as he shrugged into his coat. For Adlai Stevenson II it would always be 1965.

The pair followed a plush maroon carpet runner into the depths of the lodge to a door rimmed with glowing blue lights.

“Gotta love these portals,” Ivins said.

The door slid open. The pair stepped into what looked like an elevator and chanted in unison, “Walter Cronkite.” Seconds later, the chamber’s doors opened into what looked like a comfortably appointed old Georgetown home, but wasn’t, really. A mahogany door stood ajar. Stevenson knocked.

“Come in.” The hearty voice would have been familiar to the millions who’d listened to CBS News in the 1960s and 70s.

Walter Cronkite, dressed in a blue blazer and dark trousers, came out from behind a nondescript gray desk and shook their hands, greeting each of them by first name. He motioned them to the comfortable leather office chairs in front of his desk and went back to his chair. “Well, what can I do for you two?”

Ivins and Stevenson exchanged surprised looks.

"Haven't you been getting calls from a spiritualist conducting a séance for a bunch of desperate Democrats?" Ivins asked.

"A séance?" The newsman gave an avuncular chuckle. "Afraid I'm out of the loop these days. Want to fill me in?"

"Adlai and I have been summoned by a spiritualist hired by the Democrats to bring some of us out of retirement to do something about Donald Trump."

"Trump!" Cronkite bellowed. His jowly face turned red. "Donald Trump! He ruined my neighborhood in Manhattan when he built that garish monstrosity of a tower. The man is an utter scoundrel."

"No argument here," Ivins said. "But keep in mind: you couldn't stop him building that tower, and the Republicans couldn't stop him taking over their party, and the Democrats, bless their divisive little souls, couldn't stop him from taking the presidential election. And now that he's in office even his own Secretary of State can't stop him from trying to destroy the planet."

"Are you two going back to help?" Cronkite asked.

"Nope," said Ivins. "As far as I'm concerned, we gave it our best. And what could I do? There's certainly no shortage of pundits on the case."

Stevenson spoke up. "Walter, we were hoping that you might be able to help us find someone who'd want to go back to straighten things out. Jack Kennedy? Tip O'Neill? Bella Abzug? Paul Wellstone? Maybe Martin Luther King?"

Cronkite leaned back in his chair. He steepled his fingers and peered down at them, lost in thought. A small, tight, grin came to his face.

"You have an idea?" Ivins asked.

"As a matter of fact, Molly, I do. We need to pay a visit to the Ranch."

"The Ranch?" Stevenson shook his head. "I'm not really dressed for it. Maybe you two—"

"C'mon, Adlai." Ivins was grinning. "It's almost lunchtime and Lady Bird serves a mean chili."

"Johnson irritates me." Stevenson sighed as they followed Cronkite into the hallway. "I was his ambassador to the United Nations and, frankly, I don't think he listened to a word I said."

The trio entered the portal and chorused "LBJ."

"The old sumbitch," Ivins added. The portal didn't seem to mind.

The portal at the LBJ ranch turned out to be at the front gates, and the gates were a good five miles down the road from the ranch house. But as soon as the trio emerged from the portal they saw the rising dust cloud as a white Lincoln convertible came speeding down the driveway. It pulled up at the gate, and a grinning Lyndon B. Johnson got out and shook their hands.

"Good to see ya'll. Climb on in. We're just getting ready to sit down to some of Lady Bird's Pedernales River chili."

Steering with one hand, holding a plastic cup filled with Scotch in the other, Johnson regaled his visitors with tales of fishing and hunting all the way to the big ranch house. He didn't ask them what they'd come for until everyone had eaten at least two bowls of chili with cornbread and had insisted they couldn't possibly eat thirds.

Lady Bird brought in a pot of coffee for Stevenson and herself. Ivins was still drinking beer and both LBJ and Cronkite nursed tumblers of Scotch.

"I suppose we should get down to business," Johnson said. "It has to be business when you get a visit from a politician, a reporter, and a columnist."

The former president, who'd leaned down to pet one of his two beagles, straightened up and peered at them over his wire-rim glasses. As his guests exchanged nervous glances, his smile slowly faded. "Oh, hell. It's Trump, isn't it?"

The three nodded.

"Well, what's he destroyed now? School lunches? Public education? Equal opportunity? Head Start? Medicare? Social Security?"

"Pretty much all of it," Ivins said. "Plus healthcare, foreign relations, and the environment."

"What the hell is left?" Johnson shouted. "What happened to the Great Society? What happened to the United States?"

Under the table, a beagle howled.

"Lyndon," Lady Bird cautioned.

He shook her off. "Take it easy, Bird. I can't have a heart attack here, I'm already dead."

"And that is actually why we're here," Ivins said. "The Democratic party—what's left of it--is holding a séance and they're trying to summon one of us back from the dead to help them do something about Trump."

Johnson grinned a terrible grin. "I'd say you've found the right man for the job."

"Lyndon," his wife said.

He patted his mouth with a big linen napkin and stood up from the table. "Gotta make one call."

He gave Stevenson a meaningful glance.

"Your old neighbor?" Stevenson asked.

"Yessir," Johnson said. He headed down the hall and vanished into his library.

Lady Bird looked as annoyed as Cronkite had ever seen her.

"'Neighbor'?" asked Ivins.

Lady Bird took a deep breath. "J. Edgar Hoover. He was our neighbor back in the days when Lyndon was in Congress and we lived on 30th Place in Northwest D.C. I haven't spoken to that man after what he did to Walter Jenkins. But Lyndon. . .he never cuts a connection."

"Never know when they'll come in handy, Bird." It was Johnson again, sweeping through the dining room on his way to the front door. The beagles ltrotted behind him.

"Where are you going?" his wife called after him. She and Ivins ran into the hall.

"Back to the White House, of course." Johnson paused on the front porch, silhouetted against a rugged landscape that looked like Texas Hill Country but wasn't, really. "I'm not letting some asshole New York developer ruin all my hard work."

Everyone watched as LBJ put the dogs into the Lincoln and vaulted into the driver's seat. Dust rose as he sped down the driveway toward the ranch's portal.

"What I'd give to see the look on the faces of those Democrats at the séance when he shows up," Stevenson said.

"They don't make Democrats like Lyndon anymore," Lady Bird said loyally.

"Hell, they don't even make *Texans* like that," Ivins said. She turned to Cronkite. "You want the last word, Walter?"

The news anchor nodded and lifted his glass. "And that's the way it is," he intoned.

"God help us," said Ivins.

~oOo~

"Fire them!" came the whiny, all-too-familiar voice from the Oval Office. "I'm the President of the United States. I demand that people around here do their jobs. Which means keeping the damned carpets clean."

The White House chief of staff stood in front of the president's desk, wringing his hands. "Mr. President, that was the fourth cleaning service. I can get a new one, but it will take several days just to get their security clearances."

"Fire the security people," came the answer. "Or I'll fire you! You're fired! You're fired! You're fired!"

The chief of staff turned and fled, stepping right into a fresh pile of dog shit on the burgundy carpet just outside of the Oval Office door. *Not again!* He hopped up and down on his other foot, bracing himself against the wall as he removed the smeared wingtip. From down the hallway and up the stairs, he distinctly heard the baying of. . .beagles? But there were no dogs in the White House. The President hated dogs.

"Can't blame him," the chief of staff muttered. Holding his reeking shoe at arm's length, he limped off in search of a new cleaning service.

That night, raucous laughter rang out from the Oval Office. Guards responded, but all they found was a tumbler with a few drops of Cutty Sark leaving marks on the *Resolute* desk. Imprints from cowboy boots worn by a tall man with a long stride appeared on the White House carpets, but the trails led nowhere.

The president was apoplectic.

"Don't stay at Pennsylvania Avenue," he tweeted at 3 a.m. "Noisy, dirty--not like a real Trump property."

The next morning, the president refused to enter the Oval Office. He gathered his staff in the hallway.

"Not going in there," he snapped. "Terrible office. Disgusting desk. The place is haunted! We're all going to Mar-a-Lago. No ghosts there. Call the helicopter. Notify Air Force One."

From around the corner, the ghost of LBJ chuckled. All was going just according to plan.

His next stop was the White House pressroom where reporters from Pulitzer-winning publications, barred from a special briefing about the president's greatness, waited outside. The ghost of LBJ sidled over to a woman from *The New York Times* and slipped a big manila envelope into her briefcase. It contained papers, photos, and some of those strange little "drive" doohickies Hoover had assured him were the latest thing in communications.

LBJ watched as the reporter found the envelope, read a few pages, and then dashed into an alcove to make a call on her little handheld phone.

Johnson chuckled. Technology might change, but the FBI didn't. Hoover's operation had supplied enough damning information, some real and some maybe not so real, but plenty convincing, to blow the 45th president higher than Trump Tower.

Damn, it was good to be back in the White House.

After letting the spectral beagles out to do their business on the White House lawn, Johnson embarked on a self-guided tour of his old stomping grounds. Sure enough, Nixon--*that wimp*--had removed the high-power shower nozzles. But the secret mezzanines were still there. Johnson popped into all three of the White House kitchens to see what they were cooking these days. Seemed to be a lot of steak, which no Texan could argue with.

Late in the afternoon, the ghost slipped next door to the Executive Office Building where he left a short note for Mike Pence.

Restore funding for Health and Human Service programs and put someone who genuinely cares about our kids in charge of Education. Or you're next on the list, jackass.

He appended his famous lowercase signature: lbj.

At the Senate Office Building, he headed for Mitch McConnell's office, where he left a more diplomatic note.

"Mitch, I have long appreciated your crossing party lines in 1964 to vote for me to show your support for the Civil Rights Act. Yes, we're politicians. But we're also public servants who care deeply about the people of this country. All of them. Don't you think it's about time you started voting your conscience again? I'd strongly advise it.—lbj"

At dusk, Johnson was back at the White House where he stepped out onto the Truman Balcony, Scotch in hand, to watch his plan for Trump come to fruition.

He'd barely had time to take a sip before two burly men in white coats appeared, escorting the ranting, raving, and writhing chief executive across the South Lawn and onto a helicopter. Staff and reporters circled the landing pad like sharks.

The helicopter lifted off and flew into the sunset--headed northwest toward the new Walter Reed Medical Center, which, Johnson had read, had excellent mental health facilities.

"In your guts, you know he's nuts," Johnson cackled. That had been his favorite slogan from the

1964 campaign, and, wouldn't you know it, it was still true of the GOP leadership half a century later.

When he turned to go back inside, LBJ was startled and somewhat annoyed to find at his elbow the ghost of J. Edgar Hoover.

"Good God, man!" Johnson snapped, sloshing his drink. Recovering his equilibrium, he dished out his thanks.

"Great job. Those papers and pictures and those 'drive' things of yours seem to have done the trick. He's gone, and the Democrats and Republicans can get back to work, at least when they're not busy kicking the shit out of each other. As the generals say, 'mission accomplished.' I sure as hell enjoyed the visit, but I guess it's time to for me head back."

It bothered him that the former FBI chief made no reply, just raised a glass of what looked like cola in a silent toast. Johnson squinted, then grimaced.

That little peckerwood is recording me! Ah, hell. Damn politics! Even in the afterlife, some things never change.

The End

The historical incidents referenced in this story are true. For more information visit http://writerway.com/fiction-by-k-g-anderson/the_right_man/

I Am A Woman

Jane Yolen

I am a woman,
you can tell
by the tinkling
of the bell
around my neck,
it's time for milk,
while master walks
about in silk.

I am a woman,
fertile days
I get a good
amount of praise;
a mattress and
a sheet or two.
But other days,
red tents will do.

I am a woman,
quiet voiced.
I tiptoe and I
make no noise.
My daughters taught
just how to be,

respectful, silent
just like me.

I am a woman.
To birth a boy
is what I do
for master's joy.
But one day I
will take a knife
and slice it through
my master's life.

I am a woman,
not a toy,
and only that
will bring *me* joy.
And if I'm killed,
I will not care
for then I'll be
just earth and air.

But this one thought
I will hold fast:
I'm equal to
the man at last.

How Dangerous is Republican manic-depressive disease? Both bipolar phases are destructive, but the manic ones kill?

David Brin, Ph.D.

In early 2017, two terms gained widespread circulation: "deep state" and "weaponized narrative." Each of them was aimed at rousing fear and loathing from one end or the other of the political spectrum. We'll return to "deep state," a fiercely assertive meme promulgated by the right.

But let's start with "weaponized narrative." *Nine Nations of North America* author, Joel Garreau, defines it as using rumor, innuendo, propaganda and memes to undermine an opponent's civilization, identity, and will by generating complexity, confusion, and political and social schisms.

The general method goes back a long way, and was described in Sun Tzu's *The Art of War.* Weaponized narrative can be used tactically, as part of explicit military or geopolitical conflict; or strategically, as a way to reduce, neutralize, and defeat a civilization, state, or organization. Done well, it limits or even eliminates the need for an armed force to achieve political and military aims. Says Garreau:

"Far from being simply a U.S. or U.K. phenomenon, shifts to "post-factualism" can be seen in Poland, Hungary, Turkey, France, and the Philippines, among other democracies. Russia, whose own political culture is deeply post-factual and indeed post-modern, is now ably constructing ironic, highly cynical, weaponized narratives that were effective in the Ukrainian invasion, and are now destabilizing the Baltic states and the U.S. election process."

Let me add what should be obvious, just from reading the news and looking at a map. Moscow has been building an anti-western alliance that now stretches from Ankara, Damascus and (arguably) the Mullah faction of Iran, all the way across the Asian steppe to Manila. Geographically vaster than the old Soviet Empire—especially if you include sympathetic cooperation in Beijing—it is no longer based on communist ideology but on bald-faced oligarchy and hatred of all aspects of the Western Enlightenment, especially democracy.

Garreau continues: *"By offering cheap passage through a complex world, weaponized narrative furnishes emotional certainty at the cost of rational understanding. The emotionally satisfying decision to accept a weaponized narrative—to believe, to have faith—inoculates cultures, institutions, and individuals against counterarguments and inconvenient facts."*

I've been giving an extended, three-hour mini-course on "Threat Perspectives" at some of the intel agencies and military colleges. Lately, these presentations have drawn audience gasps, when I show 1998 slides describing methods that might be used against us in the future. These included *"imposition of disinformation upon the U.S. populace"* and *"subornation of elements of U.S. leadership castes."*

And yes, those slides were from presentations to the Defense Threat Reduction Agency and other groups, way back in the last century.

And no, since you ask. Nobody listened then. They assumed I was talking implausible sci fi, even though these have been standard methodologies used by hostile empires for millennia.

As the train conductor chided, in the movie t*op Secret*: "I warned you. . . (a lot more than) TWICE!"

==War as a symptom of political bipolar disease==

I promised to explain the "bipolar" political ailment. Please bear with me. You might recall that, under the Bushes, we had "neoconservatives" or "neocons" like Wolfowitz, Nitze, Perle, Adelman, who concocted rationalizations for both Iraq Wars and the quagmire in Afghanistan. These followers of a bizarre émigré philosopher named Leo Strauss eventually admitted that Saddam Hussein had nothing to do with terror attacks against the U.S. or its interests, or ever had Weapons of Mass Destruction.

When pressed, the neocons proclaimed that their goal was for America to assert its imperial power, not in the wimpy, mostly-peaceful ways established by Marshall, Truman, and Eisenhower, but by imposing our will directly upon the world. That word—"will"—was used with such frequency and romantic passion that many of us were reminded of Leni Reifenstahl's infamous *The Triumph of the Will.*

What surface frosting was supposed to make this aggressive international thuggery palatable? The notion that our forceful will would impose, teach, and justify *democracy* around the world, finishing a job that began with the fall of the USSR. The neocons' favorite catechism was taken straight from Leo Strauss, *"we're an empire; we should act like one."* (Never mind that this was the very mode of thinking that had torched Strauss's European homeland, wreaking hell on Earth and turning him into an ingrate-refugee.)

Ah, but the neocons' time in the sun was brief. As pain from the bungled Iraq and Afghanistan wars set in, George W. Bush and the GOP turned on the Straussians with stunning speed, tossing overboard fellows like Wolfowitz, Perle, Adelman, Nitze, when their stock of rationalization incantations were no longer useful.

At which point, that briefly-manic, sick-but-utopian era swung to the other side of U.S. conservatism's bipolar disease, a more typical grumpy cynicism, in which the GOP's sole purpose became to *prevent action* of any sort, especially if it might benefit the nation with Obama getting credit. Hence, except for Supply Side vampire guzzles for the top 5000 families, almost no negotiation or legislation was allowed. Especially not infrastructure repair, which would have released high velocity cash into the lower middle class.

Oh, but pendulums swing. Now the Republican Party is back in complete power and signs of a fresh *manic phase* are abundant. Senior military officers can read these tea leaves and are deeply worried, as men like Steve Bannon make grand, new, "philosophical" declarations in favor of violent, imperial over-reach—above all yearning for war with Iran.

The newest manic rationalizations no longer speak of "spreading democracy." That neocon patina of egalitarian proselytism is gone. Now, Bannon and his alt-right buddies foam with their own brew of teleology, racism, confederatism, and apocalyptic yearnings.

There are layers to this bitter new cake. Underlying it all is yet more supply-side-vampiric craving, the will of the party's masters. Next, the dominionist-endtimes thing is very real, and would take priority under any President Pence (take note, you "impeach now" fools).

Another layer is the "deep state" meme of hatred toward fact-centered public servants, now including military and intel officers. And finally, there is "cyclical history"—the utterly disproved insanity pushed by yet another Strauss (&Howe) in a cult incantation called "The Fourth Turning." Bosh and twaddle that makes Marxist teleology look positively scientific.

Should we be shocked? These Crazy Years were cogently predicted in the 1950s by Robert A. Heinlein.

==Do I exaggerate the manic-depressive Republican syndrome?==

In this article, Flemming Rose describes a meeting with Bannon that sounds strikingly similar to press interviews with neocons, back in early, pre-911 days of the G.W. Bush White House, frothing with justifications for a coming rampage of American imperial power. Specifically, Bannon rages that we are "at war with Islam," despite the fact that we so vastly overshadow that world, in power, wealth, science, technology culture, and numbers that comparisons are ludicrous. Oh, and our parents endured more pain and casualties during any one week of World War Two than we wimps have, across the entire War on Terror. And those parents never panicked, screeching as these neo-neocons do.

To be clear, Rose knows about Islamic Terror: "*I was the target of Islamist ire for publishing cartoons of the Prophet Muhammad in a Danish newspaper. But a war against all Muslims is not the solution.*"

Rose soon discovered that War against Muslims—very likely a trumped-up assault against Iran—is only a means to mobilize the nation and take firm hold of our military, not the end in itself:

"Bannon is angry. The object of his anger is the "globalized elite." He argued that Trump is just the beginning of a rebellion that will grow increasingly aggressive in the coming years. In a way, he told me,

Trump is not the real thing—only a premonition of what will ultimately come. "Just wait and see," he said."

Of course the stunning irony is that the elites Bannon despises—all fact-users from scientists, teachers and journalists to military officers and civil servants—are exactly the folks who stand in the way of a final takeover by the plutocrats he serves. Science, democracy and knowledge-professions will block any return to feudalism... unless they are all toppled.

Oh, please read those Heinlein quotations, again and again.

Another passage by Rose makes clearer the passionate—manic phase—the spirit of ordination and transcendentalism that has returned to the halls of the White House:

"Ronald Radosh, a social historian affiliated with the conservative Hudson Institute, wrote recently about talking to Bannon at a book party in November 2013. According to Radosh, the guy who is now Trump's chief strategist proclaimed himself a "Leninist." According to Radosh, Bannon explained his Leninist tactics this way: "Lenin wanted to destroy the state, and that's my goal too. I want to bring everything crashing down, and destroy all of today's establishment."

Further: "*What disturbed me the most in our conversation was Bannon's apparent belief that violence and war can have a cleansing effect, that we may need to tear down things and rebuild them from scratch."*

The thing about transcendentalist mystics is that they make such declarations without being able to cite even a single example of such tear-downs actually leading to a better, more vibrant, creative or prosperous civilization! Indeed, only one historic revolution achieved that, the one that handled its transitions with moderation and calm. All of our progress, across the years since 1776, has come from the positive-sum efforts of mature, negotiating adults and builders. Yes, we have had to fight, at times. But always *against* the guys who want to 'tear-down and cleanse.'

In fact, the specific target chosen by the Bannononites *is not the point!* He is very clear about his ultimate goal. And—washed free of all disguises and trappings—it is to be Nathan Holn.

The End

Drafting the President

Lou J Berger

They came for her on a Tuesday morning in late July.

Theresa Bundt shook her head, half in anger and half in sadness, dreading the argument she knew was coming. The truck outside the food bank wasn't quite warm on the inside, but it didn't matter. It had been left overnight in the parking lot without refrigeration, and the food inside was now suspect.

She needed to salvage anything she could, and she knew Ronnie, her dock supervisor, would argue against throwing anything away.

"I don't care if the driver thinks the food is safe," she said to him. "We dump the dairy and the meat. The rest, we evaluate carefully. . ."

"But. . . he began.

Theresa cut him off with a gentle hand to his shoulder.

"Please, just do as I ask."

He twisted away.

"That food is supposed to feed three hundred folks who didn't eat last night. You tell me to scrap it because it *might* be spoiled?" He reached up and lifted his ball cap to scratch his bald pate, his face crumpled in a scowl of disgust. "You don't have a clue what it means to run this food bank." He slapped his fist on a case of sour cream. "Dan Rhodes, the guy you fired, he knew how to get it done. Sometimes *men* take risks."

Theresa took a quick breath and stepped back, white-hot anger pulsing through her. The emphasis on 'men' was not lost on her.

Theresa took a deep breath. "Ronnie, you're right."

He took a step back, his eyebrows arching in surprise, and twisted the ball cap, green with a gold deer embroidered on the front, in his work-worn hands.

"There are hundreds of people who *could* eat from what's in that truck tonight. People who are hungry. But would you risk making them sick, gambling with their lives? Can they afford an ER visit? If the food isn't *absolutely* safe, we can't use it, and you know that."

Ronnie nodded as her words penetrated his frustration.

"Which is worse, do you think, falling asleep after another night of too little to eat, or sleeping in a hospital bed with food poisoning from spoiled meat?"

Ronnie looked at her thoughtfully.

"You have a little girl," she continued. "Would you feed her what's in this truck if she was really hungry, not sure if it might make her sick?

He set the ball cap back on his head. "So," he said, a defensive tone tainting his voice, "We don't have to get rid of the *whole* load, just the meat and milk?"

"Right. You've got it. Think about your little girl. After the milk and meat, it's your call. Keep what you feel is safe?"

Ronnie let out a frustrated breath, but stood taller. "Yes ma'am. I'll get right on it."

Theresa thanked him and turned to go.

"Ma'am?"

She glanced over her shoulder. Ronnie took off his cap again.

"I'm real sorry for what I said. I didn't mean it. I just care a lot about these folks. You're doing a good job."

"We all care, Ronnie. No offense taken."

Ronnie turned and barked orders at the loaders who had been standing idle, watching their exchange.

Walking back to her office, she thought about what Ronnie had said and realized that, despite accepting his apology, his words stung.

For the most part, those kinds of misogynistic attitudes had gone back into the closet after President Trump's impeachment and removal. The sight of the most fractious President ever elected being led out of court in handcuffs had done more to unify the country than anything since the 9/11 attacks, twenty-six years earlier.

Ian, her young assistant, approached and pivoted to walk alongside her. His pants were neatly pressed, as always, and his tie was impeccable.

He flailed his hands in front of him, but didn't speak. He did that when he was overcome with emotion.

"Spit it out already," she said with some amusement at his internal struggle.

"Uh. . . they're here for you."

"Who are here?" she demanded, her smile slipping away.

Ian didn't respond, just flailed his hands a bit more.

Then, through the warehouse's front windows, she saw seven black Lincoln Navigators filling the small parking lot, their emergency lights blinking in frenetic rhythm.

She glanced at Ian, but he merely shrugged and waved in a grandiose manner toward her office.

An icy shudder moved through her as she strode down the hallway, Ian struggling to keep up.

Standing outside her office door, a muscular man sporting a brush-cut and sunglasses held out a hand to stop her progress.

He touched a device wedged into his ear.

"She's here," he said, then nodded slightly, turning his mirror-shaded gaze to look directly at her.

"You may go in," he said, his voice surprisingly gentle.

"Damn right I can go in. It's *my* office," she said, shouldering him aside and turning the door handle.

Inside, an elderly, familiar man sat behind her desk, his suit pant leg riding up and showing a thin band of skin between the cuff and the top of his black sock.

Theresa strode across the carpet and put her hands on her hips, looking down into his bland face.

"Get out of my chair."

The current chairman of the Federal Selection Commission slowly stood up and walked around the desk, extending his hand.

Theresa ignored it and walked around the opposite side, keeping the desk between them.

He chuckled and lowered his trim, ninety-year-old frame into another chair.

"Ms. Bundt, I assume you know why I'm here?"

She knew. One of the biggest changes after Trump's impeachment had been a Constitutional amendment changing the process of seating a President. Gone were elections and grandiose speeches, gone were debates and primaries.

Instead of an elected office, the position of President of the United States had become another form of civic duty, just like serving on a jury.

Douglas Adams, a twentieth-century author, had once declared, "anyone who is capable of getting themselves made President should on no account be allowed to do the job."

Every four years, five Americans were nominated and then drafted into service. Each was then required to demonstrate their ability to overcome complex challenges, with the most successful being added to each of the state ballots as the only major candidate.

And the whole process was nationally televised.

Theresa leaned across the desk and hissed through her teeth. “Yes, but I don’t want to be the President. Pick somebody else.”

His genial smile disappeared. “You know I can’t do that.”

“I know no such thing. Take me out of the running. I have a food bank that needs me, and I don’t want to live in that damned White House.”

The Chairman steepled his fingers and gazed at her, his face grave. “Ms. Bundt, you have the opportunity to become the first black woman President. This isn’t something to walk away from. Do I need to remind you of your civic duty?”

Theresa shook her head, her mouth set in a thin line. “Get somebody else.”

The Chairman leaned forward. “If you insist on refusing, you would be in violation of Federal law. I am here, today, to inform you that you are, whether you want it or not, hereby drafted for civic duty, specifically serving as a potential candidate to become the forty-eighth President of the United States.”

He leaned back, letting those words sink in.

She slammed an open palm down on her desk, the sound echoing like a rifle shot in the small office.

The door banged open and the wall of meat peered in through his mirrored shades.

The Chairman waved him away and the door clicked shut.

"Ms. Bundt," he said in a gentle voice. "Your country needs you."

Her shoulders slumped. "But, I'm not what America wants in a President. I'm Black, I'm a woman, and I'm not married. I won't make it three rounds in the competition, so why make me embarrass myself?"

The Chairman dismissed her protestations with a wave of his hand. "Nonsense. We've already vetted you, checked your background, interviewed friends and family all the way back to kindergarten."

Theresa frowned. "Nobody told me they were interviewed. I'm not sure I believe you."

He relaxed in his chair. "Everybody was sworn to secrecy, under penalty of prosecution. You're one of five candidates, and your sequestration starts tonight. I'm simply here to inform you of your civic duty, remind you of the penalty if you refuse, and give you enough time to transfer your responsibilities to whomever you trust for the duration of your vetting."

Her mind whirled. Whom did she trust enough to take over the food bank? Ian? No way. He was a great assistant, but he couldn't handle the negotiations. He was too direct and, therefore, lousy at diplomacy.

"Mr. Chairman, I am grateful for the consideration, but I just won't do it."

He looked at her for a long minute, then dipped his fingers into his suit pocket, coming up with a long envelope. He casually tossed it onto her desk.

"Read that," he said quietly.

She opened it up and slid out two sheets of paper. In small print, in three columns on each page, there were over two hundred names. Many of them were familiar to her, but some were not.

Ian's name leapt off the page. Her own assistant had nominated her for this?

"I'm going to wring Ian's neck," she muttered.

"Why don't we bring him in?"

The door opened and Ian stepped into the room, a happy grin on his face. "Sorry, Boss, but I'm really not sorry."

Theresa glared. "How am I supposed to do this, Ian? Did you think of the food bank when you put my name into that website? Why didn't you talk to me about it first?"

Ian's smile slid away. "You would have convinced me not to do it. Look around. See what you've built? Three years ago, this warehouse had weeds growing out of the floor, and people were literally starving in this neighborhood. Now they eat, this place employs a hundred people, and you've brought an economy back to this part of town. You solve problems, you're a great leader, and you are too big for this job. America *needs* you."

The Chairman turned to face her, his expression solemn. "He's right, you know."

Ian inclined his head in thanks. They both looked at her expectantly.

"Fine!" Theresa said with an explosion of breath. "Let me hand this monster off." She lifted her telephone receiver and dialed a number. "Marnie, can you come into my office for a moment?"

When Marnie arrived, moments later, she was out of breath. "I was just working on. . ." her voice trailed off as she recognized the Chairman. "Oh, Mr. Pow. . . er, General! I'm a huge fan," she gushed.

He grinned, stood, and took her hand in both of his. "Nice to meet you, Marnie. Ms. Bundt here is about to ask you to hold down the fort for the next few weeks, perhaps longer. Do you think you can do that?"

Marnie turned and goggled at Theresa. "You've been drafted?"

Theresa shrugged, a wry expression on her face. "Looks like Leavenworth if I refuse, right?"

Ian laughed, and then stopped when he saw the Chairman's unsmiling face. "Really?"

"We take civic duty very seriously."

Ian's eyes grew wide. "Oh, Theresa, I'm sorry. I *should* have spoken with you first."

"What's done is done. Marnie, what do you need from me to keep this operation running?"

They conferred for twenty minutes, going over the daily operations which Marnie had mostly been running for over a year. When Marnie had no more questions, Theresa embraced her.

"Looks like this is it for a while. You sure you got this?"

"You bet, Theresa. Um, I mean 'Madame President.'"

Theresa snorted. “Miles to go, but thank you for your confidence.”

“I nominated you, too, so you know,” Marnie confided.

Theresa looked at Ian, and then at Marnie. “If this doesn’t work out, I’m gonna come back and fire you both.”

Both Ian and Marnie laughed aloud, and Ian hugged her.

“Go get ’em, Boss Lady.”

Theresa looked around her office, sighed, and grabbed her purse. “Lead the way, Mr. Chairman. I guess I’m yours.”

He took her elbow and guided her to the door, which opened as they approached. The burly man standing outside touched his earpiece and muttered “Grocery is on the move.”

Theresa turned to the Chairman. “The first thing we are going to do is change my code name.”

His eyes crinkled. “I’ll get right on that. Oh. And call me Colin, please.”

Theresa fixed him with a steely glare. “Sure thing. You can call me Ms. Bundt.”

He chuckled and they walked out of the food bank together and into a sea of flashing lights and cameras.

The road to the Presidency had begun.

The End

Dr. Republican's Monster

Jim Wright

When it began, wiser heads begged, please don't do this!

It's unnatural, they warned, this *thing* you're creating.

It will be the ruin of us all.

But, in his arrogance, Doctor Republican ignored the danger signs. The prize was all that mattered. And he would have it, no matter the cost or the consequences.

At first, his obsession seemed a horrible joke.

But slowly it took shape, a clockwork golem, all the worst, most rank, most foul, rotten pieces of modern politics, things, awful things, that should have been long buried, dug up and stitched together.

No one really believed such a beast would rise from the table.

But rise it did.

A storm of ignorant fear gave it a horrid semblance of life.

It took a shuddering breath and began to bellow incoherently.

As the creature thrashed madly against the chains that bound it down, Doctor Republican still believed. He believed the monster could be controlled, tamed, made to behave like a civilized man. In his hubris, he ignored the danger, ignored history, ignored science and reason and dismissed the pleas of more reasonable men.

Instead he dreamed of the accolades, the praise, and the glory that would now be his.

More than anything, he reveled in the power he believed he would now command.

At last, a long last, he would show them all. Oh yes. Oh yes.

But the monster could not be controlled.

And now, predictably, it has broken loose from its chains. Mad with rage and furious with pain, howling in mindless lust, it is now rampaging through the countryside, smashing, destroying, terrorizing, ripping the arms off the villagers.

From the parapet of his castle, looking down on a catastrophe of his own reckless manufacture, Doctor Republican *still* refuses to accept responsibility.

He thinks, if only I can fix his brain, it'll be OK. He'll come around. He'll be a real human being instead of this horrible twisted *thing*.

The angry villagers mass below with torches and pitchforks.

The bells ring in alarm.

The screams of the maimed rend the air. Fire. Smoke.

But Doctor Republican won't put the monster down.

This is your fault, he sneers at the crowd below. Yes, this is *your* fault. Your fault for not believing in me! Your fault for not supporting the creature! But he'll come 'round. You'll see! You'll see! *Then* you'll be sorry.

In the distance, the monster capers in mindless fury.

Gunshots ring out in a broken staccato.

There comes the sound of falling masonry.

The sky turns burnt orange and the air is thick with desperation. The situation grows more and more dire by the moment.

Oh, those stupid *fools*, Doctor Republican rages to himself as he flees to his secret lab. One day, I'll make them understand. Life! That's what matters. Life! Yes! Yes!

But, there in the dark, his fate awaits. He cannot escape the monster he has made.

And in his last terrible moments, with the monster's hands around his throat, as the castle burns and his dreams of power and glory fall to ruin around him, Doctor Republican wonders how it all could have gone so horribly, horribly wrong.

The End

A Letter from the Federal Women's Prison

Stephanie L. Weippert

June 30, 2047
Dear Marie,

Thank you for writing to me. Yes, I do remember you, though I'm not surprised you don't remember me. You were only four, or maybe five. 2017 was a long time ago. It is so nice to read about your life, it sounds great. I don't get a lot of letters here, and yours are so appreciated. Guess the rest of our family is too scared to write. Don't blame them. Sometimes I can't help but feel that the outside world has forgotten me. Forgotten us. Forgotten what things used to be like when you were little.

But this is no time to fall into a pity-party, you asked for my recollections of what happened. For history, you said, as if the real story will ever be allowed to see daylight. Maybe when we're all gone here. Whatever you do, just keep however many letters you get from me safe until the truth can come out. Okay?

Anyway, your letter asked how it started. Well, it started years before actually, on January 21st, 2017. When women from all over the country marched in our pink pussy hats to protest his election (sorry, but if I write his name or use certain word combinations the scanners will flag my letter for inspection and you may not receive it). We were strong in our numbers and we vowed to fight to keep every right that we, our mothers, and grandmothers had fought and died to win. Looking back on it now, we had no clue how far he and his cronies were willing to go to stop us.

After the march, we called, wrote letters, some of us even ran for local offices.

I'm sorry to say, Marie, but we failed. The board had been tilted too far by then. Between gerrymandering and voter suppression and redhats "monitoring" the polls, Russian hackers and God only knows what else. The final nail in the coffin was the requirement in most states for a federally issued voter ID without the requirement to make it equally available. In the cities you might have to stand in line for hours in some neighborhoods and others, you drove up to a strip mall office, and boom it was done. Minorities didn't stand a chance after that. I don't care what the official news said, unless you were white, you weren't going to vote easily. Applications from certain parts of town got "lost" a lot. Same thing for women, because if you had taken your husband's last name, your state-issued ID didn't match your birth certificate, which meant if you wanted to vote you had to bring in the husband for an in-person meeting. Yesterday, I read that to reduce election costs there's one vote per household. The article didn't say how much money it would save, though.

I'm hoping you know most of this already. I pray the basic facts are still known, but we get no real information here. If we're good, we're allowed access to the common room where we can read the *Stars & Stripes* and listen to Fox News. Manure, all of it. I mostly crochet. They like us to stay busy. Pastor Mike visits each Sunday for mandatory services and he brings us yarn and takes our blankets, hats and scarves with him to give to poor families. I finished one today with a pretty border. If you would like it, I can see if they'd let me send it to you. Pastor Mike might help. You may need to pay for the shipping, though. Don't send any money to me, whatever you do. We're not allowed money. Tell me if you want it in your next letter and I'll ask.

Now, you wanted to know how I became the felon in the family. The start of my criminal life began a month or so after what passed for elections in 2018. Then the personhood bill passed Congress and got signed in less than two weeks. This came after the law making all abortion illegal. We lost all control of our bodies then. It mandated your husband/father/nearest male relative had to be with you for doctor visits in case the two of you planned an abortion or birth control in secret.

We protested, we marched. Not that it did much good with the newly expanded Supreme Court. By then it was up to 11 judges; he appointed the new ones. It didn't matter anymore, after that.

When the fire hoses wouldn't stop us from protesting, they moved on to rubber bullets. When that didn't work, they beat us, and sent the dogs to attack us. They could scatter us easy, but we came back. Dear friends died in those marches. I am proud to say, though, that it took martial law with a military-enforced curfew and body-bags to stop us protesting. I never heard. Have they lifted it yet?

You asked why I did it. In those days, if a woman had a miscarriage and couldn't get a doctor to sign off that it really wasn't her fault, she faced arrest for infanticide. If her husband petitioned and the court okayed it, she went back home as the property of her husband for him to do whatever he wanted with her. The law didn't say that exactly, but it did strip her of her civil rights. She became a non-person.

With that fate a possibility, you can imagine how many of us wanted to escape. Canada, or Mexico, or wherever. Anywhere but here, and I helped them. A historian friend explained about a special railroad during the Civil War to help blacks, and several of us too old to have children anymore got together and pledged to help as many women as we could the same way those people did way back when.

We did it for years, and I'm proud to say the authorities have no clue how many women we saved. I stopped counting after I helped the hundredth across the border.

That damn senator's daughter brought it all crashing down, though. Not that I blame her, nobody wants to carry a rapist's baby to term and we didn't know then that the daddy wouldn't just let her disappear. We tried to save her like all the others. We lost everything instead. Her pompous father pushed so hard, they put everything into finding her.

Found her they did, at our Detroit safe house. She was supposed to leave that afternoon, hidden between the trunk and back seats of my car. (We had figured out that border guards are less watchful in the afternoon when they get sleepy from lunch.) They brought tanks. Freaking tanks! I thought we were dead. After about an hour of looking out the window at the barrel of an Abrams tank pointing at the curtains, a guy with a megaphone told us to surrender and they wouldn't kill us. I still laugh bitterly when I remember his words. Catherine's daughter, Beth, walked out the door with her hands up and one of the bastards shot her. Maddy pulled her back in, but we couldn't save her. The bullet had hit the aorta and she bled out on the rug.

After Beth died, we had to physically stop Catherine from running out there with a baseball bat. If they told you we had guns, we didn't. Hell, Marie, we had nothing bigger than a steak knife in that house. Secrecy was our thing, not violence. We had nothing to do but pray, and wait, and keep watch. The barrels never moved. Megaphone guy kept talking. He promised that shooting Beth was an accident and the man who had done it would be punished. Maddy shouted back that he was real funny if he thought we'd believe him.

All night one man or another shouted at us through the megaphone, so nobody slept. At the twenty-four hour mark, megaphone guy shut up. What a relief I thought, but next thing I knew they shot tear gas through all the windows. A couple of the ones that ran out then are locked up here with me, though they have nasty scars. As I pulled my shirt up over my face and tried to herd people to the basement, that gawd-damned senator's brat ran out yelling she was giving up and don't shoot her. I don't think they heard a word she said, because she died on the front steps.

Me, Maddy, Jo, Alex, Tasha, and Catherine made it into the basement. Thank God Jo had convinced us to put a concrete panic room down there years ago. We huddled in there and held each other as they fire bombed the neighborhood. Believe me, Marie, listening to the building above you burn down is one of the more frightening things I've ever heard. Great nightmare material, let me tell you.

Three days later, firemen found us alive and turned us over to the feds. They wanted names of more women in our group, but we only knew each other. Maddy had set things up that way on purpose. I don't know how, but that old bird held up under everything they did to her and got them to accept we weren't anything else but a small group of crazy women. They executed her, and then Jo as the second in command. My questioner told me the rest of us would live out our lives in jail. He assured me they only executed Maddy and Jo as examples. Neither one had to sacrifice themselves by admitting they were our leaders, but they did it anyway. To save the rest of us, I guess. We worked together more as a committee.

This letter is getting long. I apologize if you have to pay any extra postage. Each of us only gets one stamp a month and all electronic conversations are read by a human in real time, inbound and outbound. With our internet limited and constantly monitored to boot, this really is the best way to tell you the truth. Or as much of the truth as I can get out without triggering the letter scanning algorithms, anyway.

Give my nieces kisses from me. Be sure to read my letters to them when they're old enough to understand.

Please write soon,

Your Aunt Cindy

The End

One of the Lucky Ones

Wondra Vanian

Saying goodbye is never easy–even less so when you know you'll never see one another again.

Desmond watched through a grimy window as his father put an arm around his mother's shoulders, the other raised in a half wave. With a lurch, the train pulled away from the nearly-empty platform, and he became again a child being sent off to school for the first time.

Except, of course, that his parents wouldn't be there at the end of this day.

Smiles would not greet him to ask how his day had gone and maybe even buy him ice cream.

They wouldn't be waiting because he wasn't coming back.

When he was a child, Desmond would beg his mother to take him to the station to watch the trains pull away. For a boy who had always felt different, other, the trains represented more than high-powered boxes of steel; they were magical carriages that promised freedom from sneers and endless taunts. They were Desmond's escape plan. His way out.

How things had changed.

As the train picked up speed, the view shifted and he could watch the countryside zip by. Tall stalks of golden wheat and gentle swells quickly became a blur, but he could see them clearly in his mind's eye. They were as familiar to Desmond as his own name. More than just wheat and corn, they were home. And he was saying goodbye.

This is it, then.

He'd been away before, of course—sometimes for long stretches. Years, even. To college, to find himself. But this wasn't the same. No matter how bad things got back then, Desmond had always known that home was only a few days away. If his life turned upside down, there was always home; a place to lick his wounds, to gather his strength.

Home was a gray ranch-style tucked neatly into what passed for the suburbs in Desmond's hometown. It was a house where the big-haired, 70's bands Desmond's father loved rocked in the garage, accompanied by the clink-clatter of his father tinkering with things that usually didn't need to be tinkered with. It was the smell of the endless treats his mother baked because she believed there was nothing so bad in life that it couldn't be cured with a heavily-frosted cupcake.

Home was the place Desmond could run to when boys twice as large as him, with skin already tanned from helping their fathers bale hay, roughed Desmond up for no other reason than he was just pretty enough to make them question their own sexualities. The place where, after he caught his college boyfriend in bed with their European History professor, Desmond had spent weeks wallowing before his friends showed up to drag his sorry ass back to school.

Desmond sometimes wondered what had happened to them. To Chris, who had been all khaki and polo shirts in class, but leather and studs on the weekend. To Alex, who knew that he had been born in the wrong body but kept the promise he had made to his mother not to give up on Alexandra until after graduation. To outrageously funny Shaun, who had beaten every bully by beating them to the punch-line. Desmond sometimes wondered, but not for long because, truth be told, he didn't want to admit that, like the safety that gray ranch-style once offered, they were long gone. He was on his own now.

He turned his back to the window as the last vestiges of home rolled away. If Desmond let himself think about it, he would cry, which wasn't the wisest thing to do amid the throng of already angry, on-edge passengers. He couldn't show the fear rolling around inside his stomach. *Be strong,* Desmond told himself. *Be brave.* Head held high, Desmond held tight to one of the evenly-spaced iron poles that ran through the car and stared straight ahead.

He knew the other people squeezed into the train were staring at the laminated rainbow that lay against his button-down shirt; could feel their eyes glued to the mass-produced tag that hung from a lanyard around his neck. It had long been the symbol of gay men, lesbian women and a host of other people who didn't quite fit in. Desmond wore it with pride, even though it singled him out. Even though men in his position had been assaulted—and worse—for less.

Desmond would be lying if he said that he wasn't afraid of the burly men that filled the compartment. Their large, rough hands and sun-worn faces marked them as farmers, even without the tags they wore, the laminated sheaves of wheat that rested against their chests. Probably on their way to be tried for protesting the Presidential Work Order. They wouldn't be the first farmers to lose everything over a refusal to till the land for free, in exchange for having the land to till.

He wondered if they appreciated the irony of their situations. . .

No, probably not.

Desmond found no satisfaction in the fact that most of them had probably voted for the man who had ruined their lives. Ruined *all* their lives. It didn't matter who had voted for whom anymore; the mistake had been made and now they faced the consequences together.

It took several minutes for Desmond to realize that he wasn't staring blindly into space; he was staring into the heavily-lined face of an elderly man who wore the golden sheaves of a farmer around his neck. Unlike many of his younger counterparts, there was no hatred in the old man's eyes, only a kind of pitying sadness. He offered Desmond a tight-lipped smile that vanished the moment one of his companions spoke to him. The old farmer turned to answer and Desmond's would-be ally was lost.

The passengers scrambled to keep their footing as the train lurched to a heavy stop with a squeal of metal-on-metal. Barking at them to stay away from the doors, uniformed guards slid the doors open to allow another small group of tired-looking detainees to board. It was more of the same: coarse farmers and people whose families had probably been in America for generations but looked just a little too foreign to continue calling it home.

He almost envied them. Sure, they faced deportation but, since President Trump's first term in office, and his sweeping isolationist policies, most countries around the world had opened their borders to America's outcasts. Except, of course, the ones that had eagerly followed America's lead—countries like Great Britain, who had slammed its borders so quickly that many visitors never made it home.

A slim figure trying to squeeze through the crowded compartment drew Desmond's attention. As he got closer, Desmond could see that it was a young man, with brown hair and a scattering of freckles across his nose. A rainbow hung from the front of his jacket.

Jesus, he's just a kid. He'll never survive the re-orientation.

But as much as Desmond feared for the youngster, he was also unbelievably glad to see him. He was not alone. There would be someone who felt what he felt; who would understand the impossibility of what lay ahead. His knees weak with the sudden emotion, he clutched at the iron post for support.

The young man looked up. His eyes traveled to Desmond's shirt and the rainbow pinned there. The youngster's eyes lit up. Silently, they made their ways toward one another, meeting in the center of the compartment. Not daring to touch, a sure way to earn a beating before they'd even arrived, they stood there, staring.

It had been years since Desmond had seen another gay man in public. At times he felt like the last queer left in the state—which couldn't be true, of course. Passing a law denying queers basic human rights didn't *stop* people from being gay, it just sent them into hiding. God, how Desmond missed the community! Especially the crowded, glitter-streaked nightclubs he used to frequent. He wondered if the brown-haired boy had even been old enough to visit a club before they'd been shut down.

A sharp crack of static made his companion jump.

"Fifteen minutes to Atlanta Re-Orientation Camp," a bored voice said over the walkie-talkie clipped to a guard's belt.

Fifteen minutes. Was that all the freedom he had left? What would it be like inside the camp? Desmond hoped it wasn't as bad as the papers made out. He—

His world exploded into chaos. The train shook as the car seemed to go airborne, tilting. The crash of impact as Desmond and the others inside were tossed around like toys, colliding, smashing, then landing in tangled heaps as the train came to rest on its side. A hand closed around Desmond's. *Fuck it,* he thought and gave the hand a squeeze and pulled him into a hug. No one should face this alone.

Muffled whoops and gunfire came from outside. The guard in their compartment struggled to reach his gun but it was too late; one of the prisoners wrenched it from his hand and planted the barrel between the guard's eyes. He raised his hands in surrender.

Bang.

The guard collapsed at the feet of the angry farmers. One gave his corpse a spiteful kick.

"Heads up!" a voice from above called. A shower of broken glass rained down on them.

With the help of the camouflaged resistance fighters that had freed them, Desmond and the other occupants scrambled through the broken windows, up and out of the train. Up ahead, the engine still stood on the tracks, billowing greasy black smoke.

Some people had already taken off at a run, determined to put as much distance between themselves and the wreck as possible before word of their escape got out. Desmond hesitated. Where would he go? Home? He couldn't put his parents in that kind of danger. As he mulled over his options, Desmond managed to catch part of a conversation.

"I can't believe you pulled it off. Jesus, that was one helluva explosion!"

A man in the tan camouflage of the resistance laughed and slapped the farmer's back.

"Told you I'd fix it, didn't I?" the resistance fighter said.

"All right, boys," he called to the others. "Let's get to the safe house before all hell breaks loose."

"What about these guys?" he asked, motioning to Desmond and the younger man.

The farmer shrugged. "Does it matter? They're only faggots."

Desmond knew what was coming the moment the words left the farmer's mouth. Even before the camouflaged man raised his gun. Even before the youngster's brains sprayed across his face. He knew—as the gun turned to him, the barrel an empty circle of black, in the split second before the bullet ripped through his brain, Desmond smiled, feeling the hate that filled the souls around him, he knew. He knew.

Without doubt, he was one of the lucky ones.

The End

A Beautiful Industry

Stuart Hardy

2143: To deal with the increased demand for humanoid robots either by people who could afford them for personal use or to fill factory positions, the Chinese government construct new artificial islands in order to house factories dedicated to the manufacture of robots.

2178: The robots unite, form their own government and demand independence.

2199: The robots gain independence. The United Republic of ABCDEFG is founded, and robots, droids, circuitheads, whatever you want to call them, are manufactured at facilities on the islands by their mechanical forbearers, and are then shipped out to nexus points around the globe.

2225. . .

I saw there was a job opening at a warehouse a few states away. I didn't want to leave the wife and kids but, y'know, times are hard, and I thought we might just about make ends meet if I moved to the compound and sent a few hundred bucks home each month. They'd probably give me the job; it *was* a legal requirement to have at least 25% humans on the payroll for industrial jobs, and I was still in pretty good shape. Not many humans could keep up with the robots these days. It probably wouldn't be a total waste of time going. Just to see.

I didn't have much money so I'd have to hitchhike and hope I'd stumble into someone headed in that direction, which I did until I reached about halfway. I ended up walking down the side of the road with my thumb out for God knows how long.

When the circuithead slowed down to offer me a ride, there was a part of me that didn't think this was a bad idea and there was a part of me that was ready to refuse. I accepted because I was hungry, my feet hurt, and I was far too tired to turn down the lift no matter how much I hated those fucking things.

The truck was one of those large floating hunks of steel with a company logo printed across the side; it was one of the huge ones so there was almost no chance it was gonna be manned by a human. The second I saw it, I knew I was definitely gonna have to accept a ride from one of *them*.

Once his truck had stopped, he rolled down the window and leaned his steel face out.

"Want a ride?"

He had a strong, Southern accent, sounded like he'd originally been shipped to either Texas or Arkansas, somewhere like that. Why did they give them accents? Well. . . I mean, aside from the fact the circuitheads want to make us think they're just like us, but we know they're not! I mean. . . just look at them for Christ's sake! They made this ugly motherfucker think he's a human! Honestly, it turned my stomach!

Still, I had nowhere else to turn, had to say yes if I was gonna make the interview; it was only a few days away.

He shook my hand as I clambered into the truck. He had a good strong handshake, the type I would've liked in a human, but the plastic casings on his fingers and palms offset any appreciation of it. They felt a little bit worn and hardy though; there was almost something human in that.

I did feel uncomfortable being in the passenger seat. I'd never been inside a circuithead's truck before. I don't know what I expected but I was surprised to find he'd made it pretty homey; at least what must've been homey by robot standards. A massive flag was pinned across the back wall of the driver's compartment, didn't remember which island it represented, they all looked the same to me. This one was a dark grey, with dashes of red hidden inside an emblem of static that looked a bit like one of those old QR code things. There was a framed picture set on his dashboard of some bright green 1s and 0s. The radio was on, playing some static noise that their kind call "music". I never knew how they put up with that shit; I suppose it sounds like real words to them.

I didn't say anything for a while.

He was the one that spoke first.

"So where you headed?"

"Birmingham. Going for a job at Multishop."

"No shit! I know a guy at Multishop! Works in dispatch, name's Unit 87465, great guy. . ."

He trailed off, probably expecting me to pick up the conversation again now that we'd found a small bit of common ground, but I wasn't taking the bait. I saw his metallic smile as he tried to put my silence behind him.

"That's my wife back home," he said, gesturing to the picture of the 1s and 0s on the dashboard. "Had to sell her body a few years back to make ends meet. . . hoping she can go physical again round this time next year. . ."

He smiled and gave a bit of an uncomfortable snigger at my silence.

I don't know why I suddenly felt the need to do it, but after he mentioned his wife, I dug my wallet out of my pocket and found a picture of my family: me, Val and Luke. It was one of all three of us sitting by the barbecue on our camping trip a few summers earlier. Luke had grown a lot since then, so it wasn't exactly gonna serve as a good reminder of the home I'd be leaving behind at the compound, but it was the last time I remembered actually being happy. Last time we felt like a family.

I didn't tell the droid this, of course.

We didn't talk for a while; he just let me gaze out into the empty wastelands drifting by.

We stayed on the same road for about another half hour before turning onto a slightly more crowded main road. It was around five AM, so more cars and trucks were out. Pretty much all of the trucks were circuit jobs. Can't remember the last time I had met a human trucker. It happened sometimes, but companies just didn't want to have humans filling truck jobs anymore. When they had to hire unskilled workers like myself to meet their targets, they'd always either put us in admin, production lines, logistics, stuff like that. Droids could drive from pickup to drop-off with no sleep for days straight, but we couldn't. That, and droids never had accidents. Part of me was jealous of the guy for that.

Anyway, I started to nod off, but the humming drone of the engine kept me awake. The low static on the radio that I was ever so slightly starting to recognize as music didn't help me sleep either. It was subtle, but there appeared to be the faintest of beats hidden inside the wall of noise. Sleep just wouldn't come. My brain kept trying to hear the faint notes in the static, and I kept shooting hazy side-eyed glances at the robot's thousand yard stare, trying to picture just what was going through his head. It was genuinely frustrating me. A nap was clearly gonna be impossible.

"So, which island ya from?"

"G. One of the originals, ya know," he said proudly. "I miss G. Suppose you folks think it's all just factories as far as the eye can see, but it's not. We robots are actually big on the environment. The founders built forests and hills. . . they made fields of silicone for the young robots to play about in. . ."

"My wife and I had a little house in the suburbs," the circuithead continued. "Then, well, the economy went into deep freeze. Factories started pumping out large scale industrial units, better controls, more durable. Suddenly, they didn't see a need to keep units like me around on the island so I had to join an overseas program. Course, I was getting on at that stage, had to take whatever I could get. . ."

I said nothing.

". . . so, how about you?"

"I. . . um. . ." I couldn't tell him what I was thinking. It'd sound weird. . . I felt weird just thinking it.

"Have to leave the family behind for this job," I said. "Manual labor's all I'm good for and it's way too hard to come by these days, so I'm having to travel two states just to get it. Guy on the phone said they offer room and board for employees if they need it. . ."

The robots whistled through his teeth. "I hear that. Times ain't getting any easier. . ."

I didn't go on. I wanted to change the subject as quickly as possible.

"I've never seen the islands," I said.

"Oh you should go! They're amazing. I mean, they're nothing like your regular human tourist spots. They're a bit of a stretch for a human vacation. The islands have had their financial troubles recently, lotsa drugs, lotsa crime, corruption, bad business. . . But you've gotta see them before you die. They're beautiful, man, just beautiful. . . ."

It took me a while to respond. He got there before me.

"I know you guys think it's stupid. Our islands are all the same, but they're not. It's important to remember where you come from. That's part of why us bots are brought up in community living before we're transferred to factory work."

". . . yeah?" I said. Community living. Sounded fuckin' weird coming from a circuithead. "They don't teach us anything about you guys in school."

"Yeah, I hear that a lot. It's weird, they teach us all about you," he said.
"They could just pre-load us with blueprints and tell us to get on with factory work, but you humans are different. If we're gonna live alongside you, manufacture our children to live alongside you. . . well, we gotta learn like you do. We grow up in the foster district where all kinds of robots built for all kinds of different work live alongside each other. We go to school, we're taught the old-fashioned way, all manual like. We used to sing the island national anthem each day before empathy classes with a teacher from the human exchange program. . ."

I still said nothing. I felt so damn uncomfortable around him now that he was opening up about himself. . . no, circuitheads don't have anything to open up about, get a grip! He's just listing off stuff that's happened in his life, there's nothing in there! It's a report written in his head, little details, it's not alive!

"I miss my school friends sometimes," he said. "One kid I knew named 74111104110; he used to make me laugh so hard!"

I still said nothing. I was busy thinking back to when I was a kid at school.

We used to have these old rusted robot torsos hanging from a long tree branch on the edge of the playground. We used to hit them with sticks in recess for fun. We made a game out of it; see who could hit it so hard that the torso spun round the top of the branch. The sports teachers actually encouraged it; we had a record book and everything. I used to know a kid who hit those things so damn hard and imagined they were alive. He ended up second in those bot-thrashing league tables; used to just lose control, used to just let it all come out. . .

I made friends with him. We used to talk about circuitheads all the time. They stopped our daddies getting the factory jobs. They were why we were so dirt poor pretty much our whole lives. They stole our futures before we were even born. My family was never known for being smart, didn't have much in the way of prospects. I grew up feeling such a burning hatred for those fucking machines.

But now, just listening to this guy. . .

And what was so sickening to me was that he could sense it. The guy wasn't stupid; robots are built to be smart. They're trained to be sensitive to humans; our tone, our body language. The tension between us in that truck was like a shotgun blast to the stomach.

I could see that that smile he'd worn ever since I'd stepped into his vehicle hundreds of miles back was just as fake as everything else about him.

". . . You really hate us, don't you?" he asked.

I said nothing for a while. I could only manage an uncomfortable glance up at him. His expression wavered as he stared out at the road ahead.

. . . yeah, he was pissed with me. . . well, suppose I would be too if I were him. . .

. . . No, circuitheads don't have feelings!. . . well, they do, but they're made up feelings, y'know? They're given them in order to make humans identify with them as if they're like us, but they're not like us! They're fake! They're not real!

"S'alright, I don't mind," he said. "I'm used to it by now. . ."

He trailed off. I was sure he was about to say something to try and make me feel bad or stupid for being uncomfortable around his people, but he didn't. He just sat there; patient and polite, just slowly bobbing his head to his tunes coming out of the radio.

We didn't talk after that. It was about six hours. I got a few hours shuteye around the middle, tried distracting myself from the music and the engine and that terrifying look in the droid's eyes. I knew that his staring dead ahead with no absent-minded glances across the landscape was so he could constantly scan the roads ahead for obstructions and compute his arrival time, but I just couldn't help but think he was consciously trying to avoid looking at me.

He dropped me off a few towns away from my destination. I had a few bucks to get the bus to the factory from there. I only realised when he pulled over and told me that this was where I need to get off that I hadn't actually asked him his name. I turned as I was getting off the truck with my bag over one shoulder and asked him what it was. He told me. It was some long string of random letters and numbers, barely caught it to be honest, I don't remember any of it now. It started with a "U," I think. Honestly, how can anyone be expected to remember that shit?

He drove off without saying a word. I headed over to the bus station trying not to think about it.

I've never acted the same way around robots since. I've never been totally secure around them of course, but I'm more relaxed than I used to be.

I work with a small group of them at the factory now. They seem like genuinely decent folks. I even remember a few of their names, though I had to ask them not to take offense if I shorten their names or get them wrong from time to time, I'm just not used to being around robotkind so much. They couldn't be happier to let it slide.

We all get paid the same; we all send our money home to our families; dreaming of the day that all this running around'll be over. All of us, counting down the days until our vacations back home with our families.

It's what keeps me going, y'know? Me with Val and Luke by the lake in the summer. . .

Sometimes I think of that guy who gave me a ride, and I wonder if his wife got her body back in the end, and if he ever got to see his home again.

The End

Queens Crossing

Lou Antonelli

The young real estate broker poked at his plate, and winced.

"You know what *nouvelle cuisine* means in French?" he asked. "Small portions."

The tinkle and hum of crystal tableware and cultured voices surrounded the pair of young men. Across the table, the attorney pulled out a folder and positioned it carefully in front of him.

The waiter had just poured a lemon-flavored Perrier and as it hissed and sprinkled, the attorney nervously pushed the folder a couple of inches forward.

Across the table, the young real estate broker both smiled and glared at him.

The attorney cleared his throat.

"I'm sorry, Mister Trump..."

"Call me Donald."

"I'm sorry, Donald, I've looked at your situation and the law every which way possible, but there's nothing to be done."

Trump reached for the Perrier. "That bad, eh?"

"It's not bad, it's just not," said the attorney. "It's your father's firm. It's his to manage and operate as he sees fit. Barring any incapacity, you really don't have a say right now."

Trump leaned forward, elbows on the table. "Look, I love my father, but he's making a big mistake. He likes to do things himself, and if he moves into Manhattan, he will be biting off more than he can chew."

He looked around the lunchtime crowd at the Manhattan restaurant like he was surveying a field of prey.

"Yes, but it's his mistake to make," said the attorney.

Trump looked at him, leaned back and smiled broadly.

"Mister Springer, you grew up in Queens, right?"

"Rego Park, I went to Forest Hill High School."

"I grew up in Jamaica Estates, I went to the Kew-Forest School," said Trump. "So, we're both Queens kids, right?

Springer nodded.

"Do you think working real estate in Queens and Brooklyn prepares you for tackling the Manhattan market?"

Springer smiled nervously. "I'm not here to give you business advice. I'm here to let you know the law. And if your father doesn't want to give you a leadership role in the firm, there's nothing you can do."

Trump briefly pursed pouty lips, then smiled. "I don't even want a leadership role, I just want my own territory. I've got the energy and drive. Shit, I'm only 27! And I can do Manhattan, he can't."

"Regardless of the wisdom of his business decision, there's not much you can do." Springer cocked an eyebrow at Trump. "By the way, why *did* your father renege on his promise to you?"

Trump frowned and looked askance. "He said he was visited by some men in black suits who told him I was not welcome in the Manhattan real estate market."

"Were they mobsters?"

Donald shrugged. "None I knew, he said they said they simply represented some 'concerned citizens' who were worried over what I could and would do in the future, whatever that means."

"You have any enemies?" asked Springer.

"I thought I hadn't had time to make any enemies, damn it! I wish I knew who these people are."

"You're a bit brusque, Donald, you must have shot off your mouth or sassed someone--or knowing you, maybe disrespected their girlfriend or daughter."

Springer pushed the folder forward. "Here's my report, with my recap of all the pertinent laws and case studies," he said. "Like I said, you didn't hire me to give you business advice, but if I *were* to give you some business advice, I'd suggest you move out of your father's shadow, and start up your own firm elsewhere. Maybe you two can reconcile in the future or perhaps, if you prove yourself, he'll bring you back into the fold."

Trump scowled. “I’ve lived in New York City all my life, I don’t know anywhere else well enough to get a foothold.”

Springer pulled out a pack of cigarettes. “Smoke?”

“No, thanks,” said Trump as he picked up a pack of The Quilted Giraffe’s matches and passed them across the table. “But I don’t mind if you do.”

“Thanks.” Springer lit up and exhaled. “Do you know anything about Cincinnati?”

“It’s in Ohio, why?”

“The legal scene is packed in New York, there’s so much competition. I’ve thought about relocating, and I’ve done some research. Some cities are poised to boom in the next decade—Houston, especially—but if you want to go to a city with a healthy business climate that should grow in the next few years—and still in the Northeast—Cincinnati would be a good place to be.”

He took another puff. “I’ve thought about relocating there myself, but I haven’t quite decided yet.”

Trump rubbed his chin with a twinkle in his eye. “Well, I suppose that’s far enough away to get out of dad’s shadow.”

Springer chuckled. “Lay a guilt trip on him, say that since he’s treated you so bad, he should give or loan you a nest egg, so you can strike out on your own.”

“It just may work,” said Trump, glancing down at his plate. “Eat your food before it gets cold.”

~oOo~

Recorded Broadcast--WLTW television, Cincinnati, Ohio: February 14, 1998.

"Today on *The Donald Trump Show*, he interviews Linda Tripp, the Washington insider who *blew* the whistle on the scandal of President Wet Willy Clinton keeping an in-house prostitute. Donald will be back with us in 90 seconds."

[Camera cues in to pouting man with strawberry blonde hair sitting in an office chair holding a manila folder in his lap.]

"Today, my people, I have a very special guest... A guest like no other. She is a very spectacular guest, and she has agreed to speak with me about how she learned that President Bill Clinton was keeping a temple prostitute on the White House staff and on the government payroll. This is really, really, big, I tell you. You won't hear this anywhere else! Ladies and gentlemen, Linda Tripp."

[A rather chagrined blonde woman walks from off-stage, toward the host, who extends a small hand and grabs hers, pulling her arm towards him as he shakes it violently. He gestures to an empty seat. Tripp yanks her arm away and rubs it as she sits down.]

"Now Linda, you are a patriot, a true patriot, for making these recordings--which you have given to Special Prosecutor Kenneth Starr--where this Monica Lewinsky discusses how President Clinton--our Commander in Chief--the supposed most powerful man in the world--used her as a kept woman and had relations with her in the White House. Isn't that so?"

"Mister Trump, you make it sound much more abusive than it was..."

"Well, it wasn't appropriate, was it?"

"No, not at all," said Tripp. "But you make it sound like Clinton kept Lewinsky as some kind of sex slave. That's not the case at all. She greatly admires him..."

"Lewinsky is Jewish, isn't she?"

"Yes, but what's that got to do with..."

"Do you think it's possible she had the President in a compromising position so he could be blackmailed?" asked Trump. "So he could be controlled by the Israeli government?"

He opened the folder on his lap. "I have documents here that show that Monica Lewinsky was born in Israel and was recruited by the Mossad to be a mole in the executive branch."

"That's ridiculous," snapped Tripp. "She was born in San Francisco and is as American as you and I!"

"I beg to differ, Ms. Tripp, I beg to differ," he said, waving the folder. "I have proof here she was put in the White House to seduce the President, who was more than willing to use her as a traditional Middle Eastern temple prostitute..."

"Mister Trump, I agreed to come on this show to discuss a genuine problem with an abuse of power committed by President Clinton," said Tripp. "You are making unfound..."

"I understand, Ms. Tripp, you are concerned about catching the 'Arkansas Flu,' I understand," said Trump, turning slightly and winking at the audience. "But we can read between the lines."

He set his jaw. "You are still a great hero for letting us know about this."

He turned to the camera. "Next after the commercial break, we will talk about specifics in those Lewinsky tapes. Folks, stay tuned. Oh, here's a warning. If you are a cigar smoker, be prepared to quit."

[Fade-out to commercial break.]

~oOo~

The crowd at Gracie Mansion was bright, lively, and mostly drunk. The Mayor looked in the distance and scowled.

He nudged an aide. "What's that motherfucker doing here?"

"Councilman Halloran invited him."

"Son-of-a-bitch!"

The aide smiled. "Who? Trump or Halloran?"

"Both! Oh shit, he's seen me!"

"Want me to cover for you?"

"No, I want to look him in the eye. I haven't seen him--in the flesh--in 45 years. Only on television, and then only accidentally!"

"Oh, that's right, he grew up in Queens, too!"

Mayor Springer put on a fake smile as Trump moved closer.

"What's he doing in the city?" he side-mouthed.

"His show is on location, doing a series on big-city street hustling," said the aide.

"I wish he'd stay in Ohio. You know, I'm the guy who gave him the idea about moving to Cincinnati back in 1970," said the Mayor.

"What?"

"I'll tell you later, sometime," whispered Springer as Trump pounced.

"Jerry! It's great to see you again!" Trump shouted.

He wore a ton of make-up and a shiny golden toupee.

"You're looking good," Trump continued.

Springer poked Trump's belly. "You're looking well-fed!"

He turned and gestured. "This is my aide, Marma Shabilya. Miss Shabilya, Donald Trump."

The talk show host extended a well-manicured and plump hand. "You can call me Donald."

They shook hands. "Have we ever seen each other since that day at The Quilted Giraffe?" asked Trump.

Springer frowned. "No, I don't think so. But we've both been busy!"

They laughed.

Trump winked at the aide. "Your boss here is the one who put the bug in my ear about moving to Ohio!"

"Really?" she asked.

"It's a long story," said Trump.

"I'd love to hear it," said Shabilya.

"Can I get you a drink?" asked Trump.

She looked at the Mayor, who nodded.

"I'll be back in a while," she said, sneaking a wink at the Mayor as she walked behind Trump.

The Assistant Mayor walked up. "She's a good girl, isn't she?"

"I'll say. That's noble of her, sacrificing her brain to listen to Trump's drivel," said the Mayor.

"I know the story," said the Assistant Mayor. "You and Trump both grew up in Queens, but you suggested he move and set up his own business when Fred wouldn't let him into the company management."

"Why did you decide to stay in New York?" he continued.

Springer smiled. "In the long run, I decided I felt more comfortable home, here in New York. But Cincinnati was on my mind when I advised Trump."

"And New York is glad you decided to stay put." The Assistant Mayor patted him on the shoulder. "You've been a great mayor. DeBlasio and Bloomberg can't touch you in the next election."

The Mayor turned. "You know what's strange? We both were elected to City Council in 1971—--Trump in Cincinnati, and me here. He was mayor there years before I was here."

"Something about picking up a prostitute. He had to resign."

"Sure was, and then—--since he'd been such a tabloid sensation—a local TV station offered him his own talk show."A waitress walked by and the Mayor took a glass of champagne. He raised it.

The Assistant Mayor also took a glass. “And the rest is history!”

They clinked glasses and each took a sip.

The Assistant Mayor looked at Trump, his arm comfortably around Shabilya’s waist.

The Mayor followed his gaze.

“You know, you can’t help but wonder what might have become of that asshole had he stayed in New York City?” said the Mayor.

“Who knows? Who would have thought he’d become a sleazy talk show host?”

The Assistant Mayor snapped his fingers. “I know. He’d be mayor now! And you’d be the talk show host.”

“Bullshit!” laughed the Mayor.

“What? That you’d be a talk show host?”

“No, that he’d be Mayor! With that ego, nothing less than President!”

The Gracie Mansion crowd slowly stopped chattering and turned as the pair laughed and laughed and clinked their champagne glasses together.

The End

Small Courages

Eric M. Witchey

Easy run. Love fall. Cool air. Breathe. Out-out. In-in. Easy run. Slow run. Run again tomorrow. Out-out. In-in. Smooth path. Turning trees. Clear sky. No clouds. No contrails. Out-out. Blond-and-flannel. Up ahead. Dark-skinned daughter. Walking again today. Mixed marriage? Adoption? Pleasure to see. Been a week. No, two. Probably scared. New president. Travel bans. Walls. Saber rattling. Everybody's scared. Easy run. Out-out. In-in. They're talking. Stopped at the fork. Always a shy smile for my wave.

~oOo~

Two hundred walks since Anna turned three. A month since she decided we should take different paths around the frog pond.

"Go ahead, Anna. I'll meet you at the other side." There's no one around. The park is safe: just migrating geese, the Asian woman and her yellow lab, and the ten-o'clock running man.

It's only fifty yards of separation. Her four-year old logic is perfect. The short path is for short legs. The longer, curved path is for long legs. A month ago, the short path made me proud of her growing independence. Now, it's separation, vulnerability, and my belly burns to think of it. I wonder how much she understands?

She's so serious today. Do the kids at preschool talk about it? The sun isn't strong enough to force her tiny squint. She ignored the yellow lab. She's so cute in her little jeans. They're getting tight. I'll need to get her new ones.

She's turning back. Her cheeks are rosy from walking. "Be careful, Mommy," she says. "Look out for tearists."

"I will, Anna. You too." Her nod is grave. I've left the TV news on too much. She checks the path like she's going to cross at a light, and she's off on her adventure around the pond.

~oOo~

Breathe easy. Breathe easy. Out-out. In-in. Air moist. Cool through my beard. A little tired. Short path today. I almost shaved. Dark beard. Dark skin. Slow run. I won't shave. Easy. Not for fear. Today, I run. Blond-and-flannel walks left. Daughter walks right. What's her name? Heard it once. Anita? No. Anna. Yes. Cute. Short run today. Run again tomorrow. Out-out. In-in. Easy run. Stay right. Give her room. Little girl alone. Don't spook her. Out-out. In-in.

~oOo~

Mommy's behind the cat's tails. I hope she's not scared. I'm big. I know how to walk in the park. The cat's tails are big, but Mommy's okay. The yellow dog lady isn't a tearist. She doesn't have a beard.

The runner man's coming. He's running on my path, not on Mommy's. Maybe he's a tearist. Tearists and the orange man make Mommy cry. The running man has a beard. Orange man says tearists can be anybody. Maybe I should run. I can't see Mommy. The cat's tails are too big. He's getting close. Mommy says if we do the same stuff we always do, tearists can't win.

My shoe's untied. I shouldn't run. "Mommy?"

She's too far. She says don't show you're scared. If I yell, he'll know I'm scared. I can't let him know I'm scared.

Everybody ties their shoes. You're supposed to tie your shoes. Always.

~oOo~

Out-out. In-in. Anna ties a shoe. Cutie. Hunkered down. Sun on hair. Red tints. Her back to me. Give her room. Off the path. Two steps. On the path. Out-out. In-in.

~oOo~

I'm tying my shoe. He's running right at me. Go away. Run away. I'm doing what everybody does. I'm tying my shoe. Don't make me cry. I'm tying my shoe.

He's gone. It works. Mommy was right. Tearists can't make you cry if you do what you always do.

~oOo~

Anna runs up to me. "How was your walk?" I ask. I hug her too tight.

"Mommy, your shoe's untied."

"Just one loop. It's okay." I don't want to let her go, but she pulls away.

"I'll tie it for you, Mommy."

"No, that's okay."

"Mommy, please?"

Her gaze is intense. I laugh. Fifty yards around a frog pond, and now shoestrings are the most important things in the world. "Okay, Anna. Thank you."

The End

The Nompers

Rebecca Mix

The trouble started when the spokesman for the ICRLM—the Intergalactic Council for Resettlement of Misplaced Lifeforms—agreed to take comments.

Representatives and community members from nearly thirty planets cried out in unison. Some leapt from the dented metal chairs that had been crammed into the black-tiled room. Journalists from across the galaxy surged forward. Every alien shouted over each other, wanting to know what was to be done with the humans.

I watched as a Drunian leapt to his feet, his extra flaps of skin fluttering as he straightened. He looked like a spot of mud against the tile. Drun was a desert planet, I remembered. It was hard to keep them straight.

"What of the violence?" the Drun demanded. "Humans are cruel."

"Not all humans are violent," the spokesman countered.

The Drunian blinked, his red eyes winking like the recording lights on an old camcorder. "We can't be sure which ones are nonviolent, though," it quaffed. "Even if fifty of them are peaceful, it just takes one to ruin everything. I will not risk my planet to help some strays that should have been more careful with their own world."

I wanted to point out that Drun wasn't even being considered for taking refugees. It had no water. Other life forms rose, voicing their concerns, spewing the essence of their fears.

It had been seventy-four cycles since a planet was so completely destroyed, especially one as overpopulated as Earth. There hadn't been much the current humans could do to stop it. But try telling that to the ambassadors.

Even a Grilian showed up, arriving in an algae-coated travel tank balanced precariously on rust-covered wheels. The Grilian floated with one tentacle pressed against the glass, eyes rolling as it gestured for a translator, although I wasn't sure why. Humans didn't have gills, and a planet that was completely underwater wouldn't suit them any more than the deserts of Drun.

"Pitiful," the Flaxor mumbled next to me.

I twisted to look at him, my pen hovering over the smooth glass of my tablet. "Are you going to speak on their behalf?"

"Ach," the ambassador grumbled. "No, my district is still pissed at me over the Martian incident. Can't risk it, not if I want to get re-elected."

I sank back into my seat. I *liked* humans. A part of me hoped that the ambassador for my planet would offer at least some of them refuge.

"*I* have an objection, too," a familiar voice piped up. The Luruk ambassador rose to his feet, smoothing the fabric of his silk suit over his bumpy chest. The long, wilting red spines that protruded from his temples quivered.

The spokesman looked at the Luruk with a pained expression. "The ambassador has the floor."

"Luruk absolutely cannot take in a single human," the Luruk said, looking a little too proud.

"Oh, here we go," the Flaxor muttered.

The spokesman steepled his twelve fingers together and cocked his head to stare at the Luruk ambassador. "I will remind you, Ambassador, that Luruk is only one of *two* planets with a similar enough climate to Earth that the humans biology would not need re-programming."

"I'm aware," said the Luruk, spines trembling. "But we have to put our citizens first."

"So you would condemn them to die?"

"Oh no, of course not—we're not savages," the Luruk blustered. "I would support their relocation, just not on my planet."

The spokesman groaned. The ICRLM wanted the humans to be split equally between Cristhon and Luruk because their planets had the most similar climates, and they were both much larger than Earth. The humans could be placed there without being too much of a drain on resources.

The translator finally made it over to the Grilian, still bobbing in the tank. I watched curiously, wondering if the squid alien would have something warmer to say.

The translator turned around, and cleared her throat. "The ambassador from Grilian would like to know why the humans should even receive handouts, when the rest of us have our own struggles?"

I bit back a groan.

"He's right," the Luruk said, squinting all four eyes. "We're a planet, not a charity."

"You'll be given vouchers," the spokesman told him calmly. "Subsidies, from the council—to offset the cost."

The Luruk curled his lip. "It won't be enough. Luruk isn't as rich in resources as Cristhon. Why can't they take the whole lot?"

The Cristhon ambassador jerked to attention. Her colorful head feathers puffed out in alarm, and her wings rustled like dry leaves as she rose. "We agree that the humans need help," the Cristhakian said, her beak clicking as she spoke. Her fingers fluttered in the air. "But we're concerned of the...baggage they might bring."

"So violent," the Drun ambassador piped up unhelpfully.

I cut him at a nasty glare.

The Cristhakian nodded. "They have a different way of life from us. They're simply a different class."

The room collapsed into more arguments. The spokesman tried and failed to regain order, his face strained and a little lost. It seemed every planet that could have taken a chunk of humans had a thousand excuses on why they never would.

"Well, since we have no volunteers, we will now hear from the Earth ambassador," the spokesman said, levelling a glare at the crowd.

The room quieted. The Drun squirmed, and the Cristhakian's feathers fluffed up so high that they stood nearly on end. The humans were all supposed to be in holding, preparing to be shipped off to whatever planet the council decided they belonged on—if they decided.

If they didn't, they would be blasted into deep space, just like the Shoorians seventy-four years before them.

There were no beaks clicking, no snarling, no words as a single human shuffled to the front of the room. I leaned forward, interest getting the better of me. It'd been years since I'd seen a human in person.

She stood on two legs, covered in soft, pink-brown skin and thick, curling hair. She was small, only about half the size of the Drun, and she looked frail. I stared at the human and had a hard time believing that this was the same species who built rockets to hurtle free of their atmosphere, who had crafted bombs strong enough to blow away entire cities.

The human did not look afraid. She stepped forward and lifted her chin, smoothing the black cloth of her dress down the front. "We are not asking for much," the human said firmly. "If a planet would take us, humans will earn their keep." Her eyes flicked pointedly around the crowd, dark and quick. "You've benefited from our help before."

Murmurs rippled through the crowd. It had been humans that gave us the tablets we now carried everywhere. They'd been essential in helping establish the telecom system that allowed different galaxies to communicate.

"If your technology was so superior, you should have engineered a way to save your planet," the Luruk said dryly.

The human's face crumbled a little. "We just need a place to stay."

There was fear in her eyes, but her voice was strong. I admired her for that.

"You should have thought of that before you became planetless," the Drun sniffed.

Assenting murmurs filled the room. I leaned forward, interested, wondering if I should speak up. But I was a reporter from a tiny planet. My words wouldn't matter, and my planet didn't have room for the lot of them.

I have forgotten most of what followed. I don't remember the Drun becoming so angry that he started spitting sand. I don't remember the human remaining calm even as tears cut down her cheeks, or the aliens that leaned away from her as if her grief were a disease they might catch. Nor do I remember staring at her and wondering if my people would also be thrown away if my planet became unlivable.

Here is what I remember:

Silence, ticking through the room. The spokesman looking at the human as if she were a sick wyrmhound that he loved but still had to put down. The Drun sneering, the Luruk smug, and several other aliens looking concerned but still silent. Just like me.

I remember the human looking at the spokesman. “Please,” she whispered. “We don’t have anywhere else to go.”

The spokesman shook his head. “I am sorry, but without a willing planet, there is simply nowhere for humanity to live. We’ve done everything we can.”

Most of all, I remember the human’s wail like a siren, her cry slicing through the room, climbing higher, higher, until it cut out and then she was screaming with her mouth open, but there was no sound. She did not breathe. The human remained there unseeing, wide-eyed and still trying to scream as tears rolled down her cheeks. Silent as the rest of the room as the guards rose to escort her away.

The End

The Ten Commandments Renegotiated

Jim Wright

Bobby Lee Featherston

Somewhere in the desert, Sinai Peninsula, 3500 years ago (give or take). Trump Moses returns from The Mountain to find the people engaged in drunken revelry. He smiles.

Debauchery, fornication, gluttony, idolatry, greed, avarice.

It looks to be a better than average rally.

Thank you, thank you all. Very big day today. Very big! Just came down from the mountain. I just spoke to God. Big fan. Personal friend. Known Him a long time. Long time. He's a big supporter. Really the best God. Beautiful guy. Great ratings. Gave me these tablets. Great stuff.

The crowd cheers

I talked to God. I talk to Him all the time. Sometimes. We don't talk all of the time. But we talk. He takes my calls. Everybody takes my calls. They love me up there. God called me. Got invited up the mountain. Beautiful mountain. Good place for Trump

Hotel. Nice view. Wanted to talk about The Commandments.

The Commandments, Folks. He had a whole list of commandments. Etched in stone. Eight, ten, twenty, I dunno, I didn't count. Too many. Too many. I didn't count.

Crowd boos

God. I love God, He's a great guy, but the commandments, Folks. Too many. The regulations are strangling business. I told Him that. We've got to get rid of it, get out of the way of business. Make the Holy Land Great Again.

Crowd chants: "Holy Land! Hoe Lee Land! Hoe LEE LAND!"

God, great guy, no head for business. No head for business.

Too many commandments, Folks. But some are good. Some are fine. We don't want to mess with those, some are fine. They're fine.

The first one is big. We've got to have that one. Thou shalt have no other gods before Me. That makes sense. Like I said, God, good friend of mine. He's the best God. First in line. He called shotgun, always rides up front in the limo. Now no offense to you, no offense, Folks, but that's what it says. Best God. And we're gonna put Him first. Shotgun.

Crowd cheers wildly. Shotgun! Shotgun!

So, I left that one alone. Don't mess with what works.

Graven images. The gravy images, Folks, I don't know. We've got to stop this. Gravy images. Graven, what have you. They're bad. Some are good. But bad. You shall not make for yourself an idol, that's what God said. No idols. But I said, what about *American Idol*? That's a great show. Not great like *The Apprentice*, but okay. Good ratings. But He doesn't like idols. Gravy images. He's got a problem. Just taking up space. We're gonna take them down. We're gonna build something. Build a wall. Something great. No more gravy. No more. I like ketchup. No gravy. But *American Idol*, that's fine. That's okay. I got Him to agree to that. So we're good.

Gravee! Gravee! Gravee!

Too many regulations. It's killing the jobs, Folks. But this next one is, we need this one. This is, it's good. I love this next one. I liked it so much I just added to it. You know, can't take the Lord's name in vain. Don't do it. People think this is about swearing. Profanity. I don't do it. But it's not about the profanity. It's not the profanity Folks. It's about the lying. That's what people get wrong. God doesn't care if you swear, it's the lying. The lies, Folks. Like Crook. . .

Trump Moses's words are drowned out as the crowd begins wildly chanting,
"Lock her up! Lock her up! Lock her up!"
Trump Moses smiles and nods.
It goes on for a long time.

This next one. I told Him, bad for business, Folks. Remember the Sabbath and keep it holy. Love it. Good idea, but bad for business. It's costing. Terrible ratings. Attendance is way down. The NFL people can't be kneeling on Sunday. It's ruining the game. We gotta get rid of this one, I told Him. Big football fan. God. The biggest. Loves the game. But the ratings are terrible. Boring. We're losing jobs. So, I said this one has to go. Has to go, Folks. He didn't want to do it. No games on Sunday.

Booing

No, no, it's okay. It's okay. Remember, I dealt with Qaddafi. I rented him a piece of land. He paid me more for one night than the land was worth for two years, and then I didn't let him use the land. That's what we should be doing. I don't want to use the word 'screwed', but I screwed him.

Cheering

I told God we had to drop this one. Just drop it. Bad for business. Bad for jobs. So, we're gonna have football on Sunday. The best games. Big turnouts.

Jobs, jobs, jobs. Right? See, God, he knows. He listens to me.

And speaking of jobs, Folks. Speaking of jobs. We're bringing back, Hallmark, the greeting cards. The cards, Folks. Just talked to Hallmark, big new factory. Gonna be printing up the cards. Hundreds of jobs.

Crowd looks at each other in confusion. Cards?

Honor your father and mother. We're going to keep that commandment. That's a good one. Honor them. Unless they're liberals. Or Muslims. The Alzheimer's. I have a good brain. People say it. My children honor me. Father's Day, I get a big card. A big card, Folks, signed by all the kids. Mother's Day, a big card. Nobody loves mothers more than me. I am a mother lover. I get Melania a big card, the best card. Plays a little song when you open it. The whole works. Very fancy. We're gonna make Mother's Day Great again. Father's Day too. Bring back the greeting card jobs. What more can you say? Right? Right? Mothers. Fathers. Of course, my dad, you know, he was a hell of a guy. Taught me a lot. Made me work for everything I ever got. Loved people. Bought homes for lots of people. He loved people, good people, some of them. He loved mothers. That's where I get it. People called him a mother all the time. All the time, Folks. That's where I get it.

"Mother! Mother! Mother!"

The next one is tough, Folks. No killing. No killing. I mean, I could stand in the middle of Giza and shoot somebody, and I wouldn't lose voters. They love me. But no killing. I told God we've got to have some exemptions. It's the regulations that are killing us. This is government overreach. We're gonna need an exemption for our heroes. You can't give a man a badge and complain every time someone bangs their head or a crossbow goes off. What about loser terrorists? You can't just say no killing! That's crazy. Charlton Heston. Great actor. President of the NRA, he said, and I quote, "Thou shalt not keep a man from owning a sling. It's his right." But no killing. No killing.

Crowd boos, "Noooo!"

So, I got God to swap out this one for the Second Amendment!

"Holy Land! Hoe Lee Land! Hoe LEE LAND!"

Now this next one, Folks. Adultery. I think the only difference between me and the other prophets is that I'm more honest and my women are more beautiful. But adultery. Again, the government overreach. I love women. They've come into my life. They've gone out of my life. We can't do this, I said to God. It's crazy. All of the women on *The Apprentice* flirted with me. That's to be expected. Adultery. I mean, a commandment about gay marriage, I said I can see that. Gay marriage. It's like in golf. A lot of people—I don't want this to sound trivial—but a lot of people are switching to these really long putters, very unattractive. It's weird. You see these great players with these really long putters, because they can't sink three-footers anymore. And, I hate it. I am a traditionalist. I have so many fabulous friends who happen to be gay, but I am a traditionalist. I love women. So adultery. Bad regulation. Bad commandment. We'd have to stone half of Congress and it would be the *wrong* half. No. Can't do it, Folks. Repeal and replace. First day in office. Repeal the adultery.

Crowd holds up Tiki torches chanting, "Adult are REE! Adult are REE!"

Gee, I forgot how long ten commandments could be. It's like the movie. Great movie. Charlton Heston. Great actor. Good friend. I didn't know him. Good movie. That Ramses, great city. Beautiful house. Gold. Big statues. Very good ideas. Great movie. But too long. No stealing. God says no stealing. Thou shall not steal. See? That's the problem, it's too vague. Don't steal. That could mean anything. I asked Jeff Sessions. No stealing. Jeff and I don't agree on some things. But good man. Good ratings. He tells me he's a Knight. Very smart. If anybody knows about stealing, it's the lawyers. He didn't know. He didn't know, Folks. No stealing. Too vague. Nobody even knows what it means. I asked Wall Street. Nothing. Steal what? Money? Elections? It doesn't say. Crazy. It's gotta go.

"Cray-Zee! Crazy-Zee!"

No fake news. This is the important one, Folks. The fake news media. It's terrible. False witnesses. The failing *New York Times*. Very bad. It's so bad. Our great press secretary, Sean Spicer, gave alternative facts, but the press, so dishonest, won't report that. Washington Post. Mad Magazine. So mean. Zero integrity. False witnesses. And the leaks, we have to stop the leaks. Fake News CNN is doing polls again despite the fact that their election polls were a way off disaster. Much higher ratings at Fox. I have all the ratings for all those morning shows. When I was up on the mountain, God, He and I are friends, I'm probably the only person here who's seen His hindquarters up close. Burning bush. The whole thing. He watches them, the morning shows. I have all the ratings. They go double, triple. But they won't tell you that. Very dishonest. God is very unhappy. Fake News is at an all time high. Where is their apology to me for all of the incorrect stories?

"Cray-Zee! Crazy-Zee! Crazy-ZEE!"

We got one more. One more, Folks. No, just one. That's all, there were more, but no, too many regulations. It was a bad deal. Like the Iran thing. Had to go. I got it down to ten? Eight. Less. Obama couldn't do that. Very dishonest. One more Folks. One more. Thou shall not covfefe you neighbor's wife. . .

Crowd stops chanting

. . . I mean, don't covfefe, no cov. . . Uh.

Puzzlement spreads through the Israelites

Covfefe. . .

They turn to each other and mouth the word, covfefe? Covfefe?

Covfefe. It's right there in the stone, Folks. That's what He said. Thou shall not covfefe your neighbor's ass. Wife. Whatever. No covfefe.

At least that's what I think He said.

He's kind of hard to understand, what with the Russian accent and all. . .

The End

Illegal Citizens

Irene Radford

"*Adios, amigo,*" Mariposa Santiago del Santa Cruz saluted the dead man she shared her boxcar with. He'd died a day and a half ago, likely could have been cured with a ten dollar bottle of antibiotics. But that didn't happen in boxcars, the man was dead, the victim of a lifetime collection of neglect, homelessness, and despair. Eventually those who found the man, and then evidence of her presence, would blame her for his death, as they blamed her for everything else that was wrong in this country.

She jumped clear of the car as the train ground to a halt, landing with a knee-crunching jar. Her teeth rattled and her jaw ached. Ignoring the pain, she took off at a low run, darting from bush to bush, hugging the growing shadows. The thumb drive she'd hidden inside her panties wiggled and threatened to slip free from the spent elastic.

Shouts from behind propelled her faster, deeper into the desert. Another three minutes and the sun would drop below the horizon. A moonless night and the thick pollution had become her friends. Three weeks on the run, a thousand miles between her and home, she couldn't give up now.

An hour later she crept into the border town that was no longer marked on most maps. Only outlaws, political exiles, and *coyotes* hung out here.

~oOo~

Three weeks ago, she would never have come to a place like this. The dark, low-ceilinged room reeked of cheap tobacco, spilled tequila, stale piss, and better-than-backyard pot. She pushed back against the wall, and let her eyes adjust to the gloom.

She found the *coyote* quickly. A tall *Anglo* in a slick suit and a too-wide tie, out of style for so long that it was almost hip again. Nordic blond hair should have marked him as an outsider in this illegal haven, but the easy smile and casual way he lounged against the bar said he belonged. Nicknamed *The Viking,* he was her contact, and that information had cost her quite a bit of cash. Everyone else in the bar was too dark–skinned, or too short. And, like her, too *Mexican.*

Six rapid shots exploded outside. She slid down, making herself small, covering her head and neck with crossed arms, like in the air-raid drills back in elementary school. A few of the patrons looked up from their drinks with alarm. Most ignored the gunfire. They must consider this a normal evening's entertainment.

With a deep breath that threatened to turn her resolve into a coughing fit, she picked her way between wobbling tables and catcalls. "Hey *chica,* come have a drink with me." "*Hola, chica,* you need a real man tonight."

She hadn't appreciated that kind of attention when she had been young enough to deserve it. Here, age didn't matter so much as willingness. With long practice, she ignored them all. Only the Viking held her interest.

She stopped a scant foot away from him, waiting for him to notice her. He turned his gaze sideways almost at the moment she paused. Constantly wary and vigilant, he must know everyone here and where they belonged. She was clearly out of place. His eyes lingered where she presumed his hands wanted to grope. She grew aware of her accumulated grime from the past three days since her last shower in a flea-ridden, cash-only motel. The oozing leer made her feel truly sullied. Three weeks ago, her only dress had been new from Paris. It had been pristine clean and fit too snugly in places. It sagged on her now, and was ripped and dirty. She'd worn designer heels back then. Now her equally filthy and ripped canvas shoes barely protected her feet from the ick on the floor and the broken glass on the sidewalk.

The Viking must have recognized her desperation and gestured toward a booth. The two men sitting there caught his eye. Beers in hand, they got up and left. He raised a hand to signal the man at the bar who promptly brought two cold beers.

He remained silent until the bartender slid the bottles onto the table and backed away. She grabbed the cold, wet, glass bottle, and rubbed it across her brow, down her cheek and along her nape.

"You look like a woman who would like to take a trip," he said in perfect English with no more trace of an accent than she had.

"How much?" Mariposa asked. She squirmed a bit under his gaze and discreetly adjusted the position of the thumb drive.

"Where do you want to go, *chica?*" He pulled on his beer. "I hear Spain is fine this time of year. Or Switzerland."

Mariposa's mouth went dry and she sipped from the bottle to cover her reaction. It had been three weeks since she'd known home and safety. Paralyzing fear rode her like a jockey. Her tormentor was hot on her trail and she needed to get over the wall. *Nowhere is safe from him*!

"I need to get across the border. Only from there can I seek political asylum elsewhere."

"Now, that gets expensive, *chica*." He smiled. "It is not so easy as it once was."

"I can afford it." Obtaining the money from secret bank accounts and trusting friends had added extra miles and time to her journey.

His leer softened into calculation. When he looked at her again, he wasn't looking at her dress, but at her. He smirked.

"You might have afforded it before. But now?" the Viking shrugged.

"I have to."

"Twenty-five G's, cash. Up front."

"What makes you think I will pay that much?"

"Someone recommended me to you. Someone got you from. . . there to here. Anyone who knows my work knows my rates. You want over the wall. That's expensive. And illegal. You have to make it worth the bribes and the bodyguards. And there is risk. Expensive risk."

"I'll give you five in cash now. Another ten when you get me to safety."

"Twenty up front." His jaw firmed, but his eyes wavered. She had him.

She knew that if she gave him too much up front, she'd never make it over the wall. She might not make the end of the block.

"Five up front. Fifteen when I am safely on the other side and out of rifle range from the guards on the wall."

"You'll need to give up your ID and your passport. Your real ID, not the fake ones you've probably been using."

Every official she'd encountered for three years had demanded the same thing, but always for different reasons.

"Why, so you can sell them?"

"Won't do anyone much good to travel on *your* ID." He jerked his head toward the TV screen over the bar. The scene had shifted from a soccer game to a news alert. A bad black and white photo of Mariposa's face—younger and plumper, straight off her campaign posters—filled the screen with her name scrolling beneath it. "Wanted" flashed in an urgent cadence above her serene and trustworthy face.

Although no crime was listed, she knew that fear would motivate even complete strangers to report her whereabouts. She had to move quickly, get into hiding, or the *Federales* would swoop in, guns blazing. At her.

"Anyone with your ID is going straight to prison. From the looks of that," he nodded his head toward the TV, "you might not even make it to prison in one piece."

"They would hold me pending deportation hearings. I'd spend a year in jail while they figured out a story to fit their alternative facts. If I survived a full year in a for-profit prison straight out of hell, I might not be well enough, strong enough, or sane enough to accept deportation. I need my own passport when I get to the other side to prove who I am and what *El Presidente* has done to me."

"Handsome woman like you? They might just put you to work. Oldest profession in the world. The only job suitable for a woman like you. According to *him.*" The Viking leaned back against the bench, making the plastic creak. His too-bright smile showed teeth that had endured expensive orthodontics. He'd had one tooth capped in gold.

"Will you accept my offer?" she asked, holding his gaze.

He remained silent.

She knew the trick. People hate a vacuum of sound. Stay silent long enough, and the person opposite will likely start to babble, even confess. As a prosecuting attorney, she'd done it dozens of times. As a judge, she'd seen it even more. Keeping her face neutral, she stared at him and took another sip from her bottle, waiting for him to end the silence that hung between them like a muslin curtain.

"Five now for expenses. Fifteen when you are safe? That is not my usual rate."

"Any more up front and I won't live to see the wall, let alone get over it. Or worse, you turn me over to the *Federales.*"

"Okay," said the Viking in surrender. "I'll do it. Five now. Fifteen when I dump you within one mile of the city of your choice, on a road, after sunset." He held out his hand, palm up, rubbing two fingers together.

Mariposa fingered the leather belt pack around her waist, running one zipper open and closed, then open again. Her gaze never strayed to her backpack. She reached into the left cup of her padded bra and removed a wad of one hundred dollar bills. "You leave me on the road at dawn or you give me a gun to protect myself from outlaws."

His fingers stopped rubbing and he clenched a fist. Then he opened his hand again. "Agreed."

She slapped the bills into his hand.

"Meet me at the gas station on the corner of Mesquite and the old highway in two hours. Bring bottled water, a couple gallons worth, a hat, a blanket, and food. You're going to do a fair amount of walking to get to the wall. Wear good shoes."

The tennis shoes would have to do. She had no others. Three weeks ago, she'd had a closet full. That was then.

~oOo~

At midnight, just outside the border town, the south side still hopped with *salsa* music, light spilling through the open doors and windows of bars. Gunfire erupted periodically: men awash in testosterone. Mariposa crouched in the shadow of an abandoned gas station. It might have once been the focal point on the street, but was now just one of many empty buildings, dark and forbidding. A meeting place for *coyotes* and their clients: the poor, the desperate, and the hunted. Like her.

She touched the thumb drive that now resided in her bra. Safe.

Three weeks ago, Mariposa had lost everything in the raid. In the seconds after federal forces had burst through the heavy doors of her home, she'd watched them gun down Antonio, her husband of thirty years, as well as her aged parents and even Mindy, her ancient dog that hadn't had long to live, anyway. They had just sat down to dinner. The *zupa* was still hot, the tortillas unbroken.

The gunfire had alerted the neighbors who had called the local police. The shooters, *she knew they were government,* had fled before making sure that Mariposa, their true target, was dead beneath her husband's corpse. They wanted it to look like terrorists, outsiders, someone other than *that man's* execution squad, had struck her down, in the prime of life and likely to jump from powerful federal judge to the Senate.

She sniffed and wiped her eyes. Poor Antonio had thrown himself atop her to save her. Loving her more than life to the very end, including his own.

Movement at the front of the building caused her to crouch lower, letting the two men and three women identify themselves first.

A whispered conversation between one man and woman told her much. They needed to get over the wall to visit their daughter and her new baby. If they went legally at the official border crossing, the guards would simply take their passports and not let them return to the home they'd spent a lifetime building.

The man's voice rose in volume and pitch. The woman hushed him. All of them looked around guiltily, though they'd committed no crime. Yet.

"We're citizens, damn it. Our families have been here longer than *his*!"

More people arrived, each with furtive glances. Ten refugees, and two heavily-armed scouts to lead them. They milled about, jumping at every sound, checking their backpacks of water and food.

At last, the Viking appeared. He'd exchanged his slick suit for jeans, hiking boots, and a cotton shirt. He covered his bright hair with a sombrero. A faded serape draped over his shoulder. If he slumped to disguise his height, he'd look like any other anonymous worker.

Mariposa stood up slowly, easing her muscles into a new posture.

"Ah, our numbers are complete, now," the Viking said, jingling a wad of keys in his pocket. "Follow me. No talking. You, Mariposa, will sit up front with me." He gestured toward a sagging van, once black, now speckled with rust, parked three blocks east of them. No windows, the cab separate from the cargo hold. A refrigeration unit protruded from the top. A typical box van.

"Does the air conditioning work?" she asked.

"The journey is no longer torturous. Merely illegal," the Viking said.

Mariposa didn't believe him. She'd holed up in filthy, cash-only motels, walked endless miles, hopped freight trains, and cried herself to sleep beneath trees on her trek from home to here. A thousand miles.

If she could endure just a few more days she would, at last, be free of *Him*, intent on persecuting her to the point of death. She had stood in his way and he could not tolerate that. She'd declared his Executive Orders illegal and he decided that she should die.

When Henry II of England had done that to Thomas á Becket, the troublesome priest had become a martyr and a saint, more powerful in death than life.

She hoped someone would remember her and honor her attempts to bring law and justice back to her country.

"So, what really happened?" The Viking asked Mariposa as the lights of town grew smaller in the side mirror.

"The usual."

"Your face and name are on the news, but not your crime. You've been on the run for three weeks. That's a long time."

"*He* doesn't usually have enough focus to follow a single enemy for more than three days," Mariposa completed the thought for him.

"So, it must be dire. A federal judge seeking election to the senate. Last poll I saw two days ago placed you seventy-five points ahead of your opponent."

That surprised her. She'd been off the grid for three weeks, a lifetime in a political campaign.

"My crime is not what I did, but who I am. He has declared that all persons of Latin descent are no longer citizens—have never been citizens. We can accept deportation or acknowledge our illegal status and he will grant us guest worker permits. I would never be allowed to work as anything more than a farm laborer."

"I heard about the executive order and guessed the nuances. He does know how to cloud the issues in too many words."

"His supporters thought he meant recent immigrants and refugees. My family moved north to California in the early 1800s. I have the original royal land grant from the king of Spain. I am educated, a professional, and a woman. I graduated first in my class at Stanford, top ten at Georgetown Law. Fifteen years as a prosecuting attorney, then ten as a judge in criminal court. Lastly, I was elevated to the federal bench. Everything in my life screams denial of the stereotype he proclaims to be the truth."

He raised an eyebrow. "He needs you dead and the truth destroyed."

"He tried to kill me and failed. My existence is a major threat to his agenda. I have the truth to bring the IRS down on him for tax fraud." Dared she take the next step? It had been part of her original plan. But now?

"The IRS is beholden to no one in the government. They look only for ways to bring in the most money, respecting no one. Even *he* is not immune to an audit."

The Viking frowned in contemplation, then his grimace cleared into a smile of inspiration. "The IRS bows to no one!"

"It takes a thief to catch a thief. I bet you know who to sell this information to for the highest price and maximum exposure. It needs a forensic accountant to ferret out the depth of his crimes." She crossed her arms tightly so she could finger the thumb drive where it now resided in her bra without broadcasting its location.

"I will charge you no more money for your safe passage in exchange for that information."

"Bringing him down will cut into your business of escorting illegal citizens to safety south of the wall."

"The reward for turning in a tax evader is worth more than I make doing six trips across the border, with no expensive bribes or hired mercenary bodyguards. I can retire to the Cayman Islands on that kind of money."

"You'll give me back my deposit? I'll need all my money where I'm going to buy protection. At least *there* I can buy protection."

"Granted." He held out his hand palm up for her to shake on their deal.

"When you get me to safety," she said taking his hand. "What about my deposit?"

"When I get *you* to safety."

She didn't answer any more questions from him though he pestered her for hours. Resting her head against the window, she kept her eyes closed, feigning sleep.

Sleep did eventually come. Brief and filled with silent gunfire and blossoms of blood from the bodies of her loved ones. At least the children had made their escape right after the election. But since the wall went up, communication had been spotty and usually monitored. Miguel and Evangelina waited for her down in Mexico.

How ironic, she thought. Running for safety *south* of the wall. She no longer could claim her rights, earned over ten generations of American citizenship. An illegal citizen, running from home.

The End

During the Lockdown, After the Lockdown

Michael Haynes

Ken watches the city, still except for drones constantly crisscrossing the sky. It's the eighteenth day of the lockdown, the eighteenth night he will go to bed alone.

Irina had been called in to work over two weeks ago. The state's computers were behind on tax processing, and she was needed.

"You have your laptop," he'd said, reaching out to run a finger across her bare shoulders. "Why not just connect from here?"

"McManus said all hands on deck." She stood up from their bed. "And when he says that, everyone knows we need to be onsite, not just online."

Irina dressed and grabbed her bag. She headed for their bedroom door.

"Hey," Ken called out. "Don't I get a goodbye kiss?"

Irina rolled her eyes but came back to where Ken lay in bed. She bent down and her lips brushed his. Ken reached for her, sliding a hand up one of her legs. She brushed his hand aside. "I've got to go."

"Right," he'd said as she headed to the door. "Love you! I'll see you later." The door clicked shut.

Eighteen days and later hasn't arrived. Unless you include her face on the screen of his phone, a few minutes here and there when the towers aren't overloaded. He doesn't count that.

It's near dark and lights are starting to come on across the city. A small group of armed men in fatigues walks down the street, one of the volunteer citizen patrols officially deputized by the mayor. Ken envies their freedom, fidgets with his phone, and considers again the idea of calling emergency services with a false case of appendicitis or a heart attack or something, anything that would force them to let him outside. And, more than that, something that would justify Irina coming home. He needs to touch her, smell and taste her skin, and see the real her instead of only that phone-Irina, a shadow of the real thing.

But he knows it's hopeless. The authorities warned about faking emergency reports, that this only served to endanger people suffering from real emergencies and that penalties for false reports were severe.

Ken pockets his phone and goes to the kitchen, programs the food printer to create yet another sandwich. Ham-flavored this time.

Later in the evening, the governor is on TV. "This situation is nearing an end." He's said that for weeks and it seems to have lost meaning. He stops listening and thinks back, remembering the images he'd seen of the resistance protests in the days leading up to the lockdown. The crowds outside the governor's mansion had grown every day. Then, the counter-protesters had arrived, flooding into the city from all sides. They were there to support the local authorities, they said. Then came the counter-counter-protesters. Almost immediately they were dubbed 'Anarchists.' Within hours there were reports of multiple clashes. The next day, on a drizzly Saturday afternoon, there were explosions throughout the city followed by the scattered rattle of small arms fire. And then everything came to a halt.

Every day since then, the governor or the mayor or some other authority figure had come on the screen and said that the anarchists were being captured, reminding people that the lockdown was to ensure their own safety. And every day they repeated that "citizens' compliance with the lockdown during the ongoing investigation is greatly appreciated." Scattered praise for those militias was an increasing part of the message as the days went by.

The power flickers and dies, cutting the governor off mid-word. The power outages happen often, though not as much as before. Ken checks his phone; it's half-charged. Surely Irina is asleep by now in the makeshift dormitory set up in the Revenue Department building's cafeteria. He powers his phone down, saving the battery for morning.

Now, the only light comes from the stars. Thousands of them shine down on powerless nights, more stars than Ken has seen since he was a boy out in the Maine woods with his grandparents. He looks at them for only a moment before walking the memorized route to the bedroom. He lies down facing the empty side of the bed and falls asleep.

When he wakes and sees the ceiling fan spinning he turns his phone on. There are five new emails. Four advertisements and one from the owner of the company he works for.

Worked for.

"Already in perilous financial straits. . . exacerbated by the lengthy lockdown of our city. . . given the unknown duration of these events. . . with regret. . ."

Ken's worked for Stern and Carver all his adult life. He graduated, married Irina, and got hired there all in a matter of months. He remembers how proud Irina had been when he got the job offer, how they had celebrated with sushi, champagne, tiramisu, and half-drunk lovemaking well into the night.

He reads the email again; the message hasn't changed. He knows there are other firms where he could work but what is it even like to apply for a job for the first time in two decades? Ken wonders if those other firms will think he, only in his mid-forties, is too old to hire; if they will go with younger blood, fresher ideas, "minds straight from the great universities."

He deletes all five emails.

That afternoon, as Ken stands at the window, watching the drones fly back and forth, Irina calls.

"Hey." She smiles.

"Hey back." Ken tries to smile but it feels like he's doing it wrong.

"So, you still working on going through our movie queue?"

He had watched the last of the eighty-seven movies in the queue three days ago. “Yep, still at it. Hoping I’ll have a few left for us to watch together when you come home.”

Irina nods. Her smile weakens for just a moment and then blazes back to life. “They brought us pizza last night!”

“Who did?”

“The Guard. Dozens of boxes. I dunno if it’s a state worker perk or what.”

“Hmm.”

The air fills with silence.

“I got fired,” he says just as Irina starts to say something else.

“What?” they both ask, him with idle curiosity, her with alarm.

“Yeah, they shut down. There was something in the email about them possibly reopening but. . .”

“God, I’m sorry, babe.”

Ken shrugs. “You were going to say something?” She looks at him blankly. “When I was telling you about being fired.”

“Oh.”

“What was it?”

She scratches her cheek. “I was, uh, going to say that they even brought Hawaiian pizza.” Her favorite. “But. . .”

“Oh. That’s great! Really. It is.”

“Yeah, it was nice.”

He tries to think of something interesting to say, but his life has been static these nineteen days. The silence grows again.

"Well," Irina says. "I guess we should get going. Not hog the bandwidth."

"Uh-huh."

"Bye, then?"

"I love you, Irina."

She blinks. Someone laughs in the background and she glances away for a second. "You, too, Ken." And then she's gone.

~oOo~

Late on the twenty-sixth morning of the lockdown the governor and mayor issue a joint statement.

"We're confident," the mayor says, "that the Anarchist element that brought violence to the streets of our city has been neutralized and we're pleased to say that the lockdown will end at noon tomorrow."

The governor says the Guard and select citizen militias will remain in place, assisting local law enforcement and ensuring the safety and well-being of the citizens.

"Your compliance with these final hours of the lockdown is appreciated," the mayor says. Then, with no reporters to ask questions, she and the governor leave the podium and walk away in silence. There's no one on the screen at all for a few seconds, just furniture and curtains, and then the channel cuts to sports highlights from other cities.

Ken thinks there should be something special he could do for Irina's return, but can't think of what it should be. All the fresh food went down the disposal days ago and the food printer, while great for keeping you from having to cook when you didn't feel like it, or starving when you're not allowed out of your home for twenty-six—no, twenty-seven—fucking days, is not so great for creating anything that screams "special occasion." Or even whispers it.

He programs the printer for a cheeseburger and eats it as he looks out across the silent city. It will be strange to see people out and about again, cars and buses back on the roads, commercial aircraft sharing airspace again with the drones. How can it be that these basic facts of life just scant weeks ago will seem so alien now? Ken muses on this and wonders whether such adaptability is a blessing or a curse.

He thinks again about what he could do to celebrate his wife's return. A poem? A love song? An interpretative dance illustrating how he passed these nearly four weeks without her? A jump of fear for the beginning, when no one knew what would blow up next. Pirouetting with nervous laughter for the "extended sleepover" jokes Irina made several days into the lockdown. A swooning collapse for the awful heat wave that came during the second week. Stomp-stomp for watching yet another Jurassic Park movie, the one they'd missed in theaters because they had decided to have sex in his car in the parking lot behind the cinema. A final, awful stillness for his heart every time he saw her face in the last week, every time he saw the look in her eyes that told him she didn't miss him nearly as much as he missed her.

That evening, he finds some old papers from their filing cabinet, each of them blank on one side. With a marker he prints "WELCOME HOME" one letter to a sheet. He tapes them together and hangs them in the archway from the foyer to the living room.

The next morning, he steps outside two minutes early, at 11:58 and listens to the stillness. Down the street, another man sits on his stoop, smoking. Noon comes and goes. Nothing changes. There are no bells, no celebration in the streets. Ken waves to his smoking neighbor; the other man doesn't seem to notice. He waits outside another minute or two, just in case, before going back inside to wait for Irina.

Ken doesn't know how long it will take her to get home. The reporters have said that traffic will be a nightmare even with all the public transit lines operational.

Irina isn't home by one or by two. By four, she could have walked home but he is still alone in the condo. The "WELCOME HOME" sign is drooping and has lost its "C." Ken puts the missing letter back in place twice, but it won't stay. He thinks about getting a new piece of tape to hold it in place, but doesn't. He wonders if another letter will fall before she arrives.

At eight-fifteen Irina comes home. Her cheeks are flushed and when Ken reaches for her, her breath smells of tequila.

"The bars are open already?"

She wriggles out of his embrace and waves a hand. "State liquor store."

"Oh. Of course."

Irina notices the "WEL OME HOME" sign. "I *see* there's something missing." The emphasis lets Ken know it's supposed to be a joke. He doesn't laugh.

"Hey, I brought you something!"

From her backpack she pulls a small plastic container. Inside is a square of chocolate cake with white icing and a little blue squiggle which might have been part of a letter, but Ken can't tell which one.

He dips his finger in the icing and tastes it. It's smooth, creamy, not like the canned stuff.

"McManus apparently has a connection in the Guard. He was able to get a celebration cake brought in for us last night."

"What was the occasion?"

Irina looks at him, forehead wrinkled. "The end of the lockdown?"

"Right."

He could go get a fork but he just breaks off a little piece of the cake and eats it with his fingers, savoring the moistness and freshness of it. He takes several bites this way, the two of them standing just past the tile of the foyer. Then he dips his finger into the icing again and this time he reaches for Irina, for her lips.

She takes the offered icing but doesn't meet his eyes.

"We need to talk, don't we?" Ken asks.

Her throat moves slightly, swallowing the sweetness.

"Yes," she says. "We do."

They walk to the living room. Ken sits on the couch; Irina sits in the chair that usually is only used by visitors, and tells him what he already knows.

The End

A Sonnet on Truth

(after Spinoza)

Philip Brian Hall

When with our eyes we look upon this world,
We see as through a strange, distorting glass.
Mere leaves upon a raging torrent swirled,
Our ways of thought, inconstant, surge then pass.
When I was young, I saw truth black and white
With little evidence - a simple thing.
But now, in age, I suffer age's blight:
Polychromatic vision. Everything
Is complex, shades that morph with other shades,
Kaleidoscopes I twist until I see
The pattern all my preconceptions trade
For truth—my prejudice of what *must* be.
Of course, I can't allow, amidst this dazzling throng,
The slightest possibility I might be wrong.

The Diplomatic Thing

Esther Friesner

Connor Kelly's official title failed to accurately describe his functions within the President's staff, but if truth were not political anathema he, by rights, should have been called Chief Fire Extinguisher and Situation Spackler. He had played clean-up for so many behind-the-scenes disasters that the White House carpets were a virtual mountain range of peaks created by all the figurative bodies he'd swept under them.

This time was different. The calamity at hand was of such epic scope as to make even his sangfroid run gibbering into the night. Despite having been reduced to a whimpering toddler on the inside, he sublimated the urge to flee by glaring fiercely around the Oval Office at the ten others present, living and/or dead, and acting as if the crisis were everyone else's fault.

"Is *no one* going to talk about the elephant in the room?" he demanded.

"If it only were an elephant," one of the President's six bodyguards said under his breath. "We could handle an elephant."

"I'll say," his partner remarked. "Goddamn elephant wouldn't have done—" He glanced toward the great executive desk that was the focal point of the room. "*—that.*"

Then he threw up. Again.

Connor made a guttural sound of disgust. "Get a grip, man!" he commanded, simultaneously amping up his ire and fighting down his own urge to barf. "He doesn't look *that* awful."

"It's not how he looks," the agent said, wiping his mouth with a handkerchief. "It's knowing what she did to him."

"You ought to be ashamed of yourself. This is going to be enough of a black mark on your record when the investigation goes public without you turning girlie on us."

"*What* did you say, Mr. Kelly?" The Vice-President's chill voice sliced the air with the terse mastery of a straight razor wielded by Sweeney Todd. She took a step closer to the desk where the President's body lay sprawled lifeless across a stained blotter. "Did I hear you say 'turning girlie' as a pejorative?" Shelli Fennig's over-plucked eyebrows shot up so high that they were lost beneath a fringe of brassy blond bangs.

"With all due respect, Madam Vice-President, can we talk strategy instead of semantics?" he replied. "We have an unprecedented situation here—"

"We do not," she snapped. "The President is dead. *She* killed him." Shelli pointed to one of the sofas across the room where a slender young woman of extraordinary beauty sat quietly, knees together, hands folded in her lap, lips lightly dabbled with blood.

"And *she* is the one responsible." A second gesture indicated another, older female occupying the sofa opposite. She looked considerably less serene and fidgeted beneath the gaze of the two Secret Service agents looming over her.

"I am now in charge," the Vice-President continued. "I very much doubt we'll need any sort of investigation when the circumstances are so cut and dried. Put the guilty parties into custody, call the appropriate people to tend to *that*—" This time, it was the body at the desk that was the target of her sympathetic attention. "—and let's get on with the business of running the country."

Connor rubbed his temples. "It isn't that simple," he said. A newly-hatched headache made him testiery than usual. "What's the first item on your agenda going to be? Telling America that their President is dead because his brains were eaten by a zombie?"

"Why not?" The Vice-President tightened her narrow lips, making her look even more like a constipated iguana. "It's what happened."

"And it was his own damn fault it happened, too!" the older woman on the sofa piped up indignantly. "I *warned* him! I said that Jarah was past due for a feeding. I asked him to let us postpone this meeting, but he wouldn't hear of it." She distorted her face into the President's familiar grimace when making his wishes undeniably known, and blustered, "'I'm a busy man, Miss Taylor, and if you can't appreciate that, maybe your university should have less money for science and more for etiquette lessons.' "

"Wow, sounds just like him," one of her two wardens whispered to the other. This observation earned him a nasty look from Connor and an appreciative snicker from his partner.

"You're to be commended for such diligence, Miss Taylor," the Vice-President began.

"*Doctor* Taylor," the woman on the sofa said forcefully. "Which is another thing I told him that he didn't want to hear. He made it quite clear that Jarah and I were not going to go anywhere until he released us from the royal presence."

"There's no need to mock the dead, *Miss* Taylor." Shelli Fennig was all for acknowledging a woman's achievements as long as that woman was Shelli Fennig. "You might want to consider that public opinion will not be in your favor when you go to trial. Don't give people further cause to side against you."

"Against *me*?" Dr. Taylor laughed. "Have you forgotten who I am? How my husband and brother and I achieved a *miracle* together? We developed the formula for ZomBan! Our work short-circuited an apocalypse! We're the only reason this country—this *world*—isn't overrun with the undead! My poor Arthur lost his life when the first distribution protocol failed and *someone* I could mention tried using that as an excuse to cut our research funding." If accusatory looks could electrify, the President's corpse would have been jigging like a galvanized frog. "Maybe some people have the attention span of plankton, but there are plenty of Americans who remember that they owe my family their lives. You think *they'll* want to see me punished for what happened here? Especially when they see everything I did, trying to *prevent* this mess?" Her hand shot up to indicate one of several security cameras scanning the Oval Office. "The proof is there."

"That footage is classified," Connor said crisply. "It will not be released to the general public."

Dr. Taylor said nothing, and the way she said it gave Connor a twinge of *Uh-oh* that the seasoned Don of Damage Control could not ignore. He scowled, suspecting much amiss. "Give me your cell phone."

"By all means." She handed it to the nearest Secret Service agent who in turn passed it to Connor. He fiddled with it furiously, fingers made awkward by a mounting sense of too little, far, far too late, then threw it against the wall. "How much of the incident did you record?"

"Muddy thinking, Mr. Kelly." Dr. Taylor sat a little taller on the sofa. Justifiable annoyance had sent her earlier malaise packing. "What good would that have done? Recordings can be confiscated and wiped. I *recorded* nothing. I *relayed*. The moment I saw what the President had in mind, I initiated a feed to Jarah's family of what was going on. I have no idea what they've done with the data, but it's all beyond your control now." Her smile curved no more than a krait's fangs. "Diplomatic immunity. It wasn't enough to save their daughter from dying and coming back as one of the undead, but it *will* stop you from killing her reputation. And mine."

"You gave classified information to a foreign power?" Connor and Shelli thundered in unison.

"It wasn't classified until just now, when you pulled *that* moth-eaten bunny out of your. . . fedora. And by the way, how high *is* the security threat from the Republic of St. Cajetan?" Dr. Taylor inquired, citing the world's smallest nation, an island unremarkable for anything save it's immeasurable value as a strategic military base and for having been named after the patron saint of gamblers, document controllers, and the unemployed. "I stand by what I did. Jarah's family had the right to know how their daughter was being treated."

"How *she* was being treated? What about how she treated *him*?" The Vice-President attempted a look of genteel astonishment in the style of a British grand duchess. She achieved a goggle-eyed bit of pantomime *Well-I-never!* that would have been rejected by a melodrama director for being too overdone.

"Run the security camera recordings if you want the real story," Dr. Taylor said. "You'll see what I already told you, about how he forced the meeting. You'll also get an eyeful of him sending his bodyguards out of the Oval Office, over my objections."

"Standard operating procedure, ma'am," said one of the agents. "We're supposed to man the outside of the doors."

"Well, I'll bet he could have overruled that and ordered a pair of you to stay in the room, where you might've done some good. He didn't, though, did he? Care to guess why?"

"The President was a courageous man," Connor said solemnly.

This time Dr. Taylor laughed to the point of tears and wheezing. "Oh yes, *so* courageous!" she said when she recovered the ability to speak. "Nothing scared him except potential *witnesses* for what he had in mind."

"Have a care, Dr. Taylor." Connor placed himself directly in front of the woman who had spent years in deadly proximity to ravenous, animate corpses. There was no explaining why he believed that having his fly at eye-level was going to intimidate her.

"The only thing my predecessor had in mind was getting first-hand information concerning *that* clear and present danger to humanity." The Vice-President spat her words at Jarah, who was still seated calmly on the other sofa. "He wanted to meet the creature and see for himself whether or not it should be destroyed, just as we purified this country of its disgusting kin."

"*It* is a *she*," Dr. Taylor replied evenly. "And *she* is one of only three surviving zombies worldwide. For some reason, as yet unknown, they are unique in that ZomBan did not de-animate them, though it did radically decrease their level of feeding frenzy."

"Not radically enough," one of the Secret Service agents muttered, eying the body at the desk.

"Young man, try to understand," Dr. Taylor said. "Jarah's behavior now versus then is the difference between you feeling hungry and going to Micky D's for a burger versus you feeling hungry and tearing apart a cow with your teeth." She cocked her head and added: "You don't get fries with that."

"Okay, but what she did to the President—"

"—is the difference between you actively *starving*, and paying for a burger on your ten-minute break, but the person serving you won't let go of it until he tells you *all about* that dream he had last night."

"Oh."

"Under ordinary circumstances, Jarah survives on a nutrient formula I devised. I was not allowed to bring it to this meeting. *You* took it from me, Mr. Kelly. You wanted it held in reserve for some stupid photo op."

"We were *going* to let the press see the President sharing a toast with this young woma—" Connor caught sight of the Vice-President glowering at him. "—monster. It was intended to improve the image of zombies everywhere."

"What 'everywhere'? I told you, we have three left!"

"Three too many," Shelli growled.

"In case you were too busy feeding the homeless to keep up with the news, Madam Vice-President, let me remind you that the cause of the crisis that killed my husband was *viral*. I'll be happy to explain all the reasons why you do not destroy the last samples of a disease just because you *think* it can't come back again."

"There's no need to be sarcastic, Miss Taylor."

"There's also no need to be stupid, and yet, there he is." She jerked a thumb at the Corpse-in-Chief. "Jarah is not a monster. ZomBan made her capable of maintaining socially acceptable behavior, but only so long as her appetites are kept in check. As her long-time guardian, I have a better chance than anyone else of interceding, in the event of an. . . incident, and bringing her under temporary control. That was why I asked him to stay a reasonable distance from her, and also in view of what I'd already told him about that overdue feeding time. He refused. I believe his exact words to me were, 'There, there, honey, don't you worry. I'll protect you from this sweet little thing.' Then he took Jarah's hand, led her to the desk, sat down and patted his knee. When she failed to take the hint, America's funny uncle pulled her onto his lap and kissed her. She reacted."

"To a harmless little kiss?" Shelli Fennig shook her head. "From the President of the United States? A normal woman would be flattered."

"Madam Vice-President, that kiss was just for starters. Run the tape and see for yourself. I am not the sort of person who is comfortable with vulgarity, so I'd rather not tell you what *actually* made her—"

"I sucked his brains out through his nose." Jarah's unexpected voice sent a jolt through the Oval Office.

"It *talks*?" The Vice-President was agog.

"When I have something I wish to say," Jarah replied demurely. "I said 'Stop' quite clearly to your

President. He did not listen." She ran one dainty finger around the outside of her mouth, then licked off the last tell-tale traces of gore in a conflation of seductive and sick-making. "Sad."

"I thought that the only thing zombies could say was '*Aaarrggghhh*,'" one agent said.

"That's pirates." Jarah gave him an entrancing smile.

"But—but—but through his *nose*?" Another agent looked decidedly green. He'd been the last one on the scene. Up until that moment, he'd known Who (the President), What (killed), Where (the Oval Office), When (a quarter-to-now-ish), and Why (zombie), but only a general version of How (likewise zombie). Learning the explicit details of the event left him light-headed.

Dr. Taylor tried to soothe his qualms with science. "Jarah's method of brain-extraction is not without historical precedent. The procedure was developed by the ancient Egyptians for the process of mummification. It was likewise the go-to feeding technique for female zombies during the crisis. Much neater. The males always tore off the top of their victims' skulls and never put the lid back down." She sighed in resignation. "Men."

"I refuse to believe a word of this!" Connor shouted. "You're slandering the President of the United States of America!"

"You can't slander the dead," Dr. Taylor pointed out. "You can't prosecute the dead, either. And you *really* can't prosecute the dead when they've got diplomatic immunity. You're going to have to let Jarah go."

"Over my dead—" Connor paused, eyed Jarah uneasily, and took a different tack. "Out of the question. She killed the President!"

"Did she?" Dr. Taylor glanced at the Secret Service agents. "Gentlemen, there's something I'd like to double-check, with your cooperation and consent. You have my word that I am not going to do anything that will generate a half-hitch in Mr. Kelly's tightie-whities. I just want to stand up and take a good look at the President's body."

"I forbid it!" Shelli squawked.

"With respect, ma'am, you don't have that authority," said the agent who'd thrown up on the rug. Apparently failure to hold down breakfast was no barrier to holding a position of command. "I'll allow it."

Dr. Taylor did not touch the body at the desk. As promised, she merely looked at it for a time, then said, "We can save him."

Those four words had a rousing effect on the six agents. Orders were barked. Backup was summoned. Connor and Shelli were ignored and the consequences were filed under Be Damned. Per Dr. Taylor's direction, the President was whisked to the nearest health-care facility that could provide everything she needed for the procedure. Before she began, she took great pains to ensure Jarah's security, including the sensible step of having her brother and fellow-ZomBan developer attend the girl with a plentiful supply of her nutrient drink. He also fielded questions from the press, for the good folks of the Fourth Estate caught wind of the goings-on and attacked the hospital like a barrage of Tweet-seeking missiles

As rumors danced a merry can-can through the streets of Washington, Dr. Taylor triumphed: the President was declared to be out of danger. Although Shelli Fennig took over his duties until he recovered completely, the swiftness of his recuperation was gall and wormwood to her. It was worse when a hotshot journalist outed her plot to force the President's resignation (on the grounds of *Because That Monster Sucked Out His Brains Through His Nose and He's* **Dead**, *You Idiots*!) She ground her teeth together so hard that she broke two molars and stepped down from the vice-presidency for reasons of dental health.

She missed the White House wedding.

It was all terribly sudden and unexpected. People chattered over how precipitously the Executive branch had burst into the full bloom of love. Several theories were advanced. The most popular one asserted there was no passion like that of a man for the woman who had changed his life.

Point taken.

Jarah was a beautiful bride. No one expected any less. In life, her charm and glamour had made her the most sought-after woman in Washington society, a celebrity whose fame rested on no firmer foundation than celebrity itself. It made her a perfect match for the President.

He'd cleaned up nicely after his cerebral *contretemps.* What scraps of gray matter remained in his skull were enough to let him keep the power of speech, albeit a bit more limited than previously. His public addresses got from Point A to Point B without wandering away in the middle to chase, grab, and tear the wings off metaphoric butterflies.

The ceremony was held in the Rose Garden with a guest list representing the thick cream of the Capital's political, economic, judicial, and diplomatic communities. Dr. Taylor was both an honored guest and a safety net. She stood by to make sure Jarah and her new hubby kept up their nutrient drink intake. It wouldn't do to have the President get hungry and devour the brains of any cabinet members present.

As she sipped a glass of champagne, the Senate majority leader sidled up to her. "Dr. Taylor, I want to thank you," he said. "It makes me proud to be an American, knowing that I share that divinely blessed designation with you. I wish other women would learn from you, stop whining about how *unfair* everything is, and get down to *doing.* Whatever contribution you made to your husband's and brother's work, no matter how small, it stood us all in good stead during the zombie crisis, and now your quick thinking and God-given luck have preserved this nation by saving our greatest leader from—"

"Enough." She cut him off in mid-effusion. "Spare me the schmooze and smarminess. Oh, and ditch the condescension while you're at it. If it had been up to you and your cronies, the money that made ZomBan possible would have vanished and we'd all be surrounded by walking corpses." She stared meaningfully at him for a moment.

The Senator made a face reminiscent of a toad surprised by a proctologist. "Typical over-educated woman," he harrumphed. "No concept of proper, gracious behavior whatsoever."

"Don't mince words: Call me uppity." She took another sip of champagne. James Bond would have whistled in admiration at the cool self-assurance with which she regarded the Senator over the rim of her glass.

"Ingrate." The Senator punctuated his assessment with a moist snort and waddled away.

Dr. Taylor feigned wide-eyed surprise. "Wait. Weren't *you* thanking *me*?" she called after him.

"Is something wrong over here?" Connor Kelly popped up at her elbow.

"Nothing that matters."

"Good, because I wanted to talk to you about something important: the President will be up for re-election before we know it. People like you and me—the kind of people who really *care* about this country—are going to be facing a great challenge, getting the American public to look beyond the fact that—"

"—he's a zombie?" She finished her drink and handed him the empty.

"Er, yes." Connor twiddled the crystal stem. "That. The other men on his campaign team and I all agree that you're the perfect person to hop on board for the campaign trail and put a positive face on the situation."

"I see." She snagged the attention of a passing waiter and got another round of Veuve Clicquot. "Nope."

"What? Why not? You *have* to support him!" Connor's voice began to rise to Tantrum Threat Level Orange. "Why would you have saved him if you weren't in favor of everything he's been doing to—*for* this country?"

"I didn't do it for him," Dr. Taylor said mildly. "I interceded because saving him meant saving Jarah. If the President died, our former Veep wouldn't be the only one looking for a scapegoat. There'd be a mob of White House hopefuls shoving each other aside so the winner could strike a grand *Lo, I bring you **Justice**!* pose for the electorate."

She shrugged. "No dead President, no problem; no problem, no sacrifice on the altar of someone else's ambition. My choice also saved *me* from the time-wasting rigmarole of an investigation. I have better things to do with my life." She wrinkled her nose appreciatively over the rising spray of champagne bubbles. "Like campaigning for whoever runs against him."

The Rose Garden was awash in warm June sunlight, but the air temperature between the two of them plummeted at her words.

"You listen to me, Dr. Taylor, and you listen *carefully.*" Connor's voice was pitched low and thrumming with threat. "You *will* join the President's re-election campaign and you *will* tell America that you never could have developed ZomBan without his backing. You will stress the fact that it was only his modesty—" Dr. Taylor's short, derisive laugh interrupted him for just a moment. "—and dedication to results above personal aggrandizement that kept his involvement with the project a secret. If not, you have my word that I will use every contact I have in Congress and call in every favor I am owed to destroy your precious pet zombie."

"Are you that devoted to the man, Mr. Kelly, or is this about keeping your job? Does it pay *that* much?"

Connor smirked. "The thing about government work, Dr. Taylor, is that it doesn't need to pay a lot on the record. It just needs to be profitable."

"That's what I thought." Like a good poker player, she saw his smirk and raised it by a go-away-little-boy-Mommy's-busy grin. "And that's why I told my 'pet zombie' to marry your pet President."

The little tin god of the Oval Office grew pale. The close observer could almost read his thoughts like a news crawl as he came to comprehend how thoroughly guaranteed and unassailable Jarah's continued existence was now. If you added her former celebrity status to her beauty, her charisma, her family's diplomatic clout, and that teensy detail of her being the First Lady, you got the formula for iron-clad invulnerability. He mumbled something about allingoodfunjustjokinghahaha'byenow and hurried off in search of safety and a double shot of single malt.

As he staggered toward one of the open bars, he crossed paths with the President. In his discombobulated state, Connor Kelly accidently bumped into his employer. It was a glancing shoulder blow, but there were consequences.

"*Mon Dieu, il a perdu son bras*!" The French ambassador's wife screamed and pointed. True enough, the impact of Connor's minor body-check had caused the President's right arm to detach and drop to the ground.

Dr. Taylor sighed. Why hadn't the Secret Service listened when she'd told them to keep a *solid* no-contact zone around the President whenever he was moving? She'd warned them about the increased fragility of *post mortem* bodies, re-animated or not. Their rot did not answer to a uniform timetable. No one had ever made a study of why some like Jarah maintained their corporeal integrity so well, for so long, while some like her husband. . .

"Ugh. I can't stand political corruption," said Dr. Taylor, and went to fetch the duct tape.

The End

The Politicians

Mike Resnick

. . . Thus it was that, toward the end of the Democracy's first millennium, a wave of sentiment swept across the human worlds and colonies of the galaxy. Long had they waited for Man to re-establish what they considered to be his rightful position of primacy among the sentient races, and the prevailing mood was almost akin to that ancient credo of "Manifest Destiny." And, indeed, it was fast becoming manifest that Man had served his galactic apprenticeship and would no longer be content to play a secondary role in the scheme of things.

It was at the height of this crisis of conflicting philosophies and overviews that Joshua Bellows (2943-3009 G.E.) began his meteoric rise to power. Immensely popular with the masses, he was originally opposed and later lauded by certain elements within his own party. For if it is true that great events summon forth great leaders, then. . .

—Man: Twelve Millennia of Achievement

. . .That Bellows had considerable charm and charisma as a politician cannot be denied. However, those writings and tapes of his that still exist would seem to imply that he had neither the capacity nor, originally, the motivation to have accomplished what he

did without some powerful behind-the-throne assistance. . .

. . .Although the Democracy survived him by more than twelve centuries, there can be no doubt that Bellows was responsible for. . .

—*Origin and History of the Sentient Races*, Vol. 8

Josh Bellows sat behind a huge desk, its shining surface dotted here and there with papers and documents, a score of intercom buttons by his right arm. Immaculately tailored and groomed, he presented the ultimate picture of dignity, with his heavy shock of gray-black hair, the firm, hard line of his jaw, and the tiny smile wrinkles at the corners of his clear blue eyes. He looked every inch a leader of men, which was in fact what he was.

"So how's it going?" he asked.

The figure approaching his desk was almost his antithesis in every respect. Clad in wrinkled, crumpled clothes, squinting through lenses so thick that one couldn't see his eyes behind them, what hair he still possessed in total disarray, he seemed as out of place in these majestic surroundings as anyone could be.

"The natives are getting restless," said Melvyn Hill, pulling up a beautifully carved chair of Doradusian wood and unceremoniously putting his feet on the desk.

"The natives always look restless when you're staring down at them from the top," commented Bellows. "When I was one of them I was restless too. That's how I got here."

"That was a little different, Josh. You were restless for power. They're restless for you to exercise that power."

"I know." Bellows frowned. "But what the hell do they expect me to do? Declare war?"

"No," said Hill. "Although," he added thoughtfully, "not one out of five would be averse to it."

"I won the Governorship of Deluros VIII with sixty-four percent of the vote," said Bellows. "I think that shows a mandate of some sort for my judgment."

"I'll agree with the first half of it, Josh," said Hill. "It shows a mandate of some sort."

"You know," said Bellows, "you are the one member of my staff who continually makes me wonder about the wisdom of not surrounding myself with yes-men and sycophants."

"You're paying me too much to simper and suck my thumb and tell you that everything you do is right," said Hill, swinging his feet back to the floor with a grunt. "Someone in this damned Administration ought to tell you the truth."

"Which is?"

"Which is that you are in considerably more danger of impeachment than you realize."

Bellows just stared at him for a minute, his face expressionless.

"Nonsense," he said at last.

Hill got to his feet. "Let me know if and when you want the rest of my report." He turned to leave.

"Hold on a minute!" snapped Bellows. "Get back in

your chair and let's have this out."

Hill returned and took his seat again. "Shall I begin?" he asked.

Bellows nodded.

"All right, then. You ran for the Governor's chair based on a campaign of human primacy. So did your opponent, but it was you who began proclaiming that it was manifest destiny that Man once again rule the galaxy."

"Just politics," said Bellows.

"No, sir, it wasn't just politics. Just politics would have been promising to exterminate the Lemm, or some other race who's been a thorn in our sides. A quick little battle like the one we fought a couple of centuries ago against Pnath; it had no business taking place, but we won pretty easily and everyone felt pretty cocky about it. *That's* politics. You've done something more. You've given them a dream, a promise that our race will return to its former position of supremacy. You hammered away at it for almost a year. Now, I'll admit that you were forced into it or else you'd never have won, but your constituency put you here, and they're getting a little restless waiting for you to lead them to the Promised Land. You've been in office almost three years now; that's sixty percent of your term, and you haven't produced yet.

"So," he continued, "they're taking matters into their own hands. There have been pogroms on a number of worlds where we cohabit with other races, there have been some minor skirmishes in space between ships from our outworlds and those of various aliens, and your legislature has been dragging its feet on every recommendation you've sent them. The human race has a standing battle force of some sixty million ships and ten billion men throughout the galaxy, and they're getting restless.

"As for your impeachment, the media is just now starting to talk about it, but I've done a head count, and they're only about a dozen votes short."

"Twenty-eight votes," said Bellows.

"That was *last* month," persisted Hill. "Josh, you just can't sit on your hands. You've got to *do* something."

"Like what?" said Bellows softly. "What the hell do they want me to do—launch a sneak attack on Lodin XI and the Canphor Twins? Am I supposed to kill off every alien in the galaxy just to make them happy? I'm not the President of the human race, you know. I'm just the Governor of one world."

"Deluros VIII is more than one world, and we both know it," said Hill. "Since we moved our bureaucracy here from Earth, we've been the social, political, and moral headquarters of the race of Man. For centuries, the Governor of Deluros VIII has been the most powerful human in the galaxy; for all practical purposes, the job *is* identical to being President of the human race. If you give an order, every military unit from here to the Rim will obey it without question; if our economy goes up or down, every other human world follows suit in a year or so. We set the fashion, physically and philosophically, for every human everywhere. So don't hand me any of that crap about being the leader of one small, insignificant little world."

"All I ever promised was to give Man back his dignity," said Bellows. "I said it was our destiny to rise to the top of the heap, and it is—but not by pulling the other fellows off. We'll do it by working harder, producing more, being smarter—"

"Bunk! You couldn't deliver on that promise if your term of office was ten thousand years and you lived to the last day of it. Look," said Hill, clasping and unclasping his hands. "You were born handsome, articulate, and likable. I mean it. I've always liked you, and I like you even now, when you're throwing both our careers down the drain. You come on like a forceful but benevolent father that everyone automatically trusts. Just give the mess to Josh; he'll take care of it. The problem is that you've never had to use that thing you call a brain a day of your life. Everything comes easy to Godlike father images, and when you needed some dirty work done, someone like me has always been around to do it. Not that we've minded. But now you're Governor of Deluros VIII, and there's no higher office a human can aspire to the way the Democracy's set up. Now you've finally got to deliver instead of going after the job of the guy who's next in line above you. And if you can't make the decision and take the kind of action that's required, then let me or someone else do it in your name, or that handsome, noble face and lordly demeanor are going to get expurgated from the history book faster than you can imagine."

"Well, I'm sure as hell not going to go down in history as the man who started the first galactic-scale war!" said Bellows. "I don't plan to be remembered as the greatest genocidal maniac of all time."

"It's not a matter of genocide," said Hill. "It's simply a matter of testing the opposition, pushing and probing until you find a weak spot, then plugging the gap and looking for more. No one's advocating cutting off our noses to spite our faces; we need the other races as much as we ever did, perhaps more. But we need them on our terms, not theirs."

"We've been through all this before," said Bellows, glancing down at his appointments calendar.

"Evidently it hasn't done much good up to now," said Hill. "Dammit, Josh, I know that you've got reservations about it, but the Governorship is no place for vacillation. Sooner or later it's got to come, and it might as well be sooner."

"If it could be bloodless, I'd have no hesitation," said Bellows. "But these are sentient beings, Mel, not so many pieces on a gameboard."

"Begging your pardon, but we are *all* just pieces on a gameboard. A politician is successful or unsuccessful by virtue of how well or poorly he manipulates the pieces."

"Mel, if Man is to rule the galaxy—and I'm convinced he is—he's got to do so by exhibiting leadership in those areas that truly show his worth:

industry, dignity, intellect. No simple show of force will make us fit to rule; if anything, it goes to prove the point that we're not yet capable of doing so."

"That's beautiful rhetoric, Josh, and I hope you put it in your memoirs," said Hill, "but it's a bunch of ivory-tower gobbledegook. Religion, morality, and Joshua Bellows to the contrary, Man is neither good nor bad, pure nor impure. He is simply Man, and his destiny, if he has one, is to make the most of all of his gifts, without attempting to place values upon them. If he has a notion to grasp at the stars, then it's his duty to do so in the best and most efficient way he can; and if he fails, well, at least he did his damnedest. But Man can't just spout pretty platitudes while there's anything in his universe lacking accomplishment. I've heard it said that Man is a social animal. Some deeper thinkers have concluded that he's a political animal. I've known women who swore he was a sexual animal. None of them are totally wrong, but they haven't quite got around to the truth of it. Man is a *competitive* animal. Philosophers dream of utopias in which every need is cared for, and there is an inordinate amount of time for contemplation. Utopia, hell—that's madness! Man's living in utopia right now, a time filled with as many challenges as he can handle. But he can't start meeting those challenges until you give the word."

"And you say they're preparing to throw me out of office if I don't give it."

"They don't want to do that, Josh," said Hill. "With the magnetism you've got, they'd back any action you took. The legislature would be much happier with you than without you but you've got to play ball with them."

"I'm still as popular as ever in the polls," said Bellows. "What if I force them into a showdown, make them put up or shut up?"

"You'd lose," said Hill promptly. "Your popularity is due, in large part, to stories I've leaked to the media about how our forces are massing and how we're ready to begin reasserting ourselves. The day they find out that those are phony, you won't have to wait for the legislature; the voters'll throw you out on your ear."

Bellows excused Hill for an hour while he attended another meeting, then summoned the gnarly adviser back to his office.

"Where would you begin?" asked the Governor bluntly.

"Ah," said Hill, smiling. "Someone else told you the same thing."

"What they told me is my business," said Bellows. "Your business is to make suggestions."

Hill chuckled. "They must really have spelled it out for you, huh? Okay, Josh, how's this for a bloodless starter: Convert every T-pack so that it'll just translate Terran, rather than Galactic-O."

"You're crazy!" exploded Bellows. "Do you know what that would do to our commerce and trade, to say nothing of our Diplomatic Corps? No one would be able to understand a word we said!"

"They'd learn," said Hill softly. "Or better still, get

rid of T-packs altogether, and make it illegal for any Man to speak Galactic. Force the other races to start playing in our ball park. We're still the most potent single military and economic entity in the galaxy; sooner or later it'll become essential to their self-interest to give in."

"But in the intervening time we speak to nobody except Men, is that it?" said Bellows.

"How much time do you think will elapse?" countered Hill.

"More than two thousand worlds depend on us for medical supplies, and almost ten thousand more require produce from our agricultural planets. Now, maybe some of the others will drag their feet, but that's a hard twelve thousand worlds that will learn Terran within a month. And don't forget, this is just symbolic, simply a means of asserting our identity."

"Consider it vetoed," said Bellows. "It would cause too much confusion, kill half the methane-breathers we tried to communicate with, and I'll be damned if I'm going to cut off vital medical supplies to millions of beings just for the sake of making a gesture."

Hill took a deep breath. "All right, then. Instead of taking them all on at once, take on the biggest."

"Meaning?"

"Canphor VI and VII."

"Are you seriously suggesting that I start a war with the Canphor Twins?" demanded Bellows. "That we blow them all to hell just to get the legislature off my back?"

"I am," said Hill. "But with reservations."

"That's a comfort. I didn't know you had reservations about anything."

"Where it concerns physical or political survival, I'm the most reserved person you know," said Hill. "I do not suggest that we launch an attack on the Canphor Twins or any other worlds. We have our image to consider."

"Then what are you talking about?"

"I suggest that we repel an attack by the Canphor Twins on Deluros VIII," said Hill. "You would have no objection to fighting them under those conditions, would you?"

"None at all," said Bellows. "However, I don't think they're any likelier to attack than we are."

"It's a pity that I wasn't born with your looks and that deep, thoughtful, resonant voice of yours, Josh," said Hill with a little smile. "I could have achieved godhood within my own lifetime."

"I assume you're telling me how stupid I am," said Bellows dryly.

"Correct," said Hill. "Not that I hold it against you. That's what you've got *me* for."

"I'm not exactly sure *what* you're here for, but it's not to start wars for me," said Bellows with finality. "Consider the subject closed until such time as I personally reopen it."

Hill left the Governor's office and returned to his own, where two of his aides were waiting for him.

"Any luck?" asked one.

Hill shook his head. "He just doesn't realize how much trouble he's in, and he's basically too humane to do anything to alleviate the situation." He closed his eyes. "God save us from decent and moral leaders!" he added fervently.

"What's next?" asked the other.

"I'm not sure," said Hill, scratching what little remained of his once-bushy head of hair. "For Man's sake and for his, we ought to do something. The problem is that he can countermand anything I do."

"If he does, they'll kick him out and make you Governor," said the first aide. "What's so wrong with that?"

"You're going to find this hard to believe," said Hill, staring at him, "but I'm not totally cynical myself. I know what Man has to do, and a lot of it isn't going to be very pretty. We need a Governor like Josh Bellows, one who can convince us that everything we're trying to accomplish, and the means we're using, is not only acceptable but basically moral. If Josh told us to wipe out twenty sentient races tomorrow, we'd be absolutely sure it was the proper thing to do; if I ordered it, everybody would think I was a power-mad dictator with delusions of grandeur. The people need a leader they can love, respect and damned near worship. Josh fills the bill, so we've got to see to it that he's the one who actually gets the ball rolling."

"Did it ever occur to you'" asked one of the aides, "that the reason Josh commands so much respect is that most of what has to be done is unthinkable to him?"

"The thought has crossed my mind on occasion." Hill grimaced. "You know, it's low-down bastards like me who change history; but it's people like Josh who get the public to like it."

"I repeat: What's next?" said the second aide.

"Well," said Hill, "there's not a hell of a lot of sense trying to get Josh to knowingly take an *active* role in all this. He may have some pretty outmoded scruples, but he's not dumb, and he won't willingly let himself be pushed into anything. We'll simply have to work around him at first."

"How?"

"I am not totally without power in this Administration," Hill said softly. "Who's in command of our fleet in the Canphor system?"

"Greeley."

"Fine." He walked over to a recording device, picked up the microphone, and sat down.

"To Admiral Greeley, 11th Fleet," he began. "For your ears only." He waited the customary five seconds it would take for Greeley's thumbprint to unlock the protective clacking and scrambling mechanisms. "Greetings, Admiral. This is Melvyn Hill, Communications Code. . ." He paused, turning to his code book. "Code 47A3T98S. In view of what I'm about to say, I'd like you to check my code and voiceprint against your computer banks so there will be no doubt in your mind as to my identity." He waited long enough for such a check to have been run, then continued. "It has come to our attention, Admiral, that a number of pirate vessels which have been harassing our trade routes may well be doing so under the unwitting protection of Canphor VI. As a result, we have made a secret agreement with the government of Canphor VI to the effect that all nonmilitary vessels flying that world's colors will also have a special insignia prominently displayed on their starboard sides, the form of which is"—he looked down at some of his scribbling on a scratch pad and randomly chose a design—"an octagon within a circle. Any nonmilitary ship not carrying such an emblem is likely to be a pirate vessel. Your duty will be to demolish the first three such ships you encounter, then report directly to me. Under no circumstance is this to be discussed over subspace radio waves of any length, as we fear some of our communications may be monitored. Also, no more than three vessels are to be destroyed, as this preliminary act is merely to show any and all concerned parties that our vessels are no longer to be considered fair game. An all-out campaign will be mapped later. Good luck." He turned off the device and tossed the recording to one of his aides.

"Take this to Greeley personally," he said. "Don't leave until he's got it in his hands." He turned to his remaining aide. "From this point forward, all alien correspondence to leave this office will be in Terran."

"What if the boss says no?"

"He's got a pretty big planet to run," said Hill. "I don't think he'll bother reading anything that comes out of here. If he does, just play dumb and refer him to me."

This done, Hill settled down, went about his business, and waited for a report from Canphor VI. In less than a week it came in: *Mission accomplished. Any further instructions? Greeley* And, moments later, he was once again in the Governor's, sumptuous office.

"Suppose you tell me just what the hell is going on?" demanded Bellows.

"Sir?"

"Don't 'sir' me, Mel! The Canphor VI government is screaming bloody murder that we've blown away three of their cargo ships, and I can't get a straight answer out of Greeley. He keeps telling me to ask you about it."

"All I told Greeley was to keep his eyes peeled for pirate vessels," said Hill.

"There hasn't been a pirate ship within fifty parsecs of the Canphor system in a century, and you know it!" snapped Bellows. "I want an explanation and I want it quick!"

"I have none to make until I look into the matter," said Hill. "For the present, I'd suggest that we write a profusely apologetic note to Canphor VI immediately. I'll do it if you like, and send you a draft for your personal approval."

Bellows stared across the huge desk at his adviser. "I don't know what you're up to, Mel, but you're on very shaky ground at this moment. Past friendship aside, I won't hesitate to dump you if I find it necessary—and I'll find it necessary if there's one more incident like this."

Hill returned to his office, dictated the note of apology, and sent it to Bellows. It came back with the Governor's approval.

"Okay," he said to his secretary. "Send it off."

"In Galactic, sir?" she asked.

"In Terran," said Hill calmly.

Within hours the government of Canphor VI sent back a message that the apology was unacceptable.

"What will the Governor say to that one?" said one of Hill's aides, looking at the transcribed reply.

"I haven't the slightest idea," said Hill. "However, I don't think he'll say too much."

"Oh? Why?"

"Because I've released copies of our apology and Canphor VI's answer to the media." The intercom lit up, and Hill pressed a button.

"Hill here."

"Mel, this is Josh. I don't know why Canphor VI turned your note down, but I've got a pretty good suspicion. Did you send it in Galactic?"

"I can't recall," said Hill.

"That's it!" bellowed the Governor. "You've got two days to put your affairs in order and clear out. You're fired!"

"I wouldn't release that to the press for a few hours yet, Josh," said Hill.

"And why not?"

"It won't make the headlines until they're through

running the story about Canphor VI turning down our apology."

The intercom flicked off without another comment from Bellows.

"We haven't got much time," said Hill to his aides. "Three hours from now every human in the Deluros system will be screaming for war, and by tomorrow morning the rest of the human worlds will be out for blood too. If Josh wants to keep his political scalp, he'll have to attack—and if I know Josh, he'll procrastinate until it's too late."

"I don't see that you can do anything about it," volunteered one of the aides.

"That's why I'm your boss instead of the other way around," said Hill. "Send the following message to Greeley, unscrambled." He paused, trying to get the words straight in his mind, and then began dictating.

Admiral: The content of this message is of such import I that we've no time for code. The planned attack on the Canphor system will take place in five days' time. The delay is regrettable, but the bulk of our fleet is engaged in maneuvers on the Rim. Do not—repeat, do not—move in until that time, as you can expect no assistance from Deluros VIII prior to the return of the fleet. Should there be any doubt whatsoever concerning your orders, return immediately to base at Deluros V.

Melvyn Hill, Assistant to the Governor

Hill looked up. "What's the latest frequency that Canphor VI has cracked?"

"H57, about a week ago."

"Good. Send it on H57, but in Terran. We don't want to make it look too easy for them."

"What if Greeley attacks?" asked an aide.

"He won't," said Hill. "He doesn't know what the hell I'm talking about, so he'll come racing back to base, just in time to help fend off the Canphor fleet."

Hill walked out his door and strolled casually over to Bellows's office. He smoked a cigar, checked his watch, decided that the message would have been sent and intercepted by now, and walked in. The security agents had already been instructed that he was no longer a member of the staff, and they barred his way. After sending through his formal request to see the Governor, he was kept cooling his heels in the outer office for another hour before he was finally ushered in.

"I don't know why I'm wasting time like this," began Bellows. "I've got nothing to say to you."

"But I've got a lot to say to you, Josh," said Hill. "Especially since this is probably the last time we'll ever speak together. May I sit down?"

Bellows stared hard at him, then nodded. "Why did you do it, Mel?"

"I suppose I should say I did it for you," said Hill, "and in a way I did. But mostly, I did it for Man," He paused. "Josh, I don't want to startle you, but you're going to have a war on your hands in less than a day, and there's no way in hell you can get out of it, so you'd better make up your mind to win it."

"What are you talking about?" demanded Bellows.

"Canphor VI," said Hill. "And possibly Canphor VII too. They'll be attacking Deluros VIII very shortly. It'll take very little effort to beat them back, and not much more to defeat them. They're operating on the assumption that we're unprotected." Bellows reached for his intercom panel, but Hill laid a hand on his arm. "No hurry, Josh. Greeley will be back ahead of them, and has probably got everybody in an uproar already. Let's talk for a few minutes first; then you can do anything you want to me."

Bellows sat back in his chair, glaring.

"Josh, I'm not going to tell you how this came about. It's so simple you wouldn't believe me anyhow, and besides, you'll be able to speak with a little more forcefulness and moral outrage on the video if you don't know. But the thing is, it's started. Man's about to make his first move back up the ladder, and you're going to go down in history as the guy that did it. It won't be completed in your term, or your lifetime, or even in a millennium, but it's started now and nothing's going to stop it.

"You've got the people behind you," Hill continued, "plus the unswerving loyalty of the military. This battle won't amount to anything more than a minor skirmish, and knowing you, I'm sure you'll offer very generous terms to Canphor when it's over. But the very least the legislature will demand is that the Canphor system become a human protectorate. They'll want more than that, but I imagine you'll get them to compromise there. Whatever the result, the Canphor worlds will contribute their taxes to Deluros VIII, and our tariffs will reflect their change in status.

"And once you find out just how easy this is, it'll occur again and again in some form or another. You're going to be riding a tidal wave of sentiment, and you're either going to steer it where it wants to go or get thrown out of the saddle within a month You'll be very careful and meticulous, and you'll always pay lip service to the Democracy. Perhaps it will even remain as a figurehead of galactic power, but the handwriting will be on the wall. Man's going to wind up calling the shots again."

"I don't know what you think you've done," said Bellows, "but whatever it is, it can be undone. If there really is an alien attack force on the way from Canphor, I'll see to it that it's called back."

"Uh-uh, Josh," said Hill. "They've heard what they've been expecting to hear, and they're not going to believe anything *you* tell them."

"They'll believe me when I tell them we're standing ready to repulse any attack."

"I'm afraid not," said Hill. "There's no way you can turn it off, Josh. You'd better start thinking about how you're going to tell the people that you're the leader they've always wanted you to be."

Hill stood up and slowly walked out of the office.

Bellows spent the next two hours confirming the truth of what he'd been told, and two more hours after that frantically but fruitlessly trying to avert the coming conflict.

As night fell, the Governor of Deluros VIII sat alone in his semi-darkened office, his hands clasped in front of him, staring intently at his fingers. He considered resigning, but realized that it wouldn't have any effect on the tide of events. He even considered having Hill make a full public confession, but knew even as the thought crossed his mind that the populace would approve of Hill's actions.

Bellows was an essentially decent man. He didn't want to destroy anyone. At heart he believed that Man would emerge triumphant in the galactic scheme of things by virtue of his own endeavors.

Furthermore, Man was still immensely outnumbered by the other races. The course Hill had charted would be so perilous, so fraught with danger at any misstep. . . Man would have to divide and conquer on a scale never before imagined. He'd have to be quiet about it, too; would have to accomplish most of his plan before the galaxy awoke to what was happening, or everything would come down on his head, hard.

And yet, if Man was capable of pulling it off, didn't he deserve to? After all, this wasn't exactly survival of the fittest so much as ascendancy of the fittest. The races of the galaxy would continue to function, and under Man's leadership they would very likely function all the more efficiently.

Or was he just rationalizing? Man was capable of such splendid achievements, such generosity to other races, why did he have to have this aggressive, darker side of his nature? Or was it a dark side at all? Was Man, as Hill had said, merely making the most of every single one of his attributes, including this one? Bellows reached for the intercom button that would summon the press. As they filed into his office, he made his decision—or rather, he thought with a bemused detachment, he acknowledged the decision that had been made for him. For while he had many other qualities—goodness, judgment, integrity—all had failed him in this crisis, and he was left with the foremost quality that any politician possesses: survival.

"Gentlemen," he began, staring unblinking at them with his clear blue eyes, "it has come to my attention that a fleet of military ships has just left Canphor VI for the purpose of perpetrating a heinous sneak attack on Deluros VIII. Neither we nor any other world housing members of the race of Man will tolerate or yield to such an unprovoked action. Therefore, I have instructed the 7th, 9th, 11th, and 18th fleets to take the following steps. . ."

The End

A Modest Proposal for the Perfection of Nature

Vonda N. McIntyre

The crop grows like endless golden silk. Wave after wave rushes across the plains, between mountains, through valleys, in a tsunami of light.

Its harvest is perfection. It fills the nutritional needs of every human being. It adapts to our tongues, creating the taste, texture, and satisfaction of comfort food or dessert, crisp vegetables or icy lemonade, sea cucumber or big game. It's the pinnacle of the genetic engineer's art.

It's the last and only living member of the plant kingdom on earth.

Solar cells cover slopes too steep and peaks too high for the monoculture. The solar arrays flow in long, wide swaths of glass, gleaming with a subtle iridescence, collecting sunlight. Our civilization never runs short of power.

The flood of grain drowns marsh and desert, forest and plain, bird and beast and insect. Land must serve to produce the crop; creatures only nibble and trample and damage it, diverting resources from the service of human beings. Even the immortality of rats and cockroaches has failed.

The grain stops at the ocean's beach. No rivers muddy the sea's surface or break the shoreline. The grain and the cities require fresh water, and divert it before it wastes itself in the sea.

The tides wash up and back, smoothing the clean silver sand, leaving it bare of tangled seaweed, of foraging seabirds or burrowing clams, of the brown organic froth that dirtied it in earlier times. Now and then the waves erase a line of human footprints, but these are very rare.

The air is clear of any bite of iodine, any hint of pollution or decay.

The sea undulates, blue and green, clear as new glass. Sunlight shimmers on its surface and dapples the bare sea floor. Underwater turbines cast shadows on the sand. The tides power the turbines, tapping the force of gravity.

Far from shore, where its colonies will not interrupt the vista of clear water, a single species of cyanobacterium photosynthesizes near the surface, pumping oxygen into the crystalline air, controlling the level of carbon dioxide. Its design copes easily with the increasing saltiness of the sea.

Except for the cyanobacteria, the ocean's cacophony of microscopic organisms has followed redwoods, mammoths, and *Hallucigenia* into extinction. The krill are gone; krill would be of as little use to people as sharks and seabirds, fish or jellyfish, seashells or whales. They are all gone, too.

The water deepens beyond the reach of light. The continental shelf ends in a precipice, dropping off into darkness.

On the sea floor, the glass-lace shells of diatoms lie clean and dead, slowly settling. In a moment of geologic time, they will form white limestone.

In the deepest trenches, black smokers gush scalding chemical soup. Machines sense the vents of heat, swim to them, and settle over them to trap the energy of the center of the earth. Nothing remains for the sustenance and evolution of primordial life in these extraordinary environments.

The strange creatures who lived there, and died, were never any use to human beings.

All the resources of sea and land serve our needs.

Cities of alabaster and adamantine grace the crests of mountains and span the flow of rivers. The cities' people live rich, full lives, long and healthy, free of disease. We are well fed. We have interesting, challenging occupations and plenty of time for leisure, family, and virtual reality. We can experience any adventure, from wilderness to exotic ritual, without the expense, trouble, or danger of travel. We can experience any adventure that ever happened, any adventure anyone can imagine. The virtual experience matches reality or invention in every way: sight, sound, smell; touch and movement.

Our civilization pulses with vitality. We have unlimited opportunity: of thought, of achievement, of freedom, and of the pursuit of happiness.

Whatever we require, human ingenuity can invent and provide. And if in some unlikely but imaginable future we should wish to recreate any organism, the means to do so exist. DNA sequences, RNA sequences, are easy to write down and archive; there is no need to store messy biological material, either tough and persistent DNA or fragile and degradable RNA. We are magnanimous; we have preserved the blueprints for everything, even parasites and pathogens.

No one has bothered to recreate an organism in a very long time. We have considered the question long and hard, and we have made our decision. No creation of nature has an inherent right to exist, independent of our need.

We have perfected nature, for we are its masters.

The End

Conspiracy of Silence

Philip Brian Hall

In the Information Age, the prevalence of spurious facts, sometimes referred to as fake news, drives romance from the souls of rational men. Conspiracy theorists however remain untroubled as they possess a happy knack of disregarding inconvenient knowledge.
The Politics of Misinformation—Professor Michael Bishop, D Phil (Oxon)

Michael Bishop, Professor of Politics at Oxford University, had encountered and dismissed more conspiracy theories than most. In his judgment, the typical alleged cover-up concealed nothing more sinister than the sort of ineptitude to be expected of clerks and tea-makers over-promoted by electoral politics into great offices of state.

Sadly, callow students often ignored his sage advice. He was reluctantly obliged to downgrade their essays accordingly.

On his retirement, the distinguished academic moved to the tranquil village of Micklethwaite in Lincolnshire, to get as far as possible away from romanticists whose analysis of current affairs was invariably compromised by a tendency to misinterpret their own ignorance as a dastardly plot.

One day, out dog-walking in company with Hamish Dougal, the veterinarian, he happened to stroll along a winding footpath leading to Huttoft Wood, a picturesque copse where bluebells grew and nuthatches could sometimes be seen in spring. The escarpment offered from its summit an outstanding view across low-lying pastureland. Amid a rolling patchwork of green, hawthorn hedges were emerging into a froth of white blossom.

"It's a sad fact most people combine an exaggerated view of their own merits with reluctance to undertake research," he remarked to his new friend. "What little they know, they interpret in their own favor. As a result, when they see the manifestly undeserving preferred, it follows there must be dark forces at work."

Hamish watched keenly as his Basset signaled the recent presence of a fox. "You're suggesting authority is distrusted because inadequate officeholders can't have gained power legitimately and so must be guilty of cheating?"

"Exactly," agreed the professor, whose short-legged Jack Russell was working with eager diligence to keep up with the Basset. "In practice, the real reason the world is governed by cretins is the cretins have prevailed in a close contest with the imbeciles who were the only alternatives to put themselves forward."

"You don't have any great notion of politicians, then?"

"I'd remind you, Hamish, of the wise words of Socrates. Any man who thinks enough of himself to stand for election is unfit for office."

"Didn't he also say a good man who won't volunteer to govern will inevitably be governed by someone worse?"

"It's true, he did tend to keep all the bases covered."

"So, Michael, since you're a better man than most, now you're retired I assume you'll be standing for the parish council?"

The professor rather thought he'd talked himself into a tight corner. But when he discovered the parish council consisted of a few self-interested landowners and a sprinkling of busybodies, he began to take the idea seriously. Even Mavis Claythorpe, the village gossip, whose idea of a political platform was a step-ladder giving a more elevated view over her neighbor's garden fence, had contrived to be elected.

True, he'd not lived long in the village, but that gave him a less parochial perspective than the existing councilors. He'd contributed numerous articles to the quality press. He was the author of the standard work of reference on the British constitution, had met the last six prime ministers, and served on government think-tanks and commissions. His qualifications were close to unique in England, let alone Micklethwaite.

~oOo~

The professor wasn't sure how one went about standing, since local government had never previously merited his attention. Supposing its procedure to resemble Parliament's, he persuaded Hamish to nominate him and to collect the necessary signatures from supportive voters.

Michael personally designed and printed one hundred posters, which he distributed to every nook and cranny around the village. Having several left over, he placed a pile in the post office so enthusiasts could help themselves and display them in their front windows.

Certain he'd attract a decent crowd, the professor booked the village hall for a public meeting, advertised it in the local newspaper, and turned up early in order to put out every one of the fifty chairs the hall possessed.

To his horror, fully two score of the chairs were not in regular use. A dozen were broken beyond repair and many of the remainder bore a coat of dust sufficiently thick to have been accumulating since the early patriotic meetings of the First World War. This was an important piece of evidence. He'd ascertained a clear priority for the parish council even before being elected!

The professor didn't need to set about cleaning the chairs. No-one attended the meeting, though Hamish did have the good grace to telephone. He'd been called away to a difficult calving. After thirty minutes in splendid isolation, the professor put all the chairs away again and went home.

His canvassing was no more successful. Whether in isolated thatched cottages or slate-roofed Victorian terraces, no prospective voter upon whose door he knocked knew an election was imminent. When advised of it, they did not care; none had any intention of voting. Pressed as to policy priorities, the electorate were united in their desire to see politicians banned from knocking on their doors.

The professor rationalized all his campaign experiences as due to surprise at a high-quality candidate at last coming forward; he was sure with a little thought the voters would realize the benefits his experience could bring. They would turn out in substantial numbers on polling day.

Apart from himself, each and every candidate was an existing councilor standing for re-election. Indeed, only his candidature had prevented the old council being returned unopposed.

The professor was confident the good people of Micklethwaite would wish to thank him for re-enfranchising them. He could see the dawn of a new age of democracy and progress for the village. And all of it the result of the initiative and public spirit of Michael Bishop.

~oOo~

When the great day finally arrived, the professor presented himself bright and early at the polling station, located, just like his campaign meeting, in the stone-built village hall. Two elderly ladies were there to supervise. They were fortunate in having their knitting and conversation to occupy them, they said, since the turnout was not predicted to be high.

The professor nodded in the manner of one who knew better, took his ballot paper and proceeded to the wood-screened polling booth, where he deliberated for some moments.

At length, feeling honor would not allow him to vote for himself, he took up the blunt pencil stub (thoughtfully secured to the desk by a length of binder twine in order to protect it against theft) and marked his cross next to the name of Mavis Claythorpe. He suspected she was liked by very few residents because of her notoriety as a tale-bearer. She was likely to secure the least votes.

Folding his paper neatly, he dropped it into the slit atop the scratched, black metal ballot box, to the bottom of which it fell with a hollow, echoing clunk. He exchanged a few cheery words with the two old ladies and went back to busy himself for the rest of the day in his bookshop, the only establishment in the village enjoying less custom than the polling station.

~oOo~

The professor attended along with the other candidates when the count took place immediately upon the closure of the polls. The returning officer was a minor official sent over from the county council offices. The local policemen lent his august, uniformed presence, no doubt with a view to suppressing any tendency to riot on the part of whichever sitting candidate was to lose his or her seat.

The seal which had been formally placed on the ballot box thirty seconds earlier by the old ladies was removed with equal formality by the returning officer and the contents of the box deposited on the table from which the wool and knitting needles had been carefully removed as prescribed in electoral regulations.

For most of the afternoon the professor had been rehearsing his acceptance speech. Now word perfect, he stood a little away from the others just to run through it one more time in his head. Owing to his distraction, he was taken by surprise as the count was completed in one minute and the returning officer stepped forward to announce the result to the assembled multitude of interested parties.

It was a sad commentary on the state of democracy in Micklethwaite. The crowd was not in double figures, despite the returning officer being accompanied by his dog. The golden retriever showed more enthusiasm and interest than most, wagging his tail vigorously and panting with ill-concealed excitement.

“I the undersigned,” the official began, “being the returning officer for the village of Micklethwaite in the County of Lincolnshire, do hereby declare and give notice that the votes cast in the election for parish councilors were as follows. . .”

To cut a long rigmarole short, the result was exactly the same as the previous election, save this time Mavis Claythorpe had topped the poll with two votes, while each of the other existing members had one.

The professor, despite having outspent the rest of the field combined, knocked on more doors and posted more posters, received not a single vote. He was forced to applaud politely and alone as the successful candidates shook hands with the returning officer and departed without speeches to hold an impromptu council meeting in the pub.

~oOo~

In high dudgeon, the professor accosted Hamish the following day. He demanded to know why his sponsors had all failed to vote for him.

"You mean we were supposed to vote as well?" asked an astonished Hamish. "Surely an unnecessary duplication? Obviously we supported you, or we shouldn't have sponsored you. I'm sure all your other sponsors felt the same. Mavis Claythorpe, for example, was only too delighted to sign."

"But Mavis Claythorpe was a candidate herself!" raged the professor.

"That's right," Hamish agreed. "So were all your other sponsors. They said it was the usual thing all the candidates sponsored each other because no one else could be bothered."

"And then they all voted for themselves!" declared the professor, aghast.

"Well I couldn't say," replied Hamish. "It's a secret ballot, isn't it? Don't tell me you voted for somebody else?"

The professor made no reply. Once again dark forces had resulted in the exclusion of the meritorious and the promotion of mediocrities. The sitting members had conspired to prevent his election. They'd withheld from the public that an election was even taking place. What was more, they'd concealed from the best candidate the vital information one was supposed to vote for oneself!

He would write immediately to the local newspaper and denounce the conspiracy; the public must be told.

He wrote. The letter brilliantly highlighted in excoriating detail the darker side of Micklethwaite, and truth that only he knew. Truth that must be shared.

The editor had long ago banished all conspiracy theory to the rubbish bin. He didn't print the letter.

The End

HMO

Karin L. Frank

It started when our son, Chuck, got appendicitis.

We'd called 911 on our ancient flip-phone.

No GPS. 911 couldn't find us.

It's a crapshoot unless your GPS is registered, and, as always, there's a surcharge for that. We can't afford surcharges.

So we loaded Chuck into the back of the van and hauled him to the nearest in-network hospital.

From behind her bulletproof glass, the bored clerk dispensed the necessary forms. She used a slide tray, similar to those found in late-night gas stations.

I filled out all the forms and presented our insurance card.

The clerk's static-muffled voice told us, with a practiced wave, to: "Wait over there."

The waiting room was painted in prison beige and green. Not reassuring. The decorators had just missed bilious, but the colors were likely to mask any resulting nausea.

Chuck sat on the wall-mounted steel benches, his normally healthy, brown cheeks tinged gray. He was nearly doubled over with pain and beads of sweat dotted his forehead.

I couldn't help hovering over him. What mother couldn't? "How's the pain?" I asked for at least the third time.

He didn't get angry. He just shook his head.

"This decor isn't much of a pain killer," I said, trying to be cheerful.

"No padding on the benches doesn't help much, either." He might have matched my light tone if he hadn't had to suck in his breath as he said it.

I put my hand on his shoulder, hoping a mother's touch had miraculous pain-killing properties.

Finally, a white-clad nurse opened a door and called our names. "Mrs. Anna Turner and Charles Turner." She looked around.

"Chuck," my son said bravely. "I'm Chuck Turner." He groaned and couldn't stand up fully. I had to help him.

We entered the inner sanctum, another room—a table, two chairs and a stainless steel table. It looked like an examination room.

We waited.

The doctor entered eventually, white-coated, gray-haired. He introduced himself as Doctor Nill. He did not offer to shake hands.

The doctor palpated. He took notes. He expressed bland concern. He smiled. His pale blue eyes reflected nothing.

"Appendicitis," he said. "With a minor problem." He produced a set of forms.

The papers trembled in my hands as I read them.

"But we're insured," I said. "We have full coverage under the HMO."

"Full coverage," said Dr. Nill, "doesn't cover fully."

"Read the fine print," the ever-efficient nurse said. "Your family exhibits a series of genetic variants that partially disqualifies you for full coverage."

I read the fine print.

They weren't joking.

I considered the value of our meager possessions. "This is impossible. There have to be options."

The nurse took my son away. "He'll be fine," she said. "We'll keep him in intensive care until we operate."

"That's more or less covered," the doctor interjected.

I couldn't make up my mind if he was trying to be sympathetic or businesslike. The two tend to blend together in a doctor's bedside behavior. In my own head, I opted for businesslike. I'd read that the insurance monopoly now required a full year of internship in their offices. The insurance companies want us to never forget they're in charge.

"Well," the Doctor said without batting either pale blue eye. "There is one alternative."

"Tell me," I pleaded.

"Do either you or your husband have any headaches, backaches, rashes, sinus problems, arthritis? Any little nagging health problem that we can treat?"

"Why yes," I said. "I do have occasional pain in my joints."

"I don't see that on your chart."

"I can't take anything for it. My full coverage doesn't cover medication for non-life-threatening ailments."

"Quite so. However, I can make the claim on your behalf that it impacts the quality of your life and prescribe a medication for arthritis that your insurance fully covers. It's quite cheap to produce and very expensive to purchase. Take it for the next twenty years. By that time, of course, it will have created a stomach ulcer and we will have to operate on that. But, also by that time, your accumulated medical co-pays will have accrued sufficiently to pay for your son's operation. We can deal with payment for your ulcer at that time."

"Sign here," the nurse said holding out a new sheaf of forms.

"What could I do, George?" I asked my husband back at home as I watched red anger suffuse his cheeks. "I signed."

"They'll operate?"

I nodded. "Tomorrow."

George snatched the bottle of pills off the table and flushed them down the toilet. "We may have to pay for them." he said. "But you don't have to take them." He added bitterly, "We just have to take the shit they hand us."

We went to bed.

In the dark I whispered, “The payments will bankrupt us. It’s like being slowly bled to death.”

I felt his head nod against my shoulder. “Co-pays are a bitch.”

After an anxious day checking financials on our phones at work, we realized that the pill payments would eat up our meager food budget.

“We’ll save Chuck just to starve him to death,” George texted me.

I stared at the death sentence in clear black letters on the screen—as cold as the lump of ice in my stomach.

That evening, we returned to the hospital. We were ushered immediately past the waiting room and into the office of the receiving nurse.

“Turners?” she asked shuffling papers.

We nodded. She looked up expectantly.

“Are there any other alternatives than the twenty years of gold-plated pills?” I demanded.

She ignored my sarcasm. Why shouldn’t she? She was in the driver’s seat.

I changed tones. “Please tell us,” I pleaded.

George looked at me. I could tell he didn’t like my whining tone.

I didn’t like that sound, either. Producing it hurt my throat.

After a weary, sidelong glance, she mumbled, “We’re thinking about printing a pamphlet.”

“Alternatives?” I repeated. I couldn’t get any more words out.

She stood up and leaned on the desk. “Get the hospital a usable body part in return.” She walked away, muttering.

We stood, open-mouthed.

The insurance companies want us to never forget they’re in charge.

“They’re pushing us to only one conclusion,” George said. “One of us has to have an organ harvested.”

I leaned against the edge of the desk. “How about my uterus?”

It seemed logical. There was no way that we could afford medical care for another child. Having Chuck had demonstrated a predisposition toward pregnancy on my part, so my maternity coverage had been cancelled.

The nurse returned to her seat. “Chuck’s operation has been postponed,” she notified us. “He is being held in an induced coma until such time as you can demonstrate ability to meet the cost of medical care. The good news is that 90% of the costs of an induced coma are covered,” she smiled broadly as she slid a credit application out of a drawer. “And our office can arrange financing for the remainder.”

I glanced at the forms. An interest rate of 32% jumped out at me from the fine print.

I offered up my uterus.

“No good,” she said. “We have more uteruses than we know what to do with. It’s the one organ that doctors tend to remove while it’s still working.”

"Besides," she added, with a note of compassion in her voice. "Then you'd be on hormone replacement therapy and your insurance doesn't cover that, either."

Darkness was thinning when we got home.

We tried to get some sleep, but I don't think either of us did. Giving in to morning light, we discussed what alternatives there might be.

When my mother phoned to find out how Chuck was, we told her our predicament.

"I may be eighty," she said. "But I'm as spry as a goat. I can give 'em an organ. I'm up for it."

"Mother," I said.

"He's my grandson."

"Mother," George added.

"My doctor advised me to slow down," she laughed. "Maybe, if I let them chip a piece of me away, it'll slow me down. It's worth a try."

We took her to the hospital.

The exam lasted another three hours. We waited on the uncomfortable chairs.

"No good," the receiving nurse said as she wheeled Mother out. "She's too old, harvesting an organ could kill her and she pays taxes."

"Do you care?" Mother said sarcastically. "You'd still have your piece of flesh."

"Read the fine print," the nurse said. "Tax law is inevitable, ma'am. Voluntary harvesting of taxpayers is not allowed."

"I won't pay taxes if I give my kids everything I own," Mother said curtly. "Then you can use me."

"Not for three years. The Protection of Active Senior Taxpayer and Discouragement of Undue Exploitation Act clearly states that voluntary harvesting of active taxpayers results in a complete abrogation of all other contracts. Keeps people from doing just this kind of thing. It was passed for your protection, Granny," she added.

Stymied, we took Mother home.

That evening we sat over untasted plates of canned mac and cheese and discussed our options. To our horror, the answer seemed as inevitable as the taxes and death itself.

The body part had to belong to a derelict. "The government doesn't seem to suggest many repercussions for disposing of a non-tax-paying citizen these days," George said.

I couldn't believe I was planning the logistics of the situation. "We just have to catch one," I quavered.

"How're we supposed to do that?" His voice was no steadier than mine.

"Dr. Nill said this might help," I said and set the bottle of chloroform on the table next to the hot sauce.

That night, we drove to the bridge that crossed the river. The homeless had built a small camp there. We'd frequently dumped bags of torn clothes and worn blankets over that bridge. We had wanted to teach Chuck the meaning of charity.

"I guess now we're gonna harvest some of what we've sown," George said.

I waved a hand in the direction of all the bodies strewn about in piles of rags and cardboard boxes. "We've actually got a choice."

"A live one," George said dryly. "That way we won't have to worry about transporting the organ."

"Just about not getting killed transporting the package."

"No problem." he said. "If one of us gets killed, we've got the organ source we need anyway."

"You're not funny," I said.

We walked among the sleeping, groaning bodies.

We chose a man who looked barely older than Chuck and forlornly alone.

Trying not to breathe too deeply, I crouched down beside him while George circled around behind.

"Can I share your blanket?" I whispered to our unsuspecting victim.

"For a price," he croaked and tried to tear my blouse off.

"Goddammit," I said at the sound of ripping fabric.

George slipped in from behind like a pro and clamped the chloroformed sponge over his mouth. No shouts were raised about the ensuing struggle. It was just another rape.

We eventually stuffed the man's limp form into the back of our van and drove straight to the hospital delivery entrance.

A carbon copy of the form I signed earlier gained us immediate access through a closed chain-link fence.

"Come back in about three hours," the receiving nurse said. "We'll have the body processed by then." I was amazed. And frightened. That was all she said. Not, "What did you do to this poor man?" or even, "Did he hurt you?" just, "We'll have the body processed by then." The body, just, 'The Body.'

We had entered the dark night of medicine.

I couldn't do it. We couldn't do it. We looked into each other's eyes as the orderlies were transferring the man onto a gurney.

"No," we said in unison.

Not even to save our son's life.

"He's just drunk," I said.

"We'll take him home and let him sleep it off," George added.

"Okay," the receiving nurse said and I saw a glow in her eyes I hadn't seen before—the light of empathy.

We went home to mourn our son.

The next day at work I sat in my cubicle crying. Twenty years. Would they keep Chuck in an induced coma that whole time? Or would they do the operation at some point when we had paid enough?

A banner flashed across my computer screen.

"If you want to save your son," it read. Then it was gone. I stopped crying. I sat. I waited. "If you want to save your son," it flashed again.

Then. "Come to 11th and Market at 2300."

And again. "Come to 11th and Market at 2300."

The screen went blank, but the message was indelibly etched on my brain.

That night, we went to 11th and Market.

At 2300, a person dressed completely in white approached us as we waited on the sidewalk. "Go to this house," a woman's voice said. I thought I recognized the receiving nurse, but I wasn't sure.

We went to the house. It was in a quiet, residential district. We parked the van in front and got out. From the dark, others approached. At first, no one spoke. Then a woman whose body showed the ravages of unmedicated age said, "My husband needed heart surgery. He'd been in an induced coma for three years."

Others spoke up one by one. Everyone had full coverage insurance that didn't cover the operation or medication they needed or had needed. We looked at each other in tears and hope rushed up from my heart so mightily I thought it would choke me.

A few like the older woman had used the past tense. In some manner or other, members of this group had solved this problem.

The side door of the house opened. Another figure clothed in white beckoned us in. This time, I recognized the receiving nurse.

We filed in.

When we were all seated in a comfortable living room, she said, "Welcome, everyone, to the medical underground." She smiled. "We practice alternative medicine here. Not alternative medical procedures, but alternative methods of payment.

"The insurance companies are in charge of our lives. We must never forget that. But within those parameters, we can improvise. Insurance is a gamble. It's you, the subscriber, betting against the insurance company. And the odds are stacked for the house. Well, in one way we are no different. What we offer is a gamble also. But the odds are more in your favor than with the insurance companies."

"You get to play a game. The winners get operations. The losers, well, the losers lose."

Her face, her whole demeanor, seemed much softer to me despite the harshness of what she was proposing. She was offering us a fighting chance, a chance to take back some control of our lives.

"This is straight against-the-house Russian roulette." she added in an even softer tone. She shrugged. "It's for the desperate."

George stood up. "I'm desperate," he said. "My son's life is at stake."

She nodded. "We keep an ambulance in the garage here and one of the EMTs always on call," the nurse said and I could hear the compassion in her voice very clearly this time. "We transport the losers' bodies to the hospital and offer them in payment. Tonight we're playing for the life of Chuck Turner. But we meet once a week and each of you will find at some point that you are playing for the life of someone else's loved one."

The older woman nodded. In the subdued light of the living room I saw for the first time the steel in her bent body.

Keeping one on her lap, the nurse passed out guns to each of us. “Health management just isn’t what it used to be,” she lamented.

“Smith and Wesson. . . Colt 45. . . revolvers,” George mumbled. “How. . . quaint.”

The cold horror in his voice made the words drag.

“How. . . American,” I added and could hear the same in mine.

“We are gladiators,” the nurse declared and grasped her weapon.

I kept my eyes on George as I picked up the revolver, seeking the strength that has always been there for me. And I saw him looking at the old woman, an expression of wonderment dawning. Following his eyes, I looked at her also.

In her face glowed the strength I sought. We might not survive, it declared, but Chuck would and we would go down fighting.

“*Ave Caesar, morituri te salutant,*” the old woman yelled.

“Hail, Caesar, we who are about to die salute you,” George and I shouted together.

The sound of hammers striking empty chambers filled the silence.

The End

Being Donald Trump

Bruno Lombardi

There were eight entities in the waiting room when the blue creature walked into the office.

To be fair, he wasn't the only one who was blue, but the only other being in the room that was that particular colour was a Shuliak and, while they were indeed blue, they also had six legs, four compound eyes and two wings. In contrast, Kolli was almost human in appearance. Well, aside from the scales and horns. . .

"Yes?" asked the green half feline/half humanoid *hir* being behind the reception desk. "Can I assist you?"

"Kolli, of the House Lanxo, of the Haydo Consortium. I have an appointment?"

"Ah, yes! Take a seat! Director Tallium will be with you shortly."

Kolli thanked the receptionist and took a seat, squeezing himself between a Lwaxon Princess and a large orange crystal. In doing so, he accidentally bumped his elbows into both of them. Embarrassed, Kolli mumbled an apology.

[Raising whistle] Apology [click] Accepted [whirling sound] Colleague [sibilant sound] Hayloian [neutral whistle], came the sounds from the orange crystal, sharp and blue and tasting like copper.

<Exclamatory Interjection: Tentative Acceptance> came the telepathic message from the Lwaxon. She tilted her head and stared at Kolli for a moment. *<Query: Presence Here>*

"That's a good question. I'm not sure why I'm here either. It just seems so...intriguing. Yes?"

<Statement: Agreement>

[High pitched whistling] Agreement as well [Screech] came the song, cold and white and tasting like raw diamonds.

Kolli was called into the office ten minutes later.

~oOo~

"Tell me," asked Directot Tallium, leaning back in his chair and folding his four arms across his thorax as he did so, "What do you know about our services?"

"Not much," said Kolli. "Just what I've seen on the holi-vid ads. Mind uploading and something about. . . quantum entanglement?"

"Indeed," said Tallium, leaning forward and smiling. "Tell me; what do you know of parallel universes? Alternate timelines? Mirror dimensions?"

Kolli raised an eyebrow in surprise. "You have developed the ability to travel to those places?" came the incredulous reply.

"Indeed. Let me show you our orientation holi-vid."

~oOo~

It was an *intriguing* ten minute long vid.

Kolli was aware that much—if not all—of the technical details of the process had been glossed over but it was nevertheless still fascinating; Tallium's company could teleport your consciousness into the body of a person in a—*what was the term they used? Alternative Quantum Universe?*—and stay in it for a period of up to one-quarter standard hour. Granted, the control you had over the body you inhabited was limited at best and exactly *which* body you ended up in was somewhat 'hit or miss' (although Tallium had interjected at one point in the vid that they were getting better at 'focusing' with each passing day). Nevertheless, for a 'reasonable fee,' one can essentially "possess" the body of an alien—from a completely different universe.

"Think of the truly fascinating aspects," said Tallium, effortlessly shifting into his sales pitch voice. "You *ride* the being in question. You *become* the being you inhabit. Observe everything *through* their senses. And to a limited degree, even *control* them, albeit for an extremely short period of time. And the fee is within the budget of most sapients."

"But the ethical aspects...?" inquired Kolli, leaving the rest of the question unsaid.

Tallium dismissively waved the objection aside with his upper and lower left hands. "The being in question will have no recollection of the possession and we strive to make sure that the civilization of the possessed being is no higher than a Stage Two world." Tallium leaned forward and smiled. "And if you act *now*, you get a 10% discount."

Kolli signed all the documents immediately.

~oOo~

It was almost, but not quite, like falling into a deep pool of water.

There was the sensation of free fall, then a brief moment of *impact*, then a short period of *floating*—and then Kolli opened up his eyes to see…

He was in front of a …crowd? Of…pink-skinned bipeds?

And it was a *huge* crowd…

"So Lindsey Graham says to me," said a voice—and Kolli realized with a shock that the voice was coming from *him*—"Please, please, whatever you can do—you know, I'm saying to myself, what is this guy—a beggar—he's, like, begging me to help him with Fox and Friends—"

What is a 'Fox and Friends'? thought Kolli, as the voice kept speaking. Out of the corner of his eye, Kolli spotted a piece of paper with some words and numbers written on it being held in the hand of his?—hand.

Maybe that paper will help? thought Kolli—and then he felt a shock shudder through his body—and the hand…*twitched…*

…and slowly lifted up…

I'm controlling the hand! came Kolli's ecstatic thought, as the voice continued.

"—and he gave me his number and I found the card! I wrote the number down. I don't know if it's the right number. Let's try it—202-228-0292…"

There were the sounds of...applause...and laughter...and Kolli felt them. Felt them sweep over him and, yes, into his very soul.

Inside the body of the human, Kolli wept tears. Not tears of pain.

Tears of *joy*.

For the first time in a very long time, Kolli felt *alive...*

~oOo~

"That...was...*incredible*," mumbled Kolli between gasps of air twenty minutes later and a universe away.

"Indeed," said Director Tallium. "I take it you were satisfied with your experience?"

"For a brief moment I controlled the being!" shouted Koll. He continued, stammering as he did so, as he tried to articulate the thoughts and images and feelings he experienced. "It was... as...as...my thoughts were...influencing...even...controlling...the being. And the sensory input! Unlike any I've experienced! And...and...I'm not certain...but I think... I... think... I...was even..."

"—*sensing* the being's emotions as well?" interrupted Tallium, smiling. "So—to repeat—you were satisfied with your experience? Do you wish to try it again? Will you recommend it to all your friends and colleagues?"

"Yes to all three!"

~oOo~

"Most fascinating," said Technician Pollux twelve standard days later, as he handed a data-pad to Director Tallium. "For some reason, the—" and here Technician Pollux paused and re-read the data-pad for a brief moment—"—the *human* with the unusual skin coloration and hair is *extremely* receptive to the procedure. Completely off the charts, in fact."

"Oh?" inquired Director Tallium. "Explanation?"

"None, sir—but this makes him also very receptive to having him being manipulated by the 'rider' as well."

"So anyone ending up in his body has a better chance of controlling his movements?"

"*And* his vocal apparatus, as well. It really is quite impressive. What should we do?"

"Double the price for anyone wanting that human."

"At once sir!"

~oOo~

Donald J. Trump@realDonaldTrump.@MarkHalperin showed a focus group on @Morning_Joe me using a very bad word. I never said the word, left an open blank. Please apologize! 7:40 AM—11 Feb, 2016

"Ted Cruz is a pussy!"—YouTube video clip 9 Feb, 2016

~oOo~

"If you see somebody getting ready to throw a tomato, knock the crap out of them, would you? Seriously. Just knock the hell — I promise you, I will pay for the legal fees. I promise. I promise."—YouTube video clip 1 Feb, 2016

Trump: 'I Don't Condone Violence' Donald Trump told George Stephanopoulos on "Good Morning America" that he was not in fact looking into paying the legal fees of a man who slugged a protester . . .— See the whole picture with ABC News. 4:19 AM—15 Mar 2016

~oOo~

"I'm speaking with myself, number one, because I have a very good brain and I've said a lot of things." (Asked on Morning Joe who his foreign policy consultants are, 16 March, 2016)

~oOo~

"After I beat them, I'm going to be so presidential, you're going to be so bored, you're going to say, this is the most boring human being I've ever interviewed." (Interview on "Fox News Sunday" 3 April, 2016)

~oOo~

"Do I look like a President? How handsome am I, right? How handsome?" (Rally in West Chester, Pennsylvania, 25 April, 2016)

~oOo~

"Sir?" asked Technician Pollux.

"Yes? What seems to be the issue?" replied Director Tallium.

"I want to bring something to your attention. It's about Subject 63J in Universe 12-Alpha."

"Uh, which one is that?"

"The politician, sir? The *human* politician?"

"Oh! He's one of our most successful Subjects!"

"Yes, sir. I understand that, sir. Waiting period of five days, at last report."

"Well, what about it?"

"I'm a bit...troubled, sir. We never had a subject so susceptible before. And certainly not one being used so often. And we've been getting indications that there is, ah, 'feedback', of sorts, happening with the thoughts and memories of those possessing him into his own consciousness."

"You and your team have said—repeatedly—that the Slots suffer no ill effects. Are you saying that you were...*wrong*?"

"No, no! No, not at all!" replied Technician Pollux quickly. "It's just that my team and I think that maybe we should...perhaps...stop using him. Just for a while, you know? While we run a few more tests."

"He *is* one of our most popular requests, Technician. Do you have any evidence that there's any brain damage?"

"Well, no, sir. No evidence yet, but we haven't run any—"

"And our customers are *thrilled* to be able to act as a politician and say and do the silliest things without consequences.

"Yes, about that, sir. I understand that the world in question is a mere Stage Two world but preliminary evidence is that the polity that the politician is running for leadership for is a rather powerful one. Almost certainly in the top five powers. The consequences of—"

"It's a Stage *Two* world, Technician! Barely above stone tools and animal skins! And unless you have evidence—hard evidence—that the sapient is being adversely affected, then this conversation is over. Understood?"

"Yes, sir."

~oOo~

Donald Trump wins U.S. election in astonishing victory.

Trump will be 45th president, oldest 1st-term president, and have Republican-led Senate and House.

The Associated Press Posted: 8 Nov, 2016 4:49 PM ET Last Updated: 9 Nov, 2016 3:40 PM ET.

Donald Trump has been elected the next president of the United States — a remarkable showing by the celebrity businessman and political novice who upended American politics with his bombastic rhetoric.

Trump rode an astonishing wave of support from voters seeking sweeping change, capitalizing on their economic anxieties, taking advantage of racial tensions and overcoming a string of sexual assault allegations on his way to the White House.

His triumph over Hillary Clinton will end eight years of Democratic dominance of the White House and threatens to undo major achievements of President Barack Obama. He has pledged to act quickly to repeal Obama's landmark health-care law, revoke the nuclear agreement with Iran and rewrite important trade deals with other countries, particularly Mexico and Canada.

ANALYSIS | How Trump defied pundits and pollsters to win the White House.

"I will not let you down," Trump said in a tweet Wednesday morning: "The forgotten man and woman will never be forgotten again. We will all come together as never before."

~o0o~

Donald J. Trump@realDonaldTrump

Just had a very open and successful presidential election. Now professional protesters, incited by the media, are protesting. Very unfair!

9:19 PM—10 Nov 2016

~o0o~

Donald J. Trump@realDonaldTrump

Very organized process taking place as I decide on Cabinet and many other positions. I am the only one who knows who the finalists are!

9:55 PM—15 Nov 2016

~o0o~

Donald J. Trump@realDonaldTrump

The Theater must always be a safe and special place. The cast of Hamilton was very rude last night to a very good man, Mike Pence. Apologize!

8:56 AM—19 Nov 2016

~oOo~

Donald J. Trump@realDonaldTrump

In addition to winning the Electoral College in a landslide, I won the popular vote if you deduct the millions of people who voted illegally

3:30 PM—27 Nov 2016

~oOo~

Donald J. Trump@realDonaldTrump

Doing my best to disregard the many inflammatory President O statements and roadblocks. Thought it was going to be a smooth transition—NOT!

9:07 AM—28 Dec 2016

~oOo~

Donald J. Trump@realDonaldTrump

The FAKE NEWS media (failing @nytimes, @NBCNews, @ABC, @CBS, @CNN) is not my enemy, it is the enemy of the American People!

4:48 PM—17 Feb 2017

~oOo~

Donald J. Trump@realDonaldTrump

Terrible! Just found out that Obama had my "wires tapped" in Trump Tower just before the victory. Nothing found. This is McCarthyism!

6:35 AM—4 Mar 2017

~oOo~

"Sir!"

"What *now*, Technician Pollux?"

Technician Pollux handed Director Tallium a datapad. "Look! Look at the scans of Slot 63J in Universe 12-Alpha! In the last twelve months there has been a 3% loss of neurons and synapses in the cerebral cortex and other subcortical regions! There has been a 4% increase in insoluble deposits of protein and cellular material outside and around many of the neurons during the same period! Neurofibrillary tangles are *clearly* beginning to form in 5% of the nerve cells! Sir! We have to stop using him! At this rate, we have only—"

"Technician Pollux, did you run *unauthorized* scans? *Without* my approval?"

"Sir! I must protest in the strongest possible—"

"Technician Pollux—leave my office! Immediately! And one more outburst from you—just *one* more—and your employment here will be terminated! Do I make myself clear?"

Technician Pollux let out a long sigh. "Yes, sir."

~oOo~

"I'm...I'm...still not sure about this," said Sub-Technician Kastor, several hours later. "This is all highly unauthorized and possibly even illegal." She paused and stared for a long moment at Pollux. "And *extremely* dangerous."

Technician Pollux placed a hand on Sub-Technician Kastor's shoulder. "You saw the scans." An affirmative nod. "You saw my report." Another nod. "The fools are too intent on squeezing every single credit out of that poor demented being to care about the consequences. This is why I have to do what I must."

"But you'll be lost in that universe forever! A savage, primitive world. "

Technician Pollux's hand remained on Sub-Technician Kastor's shoulder. "I'll survive, as long as I have your support. Have you spoken to the others?"

Sub-Technician Kastor nodded her head. "I've spoken to the other Sub-Technicians. We will do our best to interfere and possibly even shut down the operation. We have several plans in place to use targeted Slots—other humans—to stop them. If we can't stop here we'll do our best to stop them on the other side." Kastor tilted her head and stared at Pollux for a long moment. "We'll need a signal that you're still alive. A code word to tell me and the others. Something innocuous that we can see while we monitor."

"Understood. Initiate the process."

~oOo~

It was, surprisingly, the very first time for Technician Pollux to try the procedure. There was a long moment of falling and another long moment of floating and yet another long moment of darkness and then—

He opened his eyes.

He was in a room—shaped, rather oddly, as a large oval. He blinked for a few moments, slowly becoming accustomed to the body and his surroundings.

There was an unusual rectangular electronic device in his hand.

Ah yes—the 'twitter' device that the customers have talked about repeatedly.

Technician—now Human—Pollux blinked for a few minutes. And then he smiled.

I know the perfect way to tell Kastor I made it. I will insert her first name in a 'tweet'...

Pollux pressed the 'send' button and then began the steps to bring the rest of his plan to fruition.

He had a lot of work to do.

~oOo~

Donald J. Trump@realDonaldTrump
Despite the constant negative press covfefe
12:06 AM—31 May 2017

~oOo~

Donald J. Trump @realDonaldTrump

Sorry folks, but if I would have relied on the Fake News of CNN, NBC, ABC, CBS, washpost or nytimes, I would have had ZERO chance winning WH

5:15 AM - 6 Jun 2017

~oOo~

"He's sent us a message!" shouted Sub-Technician Covfefe Kastor. "And it's in the code words we worked out before he left!" It had been almost seven cycles since Pollux had last communicated with her and she had feared the worst.

"Can you decipher them?" asked someone in the back of the room. There were a dozen beings in the room – all serving various minor positions in the organization and all dedicated to the Pollux's–and Kastor's–cause.

"Just a moment," said Kastor, as she pulled up the message on a screen and started tapping away on her keypad, her seven tentacles a blur in activity.

"Ok–so 'Fake News' is code for 'Bad News', the list of acronyms are the list of media agencies that he has attempted to infiltrate and the phrase 'ZERO chance' means he's been unsuccessful but will try again.

"That is... unfortunate," murmured one of the resistance members, shaking their head.

Sub-Technician Covfefe Kastor shook her head in sympathy. "If he follows protocol, we should expect another update in three cycles."

~oOo~

Donald J. Trump @realDonaldTrump

Despite so many false statements and lies, total and complete vindication. . .and WOW, Comey is a leaker!

3:10 AM - 9 Jun 2017

~oOo~

Donald J. Trump @realDonaldTrump

Great reporting by @foxandfriends and so many others. Thank you!

3:54 AM - 9 Jun 2017

~oOo~

Donald J. Trump @realDonaldTrump

It is time to rebuild OUR country, to bring back OUR jobs, to restore OUR dreams, & yes, to put #AmericaFirst! TY Ohio! #InfrastructureWeek

~oOo~

POTUS Trump Visits Cincinnati, Ohio on 6/7/17 for Infrastructure Week

3:52 PM - 9 Jun 2017 from Warren, NJ

~oOo~

“Incoming messages!” shouted a Junior Sub-technician (Fourth Class).

“On it!” shouted Sub-Technician Covfefe Kastor as she sat down and began to quickly decode the message.

“Oh no...” whispered Kastor, her voice cracking.

“What? What? Bad news?”

“Very much so, alas. The first message about false statements means that Pollux has failed in contacting other Slots. The second message – the one about 'foxandfriends'-is saying that the prognosis for Slot 63J's mental state is completely unsalvageable."

"Oh no..."

"But–the last message is the key!" A tentacle stabbed the screen. "That last message–it's telling us that there is another! Another Slot! A Slot that he can jump into!"

"And save all those... hu-muns?"

"Hu-mans—and yes!"

"But...who?"

"Check the 'twitter' feeds of the rest of the humans! There will be a message there! I'm sending you the search words to all your stations now! Go!"

~oOo~

"We found it!" yelled a Junior Researcher (Sixth Class). It had been a very stressful five cycles. "It's a 'tweet' linking to a... satirical news site?"

Sub-Technician Covfefe Kastor nodded her head. "There are a large number of such sites used by the humans. We assumed that we can easily hack the site and place messages there without arousing any suspicion. Bring up the tweet that linked to it!"

"On your screen now!"

The screen went blank for a moment–and then the message appeared.

John McCain @SenJohnMcCain Jun 14

Hilarious @DuffelBlog: "John McCain Angered Over Loss Of Hanoi Hilton Honors Points"

“Good news?” inquired the Junior Researcher (Sixth Class). A nod from Sub-Technician Covfefe Kastor.

“Very good news,” she replied. “There is another hope...”

The End

America Once Beautiful

Brad Cozzens

America, once beautiful,
the land of future dreams.
Where Industry claims profit rights
from purple mountains majesty.

In city crumbles, weed grown cracks.
Now where will children play?
A land now filled with guns and hate.
The thin blue line, it keeps us safe?

It's us and them or no-man's land,
have mercy on us Lord.
The world, it seems, that fills our eyes
Has fractures turning through it.

The fractures start to crumble as pressure
overwhelms.
Common folk can stand no more.
For once we were born equal.
Where once we stood for right.

America once beautiful,
We'll be that way again
Marching though the commons drowning out the hate.
Finding hope and holding hands,
A better future waits.

America First

Tais Teng

The new president looked across the lawn of the White House from behind three inches of bulletproof glass. The one-way mirror-glass was an inheritance of the last president and he was thinking of replacing it. French windows, perhaps?

Demonstrators dotted the lawn.

At least they are back. They trust me that much. "Don't shoot them," he instructed. "We don't do that anymore."

All colors of skin were there, he saw, all nine genders, and even a white haired lady in a wheel chair. But they all clustered in little groups, they all sat apart. *There isn't any unity, no sense of being Americans together. Look there: a Puerto Rican banker is bashing a Mormon lawyer over the head with a cucumber.*

He flinched. *Puerto Rican middle class and the Mormons, they're supposed to be the pillars of society. They voted for me.*

"Enjoying the view?" the French Minister for Foreign Affairs asked and the President came to with a start. *Don't spoil it. America has precious few friends left. Lithuania and the Republic of Togo, that is about it.*

The minister had been touring the Americas and the USA was only a short stop-over in the middle.

Three hours before he departed for Mexico and a tour of the Great Mexican Wall.

We are the seventh country he visits and only because his favorite niece and my son are such good friends, studying at the Sorbonne.

“They are my people,” the President said.

“They are demonstrating. They don’t look exactly happy.’ The Minister peered closer. “That placard. PUTIN FOR PRSIDENT! AT LEAST HE TELLS THE TRUTH SOMETIMES?”

“That is an old one and not really about me. My own son has marched with that slogan.” The president spread his hands. “Governor Schwarzenegger just phoned. Free California is thinking of joining the US again. Becoming a state once more.”

“But he is waiting to see how this works out first, eh?”

The minister was a full head shorter than the president and anything but handsome or even good-looking, yet somehow he never failed to intimidate his host. Perhaps it was his suave manner, his way of citing world-famous writers and philosophers the president had never even heard about. It might even be the way he had lifted his wineglass, swirling the contents and inhaling the rising vapors with an enigmatic smile.

The president felt sure his waiters had succeeded in serving exactly the wrong wine at the hot lunch. “An excellent vintage, of course, but not with fish, my dear President.” He almost could hear the Minister say that.

"*Mon cher ami,*" the French Minister said, "Your problem, the problem of your whole nation, is a marked lack of coherence. It's a hodgepodge of nationalities, which have no shared past at all. What you miss is a sense of history. Perhaps even. . . history itself?"

The President shook his head. "I think you're wrong," he said in the deep, careful voice that had helped him win the election. The voters had become so very tired of fist-shaking and raised finger rants. "We Americans have a fine sense of history. Any pupil can recite all the American presidents, knows of Buffalo Bill and Pocahontas, Columbus, the Boston Tea Party."

The Minister spread his hands. "But my dear friend, that's only yesterday!" And he sat back with a smug smile, secure in his ancestral pride, his country having had kings and emperors, theologians and crusaders, even Roman invasions.

The President remembered a visit to his son. Castles and churches in overwhelming profusion. Roman aqueducts. Even the smallest village boasted an inn visited by at least one crowned head. It was all so incredibly ancient! And it certainly worked miracles for their pride.

We have no pride, the President realized, because we have no past. It was the reason for his Puerto Rican chef probably spitting in his soup before he served it. For those dreadlocked gang-members on the lawn giving the finger to the red-capped truck driver screaming at them.

"You think that is it? Having no shared past?"

"Mr. President, I am sure of it."

~oOo~

Having survived four previous administrations, even the last one, Jeffrey Seager had become a kind of fixture in the White House. Presidents found him strangely useful. Though officially only a dollar-a-year advisor, his budget was, for all practical purposes, unlimited. Most of his funds fell under the heading "Miscellaneous Expenditures." Seager was the 'Man Who Got Things Done,' the ultimate fixer.

Seager listened for half an hour to the President and finally nodded. "I see, Mister President. Depend on me."

The President rose and shook his hand. When Seager left the room, he was smiling.

~oOo~

Seager sat back on his Tibetan yak-hide pouf, flicked ashes from his Brindisi de Luxe. What exactly did he need? Copywriters, con-men? History was much harder to sell than a tangible product, no matter how useless.

People just weren't interested. Scratch the con-men. Even hedge fund bankers were too hidebound. No, what he needed were daydreamers, men who were constitutionally unable to believe in the real world. Idealists. But they should be experts, too: there were just too many details that could trip him up. He was, after all, no historian. If you tell a lie, make sure you tell it well. The last president hadn't quite understood that.

He reached for his antique iPhone X. "Get me the best historian in the States. No, not the most famous, the best!" The ultimate fixer, Seager had his own army of fixers.

~oOo~

They finally found Dr. William Straub asleep in an abandoned taxicab sitting on blocks in the back of an overgrown parking lot. Books covered the back seat. Some were already moldering.

The hard-eyed man with the obligate bulge below his armpit shook him awake. Straub opened an eye, feebly waving his right hand in search of his glasses.

"You Straub? Doctor William Straub? Of Medieval European History?"

William opened his other eye. "Well, yes. Has Homeland Security finally made that a crime?"

"Save your jokes for your whitey friends. The President wants to talk to you."

"Of the bank? I told them once, I told them twice: I didn't overdraw my account! It must have been your stupid computer."

"The President, you fool, the President of the US of A!"

~oOo~

It was a masterstroke, William thought, having the President introduce the members of Task Force Omega to each other. There was a lot of clout still in the office of Chief Executive. And this particular president was so recent, he hadn't yet done anything overtly stupid.

"And this is Lloyd Quentin," the President said, his hand on William's shoulder. "Our archaeologist. He knows all about Indians. I mean the Native Americans. Especially the ancient ones."

The crew cut young man shook William's hand. His grip was firm, but not crushingly so.

No show-off, William thought, *a truly civilized human being.* "Nice to meet you." He meant it.

"I liked being outdoors," Lloyd said. "Archeology seemed a fine way to combine hobby and work." He grimaced. "I'm working outdoors all right. The Unemployment Office had me digging irrigation ditches in Arizona. It's a pity they couldn't spare the water to fill them."

"Reverend Michael Suarez. Of the Unified Church. An expert on all matters theological."

William eyed the portly fellow with some suspicion. The Reverend radiated pure reasonableness. It would be hard to win an argument with him, William thought. You just wouldn't want to win. A very dangerous man, moreover, because he probably thinks you can solve any problem with a friendly chat.

"And finally, Peter Wen, our futurologist."

The dignified Chinese gentleman smiled. It was a fine, open smile. Not inscrutable at all. "Excuse me,

Mr. President. Science fiction writer, not futurologist. It's a job like any other and harder than some."

"Err, yes." The President beamed. "Now I want you to work together. The budget is no problem. Believe me, it's huge. The sky is the limit. If you need anything, just call and somebody'll come running."

"I still think it's dishonest," William said, surprising himself. Just to fill his stomach he'd had to do several quite dishonest things lately.

This is different. It makes a mockery of all the things I still believe in and there are precious few left of those.

"It's necessary," the President earnestly replied, thinking of emperors and forests where Charlemagne himself had hunted the bristly boar. "Vital, even."

~oOo~

Just put them in an opulent movie set and keep the booze flowing. Seager believed in drinking on the job. Set the unconscious free. He leaned closer to the screen that showed the conference room of Task Force Omega. The window framed a very private beach and several palm trees. Palm trees were all-important for successful flights of imagination, Seager strongly believed. He made a mental note to request a flock of flamingos, the conservationists be damned.

"Right," William said. He spoke with great deliberation, banging his bottle on the onyx table to emphasize the most important points. "All right, you have convinced me, Reverend. Maybe a past is what

America really needs. But we already have a past. An Indian one."

"Lost for the most part," Lloyd muttered. "Of consequence only to strange people like us." He gestured, spilling half his glass. "Hell, even the Indians don't remember it anymore. How many Indian students do you think I had when they still let me teach? Not a single one! No, I think that the Reverend is right. What we need is a common past. Meaning they're no different from us. The Indians, I mean."

"The Mormons will like that," Peter Wen said. "They always insisted that Indians were the Lost Tribes of Israel. Folks just like us."

Lloyd held up his hand. "I think I have it! Look, most of the trouble, a lot of racial hatred, exists because people didn't arrive at the same time. I mean, first the English and the French, later the Irish, the Puerto Ricans, the Taiwanese. You see? Almost everybody thinks he's at least a bit more American than some other group that came later. Let's prove they came all at the same time. Somewhere around, well, the Roman Empire?"

"Wouldn't that conflict with quite a lot of historical evidence?" William asked.

Lloyd grinned. "Of course. I'll never convince you or myself. Or any of us sitting here. But we're not the people who need to believe. We have to reach the man in the street. How many people do you think can still read nowadays, William?"

"About half, I guess."

“I think you’re too optimistic. Now, how many still read books? Especially books about history?”

William shrugged. “Almost nobody. Otherwise I wouldn’t have been unemployed. They have their television, they have phones that talk and show pretty pictures.”

“You see? Nobody’s gonna yell that we’re telling lies. What we need is a nice long serial about our unknown past. A lot of nice long series. Games, too.”

“Still there’s some knowledge left,” Peter Wen said. “Common knowledge. Hard to get around. For instance, that Columbus discovered America.”

Lloyd laughed. “Just turn that around! He was an American. Everybody knows all important people were Americans. Columbus discovered Europe. I think that is it. Afterwards we colonized Europe.”

Peter Wen nodded. “And Asia, of course. The American Chinese crossed the ocean and founded the Celestial Empire. They called it China, well, because they were Chinese.”

“And Puerto Rico was a settlement of the American Puerto Ricans,” the Reverend concluded.

“Yes, I think we have the bare bones of an action plan here. We only have to. . . shall we say, flesh them out?”

~oOo~

Visiting the Cherokee Grand Casino the Israeli ambassador embraced Chief Three Coyotes Laughing and called his tribe “our prodigal sons” and “blood of our blood." He spoke at length of the joy of discovering relatives after so many centuries. His happiness that the Lost Tribes hadn't been lost after all, but flourished in this great and mighty nation. The ambassador didn't look overjoyed, he rather looked like a Frenchman who has been told that Yorkshire pudding will be served as a special treat. But the ambassadors had no choice: Israel needed those new American ground-to-air missiles.

~oOo~

"But a hundred thousand tons of bricks?" Seager asked. "I mean, there is a war going on right there! And we're supporting their enemies. How is Congress going to react?"

"Why tell them?" Lloyd smiled. "I'm quite sure their president, Grand Mullah, or whatever they call him now, can use the money."

~oOo

A hundred thousand tons of archaeological artifacts were airlifted from Iraq to the heart of Arizona. It almost broke the Pentagon budget for miscellaneous expenditures. What galled Seager the most was that the Iraqis had insisted on payment in Swiss francs.

~oOo~

"You like digging?" the reporter inquired. Lloyd smiled into the camera, leaning on his shovel. Sweat beaded his brow. These Arizona summers were *hot.*

"Sure, I like digging. And it is mighty important work, too."

"I see," the reporter said. A pause. "Important in what way?"

"This place here, we think it's Babylon. Ancient Babylon." *It's finally getting to me,* Lloyd thought, *ancient this, ancient that. I'm starting to talk like the President.*

"Babylon? As in the Bible? But I thought. . ."

"The very same. We already found several cornerstones. Foundations of the Hanging Gardens we believe. Some pottery." (Carefully copied from the jars in the British Museum.) He spread his arms. "It is important that the American People get to know their ancient heritage!" He stamped on the ground. "This here, our beloved American soil, is where it all began. . ."

~oOo~

At night the Rock of Gibraltar showed as a glowing dot of about thirty-seven degrees Centigrade on the infrared sensors of a Pentagon spy satellite. Three million Spaniards crowded the narrow peninsula to welcome their discoverer once again. It had taken the replicas of Columbus' fleet just four weeks to cross the Atlantic.

~oOo~

Still five minutes to go, the Reverend thought. Just in time. The Monsignor, he's a wily one. Well-read too. Maybe it wasn't a very good idea to make those talk shows live. Put in some delay at least. Say five minutes.

"I'm afraid there is some confusion, Monsignor. A misunderstanding. The Promised Land somewhere in the Middle East? Oh, I know our Israeli allies call their country the Promised Land. And it is. We all learned in school how the American Jews colonized the Arabian Desert thousands of years ago and of course they called it the Promised Land."

This is going wrong. I'm losing the thread of my own argument. With a benign smile, he opened the Bible, always a good way to win some time. "And the Lord God said 'I'll give you a land of milk and honey, of palm trees and condominiums.'" He closed the Holy Book, so sadly abused just now. "Now let me ask you, does that sound like Israel?" He looked straight into the camera, no longer arguing with the monsignor but speaking straight from his heart to all those listening millions, to all the faithful who were uplifted, comforted, every Friday night by his program. "No, my friends, no. It's quite clear our Lord meant California."

If that didn't bring Governor Schwarzenegger back into the fold, nothing would.

~oOo~

It wasn't the first time Peter Wen wrote for television, but his scripts for Stargate Lemuria had never been used. Not patriotic enough, the Board of Censors had declared. Barely American at all.

How sweet the taste of revenge long delayed! A series of his own, nationwide, with his name prominently displayed. Not to mention the novelizations, which he would do himself. Only some fans would buy the books, but he had insisted on "DESTINATION: THE PAST!" being brought out in paperback.

He opened his laptop and typed: Episode 12: THE COLUMBUS KILLERS. The American Time Patrol would be hard pressed this episode to prevent the assassins of the sinister alien time-traveling foe from killing Columbus and thus depriving America of her future European hinterland.

It was fun making up your own history. He had always liked alternate world stories and now he had a captive audience. All writers are liars, he thought. The suspension of disbelief. I need no suspension of disbelief now. They believe every word I write.

~oOo~

DESTINATION: THE PAST! became a smash hit. Too much of one. When the Army received the 456,386th application for training in the American Time Patrol they had to discontinue the serial. Even career officers inquired about the possibilities of transferring to the Patrol.

Polls showed that more than thirty percent of Americans now believed that the past could be altered. That wouldn't do. That wouldn't do at all.

In the final episode, the patrolmen destroyed the enemy to the last alien, leaving time once more stable and inviolate. Commander Bill Hewitt faded out with these famous last words: "Now we can rest easy, secure in the knowledge that we live in the best of all possible worlds. An American world."

~oOo~

Standing in the huge auditorium of Yale University, glimpsing the attentive audience from the corner of his eye, William Straub almost felt at peace. His first guest lecture was going well.

The Dean donned his famous fund-raising smile and nodded to his learned visitor. "So you think, Professor Straub, that you have found evidence, compelling evidence, *clear* evidence, that the Magna Carta is copied from the American Constitution?"

"Certainly. Of course, it's not all that exact a copy, but you have to remember the distance between America and England. Which was in that age close to insurmountable. The English had to rely on hearsay, the tales of intrepid American sailors, who were (sad smile) seldom very well-educated."

"Thank you, Professor Straub." The Dean turned to the audience of three thousand students and assorted scientists. "Are there any questions?"

There weren't.

~oOo~

"I think this is completely crazy!" Seager sputtered. "I know the Creationists form a major voting block and you have to take them into account, but this seems. . . sacrilegious!"

The President avoided his eyes. "Senator Marden approached me yesterday. What he gave me was an ultimatum in all but name. If we don't give in they'll blow our whole scheme sky-high. Denounce it as a terrorist plot to undermine American self-confidence."

"But the Garden of Eden!" Seager cried. "Do they expect us to produce the bones of Adam and Eve, too?"

"Well, no. I don't think they want you to go that far."

~oOo~

It seemed to be working, the President thought. Standing at the window of his study, he had a clear view of the White House lawn. The Native Americans and the Klan were still camping out there, but they were no longer camping alone. The President discovered several Taiwanese in their yellow dragon-embroidered T-shirts, at least three Puerto Ricans, a redneck patiently showing a Vietnamese fisherman the right way to barbecue a two-pound steak. Even two Rastafarians arguing with a rabbi and a Mormon.

"My people," the President said softly, feeling an overpowering fondness for all those humble voters camped out there, whose raucous singing kept him awake at night. It was the first time in two years he truly felt like the President of the United States of America.

~oOo~

The French Minister for Foreign Affairs liked to stroll through the landscaped gardens of the Louvre. The carefully manicured hedges, the marble fountains which were quite baroque and surely not in the best of taste: it all gave him a pleasurable sense of belonging, of being a part of France Herself.

God must be a Frenchmen. And if not a Frenchman at least a Francophile. He gave us so much.

He heard voices in the distance. Loud voices. American voices.

The Minister for Foreign Affairs no longer felt quite so at ease.

Those Americans. . . Losing what little sense they had and claiming that the Americans discovered Europe. That they were the first everywhere.

The biggest trouble was, they said it so often, so emphatically, that he sometimes found himself almost believing them. Last night an American "expert" had condemned the Roman aqueduct of Avignon as "a not very clever forgery, clearly copied from a Texas original."

The American divorcée rounded the corner, accompanied by a much younger companion. She looked very American, her white hair blue-tinted, her blouse striped in the colors of the American flag.

"Europe!" she shrilled. "I love it! Everything here is so incredibly fresh, so young and vital! Nothing like our weary, ancient nation."

The End

Final Delivery

Kerri-Leigh Grady

Eva has a full load tonight of twenty-four women, with their fear-soaked bodies and small backpacks of clothes, photos, and cash crammed in a space designed for ten. Four men have brought their women to the boat slip. This is a dangerous moment as the women say goodbye and load up under the shield of giant oaks and hanging moss. Eva tries to be random and choose secluded meeting points, but she worries about the noise, especially for the women fresh from delivering. They won't be able to run if they're found out. Eva can't run, either.

The men weep and whisper fervently to the wives, or sisters, or daughters they have brought to Eva, and she wills them to shut up and leave. They'll see each other soon enough, when the men get word that their women arrived safely and can pass through the wall on a "day trip" or take a "vacation" to Cuba. Eva always delivers the women safely. Always.

One thirty-something woman, well-dressed and carrying a shopping bag from Nordstrom, endures a hug from her husband. She winces—probably recent surgery somewhere on her torso—but pats his back and whispers to him with a decided nod and tight smile. Eva doesn't know her name. She doesn't want to know any of their names. It's better that way, just in case.

The man looks up, directly at Eva where she sits in the captain's chair, and she tenses, waiting for his look of disgust or dismissal, but he gives her a slow, solemn nod. *I'm trusting you*, it says. *Do right by her.*

"Miss," he says and then turns to leave.

One of the other men, what appears to be a brother or friend to a very young woman who probably only recently filled out her selective service form, cringes when he looks up at Eva, but her appearance seems a reminder of why they're here on a private dock in the middle of the night. The women seldom cringe. They seldom respond at all, beyond relief.

Finally free of her clinging man, the last of the women steps aboard, and one of the men tosses the line onto the deck and shoves the boat clear of the dock. It drifts only a few seconds before the engines roar to life and under the cover of the sound of nearby crashing waves, Eva hauls ass out of this cozy, watery hollow and into the void beyond.

~oOo~

"I'm Stella," the thirty something woman with the Nordstrom shopping bag yells over the whipping wind and the roar of the engines. Some of the women look away, refusing to respond. Others offer their names in return, though they too must shout to be heard over the struggling engine. Eva checks the GPS and turns south, and then scans the horizon for lights. She shouldn't see any until she gets to her first destination, a rendezvous. Stella thrusts an arm in the air and yells out, "Hair bands?" A few women gratefully reach out.

Eva scans the horizon again and checks the GPS. Fifteen minutes until the first stop. Assuming the first relay is there. Behind her, one of the women sings. It's an old tune, something about girls wanting some fun, and it sets Eva on edge.

This is her least favorite part of the journey, when uncertainty dogs her. She needs to offload at least half the weight at the first stop or she won't have enough fuel. There is no room for extra.

They're only half a mile from their rendezvous point, but nobody is there; she sees no lights. She isn't worried yet. They're early, and the relay might only be another runner like her. Sometimes, it's a yacht. Sometimes, it's little better than a raft with a tiny motor and no business being in the middle of the Gulf.

She cuts the engine and allows the boat to drift. It won't go far, and now she can also listen for approaching vessels. Though they're in international waters now, it's still dangerous. The Coast Guard and even the Navy patrol here. They have for decades, since women who decided they didn't want to be life-givers took their bodies—property of the State—out of the country permanently. If they get caught and end up back in America, the remainder of their shortened lives will be spent in a Women's Hospital, giving up their life, a piece at a time, continually until their final delivery.

The passengers are well aware of the danger. Some whisper in private, tense conversations. Eva keeps her ear tuned for the voice of panic. There's always at least one on these trips and the panic must be soothed before it escalates.

And there it is. Behind her, one woman's voice hisses and then rises into regular tones that threaten to increase in pitch. Eva twists to turn the chair. She keeps her voice businesslike. "It's good to be frightened. It's no good to panic."

"Why are you here?" Eva asks the woman.

The woman starts, even jerks a little, as if the idea of speaking about herself is a shock in this setting. But slowly, she answers. "I almost died with my last pregnancy." The women stir, some looking up to Eva, others out at the water, at their hands, or at each other. They are ill at ease now, but they're quiet and ready to share one last piece of themselves.

"Who else?" One other woman raises her hand. She's young, and her unlined face appears gray in the scant light.

"I'm pregnant." Everyone watches her, and she bites her lip, looking at anything but the neighbor who grasps her hand. She doesn't need to say anything else.

Eva waits as they take turns showing the scars of their deliveries—three livers, a kidney, marrow and blood and skin. The last woman to speak is missing her thumb and ring finger from her right hand. She's tall and has sturdy hands despite the missing appendages. A soldier, she explains. He was injured, and she was close enough for an emergency delivery.

Two fingers, but they only counted for one delivery, which means she would remain in the system for four more. Eva guesses she's only nineteen or twenty. She barely old enough to be out of high school, and that means she probably came up for a delivery within a few months of registering. It's a shame, but Eva is grateful the women who deliver to injured soldiers got full credit.

The women don't whisper to themselves after that. Eva watches Stella for a minute, but the woman is watching the water, canting her body away from the others. Water licks the boat, and it dips with each wave. Eva checks the GPS and scans the horizon once more. Lights have appeared, and though she's sure it's their relay, the low hum of familiar dread hits her stomach.

She restarts the engine and guides the boat slowly to the meeting point. They've drifted more than she thought they might, so she's not surprised to see a frantic light ahead flashing at them. With a relieved sigh, she flips the light switch on and off three times.

The first rendezvous happens without a hitch.

"Cuba," Eva says in a low tone to the women, and seventeen of them stand. Stella does not, and though Eva is surprised, she says nothing. The wealthy love to retreat to Cuba—it's an easy escape, and Cubans love to crow to America about receiving its refugee women. Stella could live like royalty for years if she sold the rings gleaming in the moonlight, but perhaps her husband has loftier goals. New Zealand and most of Europe would take them in.

When the women are loaded, Eva guides the boat away quickly. A yacht is much less likely to capture attention—after all, only the truly wealthy can afford one—but it's best to be as far away as possible once they turn on their running lights and begin their journey. The yacht will likely go all the way to Cuba without another relay, unless intel warns them that they'll need to relay once again farther south, near Mexico.

Eva watches the water for lights from other vessels, but the night is clear aside from the yacht retreating south of them.

The boat glides through the water now, and though the fuel gauge is lower than Eva would like, she can still make the second rendezvous and get the boat back to Father's slip, pay off the attendant, and get a few hours of sleep before she has to clean houses. She has only three tomorrow. The Morrows fired her after her last delivery required a week in the hospital to recover.

Stella's voice carries to Eva, though she can't make out what she's saying. Eva glances behind her and is surprised to find Stella comforting a woman sobbing on her shoulder. Even from here, the dim light reveals a stain from the stranger's tears on Stella's shoulder. She doesn't appear to notice, but her features are pinched.

Eva focuses on the water ahead and the GPS on the dash.

~oOo~

"This will be Mexico," Eva says in the quiet once the engine is off again, though she doesn't need to. The seven remaining women know where they're headed, and this is the last relay of the night. A green light has appeared ahead of them, and she's nervous. That's not the relay. With a second vessel out there, her rendezvous might have to change. She'll be riding in on fumes if forced to the secondary meeting point, so she prays the green light vessel disappears soon.

"I can't wait to see my girls," one of the women says. The others smile tightly at her. "They're in Belize. That's where I'm going." Her eyes shine.

"Me, too," says another. "Maybe we'll be together the whole way." She reaches out a hand, and Eva turns around to watch the green light again. It's moving toward the horizon.

She sighs with relief.

"I've changed my mind," Stella says, and even the waves quiet against the sides of the boat.

"What do you mean?" someone asks her.

"I want to go back. I can't do this."

Eva weighs whether to say something. She's had women too afraid to continue, but they usually want to turn around right away. They don't wait until they meet their relay to back out. She glances back at Stella, and the woman looks resolute.

"Okay," Eva says, but she doesn't understand. Not at all. She'd leave if she could, and if she had the money and no apparent disabilities, she'd be sunning on a foreign beach inside of a week. But some women accept, even thrive on, giving themselves up in pieces. They love to hear the State tell them this is holy, this is true service, this is a blessing, that the role of women is to give life in every way possible: with their wombs, their organs, their blood. While it is a blessing to save lives, Eva resents the women who rely on these bits of lip service for their happiness while their sisters die. She despises the ones who insist on that vision of happiness for other women.

Stella doesn't seem the type to buy into the gaslighting, but Eva has been surprised by the women in her own family. She never imagined her sisters and cousins would fall for it, but many have. Hard.

The green light is gone now, and a new light flashes where the green had been. It's their relay, and her work is nearly done.

~oOo~

When the small boat zips six women and Stella's fee away to their next relay, Eva moves to turn on the engine, but Stella stills her with a hand on her arm. "What have you given up?" she asks.

It's an oddly personal question. Etiquette says it's immodest to brag about how many lives you've saved, but Eva suspects the secrecy keeps the horrors private, and the State needs that. Unshared horrors mean no collective outrage, and that means the laws remain.

She has always shared this information with anyone receptive, though, etiquette be damned.

"Three failed natural pregnancies, five failed assisted pregnancies, six skin deliveries from my stomach and back, tendons in my elbow, three marrow donations, and a kidney."

Stella stiffens. "Did... Did you volunteer for the extra?"

Eva shakes her head.

Stella knows what this means, too. That Eva had additional obligation because her failed pregnancies were blamed on her—typically, unhealthy life choices or failed conversion therapy. This, Eva keeps to herself. She doesn't like dwelling on her ex-husband, who also endured conversion therapy, and their clumsy sex. She doesn't want to talk about the eclampsia that caused her stroke. Nor the day she was fired from her job as an accountant because the left side of her body no longer responded as it should. She doesn't want to remember Bill filing for divorce because even though she doesn't blame him, she is a mountain of rage. She nurtures that rage. It propels her from bed in the mornings, and it sharpens her mind. It is the one thing the State can't demand she give up, so she holds it close.

Eva reaches for the boat's ignition, but Stella stills her with a soft hand on hers. "Not yet, please?" The look she gives Eva is something large, barely contained. Eva wants to say it's joy or, yes, euphoria, but that seems so impossible when she's looking toward a shore that will take her piece by piece until she has nothing left to give.

With a nod, Eva sits back, swivels to face Stella, and waits. She clasps her withered left hand.

"Where would you go, if you could leave?" Stella asks.

"I'm not leaving."

Stella holds up an elegant, long-fingered hand and shakes her head. "But if you were."

Eva shrugs. "If I could go anywhere? Maybe Europe. But my job is here, and I don't have the money."

"There are jobs in Europe, so if you had the money?"

Eva laughs, and it's ugly. "Do they hire women like me in Europe?" She holds up her left hand by the wrist so the fingers curl like a claw.

Stella leans her backside against the rail behind her and studies Eva. "They'll ask for more deliveries. What do you have, one left?"

Eva's hand twitches, and she has to stop herself from grabbing the notice in her pocket. She nods. "I got my last notice."

Stella gasps. "But you're holding yourself like you're still recovering. From, what? Skin? Or kidney?"

"Kidney." Eva purses her lips.

"When is the next?"

"Three weeks."

Stella shakes her head. "That can't be safe. You don't look well enough for another delivery so soon."

"Does it matter?" Eva looks pointedly at her left hand and leg, and when she smiles, she knows it looks more like a smirk because the muscles in her face have sagged, too. "We die all the time on the table. It's a convenient time to make our final delivery."

Stella looks angry now, like she wants to smash china and kick over expensive vases. "May I ask what they'll deliver?"

Eva studies Stella. What does she care? It's too late to change her mind about aborting her escape plans. The last relay is long gone. "Uterus."

Stella's face pales and looks drawn, like she's mummifying right here on the boat. "They can do that?"

"Apparently. Maybe it's experimental. I don't know. Maybe it's a devious plan to make this my final delivery," Eva says with a laugh and then takes a deep breath because it's not funny at all. "Let's get back."

"No!" Stella yells and jumps up straight. Then she waves her hands in apology. "Not yet. I-I need to ask a favor." The way she says the last word, Eva could believe she's never used it before. She imagines someone of Stella's stature spends her life demanding, even when she's in the middle of a delivery.

"We need to get going," Eva says firmly.

"I know, but... How old you think I am?" she asks.

Eva has had enough. "Stella, if we're caught out here—"

"How old?" she demands, and Eva realizes she isn't, in this moment, a vain woman asking if she's still beautiful.

Eva studies her and realizes she's a little older than she'd first pegged her: there are only hints of crows' feet and laugh lines, but the skin on her hands has a distinct wrinkling. "Thirty-five?" she says, though the woman could pass for twenty-seven or twenty-eight.

Stella half-smiles. "Forty-four. Would it surprise you to hear I just got my first notice two weeks ago?"

Eva is a little surprised. She figured wealthy women weren't required to deliver as often as others, but a forty-four-year-old woman just getting her first notice? "Do you have children?" she asks. This is the only explanation—but she'd have to have given birth half a dozen times or more to make this possible.

Stella shakes her head. "Two failed pregnancies."

"Assisted, then?" Eva asks. It's highly personal, but Stella seems eager to share.

Stella shakes her head again.

"How?" Eva's question is breathy, and she realizes she wants to cry. How is any woman so exempted from the invasion of society into her body this way?

Stella holds up the front of her blouse to show off a modest scar by her belly button. Then she lifts her head and shows off her smooth neck. When she looks at Eva again, Eva knows she can see her confusion.

"You're unhealthy?" Eva asks.

"Not at all. Peak of health except for a uterus that doesn't hold onto babies. The scar on my stomach is what little you can see of a very successful skin graft. I had an ugly birthmark, and it was too big just to remove. My neck looks like an eighteen-year-old's neck because it is." Stella waits and watches for Eva to understand.

It's an unnecessary pause. Stella took deliveries that weren't life-sustaining. She took deliveries meant for burn and accident victims and—much, much worse—injured soldiers who could die of infection without the grafts. The rage in Eva burns hotter, and she feels as if she's growing in her chair, ready to tower over Stella.

Eva chokes back her anger, thinking of her best friend in college, who died on the table during a liver lobe delivery, and of her parents, who had to pay the bill for her death. She thinks of her sisters, who are missing giant patches of skin on their backs, buttocks, and legs. She thinks of her mother, who endured so many assisted pregnancies, she spent most of her fertile years in a Women's Hospital before the law finally allowed other deliveries besides babies. Countless women out there who give and give until they have nothing left, and then their dying bodies are harvested for everything else.

"We all do this," Stella says. "Anyone who's got enough money. We take your deliveries because we can afford them. And people who need them but can't afford to receive them... They still die." She grabs Eva's left arm and shakes it hard enough to pull her hand loose from her own grasp. "They still die."

She wants to yell, to throw Stella off the boat, but she holds herself still and tries not to let tears overwhelm her.

"He wants me to leave because now they want my kidney. You've got money? Can you buy your way off?"

"What do you want from me?"

Stella drops down in front of her, on her knees, and pulls a small bundle of money from her bag.

"This is what he gave me to escape. He says no wife of his is going to be cut up like a side of beef." She looks Eva in the eye. "I might not be property of the State if I lived in another country, but I'd still be property." Stella shoves the money at Eva. "I want you to take this. Find a new home. Go somewhere your body belongs to you."

"You already paid me," Eva says, but her lips feel numb.

"I don't need this." Stella puts the money in Eva's lap and pulls the rings from her fingers, placing them in a cup holder next to the captain's chair. "I'm going somewhere they can never touch me." She stands and walks to the bench where she had sat for their trip out here. She unlatches the small door next to it, pulls off her shoes and throws them into the water, and jumps in after them.

Eva struggles to her feet and walks as fast as her shuffling left foot will allow. “Stella!” she hisses. “What the hell?”

Stella is only a few yards from the boat, treading water. She spins to look at Eva, and her smile is unrestrained. “I’m pulling a Kate Chopin,” she says. “Go.”

“I can’t leave you out here.” Eva looks around for the flotation device usually stowed in the front of the boat, but she doesn’t see it.

“Go,” Stella says, and her voice is so free, Eva feels a pang. “Go now. Don’t even go home, just turn around and run. Go to Cuba! You’ll love it.”

Eva shakes her head. “There are other ways. Drowning is an awful way to go.”

Stella laughs. “Or maybe sharks!”

“You can’t put this on me!”

The woman’s laughter fades, and she sighs. “I’m sorry, but it’s not on you. If you try to come for me, I will dive. I will dive as deep as I can. I will stay there. I will open my mouth and take a breath, and you’ll never find me. They’ll never find me. And if they do, the water will have taken everything they could harvest. You should go somewhere you’re allowed to decide who touches you and how. Away from people like me.”

"I always get the women to their destinations safely," Eva says, and it sounds as lame as it feels to say the words. She brushes at tears on her cheek.

"You did," Stella says.

"We're saving lives?" The parroted lie shocks her.

"I'm sure you've saved a lot of women. Maybe it's time to save yourself." Stella kicks away from the boat. "I want to see the sun rise over the Gulf, and then I want to see what it looks like beneath the surface. I've taken so much from other women, but would you give me this? Consider it your final delivery to someone who doesn't deserve a damned thing from you." And then she slips beneath the water, surfacing several seconds later far from the boat before disappearing into a swell.

It's still hours until dawn, but Eva needs to leave as soon as possible. She pulls herself back to the captain's chair and sits, staring at the water. On the horizon, a large ship trudges along, casting a searchlight over the water, as if someone already knows Stella has gone overboard. Eva watches the ship to gauge its direction so she can avoid it, but its light mesmerizes her, like it's an invitation, a path to follow home. The way it bounces against the water so far away creates sharp angles from the reflected slivers of moonlight, a separate temptation.

Somewhere in the distance, a woman sings.

Eva starts the engine.

The End

No Tanks

Jane Yolen

Here comes the tanks
(no thanks!)
the bombs.

Here come the throbs
and mobs
of moms.

Here come the sirens.
There's the clown,
the one we thought we voted down.

Here come the Russians
and their hacks.
CIA not have our backs?

Here comes disasters
down like rain,
America won't come again.

We had our chance.
It's just—we blew it.
Now we have to muddle through it.

Let's secede,
start once again.
You be a Jefferson, I'll be a Paine.

Treasures

Rebecca McFarland Kyle

"Who of you can write your name?"

My fingers twitched to form the letters my mother taught me so many years ago. I was the only person who remembered my name and I dared not speak it. I froze, spellbound by the longhaired man clad in rags screaming at the crowd.

"Who of you can do your sums? Do you even know if you're being paid the right amount?"

Memories of my dad came back unbidden. *One plus one equals two…Two plus two equals four…*

The crowd shifted and I stood right in front of him.

His wild eyes focused on mine. "You remember!"

I backed up, shook my head in denial, heard a male voice behind me swearing when I stepped on his foot.

"Rebel!" shouted a woman from the crowd.

Something struck the man. Crimson bloomed from a cut on his forehead, unnaturally bright against the fog and tall gray buildings.

He raised his voice louder than the oncoming train. "We have a right to know!"

As police officers surrounded him, the man broke free.

"We were born with minds! This country is wasting them! What is the capital of Alaska?"

Light blinded me. My stomach recoiled at the odor of burnt meat. My legs shook as I ran to board the train, shoving others aside. I grabbed the first seat I could find and stared through the window, my heart pounding.

Juneau. I dared not repeat the word aloud.

Outside my window, people stepped carefully around the place where the scraggly man had stood seconds ago. It wasn't hot. Laser pistols were quite efficient.

No one wanted to be associated with that kind of activity.

~oOo~

"You okay, Guard Thirty-seven?" inquired the mechanical voice of the prison gate bioscan. "Heart rate and blood pressure are elevated."

"Yes." I managed to find enough saliva to answer. "Encounter with a rebel at the square."

"Future prisoner?"

Our facility housed a special unit of rebels: teachers and scientists who refused to give up their professions when the government made their practice illegal.

My voice rasped. "Liquidation."

The bars slid open, admitting me to work.

My mother was a scientist, my father a teacher. Now, I survived because I guarded scientists and teachers.

As I passed his food tray through the slot in the bars, Dr. Espy spoke softly. “I wonder if you could help me.”

My eyes roved to the herbs drying in his cell. Rumor had it the man knew stuff that could cure cancer, but the pharmaceutical companies didn’t want that. I didn't know if that was true. But after All-American Corrective Inc. eliminated the prison infirmary last year, he offered me some cough drops and a poultice for my chest.

The prisoners offered some tempting rewards over the decades, but I’d never accepted any until his cough medicine. Now, there was no turning back. And, sooner or later, I’d get caught. The truth was I couldn’t look in Brian Espy’s soft blue eyes without wanting to care for him. I hadn’t experienced dangerous feelings like that since I was a teenager.

“Help you how?” I murmured.

“Need to get a paper outside,” Dr. Espy replied. “Just take it to Chowman's.”

Paper shouldn’t be detected in the scans. I ate at Chowman's all the time. I'd mentioned their chicken soup to Dr. Espy back when I had the cold.

While nodding, I rasped loud enough for my backup to hear. “Hurry up and eat your lunch. I’ll be back for your tray.”

When I returned, my hands were ice cold.

“I’m here for your tray.”

My eyes met Espy's. As he slid the tray to me, he quickly slipped something wound tight and straw-thin up my sleeve. I did my best to keep my face straight.

On my break, I went to the head. In the confines of the stall with the broken vidcam, I pulled out the tube. However he'd managed to wrap the papers up, it was bendable enough for me to stick inside my boot.

You know when you do something every day, it pretty much becomes reflex? When I tried to walk out like I usually did, I quickly realized nothing was more suspicious looking than a guard who appeared to be over-thinking everything. Sweat trickled down my back. I shook in my boots. As I approached the bioscan, I rubbed my forehead and said "Headache" and the men on the gate let me through with no trouble.

I caught the crowded train into town with the rest of my shift. Good thing it was typical for me to go my own way. I couldn't have grabbed a drink with my co-workers without screwing up.

Very few non-chain restaurants operated. Chow's must have paid off the police. The food was good, though most of us had the sense not to ask where it came from in a neighborhood that had fewer rats and stray cats than most. The meat was stringy, but they had fresh vegetables from a patch outside the building, and the food tasted better than the plastic goo we got from the franchise places.

Chowman, the proprietor, surprised me. "Wondering if I could get your digits."

He had my credit information. Prepaying was the only way to make sure you got food before it ran out.

He's the contact.

"Sure." I hoped my voice sounded normal as I bent and pulled the tightly-rolled piece of paper out of my boot, and handed it over. While there were people in the line behind me, I knew all of them from the neighborhood, and suspected most would hand over their information in a similar manner. While the odds were good no one with camera-enhanced vision would come into this joint, you took care no one could steal your identity. If I lost access to my funds, I'd be sunk. Nobody wanted an old lady's body for sex, or for organs, and I didn't have much of anything else to sell after paying my medical bills.

"You're still taken care of for the month." I tried not to stare at him. My hand shook as I put it back to my side. What exactly had I handed over to the Chowman? This was more than repayment for the errand, and what would I owe him now? I collected my meal and hastened up the thirteen flights of stairs to my bedroom.

My room was once part of a two-bedroom apartment. I made it inside, pulled off my boots. and sat down on my bed, shaking hard. I took several deep breaths before I opened the paper container.

My eyes widened. Inside was three times the amount of food I'd paid for. Despite myself the smell drew me in. I used my spork to spear a bit of meat, and tasted something tender and moist. Even in the light from the street, I could see the colors: Green, orange, and yellow vegetables were in the portion, where I'd normally be lucky to find a dozen bites of meat in the sort of brownish mush we fed the inmates. Unlike the meat, the vegetables were crisp, and chewy, like I remembered from long ago. I stopped myself from shoveling in the food and reveled in the taste and texture.

This was food I remembered from childhood. Carrots, onions, potatoes, celery. I said the words to myself like a lullaby.

It was worth the price, whatever that was going to be.

~oOo~

Next day, I got to take my crew out to the yard. That was generally the job of Guard Eleven, because it was dangerous. He'd called in sick, though he had a family and couldn't afford to be off. We didn't have sick pay anymore. But I learned early on it was wise not to ask questions.

It was one of the rare days when the sun broke through the brown haze obscuring the city. The academics spread out in the paved area, turning their pallid faces to the light with expressions of delight and longing.

I kept moving, scanning the yard for trouble. My guys wouldn't cause problems, but they didn't get exclusive playtime; more hardened inmates from other blocks were out there too.

If I hadn't been looking right at them, I would have missed the flash of orange in the boulder-sized lifer's hand, as he crossed in front of Dr. Singh.

I raced forward at top speed, bellowing for the man to stop.

Everything slowed as the handmade knife, carved from a food tray, arced, striking Singh in the throat. Bright crimson stained both men's uniforms. My breath caught until Dr. Espy called out that he was fine.

Guards came from everywhere with tranquillizer pistols to sedate the lifer. Before anyone could reach him, he did himself as handily as he'd done Singh.

I hustled my guys back to their cells. Most were in shock. Some wept openly for the loss of a friend and colleague.

I couldn't figure out why anyone would want to kill one of them. They didn't cause any trouble and, truthfully, our facility was a lot better off than most for having them incarcerated here. Least we had physicians when someone got sick, instead of just carting them off feet first.

The looks on both the warden's, and my higher-level supervisor's, faces were dire. Killings were not good: they necessitated a lot of paperwork and cost the corporation lost revenue, particularly when it came to "dangerous" prisoners such as the scientists and teachers.

"Guard Thirty-Seven," Warden Two said, his expression angry. "I want you to keep a close eye on your unit and report any threats directly to me."

"The lifer's correspondence revealed he was ordered to hit Dr. Singh. Guard 11 may have been paid off as well, but we don't have the authority or the funds to look into the case," Supervisor Eight continued. "And it doesn't matter, since the perp is dead, anyway."

~oOo~

"What are you sending out?" I whispered to Dr. Espy, when he slipped me another wrapped-up piece of paper.

He paused, looking hard into my face.

Finally, he said, "Scientific findings from experiments we conduct here. We're also rewriting the textbooks burned when the teaching ban was enacted. People are still teaching their children at home in the evenings after everyone returns from work."

I remembered my Dad raising his fingers as he spoke. *One plus one equals two...Two plus two equals four...*

After that, I took whatever small items Dr. Espy had without question. Some days, I had several data capsules secreted on my person as I left the facility.

My fellow guards never looked twice at me. I was old. I'd been here for decades and never once caused a minute's worth of trouble.

~oOo~

"What happened to your crew?" I asked.

The cooks had sent me with my usual cart of meals, to discover half of the inmates cells were vacant.

"They're in isolation," Dr. Espy responded.

"What could they have possibly done?" I'd seen all manner of misbehavior in my time, but never from this crew.

"They're working on an experiment for the government."

I swallowed, and didn't ask anything else. His words were quite specific. Most of their unpaid work was for corporate entities, creating products that made millions for the shareholders. What the government might want—

I couldn't let my train of thought go further.

"If any of you want an extra meal," I offered. Such as it was, I hated to see the brown glop go to waste. If they didn't eat it, I'd dump it out for the birds. Sooner or later, one of the inmates would catch one in the yard. If we were fortunate, the inmate wouldn't make a meal of it raw in front of us.

The absent scientists stayed absent, but the extra food continued. Don't ask me why. I'd stopped asking questions, and pointing out inefficiencies, long ago.

When I was delivering mail almost a month later, Dr. Espy said, "Come here."

I approached with more eagerness than was wise.

"When you put your arm through the meal slot, keep silent."

I had to suppress a gasp as something sharp sank deep in the muscle of my upper arm.

"The vaccine will make you ill," he said. "But you won't feel as bad as others."

I walked away, not knowing how to answer. Back when I was a child, my scientist mother led the fight to convince people vaccines were not bad. But still, the epidemics came as more and more people refused to get preventative care for fear it would do them harm.

~oOo~

The outburst started quietly. The winter was cold and everyone coughed a little. Then you noticed some people didn't stop.

During the middle of the worst storm I could remember, the warden's voice came over the loudspeakers.

"Attention, employees and inmates. We're locking down the prison. Those of you on staff who are healthy will remain here twenty-four/seven to tend the population."

My backup and I looked at one another. What did he mean, healthy? Lockdowns were for riots.

"Those who do not pass the test may return home on leave until the epidemic is clear."

I stared at Dr. Espy, and saw the depth of the horror in his eyes.

I reported to the former infirmary, had a blood sample drawn, and I waited for hours. I had time.

I almost missed my number when it was called.

"You passed," said the pox-scarred prisoner who served as our lone med tech. "Get back to work."

Dr. Espy wasn't surprised when I returned to work after the test results. I didn't ask him what he'd given me, but I was certain it was beyond my pay grade.

We had been told that vaccinations were bad, but our long-lived CEOs were doing something to stay above the colds and flus that routinely sickened the rest of us.

By spring, one third of our country's population died from the pandemic.

~oOo~

"You're free to return to your homes," the Warden announced to our assembled group. The prison staff had been living in cells for three months, eating the same food as the prisoners and sharing their indoor and outdoor facilities.

Only one of us got shanked. Neither he, nor his attacker, survived.

We packed up what little we'd accumulated via the prison system's meager stores, and said goodbye to our confinement. We'd accrued our wages for that time and since we had little to spend it on, most of us were well off, financially.

I wasn't sure if I wanted to leave. Considering what news made it into the prison, I didn't expect to see the world I had left.

~oOo~

I wasn't wrong. For the first time, I got a seat instead of hanging by a strap. I didn't have to struggle through crowds getting off the train. Half the shops were boarded over. More than the usual amount of debris blew in the early spring wind, providing an odd accompaniment to the graffiti which had appeared on the walls of the city.

My stomach clenched as I approached the Chowman's and saw the place was still open.

"Chowman!" I called out the man's nickname when I entered, then stopped in my tracks seeing a young man instead of my old friend beside the cookpots and cashbox.

He nodded at me, and I approached.

"Is the Chowman here?"

"My father died."

Words bottled up somewhere behind my tongue. The young man processed my order. My cup was lighter than it had been, but I said nothing. Fewer containers of spices and other goods lined the sparse shelves behind him. Like always, we would do with less.

I headed for my apartment. Usually, I'd see people outside when the weather started to warm up. No one took in the evening air except people walking purposefully.

I climbed the thirteen flights, and used my key to the first door of my home. When I unlocked the second door, I dodged to the right when I heard someone coming out.

I put my foot out just in time to trip the man. He fell, landing hard on the bat he held in his hand.

My bat!

"That's my apartment!" I yelled as the other doors opened, revealing the faces of angry tenants.

"No, mine," he said. "Paid rent fair and square for the past two months. Came with the contents."

"He's right," a young bearded man I barely knew spoke up. "If you don't occupy your apartment for thirty days, the landlord can rent it out."

"I couldn't occupy my apartment," I snapped. "I was in lockdown at the prison where I worked."

"Not our problem," said another tenant, a middle-aged woman with two younger girls clinging to her nightgown. "We all need our sleep. Please go. You can settle it with the landlord."

Having no place else to go, I went back to prison.

~oOo~

I wasn't surprised to see the cells we'd inhabited during lockdown nearly full. Only the folks who shared an apartment with family had a place to return to.

"Welcome back," one of my fellow employees called as I trudged in. "Prison's making us an offer. We can have the cell and food for working extra hours."

~oOo~

A few days later, I got called into the warden's office. Warden and I were on respectful terms, but it's a gut-tightening experience all the same. The guards older than me likened it to getting called into the principal's office. You either did something wrong, they said, or you're fired.

I braced myself for the worst when I saw the camera and video screen in Warden's office were covered.

"There's going to be another assassination attempt on your charges," Warden Two said. "Today at thirteen-hundred."

Recalling Dr. Singh who bled out before I could help, I opened my mouth, and couldn't get words out.

"A squad's coming in," Warden continued. "They want all the scientists dead."

Cold settled in my bones. Someone had gotten wind of what they were doing. They had to know the guards were complicit, and there were only a handful of us who tended that ward on a regular basis.

Expression grim, Warden Two slid a laser pistol across the desk.

I scooped it up, my heart pounding. The things were illegal, save for the military, and prison guards weren't military. If I went through the exit scanners with one, I'd be in here with the general population.

"An escape route will be open for ten minutes after the attack, so the death squad can depart," Warden said. "Kill them all, and get your people out. A bus will be waiting out front for you. Take them to the riverfront. A boat will be waiting. The scientists will know the answers to the questions that'll get them onboard."

I nodded and left his office. I did my best to keep my steps even. The last thing I wanted to do was give anyone the impression I was fleeing.

~oOo~

I would have known something was up the minute the four men came through the airlock into the scientists' cellblock. Each of the four was clad like a typical guard, in muted brown uniform with comm unit on the chest. But they were too clean-cut and too tailored for a guard's salary, and they were too single-minded.

I braced myself, then opened fire before they could reach for their belts. They melted in a mass of goo right in front of the cells. My breath caught and I swallowed back bile. It was either them or us.

I gestured for quiet and opened the entire cellblock up from the control panel. "Come with me, or we're all dead."

Nobody asked questions. They picked up their computers, and followed.

Warden was right. The way had been made clear for us. A prison bus with the lock code already plugged into the ignition stood running and waiting by the gates.

"Anyone know how to—"I stared at the console. I'd never driven a motor vehicle. I couldn't afford one, and the prison didn't train me in transport.

Dr. Espy hopped in the driver's seat, and the rest of them quickly boarded, and belted themselves in. He hit a key code on the console which got us moving.

As we passed through the gates, sirens rose.

"Get to the riverfront," I yelled at Dr. Espy. "And step on it!"

Street level was just potholes held together by concrete and asphalt. The wealthier folk's vehicles never touched the ground, except to take off and land. The government didn't bother spending money on street repairs for the common person anymore.

I thought my teeth would fall out before we reached the riverfront.

One lone boat awaited us. Dr. Espy pulled us alongside.

A man wearing a captain's hat and a faded gray uniform appeared on deck.

He called, "What is the heaviest naturally-occurring element found on the periodic table?" He appeared to be reading from a card in his hand. I blinked at the sight. Everyone had devices which spoke to us and told us what we needed to know.

"Uranium," Dr. Espy yelled back.

The captain asked several more questions which the scientists readily answered. Then his subordinates let out a gangplank so we could board. Several of the sailors came down. As soon as we were all off the bus, they pushed it into the river.

"Why?" I stared at the bus disappearing into the dark waters. It was like watching food and shelter and all the other things the credits could buy going into the drink.

"Our movement turned off the street cams in the city," said the captain, "and destroyed the GPS unit which lets the government trace the bus. The longer it takes to find the bus, the longer it'll take to realize which direction we're headed. By the time they do, we will be out in international waters and they can't touch us."

~oOo~

The captain's voice came over the loudspeaker. "We made it."

"And we'll see our country makes it to freedom too, one day," Dr. Espy murmured to me.

We were alone at the bow.

Before I could respond, he turned to me with a surprisingly sober, almost anxious expression.

"Will you be my wife?"

"I was your jailer!"

"That wasn't your fault," he said. "And you were kind."

I realized I was the only guard among the prisoners on the ship. They'd told Warden Two who they wanted to break them out.

"Yes, Dr. Espy," I murmured. "I will be your wife."

"Brian."

He wrapped his arms tightly around me. I remembered all those feelings of belonging I'd had as a child. This was even better. We didn't say anything else for a long time.

When Brian spoke again, he said, “They did the best for us, you know.”

“Who--what--who are you talking about?”

“You remember when the government blamed science for causing disease with vaccines and making the seas rise,” he said in his whisper of a voice. “If we scientists hadn't been imprisoned, we would have been killed in the riots. They were unintentionally wise, locking up the treasure of knowledge and skill.”

The End

Remembering the Bowling Green Massacre

Steve Weddle

Where were you?
When the streets ran with blood,
When the sky cracked with bombs,
When shrapnel filled the air,
Fireflies of terror
Streaking through the heavens, thick with smoke
From Plum Springs to Rockfield,
From the Greenwood Mall
To the Prince Hookah Lounge
On Old Morgantown Road?

Where were you?
When screams of the dying echoed
Through the streets of the third most-populous city
In the state after Louisville and Lexington?
When pioneers founded the town
In 1798, could they have foreseen the horror
Unfolding in the Fruit of the Loom parking lot,
The fields near the Carol Martin Gatton Academy
of Mathematics and Science in Kentucky?

Where were you?
When we needed your strength,
Your courage,

Were you there to face the slaughter,
The likes of which never seen, never seen,
Since the Hardesty family homestead fell?
Where were you when the roughly 60,000
Of Bowling Green cried out?

Across the 35.6 square miles of the city,
As tears ran like water from the fountain
In Fountain Square? Where were you? Oh, where?

Tweetstorm

Manny Frishberg

Edd Vick

3:14AM Saturday, Oct. 31, 2020—Sri Lanka military KIDNAP US Tourists! Blackwater Intl. company picnic in Vavuniya ATTACKED! Colombo claims of Tamil collusion FAKE NEWS!

-Donald J. Trump @realDonaldTrump

3:21AM Saturday, Oct. 31—Colombo govt. has 12 hrs to release all brave American captives, OR ELSE! (I wont say what—let em guess) #nothingoffthetable #remembergrenada

-Donald J. Trump @realDonaldTrump

12:20PM Sunday, Nov. 1—Pres Trump calls for a "brief" halt to ALL election activity until Sri Lanka threat is resolved. Says: "War is no time for partisan division"

-Pres. Donald J. Trump @POTUS

7:51AM Wednesday, Nov. 4. 2020—@newyorktimes WRONG! War with Sri Lanka no "distraction." Proud to continue leading the USA. KEEP AMERICA GREAT.

-Donald J. Trump @realDonaldTrump

7:55AM Wednesday, Nov. 4. 2020—Sri Lanka not even its real name. Looked on globe in Lincoln Bedroom, its Ceylon! No wonder the Tamil want to break away.

-Donald J. Trump @realDonaldTrump #ceylonteaparty

8:42AM Wednesday, Nov. 4. 2020—Is Buddhism a REAL religion? Worship a man, not God? Don't know! Just asking.

-Donald J. Trump @realDonaldTrump #ceylonteaparty #Godisgreat

12:18PM Wednesday, Nov. 11, 2020—Happy Veterans Day. To all who serve, a heartfelt thank you for keeping my military strong.

-Donald J. Trump @realDonaldTrump #veterans #military

2:27PM Wednesday, Nov. 11, 2020—America has never been defeated in battle. Godless Sri Lankans picked a fight with the wrong hombres.

-Donald J. Trump @realDonaldTrump #ceylonteaparty #somebadhombres

11:53PM Wednesday, Nov. 11, 2020—My heart goes out to the families of our brave heroes in the Battle of Vavuniya. We shall return!

-Donald J. Trump @realDonaldTrump #EelanforTamils #WeAreAllTigers

2:13AM Thursday, Nov. 12, 2020—USA not cowed by cowardly Sri Lankan Army terrorists. We will continue to support Tamil freedom fighters. (1/2)

-Donald J. Trump @realDonaldTrump #ceylonteaparty #saynototerror

2:15AM Thursday Nov. 12, 2020—Our brave heroes will fight on till victory. USA never loses! (2/2)

- Donald J. Trump @realDonaldTrump #It'sALongWayToTrincomalee #Nosurrender

3:31AM Thursday Nov. 12, 2020—Support the brave Tamil resistance to socialistic Sinhala envirocrats. Freedom for Eelam to develop its energy future!

-Donald J. Trump @realDonaldTrump #FreeTamilOil #ItsALongWayToTrincomalee

7:04AM Sunday Dec. 6, 2020—Congress wrong to threaten military spending. Let special appropriation through! RESIST!

-Donald J. Trump @realDonaldTrump #ItsALongWayToTrincomalee

4:23PM Thursday Dec. 24, 2020—Our boys are winning in Sri Lanka. Retook Tambuttegama for sixth time. Winning!

-Donald J. Trump @realDonaldTrump #FreeTamilOil #ceylonteaparty

4:24PM Thursday Dec. 24, 2020—Just told its Xmas now in Sri Lanka. Retaking Tambuttegama a victory for God! Happy birthday Jesus!

-Donald J. Trump @realDonaldTrump #Godisgreat #FreeTamilOil #ceylonteaparty

2:18AM Friday Dec. 25, 2020 –WH is a velvet prison. Couldn't even go shopping for Barron. Have to buy online and ship to him at a SECURE LOCATION.

-Donald J. Trump @realDonaldTrump #MerryChristmas #FreePOTUS

4:22AM Friday Dec. 25, 2020—Melania is a saint for visiting the troops this holiday season. What a sacrifice. She's safe—away from the front in Pasikuda!

-Donald J. Trump @realDonaldTrump #MerryChristmas #supportourtroops

1:41AM Tuesday Jan. 19, 2021—Canceling Reinauguration tomorrow. UNNECESSARY! I am President already. MUCH too busy.

-Donald J. Trump @realDonaldTrump #FreePOTUS

3:40AM Tuesday Jan. 19, 2021—NOT TRUE that Melania has "disappeared" from Mar-a-Lago with Barron. They are in a SECURE LOCATION for their own SAFETY. Rumors are. . . (1/2)

3:41AM Tuesday Jan. 19, 2021—FAKE NEWS! We are a VERY happy family. Just ask "Tiffany" (2/2)

-Donald J. Trump @realDonaldTrump #FreePOTUS #Godisgreat #rememberflorida #saynototerror

1:45PM Thursday, Jan. 21, 2021—This great nation is going to colonize Mars. NASA is ready. Taking applications now.

-Donald J. Trump @realDonaldTrump #nasa #goingtomars

12:11PM Friday Jan. 22, 2021—Join me in welcoming my 4TH Supreme Court nominee. Make process for Roy Moore faster than for Judge Arpaio! Stop RINO delays!

-Donald J. Trump @realDonaldTrump #NoRINO

4:49AM Monday Feb. 1, 2021—@FoxNews: New poll shows @POTUS approval highest ever—much biggerer than Obama's ever was.

-Donald J. Trump @realDonaldTrump #realerandtruer

12:23PM Monday, February 8, 2021—Cowardly Tamil Eelam generals declare cease-fire. RESIST!

-Donald J. Trump @realDonaldTrump #Tamilpapertigers

2:23AM Sunday, February 14, 2021—Happy Valentine's Day, Melania! Wish I could join you and

Barron in your SECURE LOCATION. Love the tie. Thank you, Barron!

-Donald J. Trump @realDonaldTrump

3:42AM Thursday, February 26, 2021—Putting Slovenian Prime Minister on notice: Melania and Barron "MUST" be returned! Declaring NATO Article 5 against Slovenian kidnappers

-Donald J. Trump @realDonaldTrump

4:13AM Thursday, February 26, 2021—Slovenia is NATO "member"? US is pulling out. Will not support terrorists in "Europe". USA #1.

-Donald J. Trump @realDonaldTrump #USANumberOne

9:54AM Sunday, March 7, 2021—Declaring victory in Sri Lanka. Troops needed in Hawaii.

-Donald J. Trump @realDonaldTrump #VICTORY #putdemsintheirplace

3:30AM Friday, March 12, 2021—Sad to hear Scottish golf course underwater. Will sue contractors, government, neighbors.

-Donald J. Trump @realDonaldTrump #visittrumpinternationalgolflinks

3:39AM Friday, March 12, 2021—I told them not to build that wind farm. Now it's under water. SO SAD!

-Donald J. Trump @realDonaldTrump #lastlaugh

4:22AM Friday, March 12, 2021—It was NOT a heart attack! Fake news, folks. That's how they get you. Cowards all, even Fox. Sad!

-Donald J. Trump @realDonaldTrump

12:12PM Tuesday, March 16, 2021—Melania no longer @FLOTUS. Barron returned to me by Seal Team Six. Best bunch of guys in the world!

-Donald J. Trump @realDonaldTrump #SealTeamSix

6:18AM Wednesday, March 17, 2021—No better place to celebrate St. Patrick's Day in the Big Apple than @TrumpInternational.

-Donald J. Trump @realDonaldTrump #besthotels

3:12AM Friday, March 19, 2021—Great leaders don't ask other to take risks they won't. I will lead the trip to Mars myself. Less strain on my heart so I can serve the ...1/3

3:13AM Friday, March 19, 2021—GREAT AMERICAN PEOPLE for even longer. I will continue to govern from Outer Space by satellite radio while Jared Kushner acts as my. . . 2/3

3:14AM Friday, March 19, 2021—. . . surrogate here at the White House. USA can trust him. And Ivanka will remain SAFE in an undisclosed SECURE LOCATION 3/3

-Donald J. Trump @realDonaldTrump #MakeAmericaMarsAgain

The End

The Tinker's Damn

Edward Ahern

Once, not so long ago, a tinker came to the town of Bitten Apple. Townspeople who glanced at him saw a man groomed and stately. Too few stared hard and saw the clutching little fingers and an expression at once sneering and boastful.

The Tinker, who called himself Augustus, set up shop and began buying and selling all manner of things. He was a sharp trader, and told those who argued with him that they'd best be careful or he'd damn them with lawsuits and embarrassment. Such curses were feared. The menfolk in the town listened to his blustering, and thought Augustus a clever man worthy of respect.

A few years later, Augustus had become a very rich man. (The townsfolk were poorer of course, but they were too afraid to say anything) He was elected the town leader, and appointed a sheriff and constables who were in his debt.

Augustus created the damning law, which let him condemn those who disagreed with him, and forbade anyone from outside the town to take up residence. Anyone who differed with him, or who was even different from him, was banned. The town was only for the townspeople, he said.

The menfolk began to think that they'd made a mistake in electing Augustus, but didn't say anything, worried that Augustus would damn them for dissent. Besides, men never like to admit they are wrong.

The womenfolk in the town had never much taken to Augustus because he insisted they clean, breed, and be docile. Which was peculiar, because Augustus was a man who liked and left a great many women.

One woman, Servillia, was Augustus' house cleaner. She knew Augustus' damns were just bullying, because he damned her several times a day, and yet there she still was. And she, more than any other, knew that it wasn't just things that Augustus clutched at.

Servillia shopped for food every day in the town market. The other women rarely spoke to her for fear that Servillia would report what they said to the town's pompous potentate. Servillia sensed their fear, and approached groups of women, saying that she of all people should be afraid of Augustus, but she knew him to be too vain and pompous to be truly evil. Well, maybe evil in a petty way, she would say.

The women listened, and began asking her advice on how to rid the town of the festering boil they had elected. Servillia had no answer, but began to think.

A week later, she called the women together in the town square. Augustus, she said, could insult and damn individuals, but he could not banish half of the town. If the women spoke together, and held together despite his threats, they could say whatever they liked. But they would have to ignore their menfolk, who were still ashamed of their choice.

The women agreed, and began drafting a chant they could call out in front of the town hall.

"Stick to groping yourself" was suggested, but turned down because it was unladylike.

"Banish yourself, bozo" was viewed more favorably, but rejected because it missed the mark.

They finally settled on "Augie, you disgust us" because it made a nice chant and fit on the placards.

The next day, signs ready, the women marched on town hall. The constables arrested the first six women, but since the town jail only had two cells they had to stop and let the others proceed.

The women circled the town hall, chanting. The men joined in, timidly at first, then more bravely when they saw other men in the group. The crowd overwhelmed the constables, entered town hall, and carried Augustus out of the building. They carried him all the way to the town line and pitched him onto unincorporated land.

Augustus cursed and threatened all the way out of town, but everyone finally realized that this tinker's damn was worthless.

The End

Wishcraft.com

Elizabeth Ann Scarborough

On the day he sent forth the decree abolishing Social Security for the parasitic elderly, authorizing another forty billion dollars' worth of tax cuts for the job creators, and allocating another 700 billion to the construction of the wall between the US and Mexico, the Great Man jetted home to the city for a well-earned rest. What he found was an annoying surprise.

A disgusting old woman huddled against the wall of the skyscraper bearing his great family name. He held his breath before he came even with her, pretty sure she would stink.

"Hey, fella, got any spare change?"

"Get a job," he growled, though he couldn't imagine anyone would want to hire her. He turned to where his guards had been, making a sweeping motion with his hands to indicate they should dispose of her, but they were nowhere in sight. They'd been there just a second ago. No matter. He'd bawl them out and fire them as soon as they returned.

"I had a job, but the company closed when the owners got sent back to Mexico," the old gal whined.

"Everybody's got a hard-luck story," he said. "Now get off my property or I'll send you to Guantanamo. You won't like it."

"Watch who you're bullying, troll-boy," she said. "All I want is a square meal. You think begging is easy?"

"Easier than working for a living."

"How would you know?"

"Because I have done great things with my life, wonderful things. And you are nothing but a pathetic loser who is probably going to leave a stain on my marble facade."

"Maybe I lost fair and square whereas you have "won" using lies and trickery."

"Industry standard business practice," he said. "If you'd done yourself up, maybe a nose job, a boob job, a little makeup, back when you were young, you might have even been able to date someone like me, even had a little arrangement, and not be on the streets now."

"Do you seriously want me to throw up on your nice clean building, big shot?"

"Someone get this old bat out of here!" he cried to his currently invisible security team.

"Oh, I'm leaving. But I will leave you with something to remember me by," she said, and vanished--poof!--just like that. He was surprised to see she did it with a certain amount of class and gold glitter.

But then he realized he had just imagined it, though he was not a particularly imaginative man unless it involved ways to add to his personal treasury by relocating someone else's assets.

Where glitter and grime had met on the side of the building, two of his security guys now stood, looking professionally concerned.

"Come on," the great man said, for he had no time to waste with useless poor people.

He was too preoccupied to notice when something solid escaped from his lips, but the security guard protecting his rear stomped on a huge hairy spider scampering toward the nearest drain.

The Great Man's family was gone that evening and the servants were off. The security team was stationed outside the door in case he needed them so there was no one to talk to, which was okay. He just wanted to unwind. So he wrapped himself in his white fluffy monogrammed-in-gold robe, and padded barefoot on the rare hardwoods and two inch pile handmade oriental rugs, grabbed a can of Coors beer which he had ordered wrapped in the label of a hoity-toity imported brand, and plopped down in his buttery leather recliner to watch TV. He took several deep breaths first. Seeing himself on TV was--such a joy. But sometimes they said very unfair things about him.

They slandered him again with their fake news, but what really got his goat was when his predecessor came onscreen. He was on an overseas tour, where he didn't have to be nice to anybody if he didn't want to because he was retired, dammit, as in finished, over with, no longer important. And yet, there they were, the so-called "world leaders," including the dumpy German woman (women for some reason got extra nasty if you gave them a little power) who had just been so, so unfair, picking apart everything the Great Man said and never admitting that he knew what was best. They were glad-handing his grinning predecessor, maybe complimenting him but who could tell with their thick foreign accents? You'd think people in such high positions would have bothered to learn to speak proper English. But old Pearly-mouth was grinning broadly, looking totally relaxed and happy. What was the matter with those people? That has-been couldn't do anything for them anymore!

That was when he noticed something about the former leader of the free world he had never noticed before. Every time the man spoke, a pearl or a real sparkling diamond dropped from his lips. A real diamond. God knew the big man had bought enough of them as silencing presents for the women in his life. The stupid twit on the television didn't seem aware of jewels that had begun to litter his lapels and lap. He just kept on talking. The big man wondered if anyone was sweeping those up and having them appraised. So far they looked like they might take care of half the national debt.

The gems worried him, even though he was pretty sure they were just a technical trick of some kind. "Holy crap, that guy is still trying to make me look bad," he said, choking on his own words as three small snakes, six toads, five centipedes and a turd-like slug spewed onto the immaculate deep pile carpet.

He started to go to the door to yell at one of the security men to come and clean up the mess, but then thought better of it and phoned instead, adding a bullfrog, two mice, and another slug to the mess already there. When the agent came in carrying a broom and dustpan and looking furious at being relegated to housekeeping duty, the big man nodded brusquely toward the critters and walked from the room into the study which was lined with important looking color coordinated leather-bound gold-embossed books he'd bought by the yard.

One was on the floor, pages up, flipping idly all by themselves until they came to the picture. There she was. The hippie hag from earlier in the afternoon sneered up at him. Except in the picture she had wings and a wand and looked like she wasn't afraid to use it. Another nasty woman. He glanced down without picking the book up. The page it was turned to was a new chapter called "Diamonds and Toads." There was a picture of two girls, one dressed like some kind of nun, barfing diamonds and pearls, and one well-dressed like she was going to a party, barfing toads and snakes.

He picked it up. He was no fool. He'd had a German nanny who read him fairy tales until his old man fired her. She'd claimed this kind of crap used to happen in the Black Forest all the time, back in the day. So. . .apparently, he was under supernatural attack. The old woman had been an agent of witchcraft, probably hired by his defeated female opponent or maybe his predecessor, old pearly-breath.

"I'll show her," he said, burping forth a copperhead and two tarantulas.

He wasn't the leader of the Reasonably-Priced World for nothing. His aides and appointees all felt that the venomous vermin dropping out of his mouth with every word might make a bad impression, but he didn't really care what those losers thought of him. Within a day he had his solution and Tweeted triumphantly to his fans:

"I have just created a new National Terrarium for the creepy crawlies everybody so unfairly dismisses. Also a bug house and I donated a shitload of free fertilizer to the Smithsonian Gardens. This will be the largest National Terrarium anywhere, and the biggest and most magnificent bug house Ever. Also, the head gardener at the Smithsonian says my donation is the most fabulous fertilizer she has ever seen." (She hadn't said anything. She hadn't been able to close her mouth after her jaw dropped. But he figured she would have said that if she could talk.) "So certain people should know better than to mess with me. Situation handled."

Wishfulthinking@wishcraft.com replied, "*We're just warming up.*"

"*Witch!*" he texted back.

"*Ogre!*" she countered.

"Loser," he rejoined, but of course she had no answer for that. He was very witty and a good debater and no old hag stood a chance.

Sure enough, the wildlife slowed down, although it had a tricky way of coming back if he tried to put the situation in terms that supported his position. It was a good thing too because the staunchly conservative historical commission was about to have him kicked out of the Great Residence for infesting the place. They insisted on calling exterminators.

Matters did not particularly improve after that, however. People kept treating him unfairly, taking offense at everything he said, misquoting him, spreading faux news about him, somehow bungling the orders he gave them so that nothing turned out the way he thought it should.

His tweets were constantly trolled by wishfulthinking@wishcraft.com, and he was sure that was the old witch who had bugged him in front of his building. He ordered that she be found and detained to figure out who she worked for.

Someone was telling his enemies his secrets. He grew increasingly paranoid. Nobody seemed to like him. His wife didn't like the atmosphere at his office, which reminded her of the police state she came from. His daughter's husband was in trouble with the law and she, whom he loved as much as he could love anyone, was angry with him and went on a prolonged ski trip to Switzerland.

He complained aloud a lot, cursing and throwing things sometimes to emphasize his points. Only the new butler seemed to really listen, and he nodded politely and swept up the pieces. He was a real English butler, a distinguished looking gent, not like the old Black guy who came from a long line of slaves. The great man had him replaced right away. The old dude seemed way too loyal to the predecessor--he with his diamonds and pearls.

Jeeves, on the other hand, was very understanding. "You are perfectly right to feel so misused, sir, when you are doing such a fine job for our country. You might wish to speak to your security people of your apprehensions with the strongest possible suggestion that they do something about the situation." He shuddered, but only slightly. He was a genteel guy. "Those centipedes and snakes, and the toads, definitely the toads, were quite real."

"I know they were. They tasted like crap, too."

He took Jeeves' advice and spoke to the current head of the security forces—the fifth man to hold that position since he'd taken office. The man looked suitably worried, then snapped his fingers and said, "I believe NASA had something under development that may do the trick, Your Greatness. However, it's going to take more funding to finish it up so it can do what you need it to."

"How much do you need? I'll sign the order right now."

His head was down as he signed so he didn't catch the thumbs up signal the security chief gave Jeeves or the classy, subdued wink Jeeves gave him in return.

The Great Man just knew he could solve anything once he knew what needed doing, and within a week, the tech reps from the outfit providing the goods were shown into his office by the discreet route he used for other people he didn't want busybodies to know about.

Only that morning he had been tweeting about how he laid down the law to the English Prime Minister. No more trade deals or even talking about the environment until the queen let him ride in her golden carriage, as was only right for a man as important as he was. "I don't know why people don't realize that I'm the most powerful man in the world and they have to treat me accordingly. It's only fair."

The team was composed of two young women, a blonde and a redhead, both tens. They came to fit him for his suit and further explained how it would work and showed him a sketch full of measurements and angles, along with what they claimed was a swatch of the fabric.

"Here it is, Your Greatness! This will be your custom-made stealth suit, once it is tailored and programmed for you personally. It will protect you from bullets, knives, fire, and freeze rays--oh, and radiation. And any enemy of our great nation will have no idea you're wearing it. That's how you'll know them, sir. Everyone else will see this beautifully constructed suit of incredible quality, suitable to the world leader you are. But our country's enemies will see absolutely nothing, as its specially formulated fibers and nano-programming make it invisible to the eyes of individuals with certain deviancies. It might even be difficult for you to see with the naked eye until it's been programmed to your specifications and you have been totally installed inside it."

"I. . .see," the great man said. The fact was, he didn't see at all. He saw nothing. The swatch looked like her thumb and forefinger pressed together, pinching only the air in between but he was sure he could feel the fabric. They had shown him all of the technical stuff so he knew it had substance and it had to be there. It must be, like the girl said, once it was fitted on him and he was wearing it. . .If the fabric was as smart was they said it was, it would definitely know that he, the Great Man, Leader of the Free World, could hardly be an enemy to his country. He certainly didn't want anyone else to get that idea.

His second fitting was squeezed into his schedule just a week before his trip to England.

This time an entire team came to measure him and take his vital signs, do all sorts of complicated stuff they said was part of the customization process so the suit would only respond to him. Another attractive blonde directed the team, and told him that no enemies could photograph the fabric or reverse engineer it to counter its protective properties.

"That sounds good, very good," the Great Man said. "Is it going to be bulky with all this stuff built into it?"

"Oh, no, sir, not at all. It's very lightweight and sheer and drapes beautifully. You will scarcely realize you have it on thanks to the. . ." She went into more technical mumbo-jumbo and he didn't really understand a thing she said.

"That's good," he said, stroking his jutting jaw with his small but mighty hand. "Did my predecessor have one?"

"No, sir. Its development has been perfected since he left office. So it was never offered to him."

"How fast do you think you can make it?" He was thinking of the Oriental factories he'd seen when he helped his daughter choose who would make her signature fashion line. They were very fast and very cheap. "I--um--was thinking they'd be excellent for our boys in combat."

"Now that we have perfected the process, the main thing would be tailoring them to each client, sir, but. . ."

"Good to know," he said. His business imagination was scampering ahead of her, dreaming of opportunities in the private sector. A lot of things that were made for the military to begin with got leaked pretty fast.

The Attorney General had advised him that he was not allowed to make money from investment opportunities he heard about through his position, but he knew everybody did and there were bound to be ways around these little problems.

Meanwhile, he would be the first to wear this new wonder suit. Maybe they'd make a comic book hero out of him? His boy would like that.

"Can you make the cloth gold-colored?" he asked. "I want to look amazing. Let's wow everyone."

"Er—sure, sir. It's an incredible innovation. Your garment can look any way you can wish."

"Really? That's great."

His security concerns forgotten, he looked forward to debuting the stealth suit when he rode in the Queen's golden carriage, which he was going to buy as soon as she agreed on a price.

"I hope you're right about how well this thing travels," he said.

"You'll look as fresh when you de-board as you did when you boarded."

"I don't intend to wear it on the plane! I'll want to have a shower and a shave before I change."

"Of course, sir. But for times when you're rushed, you needn't worry about the suit's appearance. It will look as good on arrival as it did on departure. Also, if you wish, we can plan an entire designer wardrobe for the ladies in your family as well."

"My daughter has her own collection, but do you think you could make a suit like this one for my youngest son? He's coming on this trip. He wants to see the horses and the fancy coach."

The agents exchanged concerned glances and the girl said, "Perhaps for future engagements, sir?"

"I know, I know. It's incredibly complex," he said, waving his hand dismissively. Nobody would be looking at the kid anyway. "You just do your thing and let me know when it's done."

He sent his next in command and the chief adviser to oversee the process and report to him on how the suit was coming along. He'd explained to them how the agents said it would be invisible to traitors or his enemies, which were the same thing as enemies of the country. They both had reassuringly glowing reports, as did his own security guys. The Great Man was accustomed to seeing what he wanted to see and didn't notice the nervous glances they exchanged.

Jeeves had accompanied him from the residence to serve as his valet. Two of the agents brought the suit with them on the plane with the Great man, his advisors, and his son, and just before the carriage was due to arrive, the butler helped him into the suit the agents held up--or said they did, because, although he could not believe himself to be a traitor, the Great Man still caught no more than a glimmer of what they swore was beautiful fabric. Jeeves stroked the lapels and patted the back and everyone said how beautifully it fit--it was the best suit any leader in the world ever had worn to anything--and it protected him, too!

The day was a hot one and he really could feel how comfortable and cool the new outfit was. The carriage arrived and his people lined up to watch him get in. Most of them watched with their eyes lowered.

He stepped inside. His leg looked bare to him as he put his foot on the step. The footman made a weird sound in his throat, like he was strangling.

The Great Man looked around for the kid and saw him just getting off the plane. "Son, hurry up or you're going to miss seeing this fancy ride! This is better than all the cars in our garage, isn't it? Look! Horses!"

The boy glanced at the horses, then back at his father. "Dad, don't look now, but you forgot your pants!"

The Great Man looked down at himself. He knew his boy was no enemy and no traitor. When he turned thirteen, maybe then he might be but not right now. Right now, as far as he and his son could see, he was about to take a ride in the queen's golden carriage wearing nothing but boxer shorts printed with a royal crown motif.

He yelled for Jeeves to get him a real suit. He looked for the agents and for the staffers who'd assured him how good he looked. They'd all disappeared as if someone had gone "Poof!" and vanished them.

He was never to see Jeeves again, nor the "agents" connected with the suit. The security forces denied any knowledge of them.

The golden carriage drove away leaving him standing there in his skivvies watching it roll down the runway, looking for all the world as if a glass slipper should tumble to the tarmac in its wake, but in fact, its passage was marked only by steaming piles of horseshit.

The afternoon edition of the British tabloids accused him of being rude to the queen after he had blackmailed her into breaking protocol to let him ride in the damn thing, then stood her up. (Not that she cared. Pressing business called her away to Balmoral Castle in Scotland at the last minute, along with all of her descendants. The Great Man would have been met by the deaf and doddering Duke of Droolingham.)

Now the Great Man really didn't know who to trust. Even his son looked at him like he'd lost it.

Among the tweets about the carriage thing, one particular one stood out. *"And the press thinks your administration lacks transparency! Guess you just showed them."* Wishfulthinking@wishcraft.com"

He tweeted back something rather crude, but his usual pumpkin complexion had deepened to that of an apple just before receiving its injection of poison. He added, "*Who are you and why are you persecuting me so unfairly? I should have you arrested for treason!*"

"You still don't understand? Next time it will be as plain as the nose on your face." Wishfulthinking@wishcraft.com"

Back home again at his hotel, when asked about the much-discussed golden carriage ride, he complained that the conveyance hadn't been cleaned properly after its last use and it looked like even the Queen couldn't get good help these days, ha ha. Sad.

He pivoted quickly, telling people that climate change was faux science designed by tree huggers to retard the growth of industry and extort more money from his defense budget.

His nose grew two inches. . .

Epilogue

The Great Man's regime ended abruptly when the mysterious wooden condition of his nose (which when uncurled could wrap three times around the official residence) spread to his entire body, resulting in his death from a combination of respiratory failure and a mutant strain of Dutch Elm Disease. No further recorded tweets from wishcraft@wishfulthinking.com were found on the phone at the time of his death.

The End

A Woman Walks Into a Bar

Jill Zeller

I was in the women's bar when I thought of it. A real solution. It had to work. It was masterful and wonderful, a *coup de grâce* of monumental effect. Perhaps my idea-machine was fueled by Veronique's vodka martinis rolling off her assembly line. Veronique, my favorite bartender and enabler. Veronique, who was working this particularly special evening.

Veronique called her place of employment the Pussy Cat Lounge, but the real name of it was Patty's Place. It was a deep, dark sliver of a bar, shoved between a Russian restaurant and what used to be the best book store in town, just off Dupont Circle. The PC Lounge was always jammed by 5pm, especially on Veronique's nights.

Women's voices echoed through the place. The music when Veronique was working was always trance dance, which seemed to electrify us, get us talking and moving and excited about life, if only for an hour or two. My friend Melissa hadn't shown yet—sometimes her husband didn't let her come. Sometimes she had to lie to be able to meet me.

I didn't have a husband any more. I had a boyfriend, Sam, but he lived in California. I wanted to go back to California, but my job here was too important right now, something I had to keep as long as I could. I "always had to make a point," Sam had said, not with disdain, but with fear. "One day you're going to either die or be incarcerated for life over that point," he would say, which is maybe why he stayed in California so he wouldn't have to be here to see it.

And maybe he was right. I had hit a wall today, and maybe Veronique could see it in my eyes, because she kept the drinks coming.

She was small and moved like a ballet dancer. Her white hair was spiked high on her head, and she dyed her lips the color of currants. Tats ran up and down her arms. I tried to imagine how she lived in this city without daily attacks by men with spit and sneers. And maybe these happened every day as she got off the subway on her way to work.

And part of me thought, so what? She chose to look like that. I took those attacks every day in the office. In the board meetings. In the hallways. Behind my back as I walked the hallways. I could feel the men jeering, even as they seemed to smile and even joke with me.

But their attacks were worse. Subtle, fake, yes—patronizing, to use a shop-worn word for a shop-worn habit.

And today I did hit a wall. I slapped the wall in my office, after, and badly bruised my palm. They let me have an office, where the rest of the women were relegated to cubes. They let me have the advisory role. They let me be where I was, brief-cased and suited in

2-and-a-half inch heels—I can't take the 3-inchers. Maybe it was my PhD in public health and the papers I'd published ten years ago. And this was a "soft" job. Perfect for your token woman. Finding money. Flirting with congressmen. Keeping the coffers of presidentially designated research labs filled with dough.

With a whiff of coconut, Melissa slipped in beside me. Veronique had already plunked her glass of bitters on the bar. How Veronique knew when someone was going to walk through the door was a mystery I couldn't solve, except to say that at bartending she was a natural. After a kiss and a hug, Melissa looked at me through narrowed eyes.

I hated when she looked at me like that. I hated that my emotions poured into my face.

"So," she said, "so?"

"We had the leadership huddle today."

"And?"

"No, I'm not fired," I said and took a sip. "But I had an item on the agenda. And of course, like the last six leadership huddles, somehow we ran out of time and my issue was postponed. That same agenda item—the use of communications checklists, cost-cutting AND job-saving—has been on the agenda for six weeks. Today I finally got the last five minutes and the chair called on me, and as soon as I began to speak, financial liaison's cell phone rang, and he took the call, and everyone began to check their phones and start sidebar conversations and I sat there, with my slides on the screen like a fucking idiot until the chair adjourned the meeting."

Melissa shook her head. She'd just had her hair done. I could smell the gel. "I don't know why you stay in that job."

I turned and looked at her. "I'll tell you why I stay in that job. Because it's the best fucking job a woman can get in the government, or in any corporation, today. It's because a woman has to be there. It's because we can't just slink into our segregated bar and be girls together and not care that the old boy bar up the street is where the real power lies."

Veronique hovered near us, half listening, even though the place was busy and the drink demand was high. Something in the air, I thought. Everyone is agitated tonight.

Melissa had given up her job. There were lay-offs, and her husband told her she had to stay home with the kids. A lot of DC men were saying that to their wives these days. And since no one was hiring women any more, or minorities, or LGBT—if they were obvious about it—the men could get away with it.

The men in the office talked about why I wasn't married. Divorce was harder than ever for a woman to get without ending up in a food line at the local church, but I had done it. The ex didn't contest it, since he had traded me in, so-to-speak, for a more compliant model. Prettier, too.

Melissa touched her blond waves. I refused to go blond, although my boss hinted I should. Melissa's fingernails were a garish pink. Sometimes I thought the only reason I kept up this friendship, amid lost respect for her, was because she liked to drink with me still.

The music seemed louder, pulsing in my ear. I only heard half of what Melissa had to say about her day with the kids. Veronique leaned on the shelf behind her, a row of fine whiskey bottles glinting behind her like a polished army. She stared at me and was talking to me, but I couldn't hear her. But something she said caught me, and I tuned out Melissa's buzzing and said,

"What?"

"We're closing."

"What?"

"WE'RE CLOSING."

It was as if the music stopped, and everyone shut up and stopped dancing and stood motionless. That's what it felt like, anyway.

Melissa heard her, too, and we both stared. And inside me a small black hole opened.

"The owner's closing," Veronique said. I swore there were tears in her eyes. "The landlord jacked the rent half way to the moon. They want us out of here."

The last women's bar in town. Closing down.

We all knew the President's son-in-law owned the building. At least, his corporation did.

That made up my mind. Then and there my fate was sealed. I didn't care what happened anymore. I would not go out without a shocking fucking fight.

"When?

"Tomorrow night is our last night."

"So soon?"

There was nothing to say after that. Wiping her eyes, Veronique turned to refill another drink. Melissa stared at the place where Veronique had stood. All the color had drained out of her face.

"What do I do now?" she whispered. "What the fuck am I going to do now?"

A caged bird. A thinking thing who was not allowed to think any more.

I walked home. I took off my heels and walked barefoot. It was ten blocks but the sidewalks and tarmac under my soles kept me focused. Melissa had offered me a ride, but I turned her down. Her husband didn't like me anyway. He didn't like to think of me in their (his) Lexus.

In my basement condo on Belmont, I sat on my patio with a glass of water. I hadn't drunk as much as usual tonight, and I wanted to be sober so I could plan.

The next morning I got ready. I showered and did up my hair with blow drier and gel. My make-up was perfect—not overly done, but subtle and enhancing. I dressed in clothing I didn't really like, and wouldn't miss if I couldn't get them back, but made sure things were ironed and well-fitting.

In the subway my heart did unpleasant flops. Coffee was my breakfast, dark and strong, and it pooled inside me. I thought of Melissa's stricken face as she realized the last bit of independence she clutched at was disappearing. I remembered the track of Veronique's tear as it slid past her redcurrant lips and quivered on her chin.

I composed a text to Veronique and sent it.

My hand left a print of sweat on my briefcase handle as I laid it on my desk. I was always the first in the office, and often the last to leave. No one saw me. I closed my door and put a stickie on it: DEADLINE. I pulled the window blind up. My first meeting was at 10 am and it was an All Hands meeting, the perfect opportunity. All the hands would be male except for me.

Other than the cold, I felt light and free as I walked to the meeting, my laptop under my arm. The laptop was cold too, but I pressed it against me. This was my breakout, my chance for freedom, ever so briefly, perhaps, and my scream out to all the women who had been put back into cages by the new masculine regime.

I ignored the stares from the cubes as I passed. And as usual, when I entered the meeting room, I was the one being ignored. At least, I thought, they didn't make me go for coffee.

And as usual, the only chair was the one against the wall. Every chair at the table was occupied by a man. So I sat down, opened my laptop. And waited.

The Team Leader cracked a few jokes, like he always did, and then, like he always did, turned to me to compliment me on my hair, suit colors, even weight-control. His face, when he saw me, did a thing of blinking eyes, reddening cheeks, and a beautiful drop of the jaw.

Chairs squeaked as the rest of the men turned around and saw me. Silence, except for some shocked gasps, and a cell phone buzzing. I felt their stares like a physical blow.

Don't flinch. Don't run from the room.

Is there something wrong, I wanted to ask them. Is it my hair, or my voice? Do I have milk on my upper lip? Maybe a bug on my shoulder? Instead, I met their gazes.

That minute, before the big finish, was the best one of my life, ever. For that minute, I had the power back. Control was mine. This is one power women wield that scares the shit out of men.

"What the hell do you think you're doing?" The Team Leader broke the spell, shattered the minute of mattering.

Standing up straight in my bare feet I looked at them one by one. When I stripped off all of my clothes for this meeting, I considered wearing only the 2-and-a-half inch heels, but I decided not. Because those heels meant something to men, and not to me.

I had nothing to say. My nakedness said it all, showed that I was a woman, even if the men didn't want to know what that meant. It was enough to have that minute of dominance.

Then I walked out, crossing the office feeling like I had a bullseye on my back and the arrow would take me down before I could get away. Voices from the meeting room followed me, nervous laughter, cursing. The women in the cubes watched me go into my office. They said nothing at all.

I figured I had time to slip on my t-shirt and shorts and sandals. I left everything behind except the photo of Sam, my cell phone and my wallet. I wanted nothing else from here.

Patty's Place didn't open until noon, usually, but somehow I thought today would be different. It looked closed, dark, empty as I crossed the street toward it and for a moment my heart thudded darkly. Maybe I was really all alone. Maybe women today are so beat down, they are unable to care.

But through the door I could hear the music. Softer, but the same perfect dance beat. The door was unlocked.

Veronique ran around the bar to hug me. Her naked skin was warm. Women catcalled and whistled, clapped their hands, and danced. The place was jammed. Not one had gone to work today. And there was not a single stitch of clothing anywhere except on the floor where they had been tossed.

I danced. I don't know for how long before the police came. Someone opened the door because the Pussy Cat Lounge had become an oven. Women were dancing naked on the sidewalk and the music volume was way up. All lanes of DuPont were blocked by stunned onlookers. Women carrying babies left their cars and joined us, peeling off shirts and shorts and kicking off shoes.

I looked for Melissa everywhere. She wasn't here. I hadn't texted her, only Veronique, telling her my plan to walk into a meeting naked.

A reminder, I typed, about WHO WE ARE.

Maybe Melissa didn't get the burst text from Veronique. Or maybe she did. Or maybe her husband took her cell phone away. Her not being here was the only dark thing today. She was the type of woman I had done this for, I told myself. Maybe she'll see us on YouTube and maybe she'll smile from her cage.

The End

America Year Zero

Gwyndyn T. Alexander

The taste of ashes
in my mouth today
is bitter.

Yesterday, I awoke
full of hope,
listening for the sound
of breaking glass
as that final ceiling shattered.

Instead, we all heard
the first echo
of marching boots,
of the kicking in
of doors,
of the rattling rumble
of tanks
last seen in Tiananmen Square.

The ashes I taste
are from waving amber grain
burning in a firestorm
of hate and lies and bigotry
unleashed.

The lady in the harbor
has doused her torch.

Yesterday
I was a woman full of hope.
Today I am an unperson

in Putin's America.

Today I am small
and frightened
and tired.

Today I am ashes
and sackcloth
and mourning robes.

Tomorrow, though,
I will look ahead
to a future
I will help build.

I will ignite
the fires of hope
and anger
and love.

I will spit out
these ashes.

I will change
my cerements
for feathers.

Tomorrow
the struggle begins.

Tomorrow
I will create
and build
and strive.

Tomorrow
I will
fly.

Future Perfect

V.E. Mitchell

Retriever's log, 27 July, Year 328 of the Imperium and the fifty-seventh year of Empress Ivanka VI's reign: Recovery team, consisting of myself (Lt. Meredith Holtz), and Sergeants Bristol Tam and Jered Perez, was translocated backward to Year 1 of the Imperium following the instrumentation of the missing survey team. Our primary assignment is to pull out the overdue observers before they harm the timeline. We are the Imperium's last hope to repair the previous errors. An incomplete listing of the personnel in this unauthorized research trip to the sensitive time near the beginning of our Empire includes: Observing Historian Second Class Desmond Morrisey and four of his graduate students, plus a standard three-person team from Ministry of Time Study. Unknown is how many undergraduates Historian Morrisey may have taken, as the weight setting for his translocator boost was extremely high, indicating he took extra students, a massive amount of equipment—or both.

As per standard procedure, we tuned our translocator on the local safe house, landing downtime without incident. Evidence of the previous team was present—scattered clothes, dirty dishes, one malfunctioning data recorder—but none of the team and little of their equipment were there. High static was present on all scanning bands, but we found weak signals emanating from a large concentration of people a kilometer from our location.

We ventured onto the street, following the signals from Lt. Tam's tracker. The safe house was in a poorly maintained section of town. The block across from it was fenced off with splintered wooden boards and chain-link fencing, beyond which was a two-story-deep excavation filled with equipment. The street was crowded with internal combustion vehicles, which filled the air with their odor. The sidewalk was cracked, broken, and heaved, making walking a balancing act in boots designed for the magnetic surfaces of our slidewalks. Beyond the construction area was a series of small stores, many of them dingy restaurants, but the sidewalks improved only marginally until we traveled several blocks in a zigzag pattern.

As we approached the large concentration of population, the buildings became taller and their paint newer, the sidewalks had fewer cracks and the surroundings less trash, and the crowd density became greater. Most headed the same way we did. As I was about to remark on this, Lt. Perez palmed his data recorder and held it forward for all of us to see. "Our people are in the middle of that." He gestured towards a massive horde of people. "Chances are Morrisey's in there, too."

"How many?" Tam asked.

"Maybe twenty-five thousand total, with about fifteen thousand in a clump and another ten thousand surrounding it. They're stacked in like canisters in a sleeper."

"Our job is to retrieve our people," I reminded them. "Local conditions aren't an excuse for failure." With that, I set off briskly.

~oOo~

Retriever's log, July 27, 2347 year 1 of the Imperium (cont., Lt. Marie Horowitz, recording: My team—Sgts. Beryl Torrance and Jorge Phillipi, plus myself—have infiltrated a Trump political rally (pre-Imperium) in search of a missing Time Survey Team. History professor Desmond Morrison, an unknown number of his graduate students, and a three-person team from our agency are overdue from an observing trip to this locale. We have traced them to an indoor arena, but have little chance of locating anyone in the jostling, turbulent mob. Between the overwhelming smells of perfume, aftershave, and sweat, the skull-splitting cacophony of the sound system, the glare of the spotlights on the stage, and the all-frequency blithering of the electronic devices in use by everybody in the room, my team is blinded both literally and mechanically. None of our options are attractive, but I order strong headache relief all around and we continue our search. Once the rally disperses, we may have even less luck recovering our quarry's trail.

The current speaker finishes and a woman takes the microphone, building up the crowd to hear the President speak. Suddenly, Beryl holds up her tracker. “Emperor! Emperor!” reads the screen. The device smells like overheated microsensors.

“The other party?” Jorge asks.

“Or the professor,” I say. “Where are they shouting from?”

Beryl works with the controls on her unit long enough that I feel my nerves tighten with the tension. It should take only a matter of seconds to pinpoint a noise source; this delay measures the extreme messiness of the scanning frequencies. I search the crowd again. Our missing people have to be close, and given what they’re shouting, the people around them must be reacting. We had to get them out of here before they started a riot!

“I got them!” For all that she speaks in a whisper, Beryl’s voice is triumphant. Immediately, Jorge and I huddle around her. “There! Over on the side, halfway to the front.”

I follow her gesture and locate the group. The people around them are starting to mill, and unless I miss my guess, the uniformed guards moving toward them are event security. Whatever the professor is doing, we must get him out of here before he destroys the time line by suggesting something to the man about to take the podium. Quickly, I sketch the plan of action and wave my team forward into the heaving sea of humanity. Soon we are lost from each other.

I descend my designated staircase two steps at a time, ducking under and around broad-chested, overfed and overdressed men, heavily made-up, over-scented women. It is an obstacle course with bad-tempered, moving obstacles determined to block my way. I finally reach the section from which our quarry is shouting when someone grabs me from behind.

#

Retriever's log, 27 July 2347 (continued, Lt. Mahalia Hazelwood, recording): The shove was hard, sending me stumbling. "Get moving. I don't know what alternative facts your group is trying to spread, but get down there with the security officers while we sort through this and get your type out of my world."

I twisted to see a tall, muscular blonde digging her fingers into my shoulders. When she saw me turning toward her, she jerked my shoulder, dislocating something, and shoved me again. I barely kept my wits from the pain and bit back the scream as I stumbled into the group of people collecting on the landing. More people staggered into the group, many followed by brown-uniformed security people.

"Let's go!" snapped a hard-faced blonde with loose, shoulder-length hair. Unlike the others, she wore high heels and an expensive dress that hit her thighs well above her knees. I didn't have to think too hard about who her boss was.

We were led out of the auditorium and into a green room—literally—off one of the middle exits. Once all the doors were blocked by security, the blonde stood up on a chair with the help of a pair of burly guards. "Hello." Her voice was as hard as her face. "I am Kellyanne Conway, Special Assistant to the President, Donald Trump. You people have been showing up for the past week telling us alternative facts about the political rally happening today. We cannot have that. This is the worst type of fake news. You have built your entire futures out of whole cloth and are trying to sell them as if they are the truth." I shifted on my feet slightly, trying to find a more comfortable position for my arm while getting a better look around the room. Neither was possible, it seemed, although I confirmed that there were about a hundred people in the room in addition to the security personnel who were relieving everyone of their equipment.

"If it were just one group of you, we might think you were delusional, like those Trekkie kids. But there are many different groups, each trying to sell your own separate alternative facts with your own alternate supporting details. Well, I'm here to tell you that we have captured many of you today, and in other holding places throughout the city, where we have caught you sneaking into the city throughout the week. And each group has had its own alternative facts.

"So, today, at this rally, the President is going to show you all the Truth." With that, she stepped down from the chair and pressed a button that simultaneously dimmed the lights and lowered a screen the size of the far wall.

The view of the podium and Donald Trump filled the screen. "We've had some interesting developments in the last couple of weeks, people. Some important developments that I can't tell you everything about yet, but there are some *BIG* things happening in this country." He paused portentously, and leaned forward on the podium like he was about to confide a momentous secret to the audience. "Things like you've never seen before. Things like *nobody* has ever seen before."

"To handle what's coming our way, our country has to be strong like never before. Our people have to be strong like never before. *You* have to be strong like never before." Wild cheering and applause interrupted him for several minutes. "Our leadership must be strong like never before. *I* must be strong like never before." More applause. I'd give him that; he knew how to play a crowd. "I must take steps to defeat this threat. I must be ready to beat this menace."

I recognized our equipment in use at the podium and bit back a panicked oath as Trump resumed speaking.

His voice dropped almost to a whisper before raising to conclude on a roar. "This peril requires a god to defeat it. I WILL BE THAT GOD FOR YOU."

The End

How to Recognize a Shapeshifting Lizardman (Or Woman) Who Has Been Appointed to a High-Ranking Government Cabinet Position

Kurt Newton

1. Do their eyes nictitate while answering questions during nomination proceedings? While common in sharks, it is more pronounced in shapeshifting lizard men (or women).

2. Does the newly-appointed cabinet member walk with an uncomfortable gait? This would indicate the potential presence of a hidden tail.

3. Does the shapeshifting lizardman (or woman) only publicly appear in the warmth of daylight? At night, the cooler temperatures induce a sluggishness that is easily mistaken for drunkenness or fatigue.

4. Does the suspected shapeshifting lizardman (or woman) frequent Petco or live bait shops, or do the small dogs they are fond of "adopting" often suffer accidents? Small fluffy dogs, never cats, are one of the favorite snacks of shapeshifting lizardmen (and women).

5. Does the shapeshifting lizardman (or woman) cabinet member forego the mention of dreams in their public speeches and press briefings? This is key because lizard brains do not dream, and without

dreams they cannot understand certain basic human concepts. Other missing words to look for would be "love," "compassion," and "hope."

6. Lastly, if you do recognize a shapeshifting lizardman (or woman) who has been appointed to a high-ranking government cabinet position, do not take matters into your own hands. You will be contacted. Because we're watching you.

The End

I Didn't Say That

Jane Yolen

I never said that!
I only tweeted.
It isn't my fault
people repeated...

Fake bits of news.
Others saw through it.
It isn't my fault.
I didn't do it.

Non-White in America

Debora Godfrey

"Bishaaro is fine. Come to school quickly! Bring your bag."

That was all Ayaan had on her phone, but the principal at her daughter's school wouldn't have texted her for anything short of a crisis, and Ayaan was a doctor. "Bring your bag" was never good.

Her office was only blocks from Ahmed Zewail Elementary School, so she grabbed her go-bag and ran, still in her white coat. It only took a moment before she heard a distant muttering, growing louder the closer she got.

A policeman in riot gear flagged her down.

"You don't want to go any farther, ma'am," he shouted, "particularly wearing that." He pointed at her hijab.

Her eyes widened as she finally caught a glimpse of the signs aloft in the crowd gathered in front of the school door, amongst them "Radical Islam is the new Nazi," "What would Jesus do? Have his throat slit by Mohammad," "Muslim School Brainwashes Kids," and "No ISIS in America!"

It was a quick decision. Removing the headscarf, she stuffed it in her bag. At that moment, it was more important to get into the school than to make a cultural statement.

"My daughter's in there, along with several hundred other kids." She shouted as loudly as she could over the roar of the crowd.

"It isn't safe." The Black officer looked nervously at the throng. It took her a moment before she realized that several of its members were wearing the same uniform he was. Other police officers dressed in riot gear were milling around the outskirts, but none were moving to protect the building full of children.

"I'm a doctor. Maybe I can help. Do you know if anyone inside is hurt?"

"Yes, ma'am, at least one person." He pressed the side of the mic attached to his vest and muttered into it.

She watched a thrown brick arc through the air, striking one of the few intact second story windows. As though it were a trigger, dozens of missiles followed it, everything from fist-sized rocks to hammers. Most bounced harmlessly off the walls, but a few of them smashed into glass.

The policeman beside her looked relieved as five other officers joined them, all of them big and most of them white. "Sergeant Mitchell here is in charge. You'll have a better chance in the crowd with all of us than you will with just me."

She understood. The previous week, a Black postman had been beaten to death in New Jersey when he'd tried to help save a Syrian family from a mob. It wasn't a good time to be non-white in America.

"I'm told you're a doctor?" Mitchell handed her a vest and a helmet. "We're running a group into the school, and we can use a medic if you'll come." He pointed at a female officer, almost anonymous in her helmet and faceplate. "Officer Gonzalez will take care of you."

Things must be really bad if they were letting a civilian woman go with them. She buckled on the helmet and vest. "Let's go."

She tucked in as close to Officer Gonzalez as she could, and the small group began to push its way through the mob. She grabbed onto her helmet, as though it would protect her from the screeches and insults. The officers' acrylic shields kept off the missiles now aimed at them, so all she had to do was sidestep the debris already on the ground.

At first, she thought the goal was the front door, but the group veered off to the left and then around the building, sweeping her along with them. The mob was thinner there and less directed, not even bothering to throw anything. Ayaan thought maybe the unruly bunch was just to make sure that no one escaped from the narrow side door. It didn't really surprise her when their little squad moved straight for the small entrance.

She realized that the teachers inside must be communicating with the sergeant when the door opened just as they arrived. A large desk quickly re-barricaded the entry once they were in.

"Ayaan, thank God you're here!" Luanda, the principal, rushed over. "The kids are fine, but I've got three badly wounded staff. The first bricks caught us by surprise. Emergency Services refused to come because of the mob."

Sergeant Mitchell disappeared as Ayaan dashed after Luanda. Her friend was a refugee camp survivor, good to have around in an emergency.

~oOo~

Clear fluid leaked from the injured janitor's ears.

Ayaan shook her head. "He needed a neurosurgeon an hour ago. Try to keep him warm, that's all we can do." The guidance counselor had a broken arm, and the third grade teacher a broken leg, less serious injuries, so she stabilized them, ready for transport.

"Where are the children?" she asked Luanda, raising her voice. If anything, the noises from outside were getting louder and uglier.

"The teachers have everyone in three interior classrooms. They've set up some movies to distract them, but the kids know something is wrong."

"Any idea what started the riot?" Ayaan finished packing her instruments back in her kit, sealing permanent equipment in a bag for later sterilization.

"We've been getting some hate mail, really nutty stuff about the school's name, saying we were an ISIS training center, that kind of thing. The police said it was nothing to worry about, just some crackpots."

"Ahmed Zewail Elementary School? Didn't he win the Nobel Prize?"

Luanda nodded. "In Chemistry. We have only fifteen Muslim students at most, but I doubt anyone bothered to ask."

"Ma'am, you're the principal, right?" Sergeant Mitchell appeared at the door of the makeshift clinic, with Officer Gonzales behind him. "We've got a problem."

"Only one?" The two women joined him in the hallway. "What's happening?"

"One of the officers outside said he thought he saw someone with a Molotov cocktail. We think they're planning to burn down the school."

Ayaan's jaw dropped. "You've got to be joking! There are over three hundred kids in this building!"

"It gets better." The sergeant held out his phone. "The media have arrived."

Ayaan glanced at the headline under the video of the building they were in, shaking her head slowly.

"President Trump said we're a bunch of Islamic extremists holding children hostage? Who do they say you are?" She pointed at the officer.

"Apparently we're a paramilitary group sponsored by ISIS." Sergeant Mitchell looked down at his riot gear. "I'm afraid it might set the pack off if they see a uniform in here. I've got the rest of the squad, fifteen officers, out there to help, and there are six inside, but there aren't enough of them or us to hold off that many people."

Ayaan thought about the officers she'd seen egging the crowd on, but she said nothing. There was either enough police protection to get them out or there wasn't; worrying wasn't going to help.

The question was how to get everyone out alive. So far, no one was shooting, but there was no assurance that would last, and all it would take was one spark for the whole place to go up in flames.

One of the other officers ran up, his voice shaking. "We've got to leave the building. They've lit the fire."

~oOo~

They needed to get their message out, something to contradict the story in the media. Ayaan scrounged a sheet from the sickroom cot and paint from the kindergarten classroom. Her hand trembled as she wrote, hoping that her words would be enough. The sign had to be immediately visible, not twisted or fluttering, so she used safety pins to attach the top and bottom of the sheet to broomsticks and a rope from the gym to hold it up.

"I still don't think a civilian ought to be doing this." Like the rest of the police, Sergeant Mitchell was needed to run the internal firehoses and extinguishers, trying to soak the inner walls to slow the fire. The teachers and principal had their hands full with the students.

"I don't think we have any other choice." Years of medical training kept the strain from showing, but she was shaking inside.

They'd done the best they could. The children and the staff couldn't move from the internal classrooms for fear of being hit by something thrown through the windows, but they were as ready to evacuate as possible. Ayaan hugged her daughter quickly, then dragged the makeshift sign toward one of the front classrooms.

The message had to be legible; their lives depended on it. The sign was awkward, but it was big enough to be seen from a distance and would, she hoped, lie flat so every camera trained on the building would show what was written.

She kept low for fear of attracting more missiles, picking her way through glass, bricks, and other debris covering the floor of the second story classroom. The sharp stench of burning gasoline drifted in through the gaps in the front windows. She tied the free end of the rope to the leg of the teacher's desk, ready to poke the sign out of the nearest hole.

The rope wasn't long enough to reach the window.

There wasn't time to find more rope. She could hear the crackling of the flames and smell the acrid smoke. The only choice was to move the heavy desk despite the rubble in the way.

At first, the desk wouldn't budge, but by bracing her back against the side and shoving, she finally got it within range. The hole in the window was only as big as whatever had made it, a close fit for the furled sign. With a humorless smile on her face, she grabbed a brick from the floor and heaved it through the remaining glass, making the hole larger.

"Out, out, out," she muttered and gave a final push, and the bundle of cloth disappeared. She was afraid to look to see if it had opened correctly, but the sudden silence of the crowd told her that she'd gotten the attention they'd wanted.

The sign said, "HELP. WE HAVE 312 CHILDREN, 22 STAFF MEMBERS (THREE SERIOUSLY INJURED), SIX POLICE, AND ONE VERY SCARED DOCTOR IN A BURNING BUILDING. PLEASE DON'T LET US DIE."

~oOo~

She didn't know until later that the first firetruck had had to force its way through the crowd to get close to the building, helped by ten police officers. With the staff and the officers who'd been inside with the children, the evacuation went quickly, and two of Ayaan's patients lived. It was too late to save either the janitor or the building; the janitor died sometime before rescue arrived and Ahmed Zewail Elementary School burned to the ground.

President Trump tweeted: "Dishonest media says they weren't terrorists. FAKE NEWS! Loyal Americans saved 300 kids from ISIS; media got the story wrong AGAIN!"

The End

Desperate Resolve

John A. Pitts

DJ closed the latch on the gun case, secured the vault door, and dropped the houndstooth throw back into place, covering the square bulk of the gun safe.

He started to replace the flower arrangement, the fear of his father's reprisal a burning ember nestled lovingly in his crocodile brain. In a surge of rage, he flung the vase against the wall, where it exploded, showering daisies and shards of china over his mother's prized Persian carpet.

Resolve warred with panic as he slid the box of shells into the left cargo pocket of his fatigues, tucked the shotgun under his overcoat, and turned to face the room once again.

This is where he'd kissed Cheryl for the first time. They had been thirteen and the electric jolt of her lips against his had overwhelmed his senses, blocking out the world for the briefest of joyful moments.

He shuddered at the memories, bile rising in his throat. So much horror had passed since then.

The memories drove him through the manse, his boots echoing hollowly off the mahogany paneling.

He hated his ancestral home and everything the Chalker House represented. It had been in his family for as long as there had been a United Cascadia. Back before his grandfather—a time when Cascadia had been a part of a larger republic, a greater United

States. Back before the class wars and the purges, the pandemic and the years of fire.

The manse represented wealth and privilege -- room after room of ostentation and excess, while good folks like Cheryl and her children suffered, in the camps.

Sweat prickled the stubble on his head. His shorn head a reminder of the dead children he and his squad had buried that spring -- young bodies emaciated and balding, so far gone that when he lifted them into the truck, they weighed less than his rucksack.

Cheryl had hung herself after her boys were gone. He found her in her prison shift and tattoos, broken from the tribulation of camp life. He held her as he cut the rope free from the rafters of the warehouse. The memory of their last night together -- her body lithe and curvy, their lovemaking urgent and passionate -- shattered as the featherweight of her bony corpse fell into his arms.

He paused at his reflection in the entranceway windows. Broad leaves encircled his eyes, flaring out to the sides of his face, and down, covering his cheeks in reds and yellow. Despite the ban, a thick beard and mustache covered the remainder of his exposed face. Darien Chalker, Sr. would be horrified to see his son, dolled up like a pagan, dressed in the tattered raiment of his shattered unit, his uniform bloodied in the revolution.

The elders, including his own effing father, had known about the internment camps and the expulsions. Had known of the religious purges and the cleansings. DJ had been spared the truth, isolated in his world of privilege and class.

He waved his wrist in front of the security panel and strode out of the house, pulling the ancient oak door closed with a thud. The security net would register nothing untoward here. Only a single authorized entrant carrying a licensed and authorized firearm. A luxury of the wealthy; a privilege of the powerful.

In the yard a dozen boys and girls stood, torches held overhead, faces masked in pagan regalia -- eyes hard -- expectant.

He raised the shotgun over his head and a guttural cheer rose from the crowd. After a moment, Janice—a young woman of sixteen—raised her fist and silence returned.

Now to business.

He sighed as he walked down the long, stone stairway to the yard. How unlikely a revolution. How ironic a fall. The same computers that ran their daily lives and maintained their veneer of civilization remained blind to the inside threat—open to revolt. These newly minted anarchists and avengers knew the laws and the systems well—their parents maintained the system.

He nodded to Janice and she turned toward the lane. The crowd of children followed her, silent once more. All were below age, harmless in the eyes of the ruling committee. Only he had crossed the barrier to adulthood.

Recruiting privileged youth had been easier than he'd expected. They knew one another, trusted each other in the way that children do. Masked from the horrors of the outside world, they had played at games, pagan festivals, and fantastical reenactments of the world around them—or at least of the stories their elders had told them.

Showing them the truth, more horrifying than anything they'd ever imagined, had converted them to his cause. Only Billy Meredith had refused to join their revolution, and he'd been left to ponder his choice in the hands of the Benedictine Sisters in Lacy.

One house remained of the children of privilege. One more opportunity to arm themselves within the rules of their elders. The enlightened were allowed to carry weaponry—a law enforced by AI oversight. And while the elders huddled in their enclave, planning the coming year, forging the proverbial caskets for another million or so of the poor and unworthy, DJ and his ragamuffins marched on into the night.

Susan Slater wept as she approached her home. Her father, Senator Slater, had architected the internment camps for unwed mothers and other malcontents. He owned a revolver, she assured them—a reminder of his youth in the civil corps, where he once shot a man to death for demanding the reinstatement of the freedoms so long dismissed.

DJ and the other eleven stood at the edge of the manicured lawn, torches casting shadows over faces bedecked with feathers and sequins, leaves and silk. Susan looked back once, her china white mask hiding all but her eyes as she waved her wrist in front of the door and entered the cavernous foyer.

The door closed with an ominous click as bolts shot into place.

"She's not coming back," Janice said at DJ's elbow. "She's terrified of being sent to the camps in Corvallis. You know her brother had refused to accept a position at the university."

"I remember."

"She said the last time she saw him, her father had just watched, unwavering, while the peacekeepers took him away. Never said a word."

DJ glanced down at Janice, a full head shorter than him and stocky. "She saw the vids. She knew Cheryl like the rest of us—and the children?" He raised his voice for the others to hear.

"Oh, she'll come back out."

The chill of night slipped in upon them as they waited in the darkness unbroken by moonlight, surrounded by the orange glow of fire.

"We have to stop this," he said in a hushed voice. "Have to make them pay for what they have done to us."

Janice touched him lightly on his arm. "You will die, you know that?"

"I'm already dead." He looked down at her. "I died the moment I cut Cheryl down."

She held his gaze, her eyes shadows in the uneven light.

"You weren't there, Janice. The vids don't give you the smell of rot and death. The taste of fear and despair." He paused a moment, pushing down the bile that lingered at the base of his throat. "They raped her. We found vids. They raped the women in the camp, hell, even some of the boys." He stopped suddenly, the pain in his stomach so intense he wanted to lay on the ground and weep. Her hand gripped his arm, balancing him as he staggered under the weight of the memories. He shuddered under her touch. How long had it been since he'd had simple, physical, human contact? "Freddie laughed when we first found the vids, said he looked forward to his time guarding the camps. I shot him."

Janice tightened the grip on his arm. Freddie had run with them when they were younger, a hard boy from a hard family. "He always was a shit," she said quietly.

"Seven of us freed that camp, you know. Angel and Carmella fled with the vehicles, the weapons, and the survivors. They headed for California."

"And the camp staff? The peacekeepers?"

DJ looked away then, as the water filled his eyes. "We killed them. Dumped their bodies in a ditch and burned them. It wasn't hard. . . to kill." He looked at her again. “Not hard at all. Standing amongst the refuse and the bodies, things like that come easy.”

The children around him had heard, of course. They watched him and Janice, waiting for something to happen. They were sheep, he knew. Janice was the only leader among them. Hell, he’d been no leader until he found the vids of Cheryl being raped, of seeing the bodies of the children. Burying your heart was easy when it was already covered in the dead.

“They don’t know how thin the line is between all this—” he swept his arm back, encompassing the neighborhood. “—and the end-of-things.”

“Look.” Kim, a young girl of thirteen, thin as a rail and sweet as honey, pointed toward the house.

Susan stood in an upper story window, pushing aside the heavy curtain that had blocked the interior light. Her mask was off, that much he could tell, but her face swam in shadows. She reached toward them, touched the glass with her right hand for a moment. Only for a moment.

“Oh no,” Janice whispered just as DJ noticed Susan move her left hand upwards.

The muffled gunshot jolted them. Susan’s head snapped backwards, the pistol she’d raised etched in DJ’s retina in the afterimage of muzzle flare. He could see her standing there, head tossed back by the blast, as the image faded.

“Come on.” He looked down as Janice tugged at his sleeve. “We gotta go now.”

DJ pulled his arm out of Janice's grip, and dragged his sleeve across his eyes, knocking his mask askew. "They'll pay for that, too." He straightened his mask and pumped the shotgun, driving a shell into the breach.

He took several steps toward the unguarded civic center, weaving between the stunned and sobbing children. Once through them, he turned and shouted. "We cannot allow this to go on. How many more of us, of our friends and even total strangers, have to suffer because of them?"

"I don't want to die," a tiny voice said behind him. He turned to see Kim holding a long rifle across her forearms. "What happens if we do this? What happens if we kill them all?"

Janice strode forward then, pulling at their sleeves, lifting a small automatic pistol over her head. "Then we control the computers, we make the laws."

DJ nodded. "We get to do the right thing."

The children murmured amongst themselves for a moment, their resolve wavering with the echo of Susan's final act.

DJ cleared his throat. Fought down the panic and the fear. "We are already dead. Every breath is one more than Cheryl had, or now Susan. We have to stop them, to open all this," he turned around in a wide circle, holding the shotgun up over his head. "Why should we get to live like this when there are so many that die in pain and humiliation?"

The crying settled down and the children seemed to square their shoulders. "Let's move." Janice stepped around DJ and jogged into the darkness, toward the town center.

He watched as all the children followed her, moving past him in wavering shadows thrown by the torches. Their masks made them look wild; the light that glinted from their eyes made them feral. The anguish in their hearts gave them a desperate resolve.

"What's to stop us from becoming just like them?" Kim asked as she passed him.

"Nothing," he said. "And everything."

The End

You are Weighed in the Balance

Rivka Jacobs

Zach Adkins rested with his lower spine against the rough bark of a Virginia pine. He could hear crickets in the dark, a sound that usually made him feel safe, but now evoked sadness as he remembered happy September nights when he was a boy. He inhaled the cool, fragrant air and tried to imagine that this small patch of mountain forest wasn't an isolated stand—the last stand—but covered the slopes of all hills everywhere while fresh, clean water rippled and gurgled down pristine hollows throughout the land.

On his left, Dan Spence kicked his boots and tossed his body from side to side. He finally sat up, reaching reflexively for his rifle that lay straight beside him.

"Can't sleep?" Zach asked, his voice low. He drew up one knee and circled it with his arms, rocking briefly, his nerves sparking. He surveyed their position with eyes that had become keen in the night, listened to the coughs and restless muttering that rose and fell along the line of men and women who lay in various positions to his left and right.

Dan jumped a bit as he heard the tangled underbrush shift behind him.

"It's me," Mary whispered as she scrambled over the rim of the trench and dropped into a position on the free side of their leader. She raised the night-vision goggles to her forehead. "Met with the squad captains along Rt. 17," she said softly, a little out of breath. "No sign of troops or vehicles yet. But we picked up electronic chatter indicating Blackhawks from the Academic Security and Support Battalion are moving up from the south. Should be here in an hour or less."

"Also the 1st Battalion of the 201st Field Artillery, West Virginia National Guard," Zach said, almost to himself. "The oldest continuous unit in the United States army, now sponsored by Arch Coal, wearing the ACU patch of the corporation instead of the musket, tomahawk, and powder-horn. Along with the 156th MP Detachment—which we heard was coming up from Monaville—these troops are local. Neighbors, the people we went to school and church with."

"The ones I'm worried about are the units that served south of the border," Dan said, his voice thick as he tried to remain calm. "From Charleston. They've got five-thousand soldiers with the most up to date equipment—Blackhawks too—fresh from a twelve-month tour with the US occupation army in Mexico."

"So, do you think they'll talk to us first?" came a female voice on Dan's left, Gina Serranto.

Zach paused as he once more searched for the patience he needed to calm others, to answer questions in just the right way that allayed fear and built confidence. He had always been a thoughtful man, a teacher, a scholar, a man of peace. But he was nearing his own death; it was difficult to constantly face outward and play the part of icon and leader. Sometimes he wanted to sink into himself, shut out the world, ready his own soul. He knew they were waiting for him to respond; he could smell their anxiety. Zach sighed. "Gina, yeah, they'll go through the motions, I think. Depends where they set up their positions. Depends on what they plan on using against us."

They were dug in on the knolls just south of Blair Mountain and Spruce Creek, along the heights overlooking Blair Gap. The site where the scabs and Sheriff Chaffin and the Pinkertons had tried to ambush the West Virginia miners who were trying to unionize in 1921. Just to the west, only a mile away, was another planet—the remains of the hills of West Virginia. All around them for hundreds of miles including what once were the Appalachians, was a wasteland. Gray, black and white—like an immense boneyard, like the surface of the moon—the terrain was filled with dead, bare, immense, and crumbling mounds of debris interspersed with deep scars filled with poisonous slime. Leaden and glowing coal-ash sludge rolled in stream beds where crystal clear currents used to rush. Mercury, arsenic, and other toxic waste covered the land, contaminated every watershed including the Ohio River.

This tract on Blair Mountain, like an island, was the last few acres of natural hardwood forest left in West Virginia. It was saved in the early 2000s after a long legal battle to declare it an historical site. But in the last several years, with the Presidential Protectorate declared and voting rights restricted to property owners, the last of the national parks and historical places were sold to the most powerful energy companies and the highest campaign donors.

"Are we going to die?" Gina asked. She pressed against Dan, wrapping her rimfire Remington in her arms.

Dan shoved her a bit, as if in fun. "Hey, we're already dying from cancer and arsenic poisoning. This way, we go out fighting for the last trees and clean water in Appalachia."

Mary was spinning something between the fingers of both her hands. "Well, I'd better get back down the line," she muttered. She turned and shoved the object against Zach's chest.

"Here," she said, "I found it. It's an eagle feather. A goddamned eagle feather. Might be from the last few mating pairs in the entire country. The goddamned bald eagle."

Zach took the token, and listened as Mary pulled down her goggles. He heard her climb, heave herself out of the trench, and hasten through the ferns and brush, crunching leaves as she moved to the south. There was no light whatsoever, not even a single star in a black sky. Zach examined the feather by touch, brought it to his nose and sniffed it, rubbed it along his cheek.

"An eagle feather, really?" Dan said, his tone listless.

"The Cherokee lived here centuries ago. Some of my ancestors," Zach said. "The eagle feather was a sign from the Great Spirit. It represents balance. The unification of opposites. Harmony of the four directions, unification in the truth. Dark and light, good and bad. Don't doubt for an instant that the Continental Congress knew what the Civilized Tribes believed in 1785 when they adopted the bald eagle as the emblem of the nation. The right claw may be used for destruction, for war, for greed, and killing. The left claw, which is near the heart, holds health, life, hope, and kindness. The eagle feather represents the order of the universe, the native tribes said, and the order of the universe is balance."

"I can see 'em now, Zach, flashing your picture all over the monitors and screens in the country, 'Evil Bastard History Teacher, Tree-Hugging Hippy.'"

"Shut up, Danny." Gina shivered a little.

"It's okay," Zach said. "Wait till they find my journal. I postulated a few days ago, just for the fun of it, what if the ancient Egyptians were right about the afterlife, after all. . ."

"We love you, man, but you gotta stop with the history crap," Dan interrupted.

"No, listen," Zach said, holding the feather by the quill. "I thought, what if one of those fundamentalist Christian hardliners now running the country died—and he wakes up in a vast golden desert, and he's watching this figure walk toward him, getting closer and closer, and the figure turns out to be Anubis with a jackal's head and man's body. And the guy goes all red-faced and hysterical. 'Hey,' he shouts, 'What is this? Where's Jesus? Is this Hell?' And Anubis says, 'I'm here to lead you to Osiris for judgment.'" Zach laughed.

"Only you would find that funny," Gina said, but she smiled in the darkness.

"Thanks, Gee. I consider that a compliment." He paused, then said, "We'll give it another few minutes, then we'll get our people up and ready. We'll know in less than an hour what they plan. You all know the response routines; we take immediate action if it's gas. If the attack copters hover and the troops remain in formation, they might be willing to negotiate. We also have to see what heavy artillery is facing us. . ."

"Howitzers. . ."

"Howitzers, grenade launchers. . ."

There was soft thumping and rustling; a couple more of their recon captains stopped in front of Zach and squatted down side by side, panting. "Copters coming. Gunships," Greg Bass said between gasps.

For a moment no one spoke. Zach could feel the weight of their fear and hopelessness. He clenched his teeth, trying to scrape the sides of what was left of his own courage, to come up with any small amount to share. "We'll be fine," he finally said. "This is what we've trained for. Get everyone up. Let's get ready." He checked his watch, pressing the tiny blue light quickly. "It's just after five; won't be light for another hour. We've got some time.

In less than thirty minutes, the entire force of two-thousand men and women and some children, most of them from West Virginia or Kentucky, a handful from other states, were roused, their weapons loaded and ready as they waited behind barricades and camouflage built of branches and brush across the North and South Crests above Blair Gap.

The sky glowed an eerie yellow-green in the east. A soft breeze made the trees overhead hum. Dew-like condensation started to form on their hair and clothing and the metal of their weapons. Zach had dropped over the defensive escarpment, and was lying on his stomach a few paces ahead, on a bluff that overlooked a stream that branched from White Trace Branch hollow. He could hear the faint chup-chup-chup of the Blackhawks now. And a grinding, metallic rumble began to echo off the verdant slopes to the north.

Dan, the second in command, crawled until he was side-by-side with Zach, both flattened as low to the ground as possible. "Looks like the army has arrived."

They peered down to the right some two-thousand feet where gray dust had started to roll in great billows toward them along the winding state road.

Zach clutched his Ruger semi-automatic rifle in one hand as it lay on the grassy surface. He reached into his shirt and withdrew the eagle feather, holding it out in front of him. In the growing light, he could see it was white with dark-brown mottling. He held it higher so that it could catch the first filtered rays of sun.

Dan grasped his friend's wrist, forcing his hand down. "What the hell are you doing?"

Zach rose to a sitting position. "Once Anubis got you to the hall of Osiris," he said, "he pulled the heart out of your chest and put it on one pan of a scale. The goddess of universal order and truth would then remove a feather from her headdress—her name was Ma'at—and Anubis would put this feather on the other pan, and weigh your heart against the feather to see how much sin was in your soul."

Below them, a multitude of forms appeared in the distance, and the squeaking grumble of treads, the grinding of gears, grew louder. To their rear, behind their own line, they could hear magazines loaded, unloaded, clicked into position once more.

Zach slowly came to his feet. Dan tried to grab his legs and yank him back, but their leader and commander evaded him and was already making his way down the embankment, half sliding, half walking, pushing his way through the vegetation as he descended the mountain. Dan clutched the earth and glanced behind him. He looked once more at the scene before him, then moved himself backward on his hands and knees until he reached the escarpment; he turned and climbed up and over, joining the others. "Where's Zach? What's happening? What's going to happen?" came at Dan from different directions, in voices high and low filled with panic and despair.

"He's. . ." Dan sank to his haunches in their trench, holding his rifle with both fists in front of him. "I think. . . he's going to meet them."

Hovering in the gritty sky were copters from the 19th Special Forces Group. Cranking amidst the columns were vehicles from the 150th Armored Reconnaissance Squadron. And marching and maneuvering in formation along state Rt. 17, pressing into a forward line, were the men and women of the 77th. Zach could see them more and more clearly as he approached, his white feather held aloft. They were dressed in the pinkish-brown and gray fatigues of the Mexican war zone. Their helmets were rounded and tightly fitting, and most of them wore black gas masks, the blowers attached to their packs. Each of them carried an M9 pistol and M-18 assault rifle. On the periphery of his sight, Zach recognized the big guns—the Howitzers—being set up, the fifty-pound shells unloaded from trucks.

He locked his eyes on the soldiers in the point positions. Obscured by their gear, looking alike, it was hard to tell if they were even human. Zach skidded through the purple phlox, down the last slight rise of the mountain, and reached the side of the road. He stepped onto the asphalt only thirty feet away from the advance guard, and paused. He could hear shouts of "HALT" from among the officers ahead. The troops immediately in front of him froze, crouched slightly, raised their rifles. The sun was high enough in the east to gleam off the gun barrels and make the plastiglass of the gas masks white with glare.

Hanging his own rifle from his right hand in the downward position, Zach raised his eagle feather as high as he could in his left. He inhaled deeply, and started advancing steadily toward the opposing forces. He felt as light as air. No one fired. Except for the helicopter blades, there was no sound.

He came to within five feet of the first group of soldiers. He could see their eyes now, behind the transparent shielding of their masks. “I want to talk,” he said to them.

In an instant, a rush of wind came through the Gap. It hit Zach from behind and pushed his hair in front of him. It bent the trees on the slopes above them. It dissolved and scattered the dust still hanging in the air around them. It took his white eagle feather and pulled it out of his fingers, lifting it in circles higher and higher. Zach craned his neck in shock, watching as the feather fluttered and soared and disappeared into the brightness of the day. His left hand was still extended, his fingers still pressed together. A wordless exclamation, part grunt part cry, made him glance down again.

One of the soldiers immediately in front of him ripped off his gas mask, his gun still at ready. He appeared to be tracking the feather, his mouth open. He suddenly lowered his head and stared at Zach.

Several more soldiers pulled their gas masks onto their chests. “Hey, buddy,” one of them shouted.

"Where're you from?" Their precise formation began to melt as more weapons dropped. "I'm from Logan County, I'm from here," the voice of a young man—his eyes deep set, his face etched with uncertainty—chimed in. And a third, a young woman—a staff sergeant by her ACU patch—peered directly at Zach. She looked around at her teammates as harsh commands to "MOVE" crackled from the small field radio attached to her tactical vest. She tucked her assault rifle under an arm, reached across her chest, turned the receiver off.

"We've been ordered to terminate you all, to wipe you out. Men, women, children." she said. "I don't think we can do that."

The End

Priorities

C.A. Chesse

Tonto Gets A Pipeline
Pedro Gets A Wall
Chumpy Gets a Trump Degree
Hillary Takes a Fall

Tex Drillson Gets a Tax Break
Pussies Love Attack
Rich Kids Get to Learn Stuff
Lives Matter if They Aren't Black

The KGB's Just Fine, Thanks
The Earth is Doing Well
Ahmed's Banned to the Desert
Without a Trump Hotel

Oceans Are Big and Water
Bacardi Can Wait
No More Yellow Trade Deals
Tweet the Record Straight

White House Emails Are Private
Vote Trump and Trump Forgives
Shemale Gets a Discharge
Frederick Douglass Lives

Our Bombs are Bigger
Praise Our Flag or Face a Fight
Hurricanes Bring Ratings
So Watch Joe Get Off Light

Have No Fear of KimChi Nukes
Nor Staring At the Sun
Out Go Aides and Top Officials
Plan for Chaos and For Fun

Fritz Has Been a Good Boy
Eye for Eye and Tooth For Tooth
Democracy Dies in White Noise
Speaking Power to Truth

Headlines Are Only Fake News
For Good Health, You Can Pray
’Cause What Matters is the Crowd Size
On Inauguration Day

The Healer

Melinda LaFevers

Susan readied herself for the trek. Bags? Check. Three of them slung over her shoulder. Clippers? Check. Freshly sharpened, in one of the bags. Gun? She sighed as she clipped a holster to the strap she wore under her loose shirt. She picked up her pistol, checked the clip and safety, attached the silencer, and slid it into the holster.

She lived out in the country, and today's harvest was in a nearby field, only a mile or so down the dirt road that ran in front of her house, but you couldn't be too careful. There were too many scumbags on the prowl, and a few of them had ventured down her isolated lane. They never did it more than once.

Self defense, every single one.

She was not a woman who would be raped easily, or who would allow what little she had to be taken. With the mockery the courts had become, and no money for bribes, she hadn't reported anything. As a result, her garden was growing extra well in places. And having a good garden was crucial, especially for her medicinal herbs.

She sighed again, opened the door, cautiously looked around, and then went outside. Closing her door and locking the triple locks only took a minute.

As she walked down the road, her thoughts moved back to the past.

~oOo~

"I'm telling you, if Trump is elected, the United States will go up into flames." The elderly man's proclamation was brought on by the commentary from the news show he was watching.

"OK, Daddy, I believe you. But how will it happen?"

"I don't know. But it will happen. Mark my words. Furthermore" her father predicted, "if he is elected, your knowledge of herbal medicine will make you a very valuable commodity."

~oOo~

Susan shook off the past with a twinge of sadness. After eight years, she still missed her father. And she especially missed his wisdom. He had spent years as a sociologist, studying mankind, and that had not stopped with his retirement. He had been right on all counts, she mused. America was as close to flames as you could get, with both unrest within the country and the war on two fronts. Between watching North Korea, watching Russia, and combating the all too often terrorist attacks in the States, the military was spread thin. At least China was staying out of it. Amazingly, Trump had not only survived his first term, but had even been reelected—although there had been fraud. And terrorism. The bulk of the American "terrorist attacks" seemed to target congressmen who were Democrats or Independents and occasionally Republicans brave enough to vote against the party line. Those attacks, plus an overwhelming Republican majority in congress, had finally justified a declaration of martial law. That was a year ago. Things had gone downhill since.

Her thoughts were interrupted by a man next to the road. He was sitting on a large rock next to the tree she was passing.

"Are you the healer?"

She stopped immediately, her hand sliding under her shirt to rest on her pistol as she assessed the threat. She saw a man in old clothes, but not the worst she had seen lately. They weren't torn, and no more dirty than you would expect after a day outside. He had a beard, as many men did now, but it was neatly trimmed. He was wearing a backpack that obviously had something in it. His brow was furrowed. Fear? Worry? It could be either. No obvious weapons. She relaxed slightly.

"I don't call myself a healer. Just someone with a little knowledge of plants and their uses. Who are you, and what do you need?"

"My name is Daniel Cooper. It's my daughter, Anna. She has asthma. Ruth Baker, in town, said you might be able to help us. Can you? I don't have much to offer, but this is our only daughter. I'd do almost anything."

The story he told might even be true.

"What did she tell you?"

"She said you gave her something to help her breathe easier when she had bronchitis. Please—is there anything at all you can do to help my daughter?"

Susan remembered Mrs. Baker. The Bakers lived down the hill, about two miles away. She was struggling with obesity—now considered a pre-existing condition. Susan had brought her some mullein.

"As it happens, I am going to gather something right now that should help. Come help me, and I'll give you some."

A ten-minute walk brought them to Susan's destination. Dotting the field were tall grayish green stalks, most with a yellow flower head at the top. The leaves on the plant were fuzzy, and that is where Susan headed first.

"Do you have a knife?"

"Yes, a pocket knife."

"Are you carrying any weapons?"

Daniel shook his head no.

"A pocket knife is all I have."

"Only a pocket knife? You are either extremely brave, or extremely foolish."

"My daughter is sick."

That was good enough for Susan.

"You want to cut the leaves off at their base, but do not injure the stalk itself. Take no more than half of the leaves from each stalk. You can put them in this bag."

They both filled their bags with the large fuzzy leaves. Susan worked much faster, using her clippers expertly. When her first bag was full, she gathered flowers from the stalks. She examined a stalk and cut the entire flower head off, putting that into a bag with others. When Daniel's bag was full, she had filled her second bag with flowers, and had begun gathering more leaves. Daniel brought his bag to her.

"This is pretty full. Do I cram more in, or am I done?"

"That's good. Hold these, while I cut a few more." She handed him the leaves she had cut and cut even more leaves from another stalk. She continued until his hands were full.

"Do you have far to walk?"

"About five miles—we live in town, but at the edge."

"OK, come on back to my place."

They walked the mile or so back to Susan's place. While they walked, Susan told him how to use the leaves.

"The plant you just helped me harvest is called mullein. The leaves have a chemical compound that acts as a bronchial dilator. You will put several leaves together, tie a string around them, and hang them up near the ceiling to dry. In an emergency asthma attack, use the dried leaves to make a cigarette and have her smoke it. If she is just a little bit asthmatic, you can make a cup of tea from a spoonful of dried leaves. That will work, but it works more slowly than smoking them. When we get back to my place, I'll let you take some leaves I have already dried, as well as some of the ones you just gathered."

"Why did you collect the flowers?"

"I cover them with oil and after they have infused long enough, I use the oil for ear-aches and small skin abrasions. It has a mild, anti-bacterial property."

When they arrived at her house, Susan unlocked the door. She opened it, paused, and "felt" the condition of the house. All was calm and undisturbed.

"Wait out here. You can sit there." Susan pointed to a small bench under a tree. "I'll be right back."

She took the leaves that Daniel had carried, went inside her house and headed up the stairs. The small room, really just a finished out attic space, was her drying area. She dropped the bags of fresh cut plants on the small table, and took down three bunches of dried leaves hanging from the ceiling. She gathered a large bunch of the fresh leaves, put the ends together, and wrapped them with thread. She made a second bundle, and set it on the table next to the first one. Going to the bag of flowers, she took out the flower head that she had gathered earlier, cut it in half, and set one piece on the table. She gathered all of the fresh and dried bundles that she had set out, and took them and the second piece of the flower head down the stairs and outside.

Daniel had not been idle. His backpack was at his feet, and the contents were displayed on the bench next to him. Canned goods; tuna, peaches, and corn. A small bag of rice. A smaller bag of previously opened coffee. And. . .

"Oh, my goodness! Is that *chocolate*?"

There were not one but two bars of chocolate sitting with the goods. Daniel nodded.

"I said that I didn't have much to offer, but we can give you this. . ." he trailed off.

"Hold on a minute."

She went inside, and grabbed one of her glass jars with a lid. Going back outside, she poured a small portion of the coffee into the jar, closed it, and carefully sealed the coffee bag up and handed it back to Daniel.

"I don't drink a lot of coffee, which is good, since it is so difficult to get now. But I will certainly enjoy my next cup. I grow my own corn and peaches, so you can keep those. The tuna and the rice, I will keep, and be glad for. And the chocolate. . . I'll keep one bar. Give the other to your daughter. Now, here are three small bundles of dried leaves, two of the fresh. When you get home, I suggest that you separate them into smaller bundles to dry, so they don't mold. And, one more thing. . ." She held out the flower head.

"There are seeds in this one. I don't guarantee that they will grow, but they might. Mullein is a two year plant. The first year, it is a rosette of leaves that grow close to the ground. The second year is when it shoots up the flower stalk. The leaves may be used at any time. Now, pack up your things, and pedal us a couple of miles towards town."

Daniel packed his things into his backpack and Susan took her food inside. She locked up and wheeled out a bicycle with a goat cart trailer.

"You get to pedal, while I relax like a queen," Susan said. "But it will take you less time to get home. You can go up to three miles before I take it home again. Hand me your pack—no sense in you wearing it until you have to."

She took Daniel's pack and climbed onto the goat cart. Daniel looked at her a moment, climbed onto the bicycle, and pedaled for home.

"That's far enough," Susan said after a little while. "You should only have about a thirty minute walk left." She looked at the sun, judging its angle.

"You will get home before dark. You should have enough mullein for the next few months. If the seeds don't sprout, come back up to my place."

"I can't thank you enough. . ."

"Oh, you did. Chocolate. I haven't had that in months. You get home and hug your daughter."

Daniel shouldered his pack and walked away. She got on the bicycle, turned the cart around, and headed for home.

As she turned onto the dirt road near her house, two men stepped out of the tall grass. Their clothes were dirty and torn and both were unshaven. One of them waved a large butcher knife.

"Ooooh, looky here, Billy. What have we found?"

"I think we found ourselves an armful of loving. And that cart sure will come in handy."

Her hand grasped the pistol.

"I don't want any trouble," she said. "Just let me be."

"Oh, you won't get any trouble from us, just a little loving, honey. And some smooching. We ain't smooched on a woman in a while." Billy leered at her suggestively.

"I said I don't want any trouble."

"Tell you what, honey, you just get off of that bike and give us some loving, and we'll let you go on home. Matter of fact, we might even go home with you. . ."

His words trailed off as he first stared in disbelief at the sudden blossom of red on his dirty shirt, then he fell over. The pistol swung over as Susan hastily fired at the other man. Her aim was not quite as good on this shot. He grunted with the impact, but did not fall.

"That is going to cost you. That was my friend." The man waved his knife wildly as he stalked towards Susan. She shot once more. This time, the knife dropped from suddenly nerveless hands. The man wavered a moment more, and collapsed.

Susan looked at the bodies and sighed. At least she was out of sight of the paved road. With difficulty, she dragged the bodies over to her cart and loaded them on. Checking the area where the men had been waiting in ambush, she found a couple of haversacks. She tossed those on top of the bodies, climbed back onto her bike, and resumed her trip home. Pedaling that last two miles to her house proved to be a bit more difficult than she had anticipated, but at last she got them home, just as the sun set.

"Time to prepare a new section of garden," she thought. "Good thing the moon is full tonight."

She pedaled the bike and cart around to her garden and started digging. Once the hole was wide enough and deep enough for two, she stripped the clothes off the bodies, dumped them in, and covered them up. The clothes she would wash, rip apart, and use to make bags, ties, and anything else that she needed cloth for. She took the clothes and haversacks into the house, lit a lantern, and searched the clothes. Not much in the pockets, other than a few coins and the knife. No I.D. for either of the men.

After she searched the clothes, she put them in the wash tub. They could wait until tomorrow.

Susan turned to the haversacks next. Some food. That was good. A box of matches. Awesome. Her searching fingers felt something satiny. She pulled it out and spread it out on the table. Women's underwear. Three pairs, different sizes —and they were all bloodstained.

"They would be the kind to keep souvenirs. I think I just made the world a better place."

She looked at the underwear again, and shook her head sadly. These she would just burn. She certainly wasn't going to use them, and there were no identifying marks. She hoped the women had survived their attacks, but from the amount of blood, she doubted it.

Susan poured some water from her pitcher into a bowl and washed up.

"Tomorrow," she thought, "I'm going to pump enough water from the well to take a bath. After I plant the new section of garden. I'll need something that likes a rich fertilizer. Maybe blood-root. That would be appropriate." She finished her toilet and went to bed.

The next morning, just as Susan had gotten dressed, she was startled by a knock on the door.

"Who could that be?" she muttered.

She went to the peephole and looked out. Standing in front of her door was a woman, who had obviously been crying. Susan checked the windows and saw no one else. A bicycle leaned against a tree in the front yard. After getting her pistol and putting it on, Susan cautiously opened the door.

"Can I help you?"

"Are you the healer?

"I don't call myself a healer. Just someone with a little bit of knowledge of plants and their traditional uses. Tell me who you are, and I'll see what I can do to help. . ."

The End

Triple R Presents

Colin Patrick Ennen

News Release
For Immediate Release

Triple R
1861 Confederate Way
Winatallcosts, TX 72016

Triple R set to release best-in-the-nation suite of liberal mitigation tools

November 11, 2017

Washington, D.C.–Nationally recognized consulting/trolling firm **Triple R (Red, Right, & Righteous™)**, creator of last year's hot seller, He's-Not-A-Real-Conservative Virtual Blinders, is pleased to announce the release today of a first-of-its-kind package containing its most effective liberal deflection tools. Combining advanced technology and good old-fashioned books (with pictures!), this suite of instruments and propaganda is sure to have America's conservatives driving liberals batty and drinking their tears across the land lickety-split. From our patented **BS-tron 5000** earpiece, to innovative social media plugins, to a selection of top-notch books, the **We Won! Get Over It! Package** will have you trampling on liberals' arguments like a liberal on gun rights.

Lefty acquaintances pestering you on Facebook? Why not deploy **AxeFuscate**? This social media plugin bombards them with quotes—ruthlessly stripped of context—demonstrating how historical great men (men only, duh) obviously agree with a position that's ostensibly adjacent to yours. Or perhaps deflection is more your style: **DeflectoCon** automates, customizes, randomizes, and transmits your But Obama! But Hillary!, and Liberal Media! responses better than any human ever could. We'll also throw in our **Meme Maker Plus** (copyright Putin/Manafort Enterprises) and a curated list of validated websites and newsletters you can safely reference when the libs challenge you to "cite your source," whatever that means.

Our **BS-tron 5000** earpiece-and-microphone combo, made from the best Russian tech, is tiny, powerful, undetectable, and automatically translates incoming liberal gibberish into known lefty talking points for easy repudiation. Too taxing? Turn on the auto-refute function to have immediate rebuttals fed right into your ears. All you've got to do is repeat. A new special feature suggests Bible quotes that are sure to stymie all your heathen adversaries.

Last but not least, the books, all containing small words and lots of pictures: *The Modern Conservative's Guide to Refuting Liberal Claptrap*, by Hugh R. Amoron; *Circular Logic: A How To*, by Canby Absurdë; *Because: Why you should trust C-list celebs more than experts*, by I.M. Becile; *Disproved? All the out-there allegations you can shake a stick at*, by Kahn Spirator; and *Pfft, Science*, by Justin Faith.

Created by our brightest Moscow-based thinkers and that rascally group of Macedonian teenagers, the **We Won! Get Over It! Package** will be available online or at your local gun shop soon. Grab yours quick before the next election cycle gears up.

Trust **Triple R** for all your political communication needs. Remember our motto, *Hey, the truth is what you want it to be.*

The End

Donald, Where's Your Taxes?

Susan Murrie Macdonald and Elizabeth Ann Scarborough

(May be read as a poem or sung to the tune of
"Donald, Where's Your Trousers"
by Andy Stewart and Neil Grant) © 1960

Let the fake news wail, let the fake news whine,
Donald claims that "the truth is mine!"
His plans are bigly, grand, and fine,
But, Donald, where's your taxes?

You said when you won you'd set them free,
Your tax returns for all to see.
Now you're living in D. C.,
So, Donald, where's your taxes?

What are you afraid they'll show?
Something else that we don't know?
Your excuses, like your fibs, just grow,
And, Donald, where's your taxes?

First you say no, then you say yes,
It tends to make us trust you less
Than if you'd come out and confess:
Donald, where's your taxes?

You swore of e-mails up and down,

With a shout and with a frown.
We know you're just a Russian clown,
But, Donald, where's your taxes?

You tell your people you're straight shootin'
But the truth you keep disputin'
And meanwhile your boss is Putin
Did you pay him your taxes?

Let the fake news wail, let the fake news whine,
Donald claims that "the truth is mine!"
His plans are bigly, grand, and fine,
But, Donald, where's your taxes?

A Spider Queen in Every Home

Mike Morgan

Charlotte Hughes awoke to a gentle scratching: a peculiar, out-of-place noise, foreign to the normal murmurs and sighs of the old house. She lay still, ears straining, muscles tense. Something was wrong.

She was still groggily trying to determine the source when her alarm clock went off. The strident beeping not only blotted out the whispering rasp, but threatened to give her a headache.

Abandoning hope of sleep, she yelled at the clock to shut the holy heck up and hauled herself out of bed and into the bathroom. The dread passed, memory of the noise washed away by the realities of a workday morning.

Charlotte was still wrapped in a towel when she stepped out of the bathroom and found the spider sitting in the center of the upstairs landing. She froze.

The arachnid was bigger than any spider she'd ever seen. The meaty, pitch-black hairy body was the size of a squirrel. Its eight horribly splayed legs made it seem even more enormous. The obscene thing squatted midway between where she stood and her bedroom.

"Son of a—" breathed Charlotte, resisting a primal urge to jump backward and lock herself in the bathroom. She clutched her towel and edged around the unmoving bulk of the creature. “How the hell did you get in?”

The spider remained motionless as she reached the safety of her bedroom. Charlotte slammed the door, certain it was too big to squeeze under, and dressed.

She grabbed a high heeled shoe and pulled at the door handle. Peering around the chipped paintwork, Charlotte saw the spider hadn’t moved. Its fangs twitched, each one as substantial as the end of her little finger.

Time slowed as she advanced, stiletto held high. Charlotte believed the monstrosity would spring the exact moment she struck, hurling itself out of the way with a speed no human could hope to match.

The thing made a god-awful mess when she killed it.

She left the shoe impaled in the creature and took another shower. She really hated spiders.

~oOo~

Charlotte’s boss at the Department of National Statistics spent the day making suggestions, checking her work for anything that couldn’t be allowed to be true. After hours of managerial review, Charlotte had little of her original data left and was relieved to leave.

She spent the short journey from the office tower in Moline, Illinois to her home in Davenport, Iowa listening to modern glissom tracks, not really getting what fans saw in the musical genre. Perhaps she wasn’t one of the cool kids anymore.

The view through the windows of her personal transport pod added to her gloom as she crossed the high bridge over the Mississippi. She hated the twice-daily sight of tent cities lining the broad river's banks. The supposedly temporary camps had been nestled in the shadows of the rusting metal flood barriers for years.

Not soon enough, her transport pod parked itself in the old garage at the bottom of her yard. Charlotte tried to force the faces of the out-of-state refugees from her mind as she went through the ritual of plugging the vehicle into the garage's outlet.

After checking the pod was charging properly, Charlotte trudged wearily to her backdoor. A light breeze made the power line leading from the Victorian foursquare to the garage swing loosely overhead. The cable was wired up to the microbial fuel cell in the basement, carrying current generated by billions of microscopic algae.

She knew she should feel grateful to live in a home fitted with its own power supply, especially when so many lived in tents. She knew how privileged she was to be a government epidemiologist in a time of spreading, mosquito-borne diseases, near the top of the carefully vetted resource reallocation lists. Nonetheless, she detested the cell.

The fuel cell's microalgae had to be fed water mixed with nutrients, and human waste was the perfect source. The sludge-filled tank in her basement was hermetically sealed, but Charlotte swore she could smell her effluent fermenting.

To distract herself from the thought of the all-pervading stink, she loosened her necktie in the ferocious heat of the early fall evening. How many more weeks it would take for the temperature to cool?

Charlotte's elderly neighbor, Scarlet Kirkpatrick, waved theatrically from the other side of the chain link fence separating their gardens. The extravagantly-muscled widow cried cheerfully, "Come over for a drink!"

She was sat on her garden patio, cocktail in hand, wearing a swimsuit that showed far too much wrinkled, heavily tanned skin. Charlotte suspected the outfit was a way for Scarlet to show off her huge, dramatically defined physique. Since retiring from wrestling, bodybuilding had grown to become the woman's passion, one she pursued with undiminished fervor even in her seventies.

The exhausted statistician hesitated, one foot on the wooden steps leading up to the rear of her house. Scarlet had the local infotainment broadcast blaring away, its upbeat tunes interspersed with short, equally optimistic news-bites. Charlotte weighed the extent of her tiredness against her need for a cocktail.

Booze won out.

~oOo~

A reassuring voice on the broadcast channel explained how the presence of US troops in Canada was a humanitarian relief mission; Uncle Sam was rescuing its neighbor. Protestations from the former Canadian government that the push was an invasion were untrue, as all right-thinking patriots would surely agree.

Scarlet sipped at her colorful drink and commented wryly, “Rescuing Canada from what, though? I’ve never been terribly clear on what is threatening them. Other than us, of course.” She flexed a bicep, grinning at the way the muscle jumped.

Charlotte steadfastly ignored her neighbor’s antics. Scarlet’s sculpted frame always made her feel self-conscious about her own far-from-impressive, rather dumpy, build.

The former wrestler’s words were no more reassuring—people were locked up for less, although not usually people as rich as Scarlet. Her husband had been a high-level party apparatchik before choking to death on a piece of vat-grown shrimp-on-a stick at a political fundraiser, and he’d left her a fortune.

On a completely unrelated topic, the broadcast explained how the new Canadian regime was authorizing the relocation to sunny Saskatchewan of a hundred thousand Americans displaced by rising sea level. Lately, when a storm submerged a coastal area, the waters seldom receded.

Charlotte ignored Scar’s question about Canada, choosing to take a long draught of her own orange-and-pink beverage. Scarlet always did a good job of layering the different liquors so they sat in distinct strata. She'd initially acquiesced to these after-work sessions because she'd felt sorry for the lonely widow. Now, she looked forward to them. Scarlet's talk might be incendiary, but she had a lifetime of colorful stories and she knew how to mix a drink. Charlotte even picked up groceries for the former wrestling pro and helped fill out the complicated bill pay screen for her quarterly citizenry fees.

Scarlet's calico cat, Leonard, came to sit under Charlotte's patio chair. He seemed uncharacteristically jumpy.

Another spider, as big and hairy as the one she'd killed that morning, slunk through the monkey grass bordering Scarlet's patio. Charlotte was about to shriek this discovery when the spider pounced. The lunge was too fast to observe clearly, but Charlotte had no trouble seeing the thrashing, fourteen-inch-long, bright yellow-and-red centipede it caught.

"Oh yes," drawled Scarlet, "I bought a spider queen." She added, "For pest control."

"A spider queen?" Charlotte stared, aghast.

"Oh, no, no, that's a small one, a male hunter. The queen acts as a general. It's much more impressive."

The spider contentedly snacked on the centipede, twisting legs off and guiding them into its maw. Charlotte tore her gaze from the grisly sight to regard Scarlet. Her neighbor took that as her cue to inexpertly sing the advertising jingle for the over-sized creatures, an excessively cheerful song that insisted on repeating the refrain, “a spider queen in every home!” more than seemed reasonable.

Charlotte asked, “What?” in a tone that she hoped conveyed how profoundly surreal she was finding the conversation.

“It’s the definition of environmentally friendly. A natural extermination method.”

Charlotte felt an expression creeping across her face that she feared was one part incredulity mixed with three parts ‘You be crazy, lady.’ She blurted, “Those do not look natural.”

“They are from a lab, admittedly.”

“Hardly what I’d call a green solution, then.”

“Oh, come on. Bioengineering is the only technology keeping us going now all the fossil fuels are gone.” She laughed. “Even our homes are powered by poop.”

“Fuel cells are not powered by poop. They’re powered by algae.”

Scarlet rolled her eyes. “If you say so, dear. But look, I must do something about these invasive insect species. They’re spreading all over and getting bigger every year. I saw a centipede ambush a rabbit last week. They have venom, you know.”

“I assume you mean the centipedes.”

“Quite,” replied Scar, unamused, “They could hurt Len.” She reached down and stroked the cat. “The situation is far from funny.”

“I didn’t think they’d reached this far north.”

"Well, when the weather here is the same as in their native habitat, it's no surprise they spread our way." Scarlet leaned toward Charlotte, secretively. "They're called Peruvian yellow-legs or Amazonian giant centipedes. Now, I have no issue with them living down south, in places where people might reasonably expect to stumble across monstrosities like that. But I'm not having them set up home in my garden." She poured herself another glass of mixed-drink nirvana from the pitcher and added, "I read all about them in the spider brochure. Do you want to have a look?"

Charlotte did not want to look at the brochure. "I found one of your spiders in my house this morning."

"Oh, you're welcome, dear."

"That wasn't the reaction I was hoping for."

"They work tirelessly for our good." Under her breath, Scarlet muttered, "And they eat what they catch." She continued more normally, "There's nothing to be worried about. These spiders are completely safe as far as people are concerned. They're re-engineered *lycosidae*. You know, wolf spiders."

"I can see they're ridiculously overgrown wolf spiders. That's not my point. I'd be obliged if you kept them out of my home."

"Very well. There's a setting for the queen that controls the maximum patrol distance. I must have forgotten to enter it."

"The queen has settings?"

"Well, of course she does," said Scarlet, as if that were the most natural thing in the world. "She directs the males through pheromones."

"Scar, exactly how many of those male spiders are there?"

"The order came with fifty. At least to start. They breed, obviously."

"Fifty? And they breed?"

Scarlet had the effrontery to arch an eyebrow at her. "They'd hardly be worth the investment if they weren't sustainable. I'd be forever buying replacement stock."

Charlotte tried to concentrate on her drink, but it was hard to ignore the sounds of the dutiful arachnid cracking through the centipede's exoskeleton.

~oOo~

"Did you hear?" asked Scarlet, blatantly changing the subject, "The city council is tearing up all the oaks along our road. Replacing them with palm trees. More suited to the current climate, they say. We'll end up looking like Florida. The climate—"

"The climate isn't changing. The studies show. . ."

"Yes, but dear, the results of those studies are not to be trusted, as you can testify."

"I have no idea what you're talking about, Scar." She fiddled with her cuffs in an attempt not to look like she was lying.

Charlotte's boss was always so very thorough in sifting through her studies for anything that required factual adjustment. It was the only way to ensure government funding continued. And if it happened to the epidemiological studies Charlotte performed, the same process of 'oversight' surely occurred on ones related to climate change.

Feeling lightheaded, Charlotte excused herself. She was tempted to blame the alcohol, but it was just as likely caused by the incessant heat. She longed for the days when Iowa had had seasons. She turned in early, deciding to write the rest of the day off.

Gazing up at the whirring ceiling fan, Charlotte couldn't decide what was worse: the occasional super-sized carnivorous centipede loose in the back yard or giant spiders on the prowl. It was the spiders. Definitely the spiders, with their calculating gazes and twitching fangs.

Again, she heard faint scratching. Charlotte felt certain it was coming from the outside wall of her bedroom. The source seemed to move about with the tell-tale skittering of sharp claws. She assumed it was a spider, but had to admit to the possibility it was one of the black-furred squirrels that infested her neighborhood. It could even be a mouse. There were certainly enough of those.

The noise came once more, stubbornly refusing to provide a definitive clue as to its cause.

After a few minutes of pressing an upturned glass to the wallpaper, she admitted defeat and returned to bed. Whatever it was, it must be outside. Fortunately, she always kept the windows sealed shut to let the AC pretend to work.

Drifting off to sleep, she cursed Scarlet. Most likely, the racket was caused by one of her wandering beasts. If the gene-patented pest-hunting bug damaged the house, she'd sue or at least insist on stronger drinks.

~oOo~

The next day was much the same as normal. Leaving for work, Charlotte made certain to shut the back door. She rattled the handle and checked the lock. No spider would let itself in today.

Her manager spent the day torturing her with countless alterations to survey results from Oona virus sufferers. All she could think of upon returning home and climbing up the rickety wooden steps was opening a bottle of Iowegian red and luxuriating in air-conditioned bliss.

It took Charlotte several minutes of fruitless searching in her handbag and rooting through the pockets of her thin linen jacket to concede that she'd left her house keys on the kitchen table.

Damn it, she'd locked herself out. At least Charlotte knew herself well enough to arrange a system for situations like this. She'd ask Scarlet for the spare key.

~oOo~

Scarlet seemed pleased and amused to have her call round. She handed over the key wordlessly, after quickly finding it in an immaculately-arranged kitchen junk drawer.

Charlotte was grateful Scar didn't make fun of the situation. This had to be the third time in the last six months she'd left her housekeys on the kitchen table. It was the stupid pod's fault, with its keyless ignition and biometric handle sensors; carrying around a bunch of keys wasn't necessary for traveling. She should really retrofit the house with an access pad, but it was expensive.

"Since you're here, would you like to see the spider queen? She's in the basement. I am keen to show her off."

Charlotte wasn't afforded a chance to decline. Scar provided white wine for the show.

On the way to the basement stairs, they passed along a hallway lined with framed pictures of Scar in glittering wrestling costumes, quickly reaching a living room packed full of weightlifting equipment and stacked cans of protein supplement. Scarlet saw Charlotte's reaction.

"I suit myself these days. Why hide my gear in a spare room when I use it three times a day?"

"Do you miss the ring?"

"I miss the feeling of family I had with the other wrestlers. I hear from those old dames more often than my daughter lately, and half of them are dead."

Scarlet opened the entrance to the lower staircase and they trekked down, trying not to spill wine. Scar steered Charlotte around a corner to the front half of the basement, a finished room with brightly painted drywall and a large, exotically patterned rug. A couch and entertainment screen took up some of the space, but Charlotte's eyes were drawn to a small cheerful cat basket arranged in the center of the rug. It was one of those beds shaped like a rounded tent, with a small opening in the front and a cushion inside.

Len was not, however, using the basket. He sat in front of it, one paw batting at a plastic ball. Something else was inside the enclosed piece of cat furniture; something with two long hairy legs poking out through the opening and six more legs hidden away inside.

"Oh my God, Scar, it's the size of a woodchuck."

Scarlet shook her head. "Don't exaggerate. Three fourths the size of a woodchuck at most."

"I've seen smaller dogs."

Scarlet chuckled.

Charlotte remembered killing the spider and hoped the queen didn't hold a grudge.

Len batted the ball toward the spider queen's limbs and, incredibly, the creature knocked it back. "They keep themselves amused for hours. I'm so glad Len has a friend. Not surprising really. Arachnids are astonishingly intelligent, just like felines. Did you know spiders are second only to humans in the number of ways they know to catch and kill prey?"

"Is that true?"

"Yes, it is," snapped Scarlet. "People wax lyrical over sharks, but you don't see a great white laying an ambush or luring its victim into a trap. Sometimes, reality is simply reality, regardless of prejudice."

"Was that a crack directed at my job?" It was her turn to be annoyed.

"Dear Lord, Charlotte. I bite my tongue each time you mention your occupation, but enough is enough. You do important work. You track the spread of diseases and the effectiveness of drugs developed to combat them. You shouldn't twist the data just because the conclusions of your research don't fit with your paymasters' ideological views."

A bitter taste filled Charlotte's mouth. "I don't do that."

"You might not, but the folks you work for certainly do and you take their money."

"You're being unfair."

"Am I? What about Oona? If we believed the guff put out on the info-network, we'd think it was a mosquito-borne virus that only harms foreigners or unsanitary poor people here. But you know that's not the reality. Mrs. Scott-Martin in our own parish has a daughter with birth defects caused by it. But is our city using mosquito control measures? No, certainly not. Because the government says Oona is not a threat in the Midwest. That's political prejudice directly impacting public policy and causing harm to our fellow citizens. What's more, your department is responsible."

Charlotte shook her head. "People don't want complicated truths. They need something simpler, something they'll listen to. It's better to trick them into paying attention to one thing than tell them a dozen facts they'll ignore."

"But you simply tell people what they want to hear. That's not the purpose of science. And it doesn't solve the problems we face."

"People get angry and scared when you tell the truth. They shove their heads in the sand and ignore you. What's the point?"

Scarlet opened her mouth to say something, but they were both distracted by an eerie clicking noise. Charlotte's eyes flickered up. She backed hastily up the stairs, unable to look away as she climbed. Fat-bodied, black-haired spiders clambered out of the hole of the open ventilation grill leading from the first floor, crawling upside-down onto the ceiling.

"We shouldn't shout near the queen," said Scarlet softly. "We're a little intimidating. Poor thing got frightened."

"I'm leaving," said Charlotte, shocked at how hoarse her voice sounded. "I'm leaving this madhouse. Thank you for the key and thank you for the wine, but enough is enough. Keep them out of my house. I swear to God, I will kill them."

Scarlet's face fell. "I'm sorry. I had no idea you were so scared of spiders."

"It's not— Look— Just keep them away from me."

Scar's voice was a whisper. "No good decision was ever born of fear."

On her way out, Charlotte put the glass down on the kitchen table more forcefully than she'd intended, breaking the stem. She threw the glass in the trash and left feeling guilty.

~oOo~

The scratching returned with a vengeance that night. It seemed to have spread to the spaces under the floorboards.

Enraged, Charlotte got down on all fours and tried to pinpoint the source of the unnatural sound. It was worse than ever; Charlotte's skin itched with every echoing scrape.

By four-thirty in the morning, she was convinced Scarlet had sent an army of spiders to seek revenge for their harsh exchange. They could be chewing through wall insulation, through wires, insinuating themselves into every nook and cranny of her home, infesting the very fabric of the building.

Charlotte was still awake when her alarm clock started its insistent shrieking.

~oOo~

It was no surprise that Charlotte failed, once again, to pick up her house keys that morning, not even the spare set she'd borrowed back from Scarlet. Equally, there was no great amazement in the fact she didn't notice her lapse until she returned home, utterly ragged. She had proposed a re-examination of the Oona virus data to her manager. He had flatly denied her request.

A frantic call confirmed the locksmith had already shut up shop for the day. Annoyed with her entirely predictable failings, Charlotte grabbed the heavy plastic birdbath from the backyard and decided to break her way in through a dining room window, the only ones low enough to the ground for her to climb through. The birdbath rebounded from the shatterproof glass without leaving a scratch.

Left with no alternative, she was forced to knock on Scarlet's door again, to ask for her emergency spare key, the backup to the backup. She wasn't looking forward to the encounter. The conversation of the previous evening was still fresh in her memory, and she had never developed a liking for the taste of humble pie.

Oddly, her neighbor's back door swung wide with the pressure of her knocking. Scarlet didn't leave the door unlocked overnight, at least not intentionally. And she hadn't left it ajar for the patrolling gen-engineered spiders, because there was a freshly installed cat flap.

Charlotte poked her head inside Scarlet's kitchen and called out, "Hello? Scar? You in? Yoo-hoo."

She found Scarlet's body in the living room, collapsed beneath a barbell loaded with a prodigious number of metal plates. Her face had a grayish hue.

Charlotte reached out to check for a pulse, but then hesitated. After a few seconds consideration, she realized there was no point. Her neighbor had plainly been dead for many hours. Looking at Scar's waxy skin and glassy eyes, Charlotte could only imagine she'd passed on not long after their argument.

She dialed 911. Waiting for someone to answer, her mind drifted to potential causes of death. Had the queen bitten Scar? Charlotte couldn't see a bite mark anywhere on the bodybuilder, but that didn't mean there wasn't one.

Len was nowhere to be seen.

~oOo~

In the paramedic's professional opinion, heart attack was the culprit. The autopsy would tell them for sure.

"What should I do about the spider queen?" she asked.

"Spider queen?" He exhibited only mild interest.

"She bought a spider-based pest control system."

"Oh, yeah. I saw the commercial." He shrugged unhelpfully, packing away his equipment. Now he'd confirmed Scarlet was indeed dead, his duty was over. From here on, the police would take care of things.

He said as much to Charlotte, adding, "Best not to do anything. You'll make a statement about how you found the deceased. Then the cops will contact the next of kin. It'll be their call, what to do about the spiders. But, hey, aren't they a good thing?'

"A *good* thing?"

"Yeah. They'll keep on scouring the local environment for non-native species, regardless of whether their owner is still alive. They should be just fine. They feed themselves, after all."

"That wasn't my worry."

He blinked at her tone. “Sorry, ma’am. It’s really nothing to do with me. Now, if you’ll excuse me. I’ll wait outside until the cops arrive. They said they’d be here soon.”

~oOo~

The police interview was brief. Scarlet’s corpse vanished in a black bag strapped to a stainless steel gurney.

Charlotte explained the issue with the spiders scurrying across, or perhaps inside, her walls, but the police officer was unsympathetic.

“Did you know Mrs. Kirkpatrick well?” the female officer asked.

“I’ve known her— knew her— for about seven years,” stammered Charlotte.

“Finding her there must have been quite a shock.”

“Yes. But it’s not shock making me imagine things. I heard the sounds before I found Scarlet.”

The officer smiled and nodded. “Unless you see one on the outside of your residence, ma’am, there’s not much we can do. Even then, who would I cite?”

Charlotte was released to go back to her life. Fortunately, the cop let her extract the emergency backup key from Scar’s neatly-organized junk drawer first.

Walking out of Scarlet’s home for the last time, Charlotte kneeled and flipped the catch on the cat flap, locking it shut. The spiders could make do without their queen. Maybe they’d leave without her guidance.

~oOo~

Night fell, and the scratching in her bedroom wall was worse.

Charlotte sat on her bed, nagging at a fingernail nervously. She'd tried going outside with a flashlight, but there hadn't been anything scuttling along the siding. Unable to gather any evidence of arachnid infiltration and worried she hadn't used enough mosquito repellent, she'd retreated inside.

The more she thought about it, the more she knew she had to do something. Her home was being invaded and the authorities couldn't see any crime being committed.

Charlotte needed to attack the problem at its source.

To do that, she needed something long and heavy, with a good grip. Her high school grass hockey stick came to mind. As best she remembered, it was languishing in a box of sporting gear in the garage. She went to fetch it.

~oOo~

With each step down the path to the transport pod's glorified shed, Charlotte expected to see a fat spider dart across the beam cast by her flashlight. It wasn't until she reached inside the side door and flicked on the main light that she understood why she hadn't seen any.

Next to the pod, one of the creatures stirred, a leg lifting and moving with deliberate aim. It took

Charlotte a second to make out what was happening in the sudden glare of the naked bulb; then, she recoiled.

The spider prodded at a rat. It steered the terrified animal farther into the garage, toward *another* spider.

She'd known intellectually the re-engineered spiders cooperated. Seeing it in action was another thing altogether.

The second spider wasted no time in catching the base of the rat's tail in its jaws. Delicately, it carried the writhing animal in the direction of the sliding metal shutter.

In most garages, there wouldn't have been a way out for the huge bug. But this garage had a ramp leading to the alleyway and, when the concrete had been poured, the contractor hadn't done a very expert job. The slope was higher in the center than at the sides, leaving large gaps under the shutter's straight slats on the left and right.

Now she saw how those gaps allowed the spiders easy access. First one spider and then the other slipped away. Charlotte slapped the door control and waited impatiently for the wide metal panel to rise so she could follow.

She watched the two spiders join up with a group of other arachnids, adding their rat to a growing herd of livestock. One of the spider shepherds pushed forward a pile of food scraps.

"You're fattening them up for the slaughter."

Charlotte strode back into the garage and tore off the lid of the box holding the sports equipment.

~oOo~

Technically, Charlotte was now a burglar. The police had locked Scarlet's house when they left earlier but, just as Scar kept a couple of Charlotte's spare keys handy, Charlotte was the possessor of one of Scarlet's.

She stood in the kitchen, checking both the back door and its flap were still shut. Charlotte didn't want to give the queen the chance to summon reinforcements. That didn't mean the house wasn't full of male arachnids.

The time had come to put an end to the reign of the spiders.

~oOo~

The spiders were waiting. A dozen drones scurried into the hallway to block her path.

Charlotte jabbed the hockey stick again and again, crushing limbs, thoraxes and abdomens with each solid blow.

The spiders reared up, but they didn't spring at her.

She pressed forward, lashing out brutally until every one of the creatures had been pulverized.

So what if they hadn't hurt a person? Like Scarlet said, they were smart. What she'd seen confirmed that. Given time, they'd work up to killing people.

Charlotte yanked open the door to the basement staircase and clicked on the lights. “I’m coming for you,” she hissed, carefully beginning her descent.

She scanned every surface as she made her way down to the bottommost corner, not encountering any more males. A quick glance behind confirmed nothing was sneaking up from the rear.

Then she rounded the stairs and stepped into the basement.

The queen had not moved from her cat basket throne.

The spider monarch inspected Charlotte. The hockey stick-wielding statistician could see in sickening detail the creature’s two enormous main eyes and its lower row of four smaller ones.

“You’re grotesque, you know that?”

She edged closer. Six more males slinked out from under the threadbare couch, taking up position in a line between them.

“Did you kill Len? I bet you did,” whispered Charlotte, adjusting her grip on the stick. “And plenty of other pets.”

Scarlet had claimed the queen and its foul progeny were harmless to people, programmed deep in the chromosomes not to attack. “I don’t believe you can control yourself. I think you’re a predator. I think you’re a murderer. This is my world and I want no place in it for you!”

Charlotte howled, then slashed sideways with the stick, obliterating three of the patrol spiders.

She stepped back warily, anticipating a counterattack. It never came.

The queen emerged from the cat basket and backed away. Charlotte couldn't believe how large the creature was. Her top lip twitched with revulsion.

A stream of male spiders, at least twenty in all, emerged from everywhere, falling in behind their retreating sovereign. The queen was calling forth its surviving underlings and they were leaving.

Charlotte started after them.

A reverberating clang of steel striking concrete made her stop and whip her head around. It sounded like something large and metallic tipping over in the utility room.

The microbial fuel cell cracked wide. A wave of brown sludge sluiced out under the utility room door, across the base of the staircase, and onto the floor. She gagged from the rank smell.

The spiders were cutting off her escape, leaving her stuck in the filth.

Something inside her snapped. Charlotte leaped *toward* the approaching swell of diluted excrement, before it could deepen. Her first stride carried her halfway through the spreading lake. The next brought her to the base of the stairs. A third won her a step higher than the incoming tide.

She turned to look at the spiders. "You used a distraction. You thought up a plan and then you carried it out."

They ascended the far wall, clear of the advancing fluid, walking up the sheer surface with silent dignity. Reaching the recessed window, they stepped onto its ledge; the queen nimbly lifted the catch of the frame. In moments, they had nudged wide the window and marched through.

"You might have driven me back for a few seconds, but you're the ones running away. The way I figure it, I won. Yeah, *I won.*" Charlotte barely believed it.

"And don't come back!"

She frowned, a nagging worry buzzing round her mind like an Oona-ridden mosquito. The queen had smelled what was in the cell, that was obvious enough. The problem was, how had the spider known it could be used against a human? How intelligent were they?

~oOo~

Charlotte returned to the kitchen. Immediately, she heard a scratching from the back door.

With a moan of frustration, she turned the lock and swung the door wide, ready to bring the hockey stick down.

Len sauntered in.

Charlotte lowered the weapon shakily. Once she had her breath back, she filled the cat's bowl.

"Scarlet's daughter will arrive tomorrow. Ursula will take care of you." Len paid her no attention, more interested in his food.

She considered leaving a note for Ursula, explaining about the ruined fuel cell. But any explanation would be an admission she'd broken into the house.

Charlotte decided to keep quiet and slink back home.

Bone tired and muck-splattered, the epidemiologist locked Scarlet's house and began crossing the few scant feet to her own yard. The only thing she had to do now was get a good night's sleep. Relief made her light-headed.

She took two steps before a harsh chewing sound set her teeth on edge.

Casting about in the darkness, she finally located the source of the noise; the same rasping she'd been hearing every night.

It was coming from the eaves under the side of her roof, a few feet from her bedroom window. A ragged chunk of material the size of a tea saucer fell from the top of the siding, landing near her feet.

Stubby yellow-and-red legs curled around the raw opening. Long antennae followed as the giant Peruvian centipede began to explore the freshly-exposed terrain of the wall's outside.

The fifteen-inch-long venomous monster must have burrowed its way into the base of the house days ago, getting trapped in the wall cavity. Charlotte imagined it growing increasingly frenzied in its attempts to escape, working its way up.

The spiders weren't the cause of the scratching in her wall.

She stared at the arthropod's unsteady descent, thinking of Scarlet. Some facts weren't up for debate, the old lady had insisted.

Blood pounding in her ears, Charlotte gripped her hockey stick and waited for the centipede.

The End

Trickster Times

Jane Yolen

We live in the time of the Trickster,
Coyote, Rabbit, Raven, Anansi,
the merry pranks of Eulenspiegel.

We laugh even when they poke a stick
into our private holes. Laughter
is no medicine but a panacea.

The stories our grandchildren will tell:
the stone lady taking her lamp back to Paris,
the fat old man on a throne of bones.

We will not be there to hear the tales.
But they will be told around the fires,
wine will be spilled on the earth,

and the children will shake rattles at the corpse.

About the Authors

Ed Ahern resumed writing after forty odd years in foreign intelligence and international sales. He's had a hundred sixty stories and poems published so far. His collected fairy and folk tales, *The Witch Made Me Do It* was published by Gypsy Shadow Press. His novella *The Witches' Bane* was published by World Castle Publishing, and his collected fantasy and horror stories, *Capricious Visions* was published by Gnome on Pig Press. Ed's currently working on a paranormal/thriller novel tentatively titled *The Rule of Chaos*. He works the other side of writing at Bewildering Stories, where he sits on the review board and manages a posse of five review editors.

Gwyndyn Alexander is a New Orleans poet and artist. She alternates between creating words and creating costumes, and often confuses the two. She is the benevolent dictator of a tiny nation state consisting of one husband, one cat, and an embarrassing amount of glitter.
Her work can be found at : https://www.amazon.com/Gwyndyn-T-Alexander/e/B00N7BMYGC/ref=dp_byline_cont_book_1 and https://www.etsy.com/shop/FeatherInYourCapNOLA

K.G. Anderson grew up in the Washington, D.C., area, surrounded by politics and politicians. After college she worked for several years as an East Coast newspaper reporter. Her short fiction—urban fantasy, space opera, alternate history, Weird West tales, near-future science fiction, poetry, and mystery—has appeared in anthologies including *Second Contacts, Triangulation: Beneath the Surface, The Mammoth Book of Jack the Ripper Stories, Triangulation: Appetites*, and *Alternative Truths*, as well as online at *Metaphorosis, Ares Magazine*, and *Every Day Fiction*. K.G. attended the Taos Toolbox and Viable Paradise workshops. She currently lives in Seattle where she designs, writes, edits, reviews, and produces what they call "content," most of it for the web. More information at writerway.com/fiction

Lou Antonelli's collections include *Fantastic Texas* published in 2009; *Texas & Other Planets* published in 2010; and *The Clock Struck None* and *Letters from Gardner*, both published in 2014. His debut novel, the retro-futurist alternate history *Another Girl, Another Planet*, was published in 2017 by WordFire Press.

He has been a finalist for the Hugo, Dragon and Sidewise awards.

His first professional science fiction short story, "A Rocket for the Republic" (*Asimov's Science Fiction* Sept. 2005) was the last story accepted by Editor Gardner Dozois before he retired after 19 years.

"The Yellow Flag"—his 100th published short story (*Sci-Phi Journal* Aug. 2016)—set the record for all-time fastest turnaround in genre fiction. It was written, submitted and accepted between 1 p.m. and 5 p.m. on May 6, 2015.

His story in this anthology, "Queens Crossing," is his 113th story published since 2003.

A Massachusetts native, Antonelli moved to Texas in 1985 and is married to Dallas native Patricia (Randolph) Antonelli. They have three adopted furbaby children, Millie, Sugar and Peltro Antonelli.

Lou J Berger is a Denver-based author with over a dozen short stories published in a variety of venues, including *Galaxy's Edge Magazine*, *Daily Science Fiction,* and several noted anthologies.

His website is www.LouJBerger.com and his Twitter account is @WriterLJBerger.

David Brin is an astrophysicist whose international best-selling novels include *The Postman*, *Earth*, and recently *Existence*. Dr. Brin serves on advisory boards (e.g. NASA's Innovative and Advanced Concepts program or NIAC) and speaks or consults on a wide range of topics. His nonfiction book about the information age—*The Transparent Society*—won the Freedom of Speech Award of the American Library Association.

His new novel about our survival in the near future is *Existence*. A film by Kevin Costner was based on The Postman. His 16 novels, including NY Times Bestsellers and Hugo Award winners, have been translated into more than twenty languages.

(http://www.davidbrin.com)

Adam-Troy Castro made his first non-fiction sale to SPY magazine in 1987. Among his books to date include four Spider-Man novels, 3 novels about his profoundly damaged far-future murder investigator Andrea Cort, and 6 middle-grade novels about the dimension-spanning adventures of that very strange but very heroic young boy Gustav Gloom. Adam's darker short fiction for grownups is highlighted by his collection, *Her Husband's Hands And Other Stories* (Prime Books). Adam's works have won the Philip K. Dick Award and the Seiun (Japan), and have been nominated for eight Nebulas, three Stokers, two Hugos, and, internationally, the Ignotus (Spain), the Grand Prix de l'Imaginaire (France), and the Kurd-Laßwitz Preis (Germany). He lives in Florida with his wife Judi and either three or four cats, depending on what day you're counting and whether Gilbert's escaped this week.

Christine A. Chesse was born into an evangelical home and raised in Houston, Texas. She attended Second Baptist School (which also produced Ted Cruz). Initially a Republican, she voted for George W. Bush. Twice. She has since come to the conclusion that God is probably not honored by devotion to the Republican party, and a candidate's ability to pose for "Bringing Prayer Back to the White House" photos is not, in fact, a sign that God's unerring will is being enacted from that house. She writes LGBTQ+ romance under the name C.M. Taylor and has a husband and three children. You can visit her at cmtaylor.dreamwidth.org.

Brad Cozzens is a 52 year old father of two boys, Dylan Freeman and Jacob Cozzens. He is the author of “America Once Beautiful.” Brad lives in Eagle, Idaho with his friend of 38 years, his wife Sheilah Kennedy. He is the youngest of four who shares a love of cooking with his siblings, given to them by their late mother, Gail. Brad does not have a website, but he can be found on Facebook at https://www.facebook.com/bradley.cozzens

Colin Patrick Ennen lives in Albuquerque, New Mexico, where he wrangles mutts at a doggie daycare and contemplates becoming a hermit. He is, himself, a recent puppy parent (Shylock). Colin eats waffles every Saturday morning, dislikes most odd numbers, and may be allergic to spinach. As a longtime fan of the Boston Red Sox and Texas A&M Aggies, you’d *think* he’d be used to disappointment, and would thus take copious literary rejections in stride… Anyway, he keeps on, taking inspiration from writer heroes such as Shakespeare, Poe, Twain, Tolkien, Vonnegut, and Douglas Adams. “Triple R Presents” is his first sale. He tweets as @cpennen.

Bobby Lee Featherston is a refugee from Texas. He escaped in the dark of the night, joining the Navy when he was 16 and now he operates a small organic farm in Prosser, Washington, and has been known to speak lovingly of Cushaw squash and share recipes for strawberry-banana squash jam with his patrons at the farmers market. He is often found in the company of his dogs, Jules and Verne. Bobby Lee hates cats.

Karin L. Frank is an award-winning author from the Kansas City area. Her poems and prose have been published in both literary journals and genre magazines in the U.S. and abroad. In particular, her science fiction poetry has been published in Asimov's Science Fiction, Tales of the Talisman, Dreams and Nightmares and Scifaikuest.

Nebula Award winner ***Esther Friesner*** is the author of over 40 novels and more than 200 short stories. Educated at Vassar College and Yale University, where she received a Ph.D. in Spanish. She is also a poet, a playwright, and the editor of several anthologies. The best known of these is the *Chicks in Chainmail* series that she created and edits for Baen Books. The sixth book, *Chicks and Balances*, appeared in July 2015. *Deception's Pawn*, the latest title in her popular *Princesses of Myth* series of Young Adult novels from Random House, was published in April 2015.

Esther is married, a mother of two, grandmother of one, harbors cats, and lives in Connecticut. She has a fondness for bittersweet chocolate, graphic novels, manga, travel, and jewelry. There is no truth to the rumor that her family motto is "Oooooh, SHINY!"

Her super-power is the ability to winnow her bookshelves without whining about it. Much.

Manny Frishberg was born just south of New York City and has made his home on the West Coast for over 40 years. He spent the first half of his life learning how to write and the second half learning what to write about, He is now spending the third half of his life making up stories, just like when he was eight years old. His stories have been appearing in anthologies and magazines since 2010.

When he is not doing that, he writes about things he hasn't made up for several magazines, and provides freelance editing and writing coach services. An independent editor, his anthology, *Horseshoes, Hand Grenades and Magic* was published by Knotted Road Press in 2016. He and his partner make their home near SeaTac Airport.

David Gerrold was a runner up for this year's one-line biography award, coming in only six votes behind Vonda N. McIntyre's one-line bio.

Debora Godfrey, like many aspiring writers, started early. Her first poem was in a publication called "Death in Room 106" a reference to both her eighth grade classroom and the subject matter of most of the content. Junior English was spent writing a long Russian spy novel in class, with the constant danger of Miss Self actually catching her writing about a subterranean shootout in Paris, rather than *The Red Badge of Courage*. More recently, she has attended the Rainforest Writers Retreat, where she is the reigning Soup Goddess. "Non-White in America" is her first professionally published story, and is dedicated to a time when this would truly be a work of unrealistic fiction.

Kerri-Leigh Grady is a graduate of Seton Hill University's MFA program and holds a BS in computer science. She's a nerd with an unnatural love of dark humor, gadgets, chickpeas, cross-choking her friends, artsing and craftsing, archery, and planners. This week, she lives in Virginia. If there's a next week, she hopes she's still in Virginia. She kinda likes it there.

Yorkshireman ***Philip Brian Hall*** is a graduate of Oxford University. A former diplomat and teacher, at one time or another he's stood for parliament, sung solos in amateur operettas, rowed at Henley Royal Regatta, completed a 40 mile cross-country walk in under 12 hours, and ridden in over one hundred steeplechase horse races. He now lives on a very small farm in Scotland, but once upon a time lived in an English village.

Philip's had short stories published in the USA and Canada as well as the UK. His novel, *The Prophets of Baal* is available as an e-book and in paperback.

He blogs at *sliabhmannan.blogspot.co.uk/*.

Stuart Hardy is British internet comedian and TV critic from the Youtube channel "Stubagful" where he's known for his popular *Doctor Who* reviews series "He Who Moans". He also makes bizarre horror cartoons and adaptations of his speculative short stories about technology and social media and the way in which they affect society and the online political discourse. He's also worked as a satirical sketch writer and commentator for various community and student radio projects over the course of the last ten years. His primary influences include Charlie Brooker's *Black Mirror*, Douglas Adams, Philip K. Dick, and the short stories of Robert Shearman.

Michael Haynes lives in Central Ohio where he helps keep IT systems running for a large corporation during the day and puts his characters through the wringer by night. An ardent short story reader and writer, Michael has had stories appear in venues such as *Ellery Queen Mystery Magazine*, *Beneath Ceaseless Skies*, *Nature*, and *Daily Science Fiction*. He is the Chair of the Cinevent Classic Film Convention and enjoys geocaching, live music, travel, and photography. His website is http://michaelhaynes.info/ and he tweets at @mohio73.

Rivka Jacobs has lived in West Virginia for thirty-eight years. She was born in Philadelphia and grew up in South Florida. She's sold stories to such publications as *The Magazine of Fantasy and Science Fiction*, the *Far Frontiers* anthologies, and the *Women of Darkness* anthology. More recently she placed stories with *The Sirens Call* eZine, *The Literary Hatchet*, *Fantastic Floridas*, and *Riding Light Review*. Rivka has a BA in history, MAs in sociology and mental health counseling, and a BSN. She most recently worked as a psychiatric nurse in a forensic psychiatric hospital. She is currently semi-retired, living peacefully with four Siamese cats in a double-wide mobile home.

Born on Friday 13, ***Rebecca McFarland Kyle*** developed an early love for the unusual. Dragons, vampires, and all manner of magical beings haunt her thoughts and stir her to the keyboard. She currently lives between the Smoky and Cumberland mountains with her husband and three cats. Her first YA novel, *Fanny & Dice,* was released on Halloween 2015. In 2017, she will be editing a charity anthology, co-editing a political anthology, and releasing works in young adult, urban fantasy, and dark fantasy. You can find her online at: http://rmkyle.abckyle.com/

Melinda LaFevers is a renaissance woman with a wide variety of interests, hobbies, and talents. She is an Arts in Education residency artist, with two programs, Life in a Castle and Life in a Log Cabin. As a performing artist, she sings traditional ballads, tells stories, and plays a variety of instruments, including a lap harp, bowed psaltery, and more. The first story she sold is "The Oldest Profession?" in The Ladies of Trade Town. It was written in fifteen minutes after a flash of inspiration. Other stories may be found in the following anthologies: *Dreams of Steam IV: Gizmos*; *I Didn't Quite Make it to Oz*; *Luna's Children: Stranger Worlds*; *Potters Field 5*; *A Tall Ship, A Star, And Plunder.* She writes poetry, music, songs, speculative fiction, and non-fiction. Her hobbies include spinning, weaving, and learning new things, to name a few. As "The Renaissance Herbalist" for *The Renaissance Magazine,* she has studied and written about the traditional uses of plants and what modern science has discovered about those uses. Her blog, “Melinda's obscure thoughts,” may be found at https://melindalafevers.wordpress.com/

Emma Lazarus (July 22, 1849–November 19, 1887) was an American poet and Georgist from New York City. She is best known for “The New Colossus”, a sonnet written in 1883; its lines appear inscribed on a bronze plaque in the pedestal of the Statue of Liberty installed in 1903, a decade and a half after Lazarus's death.

Bruno Lombardi was born in Montreal in 1968. He has had a rather distressing tendency to be a weirdness magnet for much of his adult life. If your friend's cousin's brother-in-law tells you a story and swears it's true and that it 'happened to someone he knows', it was probably Bruno.

His hobbies include attempting to dissuade the cults that form around him, managing the betting pool on the next Weird Thing, and being a slave to his cat, Mynx. He currently lives in Ottawa and works as a civil servant for the Canadian government.

He has also met lots of people off the internet and has yet to be murdered by any of them; his cat, on the other hand, has other ideas.

"Snake Oil," published by Daverana Enterprises, is his first published novel. A second edition of "Snake Oil," published by Martinus Publishing, is now available. His short stories have been published in a variety of anthologies and magazines, including *Weirdbook* #33 and *Occult Detective Quarterly* #2

Bruno does not have a website, but he can be found on Facebook at https://www.facebook.com/Bruno-Lombardi-Author-Page-434916096583689/

Susan Murrie Macdonald is a wordsmith: rejection slip collector, proofreader, copy editor, journalist, blogger, occasional poet, storyteller, and would-be novelist. In addition to being a regular contributor to Krypton Radio, she is the author of several short stories. Her most recent work can be found in the *Gothic Fantasy* series from Flame Tree Publishing and in the first two books of the popular *Alternative Truth* series from B Cubed Press. She is writer, editor, publisher, and maid-of-all-work for Highland Heather Press. Her first children's book is *R is for Renaissance Faire.* She is, of course, working on a novel (isn't everyone?) and researching her second children's book.

Susan Murrie Macdonald enjoys Highland Games and Celtic festivals, being a member of Clan Murray by birth and Clan Donald by marriage. She has won the Arkansas Scottish Festival's annual poetry contest twice, once in 2014 and again in 2017. She also enjoys attending Renaissance Faires, science fiction conventions, and Native American pow-wows. She lives in Tennessee with her husband and two teenagers (son off at college, daughter in high school). She was an extra in the time travel movie *Time Boys.* She can be reached through her website https://mrssusanmacdonald.wixsite.com/author, or her blog, Assorted Scribblings of a Minor Author (https://mrssusanmacdonald.wordpress.com/).

Vonda N. McIntyre writes science fiction.

Rebecca Mix is a speculative fiction writer, book lover, and hoarder of houseplants. She lives in Michigan with her boyfriend and two cats that might be possessed by friendly but troublesome demons. For more stories like this one, visit her at rebeccamix.com and send her neat puns at @rebeccarmix on twitter.

Mike Morgan lives in Iowa with his wife, two children, and increasingly infirm cat. After various careers in the UK, Japan, and Texas involving accountancy, freelance illustration, non-fiction writing, editing, and teaching, Mike now does improbably complex things on computers for a living. When he's not worrying about the cat or tidying up his kids' toys, Mike gets overwrought about politics and tries to write short stories. It's possible his two hobbies get muddled together from time to time. He has written for several publishers, with stories in various comics, anthologies and magazines in the UK and the USA.

For news about his writing, feel free to take a look at his website, https://perpetualstateofmildpanic.wordpress.com/, or follow him on Twitter at @CultTVMike, where he posts about all things science fiction.

Kurt Newton's imaginative works have appeared across a wide spectrum of genre and literary publications. He is both a poet and a short story writer, and sometimes his brain confuses the two and spits out a piece like the one presented here. He is the author of several collections of poetry and short fiction, and two novels, most of which can be found in unmarked boxes stored in a storage space under the stairway of his home. His more humorous pieces can be found at *Zetetic: A Record of Unusual Inquiry, Intrinsick* and Empty Sink Publishing.

John A. Pitts learned to love science fiction at the knee of his grandmother, listening to her read authors like Edgar Rice Burroughs and Robert E. Howard during his childhood in Kentucky. His favorite place in the whole wide world was the library where he could become so lost in story that he didn't want to ever leave.

He lives his life surrounded by books and story. A collector of myths and legends, John relishes the moment when an audience gasps or cries, laughs or winces at a particularly vivid tale. Selling his own tales still comes as a surprise to him.

The first three books in the Sarah Beauhall urban fantasy series are out from Tor Publishing (http://us.macmillan.com/TorForge.aspx)

Black Blade Blues, 2010, *Honeyed Words*, 2011, *Forged in Fire*, 2012.

His first short story collection, *Bravado's House of Blues*, came out fall of 2013 from Fairwood Press. The fourth book in the Sarah Beauhall series, *Night Terrors*, has been published by Wordfire Press in April 2016, with early conversations about book five in the works.

John has a BA in English and a Masters of Library Science from University of Kentucky. He is a member of the Science Fiction and Fantasy Writers of America and the Dark Forces Defense League. He is said to have the hair of a Greek god.

Irene Radford is the daughter of a sailor man who saw the Far East before the skyscrapers buried the mysterious orient in western glass and steel. He brought home the stories of other worlds and forever changed the perspective of his petite bookworm of a daughter. Now, grown into a leading voice in F&SF as both a writer and editor she passes on this gift of the story, bringing perspectives that not only span her own life, but the generations of storytellers that preceded her.

You can keep track of Irene on her website www.ireneradford.net, where you can sign up for her newsletter, on FaceBook at https://www.facebook.com/phyllis.i.radford, on twitter @radford_irene25, or share the process of finishing a book on her patreon page https://www.patreon.com/user?u=5806073

Mike Resnick is the author of 77 novels, more than 280 stories, and 3 screenplays. He has edited 42 anthologies, and currently edits *Galaxy's Edge Magazine* and Stellar Guild Books. According to *Locus*, Mike is the all-time

leading award winner for short fiction. He has won 5 Hugos (from a record 37 nominations), a Nebula, and other major awards in the USA, France, Japan, Spain,

Catalonia, Croatia, Poland, and China. He was Guest of Honor at the 2012 Worldcon. His daughter, Laura, is also a science fiction writer, and won the 1993 Campbell Award as Best Newcomer.

Elizabeth Ann Scarborough is not a fairy godmother. She just writes about them and how they mete out social justice, kind of like warriors, only with more glitter. Scarborough is a Nebula award winner for *The Healer's War*, very loosely based on her experiences as a nurse in Vietnam during the war. She's the author of 40 books, 16 of which were co-written with Anne McCaffrey. Currently she's finishing the sixth novel in her SONGS FROM THE SEASHELL ARCHIVES series. She lives in Washington state with two black cats, Cisco and Pancho, sings shanties with the group Nelson's Blood, and designs and creates beadwork. She can be contacted through http://scarbor9.wixsite.com/beadtime-stories, and on FB at https://www.facebook.com/Elizabeth-Ann-Scarborough-162538643771710/?ref=aymt_homepage_panel

Tais Teng (1952) is a Dutch writer and illustrator. His stories are often rather satirical in a Robert Sheckley way. As a cover artist he has drawn everything from talking teapots to beautiful ladies with bat-wings and rather bad characters. Websites stories: http://taisteng.atspace.com/ Illustrations: https://taisteng.deviantart.com/

Next year Spatterlight Press will publish his novel *Phaedra: Alastor 824*, set in the universe of Jack Vance.

Wondra Vanian is an American native, now residing in the United Kingdom. She left her job working for The Man in 2014, both to pursue a career in writing and to concentrate on finding happiness while living with chronic illness. An author first, Wondra Vanian is also an avid gamer, a photographer, a cinephile, and mother to an army of fur babies.

Edd Vick, the son of a pirate, is a recovering Texan now living in Seattle. He is a bookseller whose library is a stuffed three-car garage. His stories have appeared in *Analog, Asimov's, Year's Best SF*, and about forty other magazines and anthologies. You can find him at eddvick.com.

Steve Weddle holds an MFA in creative writing from Louisiana State University. His debut novel, *Country Hardball*, is published in North America by Simon and Schuster. The follow-up to Country Hardball, "South of Bradley," appeared in the November 2015 issue of *Playboy* magazine.

Stephanie L. Weippert is bibliophile—full stop. Leave her alone for ten minutes and she will be reading or writing.

Stephanie is married and claims she and her husband are naturally insane in a fun and harmless way. Together they do filking and other musical hobbies. Their teen boys often drive them toward the not-fun insanity (Nature or Nurture?–you decide).

With former careers as a legal assistant and a licensed massage therapist, Stephanie now gets to make writing a full time endeavor thanks to her awesome husband.

Stephanie signed with TANSTAAFL Press in July of 2015. Her Patreon can be found at www.patreon.com/stephanieweippert, where she records audio files of her short stories.

Eric M. Witchey is a popular writer, teacher of seminars, and conference speaker. He has worked as a fulltime freelance writer and communication consultant for more than a quarter century. In addition to many contracted and ghost non-fiction titles, he has sold novels and more than 140 stories. His stories have appeared in 11 genres, and he has received awards or recognition from New Century Writers, Writers of the Future, Writer's Digest, The Eric Hoffer Prose Award Program, Short Story America, the Irish Aeon Awards, and other organizations. His How-to articles have appeared in *The Writer Magazine*, *Writer's Digest Magazine*, and other print and online magazines. When he is not writing or teaching, he wanders about the Northwest wilds and tests his intellect against trout brains the size of a pea. He says the humiliation is good motivation to return home and write.

Jim Wright is a retired US Navy Chief Warrant Officer and freelance writer. He lives in Florida where he watches American politics in a perpetual state of amused disgust. He's been called the Tool of Satan, but he prefers the title: Satan's Designated Driver. He is the mind behind *Stonekettle Station*. You can email him at jim@stonekettle.com. You can follow him on Twitter @stonekettle, or you can join the boisterous bunch he hosts on Facebook at Facebook/Stonekettle. Remember to bring brownies and mind the white cat, he bites. Hard.

Jane Yolen, who has been politically active most of her life (including being a delegate to the 1972 Democratic Convention pledged to McGovern) is often called "the Hans Christian Andersen of America." She has over 360 published books including *Owl Moon, The Devil's Arithmetic, How Do Dinosaurs Say Goodnight* and two books of political poems—*The Bloody Tide* and *Before/The Vote/After*. Her works, which range from very young rhymed picture books to novels and poetry for adults and every genre in between, have won an assortment of awards including two Nebulas, a World Fantasy Award, a Caldecott, the Golden Kite, three Mythopoeic awards, two Christopher Medals, a nomination for the National Book Award, the Jewish Book Award, the Kerlan Award, and the Catholic Library's Regina Medal, as well as six honorary doctorates. One of her awards set her good coat on fire. She lives in Massachusetts most of the year, but Scotland in the summer. She writes a poem a day.

Jill Zeller, the author of numerous short stories and novels, lives near Seattle, Washington with her patient husband, two self-absorbed cats and their thralls, two adult English Mastiffs. Her works explore the complex geology of reality. Some may call it fantasy but there are rarely swords and never elves. For more, http://jillzeller.com.